The
Trinity
Cat

and Other Mysteries

The
Trinity
Cat

and Other Mysteries

by **Ellis Peters**
(Edith Pargeter)

Edited by Martin Edwards and Sue Feder

Crippen & Landru Publishers
Norfolk, Virginia
2006

Crippen & Landru Publishers
P. O. Box 9315
Norfolk, VA 23505
USA

Email: Info@crippenlandru.com
Web: www.crippenlandru.com

CONTENTS

INTRODUCTION

Long before Ellis Peters earned international fame with her books about Brother Cadfael, she wrote regularly for the British magazine market. Not all her short stories are mysteries, but many of them are, and I believe that the best of her previously uncollected short crime fiction appears in this volume. This view was shared by my co-editor, the late Sue Feder, whose expertise in Peters' work was unrivalled.

In gathering these stories together, Sue, publisher Doug Greene and I combed through material published over a time span of four decades, ending with the 1990s—and there may yet be a wealth of undiscovered work lurking in obscure magazines, especially from before the 1950s. Several of the early stories included here first appeared under the author's real name, Edith Pargeter. The Pargeter name was primarily associated with historical fiction and sequences of novels— notably *The Brothers of Gwynedd Quartet* and *The Heaven Tree Trilogy*— and as she focused increasingly on the mystery genre, loyal readers who expected a Pargeter book to conform to precedent no doubt became restive. At the outset of her career, she had used pseudonyms—Jolyon Carr and John Redfern—for writing mystery novels (now very elusive) that she later came to regard as apprentice efforts. It was a logical "branding" decision to adopt the Peters surname, coupled with a sexually ambiguous first name, for crime novels starting with *Death Mask* (1959).

The stories divide into three broad categories. There are long stories of romantic suspense, with decent young men and attractive young women in the lead roles; they were serialised over two or more issues of the same magazine. These tales were written for the British women's magazine market during the 1950's. There are short-short "twist" stories, many of which were published during the middle 1960's in an American newspaper supplement called *This Week*. And there are the later stories in which Peters experimented with a range of different themes and settings.

Like many of Peters' admirers, I was long unaware of how prolific she had been as a writer of short stories, although I had enjoyed one or two anthologised tales, notably "The Trinity Cat." One of the short-shorts, however, is the story which first drew my attention to her earlier uncollected work. In compiling *Mysterious Pleasures*, a celebration of the Golden Jubilee of the Crime Writers Association, I wanted to include stories from past winners of the CWA Cartier

Diamond Dagger, which is awarded for those whose crime writing careers have been noteworthy for "sustained excellence." Peters won the Diamond Dagger in 1993, but her few short stories about Cadfael were well-known, as is the collection of longer tales, *The Assize of the Dying*, while the stories in *The Lily Hand*, which Peters regarded as the best of her story collections, fall outside the genre. Exploring the possibilities in collaboration with her agent, I was delighted to encounter "Guide to Doom." This sharp little piece—originally entitled "A Tour of the Castle" and published later as "Please Don't Scream"—strikes me as an excellent example of Peters' talents and is, so far as I know, the only one of the group of pre-Cadfael stories in this book to have been reprinted in recent years. Such an intriguing discovery encouraged me to delve deeper and Sue's diligent researches yielded several unexpected treasures. My hope is that other readers, familiar only with Cadfael, will find fresh delights in the pages that follow.

One hidden gem is "The Man Who Held Up the Roof," which Sue found lurking in an agency file. If it has been published before, we have not been able to trace any evidence of when it appeared—or, even, when it was written.

Of the stories that were originally serialised, "At the House of the Gentle Wind" deserves special mention. It was first published, as by Pargeter, in 1956; apparently she toyed with an alternative title, "The Hypocaust" before she (or some unknown editor) opted for something more evocative. Keen Peters fans will spot that the essential elements of the plot were re-worked and expanded to form a novel, *City of Gold and Shadows*, an entry in her long-running series featuring members of the Felse family, which appeared under the Peters by-line in 1973. Even by that date, she was still a mid-list writer, yet to be elevated to the ranks of the best-sellers, and she must have thought it unlikely that "At the House of the Gentle Wind" would ever see the light of day again. Writers are apt to be thrifty creatures, and Peters is one of many to have re-used short story material in novel form (in another story gathered here, incidentally, she borrowed a plot device most famously associated with Sir Arthur Conan Doyle.) That the events centre around a timeless archaeological site is one of the reasons why she was able to return to the story after so many years and turn it into something fresh (and ultimately, when the Felse books were reprinted as publishers rode on the back of Cadfael's immense popularity, no doubt much more financially remunerative.)

For the most part, the serialised stories are devised with skill so as to conform to stringent editorial requirements without an undue sacrifice of plausibility. "A Present for Ivo," for example, is a pleasing holiday story tailored to the Christmas market; the first instalment it appeared in *Everywoman* magazine in December 1958, surrounded by advice on "a gay way to disguise any present shaped like a bottle or in a bottle!" and advertisements urging readers to "make it a real Christmas for the family with Batger's original Chinese figs." These stories are straightforward pieces of light entertainment, reminding us that Peters was, above all, a highly professional writer, a craftswoman who knew what readers wanted, and made sure she delivered it.

Most of the later entries first appeared in that excellent and much-missed British series of annual anthologies, *Winter's Crimes*, while "The Frustration Dream" was included in a CWA collection, *2nd Culprit*. These stories see Peters in increasingly laid-back mood. The relaxed style is the product of a confidence that comes with commercial success on a scale that presumably she can never have anticipated; when she created Cadfael, she was already in her sixties and it took several years for the books to capture the public imagination (she rightly resented any suggestion that she had jumped on the bandwagon set rolling by *The Name of the Rose*; she had published seven Cadfael novels by the time Umberto Eco's book achieved celebrity.) "Come to Dust" is a very amiable piece of work, and "The Frustration Dream," her final short story, offers a rare excursion into the realm of the supernatural.

Ellis Peters was a modest woman and she was conspicuously modest about her work in the short story field—perhaps this is why she kept few records of it: understandable, although maddening for would-be bibliographers! In an interview with June E. Prance, quoted by Margaret Lewis in *Ellis Peters: Edith Pargeter*, she said:

> I'm not terribly good at short stories. I've written quite a few but I found them quite difficult. I need the elbow room of the novel. I need space for descriptions and for dallying with things like the weather, and for people to contemplate. That's hard to do in short stories.

Hard, yes, but she demonstrated herself that it is far from impossible. My guess is that, in some respects, the discipline of writing short stories, even to meet the demands of formula, sharpened her skills and helped her to avoid an excess of romanticism that would have weakened her work and made it date more obviously.

Bringing this book to publication involved an extensive and agreeable collaboration by email between Sue, publisher Doug Greene and myself. Despite serious illness, Sue provided helpful comments on the first draft of this introduction and allowed me the opportunity to study her unpublished bibliography of Peters' stories. In all the views that she expressed, her love of the author's writing shone through. It is sad that Sue died before she had the opportunity to see the finished volume, but some comfort to know that she participated in its compilation with such obvious relish. I am equally grateful to Doug Greene for the enthusiasm which he has brought to this project; this has included expanding the book so as to accommodate a lengthy story that Sue and I both liked very much, "A Lift into

Colmar." Crime fiction fans everywhere owe a considerable debt to Crippen & Landru for giving so many lost stories a new lease of life. Finally, a word of thanks to Ellis Peters' agent, Rosemary Scoular, and her estate for their co-operation and support throughout.

It is our belief that Ellis Peters' virtues are evident even in the slighter pieces included here. Her plotting may lack the dazzle of a Christie or a Berkeley, but it is always workmanlike, while her settings are customarily atmospheric. Above all, we read Peters for her people, for characters are created with the warmth and humanity that was her hallmark and for whom we therefore feel an immediate liking and sympathy. These stories are full of them.

Martin Edwards

DEAD MOUNTAIN LION

Toiling up the ash-white traverses of the Langkofeljoch, with his eyes bent steadily on the zigzags of the path ahead, Edward Stanier came over the brow of the pass and looked up from the sudden grey heaving of rock round his elbows, into a boiling cauldron of cloud. The cliffs of the Langkofel soared clean out of sight, foaming with leaden coils of cloud, and screaming with ravens.

Edward stopped and, turning his back on the forbidding cavern of the Langkofelkar, looked back down the dizzy chute of scree, into the rock town behind the Rifugio Passo Sella.

Down there was the warmth of July, and the drowsy sunset of Italy. Up here he stood on the edge of a slanting snowfield, with the vaporous hands of an imminent storm brushing damply at his shoulders. Against his will he felt a small contraction of discomfort inside him. It was all downhill now to the Rifugio Vicenza, low down there in the invisible bowl of the group. Surely there wasn't a shadow of risk attached to the mere slither down the scree and snow to find it, and with it his bed for the night.

Still, he had to admit that he disliked the look of it almost as much as he disliked the idea of turning back. He could tackle anything, provided he could see it; but here the limit of vision went backward before him grudgingly, a step at a time. Between the twin copper cliffs the palpable presence of storm coiled and writhed, and the ravens screamed and wheeled in it invisibly.

He had come all the way up from Bolzano in the orderly manner he preferred, sticking to his timetable as tenaciously as he stuck to his syllabus all through a three-year tutorial; and if he did not reach Vicenza tonight his whole programme would be thrown out of gear. The very thought made him give a determined hitch to his rucksack and plunge on.

Within the darkening shelter of the Five Fingers a tall snowfield slanted upward and instantly he stopped in his tracks, for somehow at this hour he had not expected the Langkofelkar to be inhabited.

There was a girl on the snowfield. She was not paying any attention to him; she had not yet seen him, nor heard his approach. She was wholly absorbed in what she was doing, and to Edward's staid mind her occupation was so astonishing that he became wholly absorbed in it, too, and stood staring like a halfwit.

She was dressed in slacks and a thick orange-coloured sweater, with her trouser-ends tucked into multi-coloured socks above ski boots, and she was engaged in running full tilt up the steep snowfield as high as she could before losing impetus, and then sliding down again, eccentrically poised with spread arms on the dimpled and soiled surface.

She was playing devotedly, in the middle of a terrifying solitude of rock and stormcloud, as unimpressed by the vastness and violence of the Dolomites and the crying flight of the ravens as a child, or a cat. And, indeed, there was something of both child and cat in her perfect concentration and absolute unselfconsciousness. Edward held his breath, and did not realize that he was holding it for fear she should become aware of him, and be disconcerted. Children and cats do not like being watched.

She was young, and beautifully built, strong and slender. She had hair of the light, honeyed gold which is not uncommon in North Italy, and her face was oval and smooth, and tanned to a deep bronze-gold, noticeably darker than the hair. This gold and bronze colouring was all he could see of her, until she took a wilder plunging fall, rolled down the snowfield, and sat up in a flurry of white, beating snow from her sleeves. She was facing the rocks where he stood, and she saw him.

He need not have been afraid; she was not startled. She got up unconcernedly, and came towards him at a light run and said in a clear, rather high voice: "*Buona sera!*" as if they were meeting and passing on some frequented road; and then as blithely, in case he had not understood: "*Bon soir, monsieur!* Good evening!"

Edward, who had never been more taken aback in his life, nevertheless managed to reply with correct gravity: "Good evening!"

He shifted his rucksack uneasily, and looked down the wavering track which was trodden downhill through the snow.

"Where are you bound for?" she asked.

"The Rifugio Vicenza. And you?"

"Oh, back to Sella," she said, shaking back the heavy, soft mass of her swinging hair. "I came up here only for an hour, to get an appetite for dinner. From where have you come today?"

"From Pordoi." It did not sound a very impressive day's work; he wondered how he had managed to take so long over it.

"To Vicenza is too far," she said, shaking her head gravely. "The weather is not good, and it will be dark before you can reach the *rifugio*. You should turn back to Sella."

"How long does it take from here to Vicenza?"

"Even in good conditions, more than one hour. Down to Sella it is only half an hour, and very easy. I think you should not go on tonight, it will not be safe. At the Rifugio Sella they will find you a bed. I am staying there myself. It is full, but they will not send you away."

He knew that she was giving him sensible advice, but his mind could find only dismay in such an adjustment of his holiday.

"I'm going back now," she said. "If you are wise, you will come, too." But she did not wait to see if he would follow her.

Edward turned resolutely, and walked across the almost level basin towards the next broken barrier of rocks. He began the descent gingerly, but maintained it for no more than five minutes. Darkness was closing too quickly upon the Langkofelkar. The girl was right, he ought to go back. It was the only sane thing to do.

He went down the slope more soberly than she had done. The first drops of a heavy shower spattered round him as he drew near to the large white bulk of the *rifugio*.

He clumped into the wide wooden hall. People and dogs were seething in and out of the doors as furiously as the cloud boiled in and out of the darkening blowhole of the mountain above. Most of the people, Edward judged, were Italians, and of a certain quite clearly indicated kind. Not the rich and fashionable, but the comfortably-off and self-confident. The few who were just coming in, in climbing kit of the cheap, unaesthetic but efficient ex-army type, struck him as being the few foreigners, Austrian, German or English. The rest were better-dressed, but for admiration rather than action. As for the dogs, they were mostly a litter of half-grown boxers which seemed to belong to the house. Children shrilly pursued and tormented them. The din was almost confusing, after the immense quietness on the mountain.

He used his best German on a girl behind the counter in the little shop, where all the musical boxes and wooden toys from the Val Gardena waited for purchasers. She told him that the rooms were all taken, but hesitated and glanced at the darkening windows, and he knew she would not turn him away. There was a bed in one of the top landings.

It proved to be a large corner in a wilderness of dark recesses like open rooms, warm still from the hot sunshine which had poured upon the roof most of the day. A bathroom was not far distant, and the place had more privacy by far than he would have found in the chalet used by the climbers. He accepted it gladly, and shut himself into the bathroom to wash and shave, in some haste, for the gong had already sounded for dinner, and he was hungry.

The dining-room at the Rifugio Passo Sella was large, bright and noisy. As soon as Edward entered, he was met by a very diminutive waitress, with a flashing smile, who waved him after her to a table in a corner.

It was laid for six people, but only one person was yet seated, an elderly, lean-faced man, with cheeks the colour of teak, and far-sighted blue eyes. He was dressed in an ancient and disreputable tweed jacket, knickerbockers, and a khaki shirt without a tie, and his large hands, knotted before him on the plastic tablecloth, were like the roots of trees.

"Good evening!" said the elderly man. "*Thought* you were English! Sit down—where you like!" He pushed the carafe of red wine across the table. "Staying long?"

"Only overnight. I was a bit too late to get over to Vicenza, or I shouldn't be here now. The weather was against me."

"Oh! Just walking!" A little of the bright, speculative interest faded out of the blue eyes. "You don't climb?"

"I'm afraid not."

"Pity! But you couldn't have better country for learning," he said, brightening. "I've got a couple of keen beginners up on the Grohmann today. I'd have been with 'em now if I hadn't pulled a muscle on the Sella yesterday. Why not stay a few days, and join up with us?"

Edward devoted himself to his soup, and muttered apologetically that he had to get over to Siusi as soon as possible.

"All your party are English?" he inquired.

"Yes. Palgrave and his wife have been coming out here with me—various places, you know—for several years. This year we brought out two of my undergraduates. Promising lads, too! Climbed with 'em in England often, but they're new to the Dolomites."

Edward warmed to find himself in the company of a fellow don. They exchanged names, and plunged into involved comparisons of provincial universities.

Professor Lacey's light blue eyes roved round the room speculatively. "I see our star turn's missing!"

Edward suppressed a guilty start, convinced for a moment that this sharp old gossip had probed the recesses of his mind, and surprised the image of the golden girl inconveniently insistent there. But when he followed the shrewd gaze he saw that his companion's thoughts were elsewhere. He was watching the antics of a large party of obvious Italians, round a table in the middle of the room. They were all of them notably overdressed, and were making a considerable amount of noise. There was only one vacant place, a pretty, distrait little dark woman sitting anxiously beside it, her eyes forever on her watch.

"Her husband," explained the Professor simply. "It seems very quiet without him," he added.

"Why, who is he?" asked Edward.

"Oh, just one of those people with over-active glands. We always call him the Lion. The rest run after him making adoring noises. They're all from the same place—somewhere in the Veneto; I think it's Padua."

He sniffed; his opinion of the Paduan party was plainly not a very high one. Probably none of them climbed.

"Pretty wife he's got, at any rate," said Edward, watching her look sadly from her watch to the empty chair beside her. "Fond of him, too!"

"Best-looking of the whole bunch, and the only one he never takes any notice of. There isn't a woman in the place he hasn't made a pass at—most of them successful! Until Olimpia arrived, he didn't mind handling three or four at a time. But, of course, with Olimpia in sight, the rest more or less vanish." He lifted his long nose, sniffing appreciatively in the direction of the door. "Speak of the angel! Now *there's* a woman!"

The golden girl from the Langkofelkar came in slowly, and moved to her place on the other side of the room. She had changed into a black silk skirt, and sandals, and a matt white blouse cut very low on the shoulders, and out of its thick opaque whiteness her golden shoulders sailed with the aplomb of a lily growing. Her arms were long, rounded and beautiful. Her skin was as sleekly smooth as polished bronze.

The only disquieting thing about her was the presence at her shoulder of a large man in an expensive summer suiting, a bulky blond of impressive physique and indeterminate age. Somewhere between thirty and forty, clean-shaven, heavy-featured, one of those inert faces behind which a formidable temper can sometimes conceal itself. Worst of all, his hand at the girl's elbow was casual and possessive.

Edward's eyes followed her steadily until she was seated. He swallowed hard, and asked as casually as he could:

"Who is she?"

"That's Olimpia! Signora Montesanto—I'm afraid!" Edward caught Professor Lacey's too penetrating eye, and quickly averted his own.

"Yes," said the Professor with candid sympathy, "he's her husband. Sometimes I'm not sure that she's any better pleased about it than the rest of us. A lovely creature, isn't she? There isn't a man in the place who hasn't made a play for her."

"Including your Lion," said Edward, struggling manfully to look no more concerned about Signor Montesanto's unwelcome existence than the next man.

"Oh, he can't understand that any woman could resist him."

"*She'd* have made a magnificent lioness," said Edward, on an irresponsible impulse.

"So the Lion seems to think. I must say, she hasn't shown any sign of thinking so herself, for all the success he's had elsewhere. No doubt she's found out that it's the only way to keep the peace, with a possessive person like her husband around."

Some of the tables were already emptying. Giulia Leoni was twisting a handkerchief between her anxious fingers, and looking over her shoulder towards the door at every sound of a step entering the wooden hall. She was certainly no lioness. A charming little black kitten, perhaps, nothing more deadly than that.

They were halfway through coffee when a red head was thrust in at the door, and dark young eyes in a dirty face signalled across to them imperatively.

"Young Crowther," said Professor Lacey, stubbing out his cigarette without hesitation. "Something wrong!" he added in the same quiet tone, and got up and made for the door. Edward went after him, because the boy's eyes had seemed to include him in the summons. He began to talk, in a soft, laborious voice of shock, the moment they were within range.

"Prof, something ghastly's happened! He *would* climb alone! My God, of all the idiots! And who's going to tell his wife?"

The big, brown, quiet woman who was kneeling in the middle of the floor said kindly, but firmly: "Shut up, Bill! Go and get a drink, and bring one for Tony, too."

There were four of them grouped round something on the floor; the woman, who must be Mrs. Palgrave, and a shaggy middle-aged man in a dark green sweater, who was most probably her husband; the other undergraduate, a thickset boy in an ex-army windproof jacket; and the guide Johann, who was slight and wiry, and looked the part rather less perfectly than Lacey did.

They were bending over a long bundle, the unmistakable shape of a man, from which Johann was just carefully unwinding the nylon rope which had afforded a means of carrying the burden.

"Took us all this time to get him down the scree," said Palgrave, looking up sombrely into Lacey's face. "We marked out the position we found him in, in case they can make anything of it, but Bill's right, it looks as if he was fooling about on the Grohmann by himself. Betty tried some photographs, too, in what was left of the light."

"We'd better get the doctor, at any rate. He's in the dining-room now."

"I'll go," said Tony promptly, and made for the door.

"And the manager! Ask Sabina to find him." Lacey watched the layers of padding fall away with the rope, and asked: "Dead?"

"Stone dead! Dead when we found him."

The figure took shape, seemed to grow larger. Edward saw the body of a big and shapely man, a young, lusty, arrogant body, in well-made mountain clothes of a rough light cloth, good boots, a white silk shirt open about a brown, brawny throat. A sweater was pealed away gently from the face. One of those bold, over-pronounced faces, full of bone, with large, deep eyelids, half-open upon dark eyes, a strong jaw, and a mouth whose forward thrust suggested large and immaculate teeth. He had a short russet beard, nicely trimmed about the full and passionate mouth.

They stood looking down at him for an instant in awed silence. "Better a live dog!" said Professor Lacey, and added upon a sharper tone: "He doesn't seem to have had much of a fall!"

He fell on his knees beside Johann, who was already unbuttoning the tweed jacket. "Not a mark on him! No obvious fractures! What the devil *did* happen to him?"

They had all drawn closer, Edward fascinated but silent on the fringe of the circle.

"The snow under him," said Mrs. Palgrave suddenly, "it was hardly dented! Close to the rocks, too—if he'd fallen far he'd have been embedded in it feet deep. There must be nearly two metres of snow there—"

Johann turned back the jacket. There was a thick pullover under it; he felt at it above the dead man's heart, and drew back his fingers faintly stained. He turned up the pullover to disclose the soft white shirt. Close above the heart was a small, neat, unmistakable hole, so small that in the dark wool they had failed to see it at all. There was hardly any blood, only a few stained inches of silk. The wool had absorbed the rest as it oozed out from the wound.

"No," said Professor Lacey, softly out of the stunned silence. "He didn't fall far—just off his own two feet. Somebody put a bullet in him at pretty short range. I think," he said, "I'd better go and break it to the manager that we're going to need the police."

Edward never knew how far the police had to come but by nine o'clock they were there and in possession. The small points of light moving about high in the air to westward were the torches of the policemen plying up the traverses to the col. Within the house the little office was given over to the use of two more officers, the only refuge anywhere within doors from Giulia's tears and despair.

The English party told their story first, and it was brief enough. They had been all day up on the Langkofelkar. They had been entirely absorbed in the pitches of their climb and the coaching of the novices, and had seen no human beings below them, nor heard anything which could make them think of a revolver shot. Descending, in light considerably worse than they had expected, they had found the body. They had thought it best to bring it down with them, but had marked out its position with stones, and left a coloured handkerchief wedged flaglike into a cleft of the rock above to make discovery easy.

The deceptive light had prevented them from seeing too clearly, and the very meagre flow of blood had all been absorbed within his clothes. Moreover, as they realized now, his jacket had been buttoned after he was shot, for the cloth was not marked by any hole over the spot where his pullover and shirt were perforated. Not until they had eased him laboriously all the way down the scree, and brought him into the light of the hotel, did they discover how he had died.

Edward, for his part, had come from Pordoi the long but easy way. At the top, about a quarter to seven, he had encountered Signora Montesanto, who had advised him to turn back to Sella because of the bad weather and the fading light, and after a very brief pause for consideration he had done so. That was all he knew.

When they had made their statements, which Professor Lacey translated into Italian, they were dismissed from the office. The dining-room was a chaos, the boxer pups unchecked under everybody's feet, the doctor, an inoffensive little man on holiday from a practice in Cremona, in weary attendance on Giulia. As soon as she was fit to answer questions the police would see her, so that she could be put to bed, and escape something, at least, of the horror of the evening. Meantime, she sat clutching at the nearest friendly arm, her handkerchief at her lips, the tears raining effortlessly from her large, purple-black eyes.

Several of the other Paduan women were also in tears, but voluble between their bouts of weeping, and the noise they produced sounded to Edward as bitter and angry as it was shrill. The men of the party were nervous and sullen, padding backwards and forwards between the bar and their table, and accosting one another in sudden explosive outbursts as they drank.

"They sound as if they're quarrelling," said Edward, in Professor Lacey's pricked and capacious ear.

"They are. Not much comradeship left in that little fraternity now. All the women were jealous of the least attention the Lion paid to any other woman, and the husbands divided their time between envying him, being scared of him, and hating his guts. He was an eminently murderable person," sighed Professor Lacey, almost with respect, almost with regret, "in spite of being irrepressibly likeable."

"How did a man like that manage to get into the Langkofelkar entirely alone? I suppose he did! I should have thought there'd always be a few of the faithful under his feet."

"Oh, he could kick when he liked. People didn't hang around the Lion when he told them to go to hell! Everybody claims to have been miles away all afternoon, and they're all busy casting doubts on the claims of all the others. Nobody seems to have seen the Lion turn back from Rodella and go up into the Langkofelkar."

"That could be true enough," said Palgrave, looking up from his belated dinner. "In country on this fantastic scale it's amazing how you can lose a hundred people—all still within sight."

"Oh, it could be true! So he came back alone and unnoticed—or maybe he didn't come back, but worked up along the contour from Rodella, and on to the scree from there."

"Did he leave his wife with as little ceremony as the rest of the party?" asked Edward.

"With a damned sight less. Why should he waste finesse on her? He already had her. Besides, Giulia doesn't walk. Everybody knows it. No, he brought her here, and after that she had to fend for herself. It would have been rather a sensation if he *had* been seen out with her, as a matter of fact."

"Then where did she spend her afternoon? I suppose they'll have to ask her, too." She was gone from the dining-room, as he saw when he looked round again; she must be in the office with the police at this moment.

"She took one of the cars, and went off down the valley by herself after breakfast. It seems she's been down in Santa Cristina, shopping. I saw her bringing the parcels in when she got back, about twenty past seven or somewhere around that time."

The red-headed Bill said, somewhat uncomfortably: "There's a path up from Santa Cristina—it works up round the back of the Langkofel."

"It's two good hours' walking, and the scramble at the end," said Tony. "And Giulia doesn't walk. And even if she really could tackle ground like that, she couldn't have got back to pick up her car in the time."

"How do you know she couldn't? We don't know what time he was shot."

Edward looked at the Professor, who certainly would not have forgotten to sound the doctor upon the subject. "What time *was* he shot?"

"He's too cautious to commit himself too deeply. Probably between half-past four and half-past six, he says."

"So, on the earlier limit, it *would* be a possibility for her to walk back to Santa Cristina, pick up the car, and still be back here by twenty-past seven."

"It would for anyone but Giulia. Maybe she's not so helpless on her feet as she claims, but no one's ever seen her take more than a peaceful little promenade on the grass verge along the road."

"You didn't notice her shoes?" asked Mrs. Palgrave.

"No, I can't say I did. She wears good stout walking shoes. They're the thing here, and you can trust all that party to do whatever is the thing."

"She wouldn't have hurt him!" said Tony, suddenly laying down his fork as if his appetite had suffered a serious check. "She's crazy about him. And look what she's put up with already, without a murmur of complaint!"

Giulia came out of the office, her handkerchief to her eyes, the sympathetic arm of one of her friends supporting her tenderly towards the stairs. It was curious that they all looked at her shoes now. They saw foolish little sandals, with three-inch heels. Exactly the shoes one would bring to Sella to support a reputation for never walking anywhere.

The manager, hovering anxiously upon the threshold of the office, lifted an imploring finger, and whispered: "Signora Montesanto!"

Olimpia rose, smiled at him reassuringly across the room, and crushed out her cigarette in the ashtray. She walked towards the open door and the waiting policemen with the beautiful, alert vehemence with which she had launched herself down the snowfield.

Edward said: "I suppose there wouldn't be any objection to our getting a breath of air, would there, provided we stay within call?"

He went towards the door, and since no one attempted to stop him, opened it and went out into the night. He took the path which lay between the hotel and the little chapel, and walked into the cold, pale, stony borders of the rock town. Far above him the vague shape of the Langkofel, fantastically high and close, blotted out whole galaxies of stars.

He lit a cigarette, and found himself a sheltered corner among the rocks. The air had almost the snap of frost, and he was shivering by the time he turned back slowly towards the *rifugio*.

Out of the dimness something white moved vaguely towards him upon the path. His senses leaped to recognition as if he had willed her rather than merely encountered her. After the whiteness of her blouse he was aware of the light, amber gleam of her eyes. They had not kept her long; but then, she had nothing to tell them. He heard her sudden, indrawn breath, the long, soft sigh.

"Oh, it's you!"

The high, clear voice could be almost as still as silence itself.

"You'll be very cold!" said Edward, disturbingly aware of her naked golden shoulders so close to him. "I'll go and get you a coat—or, if you'll have mine—"

The short hair tossed violently as she shook her head. "No, not cold! May I have a cigarette, please?" As he sheltered the little flame of the lighter assiduously between their bodies, his heart thumping at her nearness, she shut her hand suddenly over his, and clung to it with cool, tremulous fingers. In the pure oval of her face her eyes clung to his as fiercely. "Not cold—just afraid!

"You're very kind," she added softly, "and I am glad you are here. But there is nothing you can do for me except be here, and be kind."

He did not know how it had happened, but his arm was about her shoulders, and he was trembling as violently as she, and stammering incoherent reassurances into her ear. They clung together in the hushed and magical night.

"You can tell me," he said vain-gloriously. "You can trust me! If there's something frightening you—"

He held her to his swelling heart, and waited.

"If I'd known—if we *could* know what people will do—I wouldn't have let him out of my sight today! Ever since I married him it has been like this! He looks for wrongs, wrongs, wrongs, everywhere, always. But I have grown used to that," she said in a shuddering whisper, "and I thought it would just go on like that always. I never thought that something bad would happen—like this!"

"You think your husband may have—may know something about Leoni's death?" Edward baulked at the word "murder." She lifted her beautiful face, so softly and deeply moulded in the darkness, and he saw the fixed golden shining of her eyes.

"We were out together all morning on the Cir. We went at dawn. When we came back to lunch I was tired, and so was he, and I went to my room and slept. When I dressed and came down to look for him I could not find him. I thought I would just go up to the col before dinner. It was after five o'clock, I know, when I went out, but I am not sure how much after—perhaps Sabina will know, she saw me go out. When I came back—you know when that was—Tonino still had not come in. He did not come until almost eight o'clock."

"But he must be able to prove where he was all the afternoon," said Edward reasonably.

"He *says* that he took the meadow path over the pass, by Valentini's Inn, and went down towards Ganazei. You know that path? For a long way it is so open you could see and recognize a man on it as much as half a mile away from you. There are huts, too, and part of the meadow is only just being mown. Do you think a man could go that way, and meet nobody? Oh, it is possible, it could happen to one man in a thousand men, but—"

"But you're afraid he was up there in the Langkofelkar with Leoni! Is that it? You think he was there when you climbed up the same path, and that he waited until we'd both gone before he ventured down?"

"It could have been like that," she said, almost inaudibly.

His eyes dwelt upon hers in consternation and dismay. "*Has* he a gun?"

"Yes. I have seen it—but I do not know about guns. It is only small, but I don't know the … calibre? Is that right? It may be the wrong kind of gun. Only, I am afraid—"

Edward was shaken with a tremor of alarm which seemed to originate within his own heart rather than in any look or word of hers. He took her suddenly by the shoulders, aware of the silken unexpectedness of her cool skin under his palms, but past anything so trivial as embarrassment. "He won't hurt *you*? If there's any fear of that—if there's any possibility—"

Olimpia smiled, slowly and wryly, with the smoke of the cigarette curling from her lips. She looked at him steadily, and he thought he saw amusement in her eyes, but was sure he saw tenderness. "You are very sweet," she said, so softly that he hardly heard the words.

"But if he's crazy with jealousy like that—if he thinks that—that you—"

"He thinks I have betrayed him with Paolo Leoni," she said, in a voice which had strongly recovered its calm, "and with at least a dozen men before him. I think he has dealt with Paolo for it. But that is not the kind of thing one tells the police unless one is sure."

She dropped the butt of her cigarette, and put her foot upon it. Her hand closed tightly over his for a moment, and she was turning abruptly away when he caught her back suddenly into his arms.

"Olimpia—"

He didn't know what he had wanted to say, he was groping without any words, her startled face upturned to him, glimmering in the dark, the rich, soft lips parted, the shining eyes wide. He felt for her mouth partly out of sheer desperation, because he was at a loss for anything to say which would not be utterly fatuous. Her mouth quivered, made to maintain its startled quiescence, and then could not. She fastened upon him insatiably, clinging and trembling.

Somewhere not very far distant, upon the path, a stone rolled and a foot stumbled. A voice, heavy and still like valley air, said loudly: "Olimpia!"

She pulled herself out of Edward's arms. Her face was quite calm. She shook her head, forbidding him to accompany her, but she made no secret of his presence, for as she walked firmly towards her husband she called back: "Good night!" over her shoulder in deliberate English.

Edward stood where she had left him. He strained his ears to catch the tone of the encounter, ready to spring to her rescue at the first hint of a threat.

The deep voice, inexpressibly weary and bitter, said with the faintest note of surprise: "An Englishman this time?" copying her firm pronunciation. "Well, why not? I have been cuckolded in every other major language." It was, in its way, a blow, but it was not the voice of a man immediately dangerous.

They were gone. For an instant, when they reached the light from the windows of the dining-room, he saw them as two black shapes silhouetted on the yellow, walking apart, scrupulously drawn back from touching each other. Their careful movements infected him with a totally unexpected frenzy of pain.

Then they vanished, and he was alone. Far up the scree the torches of the police were threading a zigzag way downward, like arrested lightning flowing painfully towards the earth.

Edward watched the police thread their way through the rocks towards the *rifugio*, which was still blazing with lights. They had not the knowledge he had just acquired, nor his urgent reasons for wanting the case cleared up at all costs. For the only possible way to extricate Olimpia Montesanto from her unbearable situation was to prove her husband a murderer, and wrest her away from him once and for all, or prove him innocent, and set her mind at rest.

He stood looking back towards the lighted windows for a few minutes after the policemen had passed by, and then he swung round suddenly, and began to stride rapidly up through the rocks towards the base of the zigzag path which climbed the scree.

The sky had cleared, and stars, very small and pinched, pricked the dark blue expanse of sky with pinpoints of light. The *rifugio* was only a tiny lamp below him now, shining upon a short, lambent, pallid coil of road. Suddenly he saw himself for the incredible fool he was, charging romantically up a mountain at eleven o'clock at night to find some evidence which would put a man, hitherto unknown to him even by name, in goal, and set his wife free—free for what? Free to accept Edward Stanier's protection and admiration? He was appalled by the unexpectedness of the vision.

The rocks soared about him quite suddenly, a sort of closing in of the arms of the mountain round his strenuously bent shoulders. The cliffs were awesome in the night, and the silence was withering.

The first glimmering snowfield fell away on his left, within the arena of rocks. He was glad that his climbing boots were Italian, and almost certainly of the same pattern as many which had passed this way already, probably including some of those worn by the policemen. He must not cut up the marked area of snow too crudely, but if he took care his tracks would pass among the rest.

It had not occurred to him until then that someone might have been left on guard there, and he halted for a moment in his reckless slide down the snow, in consternation at the possibility. But no, on second thoughts it was unlikely enough. The night was already very cold; before morning there would be several degrees of frost up here; and who was likely to invade the mountain at night, in any case?

The place was not so hard to find. There it was, the shape of a man roughly marked out on the dimpled surface and a flutter of coloured cloth above.

Stepping lightly and steadily, to leave no deeper indentations than he need, he went inch by inch over the ground where the body had lain.

One of the stones placed by Johann's party heeled away silently. He righted it, playing his torch closely into the hollow; and in the thin beam of light he saw something black in the crumbling whiteness within.

He pulled out a soft, narrow leather strap, a bit of black kid about eight inches long, with two small steel half-hoops sewn into a loop in one end of it. He did not know what he had expected; it meant nothing to him now that he had it. Just a strip of kid, with a few frayed threads of cotton where it had been sewn to something else. And yet there was something about it that made his fingertips tingle as he held it.

The leather was fresh, supple and brightly black, and his cold hands could detect in it none of the internal stiffness of damp. It could not have kept this condition for so much as a single day in the hollow of snow. Either one of Johann's party had shed the thing when they lifted the body or else it had been dropped by someone shortly before Leoni was shot. So shortly, thought Edward, shivering in the thin, frosty wind, that he could hardly be anyone else but the murderer.

The place was neither on nor near any path; he had had to swing inward a long way from the track to reach it. He could hardly believe that some other, some innocent person had chosen exactly the same spot to linger in, on the same day. No, what he had in his hand belonged to one of the climbing party who had moved the body, or to the murderer.

He found nothing else, though he hunted doggedly for ten minutes more about the disturbed area of snow. He was shivering violently with the cold, and it was growing very late. He pushed the strap into his pocket, for more exact examination later, and began the laborious climb back to the col.

It was past midnight when he crept quietly through the town, but the lights were still on in the hall and the office, and the doors still unfastened.

He got himself to bed and lay for a long time sleepless, trembling and trying to get warm.

Tomorrow he must somehow contrive to get a word with Olimpia alone, and show her the strap. If she could connect it with her husband, there would be something, at least, on which the police could take action.

When Edward came downstairs next morning, the dining-room curtains were still closely drawn, so he went out and strolled back and forth on the green verge of the road, where he could keep an eye upon the stairs every time he passed the door. The first sunlight, salmon pink, flushed the upper cliffs of the Langkofel. It was going to be a beautiful day.

Professor Lacey came out with the rest, hitched his shapeless hat, decorated with a frayed end of nylon rope, forward over his mahogany brow, and sniffed appreciatively at the glittering air. Then he went back to muster his party, and presently they emerged in a tight little organized knot of British efficiency, and made purposefully for the dining-room, which was now open.

They called a greeting to Edward as they approached the doorway, and lingered as though they expected him to join them at once; but he did not go in until he had seen Olimpia come down the stairs and enter the dining-room, her husband close at her elbow, his hand touching her arm. No luck there! She passed in through the little anteroom as though she had not seen Edward standing in the sunlight beside the road; but he felt in his heart that she had, that she was deeply aware of him, and would have come to him if she could have shaken off that forbidding hand.

At least from his place at the corner table he could watch her across the room. While he fended off the Professor's efforts to inveigle him into their plans for the day's climb, he was covertly studying the slender, erect figure, the long brown hands and the swinging honey-coloured hair. She was in knickerbockers and a white shirt this morning, her hooded windjacket hanging on the arm of her chair. So they were going out, and on an active expedition, too.

The thought terrified him. How could he let her go off into the desolate lunar craters of disintegrating rock about these mountains, alone, with a wretched unbalanced creature who had probably killed once out of his insane jealousy, and might do so again? He could not bear to think of the miles and miles of faint, bewildering greys and greens and pinks of stone and scree, unpopulated, deceptive, silent, where a body could lie for weeks and weeks undiscovered since only colour and movement together ever served to call attention even to the living.

The Professor was nudging him, urging something, he didn't know what, he hadn't been listening. Distrait, he parried at a venture:

"Perhaps we shan't be allowed to go off the premises. I mean—the police—"

"My dear fellow! Approximately one hundred and eighty people, most of them with only the flimsiest acquaintance with the Lion!—How can they all be kept here? No, we can all go where we like, as long as they're reasonably sure we're coming back again. You'd much better come with us."

Edward fought them off with much more decision than he could ever have shown for his own sake. His eyes were on the silent couple across the room, the girl with her warm bronze skin exquisite against the white silk of her shirt, and her eyes cast down desultorily upon the plate she had hardly touched.

He wondered that the tension between himself and her was not as perceptible to everyone in the room as it was to him. She kept her eyes resolutely lowered because if she raised them it would be to fix their wide, golden, fearful appeal upon him, and that look would be one Tonino would read instantly, and translate into something shameful.

Edward had to let them pass through the doorway before he dared excuse himself hurriedly and follow. They were going towards the stairs again. He saw Olimpia check suddenly, heard her say something about stamps, drawing her arm from Tonino's grasp with an easy and natural recoil towards the little shop; but instead of going up the staircase without her, he came back at her heels, stood by her at the counter, still touching her remindingly with the ends of long, inexorable fingers. He was not going to let her out of his sight, that was plain. "Neither will I!" said Edward grimly to himself. "Not until I can get her safely away from you!"

He met her eyes full for an instant, light yellow flames of fear in the mask-like calm of her lovely face, and flashed back at her, as convincingly as he could when the greater part of himself was a molten panic of infatuation and bewilderment, his service and reassurance.

He watched them move off across the road, and take a thinly-trodden path diagonally over the open meadow, heading straight for the cliffs of the Sella, which loomed immense against the washed blue sky, palest pink above, shadowy russet and bluish grey below. As soon as he was sure of their direction he went back into the equipment room, where the English party were just girding themselves with the most casual set of ropes and *kletterschuhe* he had ever seen.

"Is there a quick way up into the Sella plateau this side? There's a path that makes off directly into the cliffs just opposite here. I wondered about taking that. It must take hours off the Val Lasties route if it's practicable."

"Oh yes, much the most direct way up." Professor Lacey knotted a pair of dingy tennis shoes at his belt, and looked round with mildly quickening interest. "Just across the meadows here—the path's liable to vanish, but keep more or less on the contour, and scout along the cliff there, and you can't miss it. Takes you up to Piz Selva in a few hours. Interesting route, too!"

"Is it very difficult?"

"Hardly a scramble. Where it gets rather steep and exposed there are wire ropes fixed and some hand-holds."

"Only you have to watch out for the ropes in places," supplemented Mrs. Palgrave cheerfully. "Some of them aren't too safe. There's a lot of weathering on those faces."

Edward withdrew with somewhat nervous thanks, and went out to the vast green undulation of meadow again. The two dwindling figures were walking steadily along the invisible track, some distance away now, their faces towards the mountain, but the space between was so open that he could not follow them without becoming as conspicuous as a sore finger against the empty sweep of grass.

After a few irresolute moments he set off uphill by the road, cutting the corners of the boggy grass, towards the crest of the pass. He had not thought what he could do. The first thing was to be close to her, and feel the desperate valour her eyes had given him filling his mild heart with fury and resolution.

He lost sight of them from time to time from the undulations of the cliff-face, which leaped out of the meadow almost as cleanly as a wall, with only here and there a few fallen boulders to soften its fabulous outlines. He dared not go many yards from the shelter of the rock, for fear of becoming visible to the two who were gradually converging with him across the meadow.

He slowed down, edging yard by yard along, and waiting for the first sounds of their nearness. They were not speaking at all. Presently he could hear their steps in the grass; and for a moment, before they vanished into the rock, he saw Olimpia's face clearly, intent, aware, and very still, the eyes flaring unfocused, as though all her powers were concentrated on listening. Listening, he thought, for him.

When their leisurely, deliberate movements no longer sent him any echoes, he ventured along the cliff perhaps twenty yards more, and came upon the gully, doubling steeply backward into the rock mass. It was narrow enough to be easily missed unless one looked back at the right angle, complicated with masses of fallen stones for a while, but clear of scree, and he could move silently and fairly quickly up it, for there was plenty of cover.

From rock to rock and corner to corner he pulled strenuously upwards until he could hear them moving ahead of him and catch an occasional glimpse of them as they bent their backs in the long, easy, untiring stride of practised mountaineers.

Once they halted, and sat down where there was an open window on the pass, to smoke their first cigarette; but as soon as the ends were trodden out against the stones they were off again. He stayed in close attendance on them, dangerously close, wherever there was cover, but sometimes he had to fall back as much as a hundred yards to remain hidden, and then his fear began to beat upward in his throat urgently, tugging him onward towards her for dear life, her life, which had become so crazily dear to him.

They were well up now, and coming to some of the more exposed places, where the path, if it could be called a path, crawled outward to the exterior faces of the group.

At any other time he would have been gravely discomforted by the plucking of the air, and the almost sheer drop of several hundred feet on his right hand; now he was too furiously intent to notice his own uneasy situation. Compared with the two people he was shadowing, he was an abject amateur. To them this was indeed an easy scramble, and nothing more. Edward watched Olimpia's movements whenever the chance offered, envious of her case and precision. He knew how her mind leaned back to him in its anxiety, and yet her body seemed as relaxed and competent as a cat's.

Her husband went before her, leaning back to give her a hand occasionally where the reach was long and difficult. Now the route had tacked, and they were crossing Edward's position on a higher level. He clung flattened against the rock, listening intently as the methodical, measured movements of their feet were stepped out above his head.

For the first time within Edward's hearing, Tonino had spoken to her. Her high, clear voice, curiously flattened and wary, said something mildly in return; it sounded like an obedient agreement to whatever he had said. Then a foot slid suddenly along the rock, a protesting sound; there were two cries so simultaneous that they might have been only the two dominant tones of a dreadful natural disharmony. Then a shadow flung outward on the air above Edward's head like a swooping bird, and something went by his cringing shoulders with a rushing sigh, turning, plying its arms vainly against the unsustaining wind, down, down, over the sheer edge of the cliff-face, plunging towards the meadows far below.

Crouched hard against his rock, frozen with horror, he saw something else fall with it, something tiny and thin and between black and bright, that rang on the edge of the fall with a metallic note, and bounced outward from his sight to vanish after Tonino Montesanto's body.

His senses, recoiling in self-defence, slammed a door upon reality and left him hanging there blind and deaf for a moment, and then he tore himself out of his paralysis to hear the thin, terrifying sound of Olimpia screaming. He forgot the nine hundred feet of vertigo below him, and the thirty-seven years of physical mediocrity behind him, and clawed his way up to her with heroic haste. She was spread out against the rock, her face pressed into her shoulder, wailing like a crazy child. Not far above her right hand he could see the place where the iron staple was newly broken out of the rock.

He came to her side very gently and warily, anchored her to the rock with a firm arm, and began to talk to her softly, choosing words so calm and tender that she had to hear their authoritative sound, if not their sense.

"It's all over now, you're quite safe with me. I'll take you down again safely. I'll take you home. Don't worry any more. I'm with you."

She braced herself a little, and drew closer to him, huddling against his breast.

"It wasn't your fault. Don't think of it, it's all over now. Just hold on to me."

"He tried to kill me," she said indistinctly into his coat, her voice a child's whimper of protest against injustice. "He leaned down to give me his hand—and he took hold of the iron hold instead, and broke it out, and it fell—I don't know what happened—he must have lost his balance—"

She detached one hand from its frantic clutch on the rock, and took hold of his coat instead, clinging convulsively. "He wanted to kill me!" she sobbed, relaxing from her quivering rigidity into the sustaining circle of his arm. "He was smiling, and then he pulled the staple out and let it fall—and all at once he slipped, and the smile went away from his face—and then he fell, too—"

He held and soothed her until she ceased to tremble, and visibly drew herself together again, raising her face dazedly to his.

"He was mad, wasn't he?" she said suddenly, when they were nearing the last stony cleft which brought them into the meadow. "It wasn't his fault—he didn't know what he was doing."

"No," said Edward tenderly, "he didn't know what he was doing. He wasn't normal."

He knew he had to find the body. When they reached the grass he wanted to leave her sitting against the safe, solid rocks while he prospected to the left, where he was pretty sure it would have fallen; but though her knees were shaking under her, she would not be left alone. She followed at his elbow, her hand reaching out to him, so that he turned back impulsively and gathered her to him again. Her face was too still, her eyes too hectically bright in it. He was afraid she might collapse in the reaction from terror and shock.

What was left of Tonino was lying in a small, hard field of stones below the sheer face, about thirty yards to the left of the mouth of the cleft. He looked remarkably intact still, only without bones, as limp and abandoned as a rag doll, and insubstantial inside the deflated bulk of his windjacket. Not ten yards from him the iron staple was lying in the thin grass between the stones.

"He's dead?" asked Olimpia, through stiff lips.

"Instantly. Maybe before he even hit the ground. He wouldn't know, Olimpia, he wouldn't have time to feel anything but one great blow. You mustn't think of it. You have to think of yourself now."

"I'm all right," she said, and swayed on her feet.

He got her to a comfortable spot with her back against a smooth stone, and wrapped her in her own jacket and his, and told her to shut her eyes and wait there while he ran to the *rifugio*, and not to try to move until he came back with help.

He thought for fully five minutes, as he ran across the meadow, that she was going to obey him. But at the end of that time, looking back again, he saw her stumbling after him at a reckless run, and calling after him with a sad little cry.

He turned back, sick with devotion, and took her into his arms. She was crying, the tears pouring from her eyes; and her face had recovered something of its live warmth with the relief of it. She was ashamed and apologetic, flushing under her tan as she entreated: "Don't leave me behind! I'm sorry!—I'm so sorry! But don't make me stay there—"

He kissed her wet cheeks, not like a lover at all, more like a father picking up a hurt child; and slowly, gently, he helped and coaxed her all across the interminable waste of meadow towards the *rifugio*.

The porter, Edward, and four policemen, went out to bring back the remains of Tonino Montesanto. It was not quite noon when they picked him out of the blood-stained stones, and went carefully over his disarticulated body, picked up the fallen iron staple he had wrenched from its place the better to tip his wife to her death, and put together the whole story of the morning from Edward's account.

The police officer in charge—Edward never knew what his title might be— felt at the deep inside pockets of the gaberdine windjacket before he unzipped it.

His hand halted upon the left breast, felt along the outline of something hard there. He was interested.

What came out of the pocket was a small, snubnosed revolver, which he lifted forth in the folds of a handkerchief, and regarded with alert satisfaction. The make and calibre, to judge by his face, was right. There was a silencer grooved into the barrel. The individual markings and the fingerprints, if any, should settle the matter.

Edward wondered where the gun would have been by now, if it had been Olimpia, and not Tonino, who had fallen. With all the terrace of the Sella for its grave, it would have taken some resurrecting.

Had Olimpia known more than she had confided to him last night? Had she discovered more since then, enough to make her death desirable for other reasons besides Othello's demented vengeance? He was never going to ask her. She was alive, and out of her nightmare. That was all that mattered.

They carried the stretcher back to the *rifugio*, decently covered from sight, and it was taken into the little office and the policemen went in after it, and shut the door on all the rest of the world. And yet within an hour or two the news had gone round.

The gun which had shot Paolo Leoni was the one which had been found, wiped clean of all prints, in Tonino Montesanto's pocket. There was no mystery now, it was all over. The murderer was dead, as dead as his victim. A wretched husband unbalanced by groundless jealousy—they knew well how to understand a tragedy like that.

Giulia Leoni came down in the afternoon, when it was quiet in the sun by the little chapel. She was drawn with weeping, but quiet and calm, her pretty dark curls conscientiously arranged about her little erect head. She went steadily out of the door, and over to where Olimpia was lying in a deck chair on the grass with Edward protectively beside her.

Olimpia had eaten nothing, but had obediently drunk the brandy he had given her. Giulia appeared beside the chair very gently and solicitously. She said: "Signora Montesanto!" in the most limpidly sweet of voices, and poured out a flood of Italian far too rapid and unemphatic for Edward to follow. He thought how kind and how brave it was of her to come straight to her fellow-victim like this, and offer her sympathy in this childlike manner.

Olimpia looked up, startled for a moment, through her long, bright-gold lashes, and a faint smile touched her lips.

Edward could not tell what she answered. He felt the play of certain feminine undercurrents.

Giulia had a quaint, vindicated dignity now, something she would perhaps never lose again. Drawing back a step or two for departure, she looked at him for a moment. She smiled. She made some last soft remark to Olimpia, and turned, still smiling, and walked back towards the house.

Olimpia sat looking after the slight, upright figure. She said tranquilly: "Giulia is very pretty, and quite sensible. She will not be a widow for long."

He was trying to run to earth a word Giulia had used, and which he was almost sure he ought to remember.

He was still thinking warmly how good women could be to one another, when he went in to tidy himself for dinner. It was quite a shock to him, when he remembered and looked up the elusive word. He had heard it before, all right! A man in the market at Brescia had once said it in his hearing to a woman at one of the stalls, and it meant, quite simply, "whore."

It gave him a nasty jolt to think how mistaken he had been in Giulia, and for a few minutes he was filled with an illogical fury against her. Then he remembered Olimpia's compassionate forbearance, and recalled with shame the legacy of shock and grief under which the poor little woman was labouring.

Olimpia came down to dinner in the black silk skirt and another white blouse, against which her bronzed arms and throat glowed enriched and polished in the lamplight. She sat at her table alone, declining, though graciously, all offers of company, even Edward's; but for him she said, softening the brief banishment: "Afterwards we will go for a walk. Please! Then we—"

She never completed whatever she had been about to say. Her eyes had a look of astonished discovery, as if even the pronoun had taken her by surprise.

He sustained the eager questions of the English party, not long returned from their day's climb to a mystery resolved, on the strength of that "we."

Afterwards Olimpia rose, and in leaving the room turned and looked at Edward from the doorway.

She came down buttoning a short woollen jacket, and hugging soft kid mittens under her arm. As soon as they were on, she slipped her hand into his arm, and they went out together, and turned towards the saddle of the pass.

Olimpia halted suddenly, and her gloved hand was drawing his head down to her, and her lips feeling softly, imperiously for his mouth.

She shut her long, strong arms round him wildly, arched against him into violent stillness.

"You saved my life," she whispered. "If I hadn't known you were there, close to me, I should have died of terror. Oh, Edward!" Feminine to the bone, she said self-reproachfully: "What must you think of me, that I throw myself into your arms like this, after so short a time?"

"I think you love me—I know I love you. What has time got to do with it, when so much has happened to us?" Was it really Edward Stanier speaking? His face flamed for his own audacity, but as much with triumph as embarrassment. Her hair was soft, like live silk; it seemed to quiver as it stroked his face, and smelled of lemon-blossom. He was faint and tipsy with the sweetness of her mouth, and her eyes, whenever he opened his own, opened responsively to receive the close, unfocused gaze, a luminous haze of gold, rapt, placid and satisfied.

"A cigarette?"

"Light it for me, please."

They stirred out of the trance slowly, and stood apart, smiling. He lit the cigarette, and transferred it from his lips to hers.

He watched her fondly, still a little drunk; and it was in the absorbed solemnity of drunkenness that he found himself dwelling upon the little elaborate glove in the glow of the cigarette. A pretty little mitt, the palm of black kid, the back of cherry-red, the wrist encircled with a thin black kid strap about eight inches long, two half-loops of chromium or steel making an unusual buckle in front.

For an instant the night was absolutely silent, with a silence which hammered his senses like the explosion of a gun. He held his breath, and his fingers felt instinctively at his inside pocket, where he had left something lying quite forgotten all day. He slid his gaze down, wincingly, reluctantly, towards her other hand, which at that very moment was rising innocently to touch his cold cheek. He felt the sweat break out along his hairline as chill as frost.

There was no little black kid strap on this wrist; only a few frayed threads of silk along the seam marked where it had once been.

When he closed the door of his room his legs gave under him, and he had to sit down quickly on the edge of the bed. Heat broke out through his body as intense as the first bitter cold. He wiped his face, and watched his hands trembling. The taste of her love-making, terrifyingly sweet, was still on his lips.

So Giulia had known what she was talking about, after all. The rest might say that the Lion had pestered Olimpia without result, but Giulia knew better. There had been results, all right! Once, at any rate! Yes, probably only once, that was what had baffled the Lion. He couldn't realize that there could be a woman who lived just as he did, taking whatever she wanted wherever she found it, and then throwing it away.

She had been quite ready, perhaps, to jettison Tonino, but not for an easy creature like Paolo Leoni. And a man like that might easily become a serious nuisance to a woman who dared to tire of him before he tired of her. Maybe he only bored her. Maybe he threatened, in his baffled indignation, his offended maleness, to talk to her husband, since he couldn't talk sense into her. Either way, he got his one more meeting. And he was dead.

Edward thought of Olimpia as he had first seen her, pleased with her solitude, eased of her encumbrance, gambolling in the snow with all her heart and mind. The gun must have been in the pocket of her slacks then, the gun she had planted on Tonino this morning, when for five minutes she was left behind with his body.

And Edward knew the rest of it, too, the part Giulia didn't know. It wanted only one bit of the puzzle orientated correctly, and all the rest fell into place. The summons of her eyes pulling him after her to the mountain, the chosen witness— not only for his lovesick gullibility, but also as a sort of favour, because he had already been chosen for something more than a witness. Olimpia liked him.

She had persuaded him back to Sella in the first place as much because she liked him as to avoid the possibility of a premature discovery of the Lion's body. This time she even liked him enough to shrug off Tonino in his favour, it seemed, especially as Tonino was beginning to offend her a little with his tragic forbearance and his tedious unhappiness.

It had been childishly easy; he saw that now. The pitch of the climb carefully chosen, the husband unwarily leaning to give her a hand. A little jerk outward when he was least expecting it, and the iron hand-hold wrenched from its already precarious anchorage on the rock and tipped down after him. Yes, after him! Edward realized now more clearly the order of that fall. And then she had nothing to do but stand there huddled against the rock, screaming delightedly into her own shoulder, her eyes closed in the satisfaction of artistry, until the sweet besotted fool of an Englishman came panting to her rescue.

But who was going to believe it now? What was there to show for it all but a little black kid strap from a glove, and if it was what he said it was, and he'd found it where he said he had, why hadn't he handed it over to the police? And in any case, whose word was there for it but his?

He thought of what it would be like to come out with this accusation before Olimpia's wide, wounded eyes, and a fiery sweat broke out all over him. Even if he could do it, even if he had the courage, even if they believed him, it could never be made good against that invulnerable serenity of hers. She would have nothing to do but fold her hands, and endure the torrent of words, and make it clear in her lovely, resigned silence that he had attempted to extort for his serv- ices a reward she was not prepared to grant, and had taken this method of avenging his slighted masculinity. She wouldn't even have to say it; that was the kind of conclusion to which people leaped where Olimpia was concerned. And at the end of everything, with her wild, candid kisses still burning on his lips and cheeks, did he even want the truth at that price?

So when everything was said and done, there was only one course open to him. Only one! Ignominious but inevitable!

He packed his rucksack, and lay down fully dressed on his bed, and even slept a little. At dawn he washed and shaved, and crept down to the office to wait for the porter. They were used to people rising and paying bills at short notice, and the police were no longer interested. By seven o'clock he was striding down the valley towards Plan de Gralba, to catch the early bus over the Passo Gardena for Brunico and the north.

He went down the road as if the devils were after him for the first mile, and then inexplicably his feet began to drag. He could hardly feel proud of himself. He was turning his back on a duty, he was going to be haunted for years by uneasy speculations about all the other poor devils who were destined to blunder along after Paolo and Tonino, and come to the same sticky end. But what else could he do? He was astonished to find that his walk had slowed to a stubborn crawl and, at every panicky spurt he put on, his implacable conscience jammed on the brake. But they'd never believe him. Why should they?

It was at this point that it dawned upon him that he was afraid of her. He stopped in his tracks, digging his heels indignantly into the turf by the roadside. He could throw overboard all the arguments of chivalry, for do what he would, Olimpia needed no help to protect herself from him. He just hadn't the courage to face her.

The realization fired his gentle heart into a totally unexpected anger. Not only had she made use of him as an assistant in disposing of her husband and her lover, and fooled him to the hilt, but she had brought him face to face with a mirror he had probably been avoiding all his life. He was afraid to tell the truth, because it was going to put him in a dubious position, and he might not be believed! As if that altered the fact that it was truth! So he was that kind of timorous soul, was he?

It confused him a little to find that he had turned, and was striding back up the white road as hard as he could go. He didn't pause to examine his motives too closely, and it was never at all clear to him whether the deprived ghosts of Paolo and Tonino had really had any hand in turning him, or whether his own galled self-esteem had done the job single-handed. He hoped it was his sense of duty to society, but he wasn't going to look too closely. He had more than enough on his mind.

The first climbers were out in front of the chalet when he reached the *rifugio*, and Professor Lacey was sniffing the air and measuring with his alert old eyes the day's possibilities. A terrifying air of normality had already settled over the house.

Before his courage could fail him, he approached the Professor, with so abrupt and strained a note that the old man stared and bristled like a pointer.

"My dear chap, the porter said you'd left. Did you miss the bus?"

"Not exactly. I had to come back. Professor, would you mind coming and interpreting for me? I've got to talk to the police."

"The police? Something new?" The blue eyes brightened with glee and widened with anticipation. "Surely they'll have gone by this time? But, of course, anything I can do—" He abandoned his study of the weather and was through the door ahead of Edward, and panting at the office doorway in a moment.

The police were still there, clearing up their records at leisure. They received Edward with alert interest. He began abruptly: "Tell them, will you, that I've got something to say about the case, and I should prefer to say it in the presence of Signora Montesanto, if they wouldn't mind asking her to come." He owed her that much, at any rate; or perhaps the debt was to himself. At least he kept his story obstinately to himself until the door opened upon the morning vision of Olimpia, fresh as a flower, with a white ivory necklet round her bright bronze throat, and the innocence of spring in her serene and dewy smile.

That was his worst moment. When her eyes lit on him, and brightened, and she exclaimed: "Why, Edward!" he felt like a murderer himself.

He had almost hoped that she would have got up early and asked for him, and finding him gone, suspected her immunity here, and slipped quietly away to new pastures. He ought to have known that Olimpia never ran away; it looked bad, and would have inconvenienced her, and besides, there is always a better way of dealing with any situation. Several better ways. She had only to pass her slender brown hand over the facts, and the appropriate arrangement would come to her fingers naturally.

"You sent for me?" she said, composing herself serenely in the chair they offered her. She looked at Edward again, and more softly, and knew what was happening; and when he raised his head and looked miserably into her eyes she gave him a sweet, tantalizing smile. Good God, what chance did he have, when she even began by teasing him?

She wasn't angry or alarmed. She didn't feel guilty at all. She had only broken other people's rules, not her own, and to wind her way out of a contretemps of this kind was normal exercise for her. She might even repay him good for evil by turning the whole thing into a silly misunderstanding, and getting him out of it gracefully, into the bargain. If she did, he'd never be able to bear the sight of himself again.

Forcing himself to face her, he told his story, pausing to give the amazed Professor time to translate. With all those unbelieving eyes upon him, and Olimpia wide-eyed in silent horror, it was the hardest thing he'd ever had to do in his life, but he went through with it; and when the little black kid strap was on the table in front of the police, he turned his head, and looked despairingly at Olimpia again. "I'm sorry! I couldn't do anything else."

"But I don't understand. Of course that's mine, it's off one of my gloves. I lost it two days ago, after we came back to lunch. If you had it, why didn't you give it to me?" Her lips were quivering with hurt and bewilderment, but her eyes laughed at him gently. "I'm sorry if you didn't think I was appreciative enough—after all your kindness to me—but I didn't think you'd try to make trouble like this—I didn't think you wanted to hurt me."

The policeman questioned her in rapid Italian, and she answered as promptly and directly. The Professor, wild-eyed with excitement, translated breathlessly: "She says she told the whole truth before; she doesn't want to change anything. She lost the strap, and she hasn't seen it since. She says Tonino must have picked it up somewhere, and put it in his pocket until he could give it to her. She—my dear chap, she hasn't *said* it—but they seem to have the impression that, for private reasons, you've—well, developed a grudge against her. Last night, apparently, she thinks you—rather expected more of her than she felt like giving—"

He had known how it would be!

No one could manipulate truth as expertly as she did, with such appropriate silences, such wounded reluctance to wound. She had an answer for everything; and, of course, what could be more probable than that her husband, observing something of his wife's shed along the road or in the hall, should pocket it until he could give it back to her? His one bit of evidence, and she blew it away delicately, like a bit of thistledown! Not a word too much, no counter-accusations against her accuser. She could not believe that Signor Stanier was insincere or malicious, it could only be that he was terribly mistaken. No, it was the police who suspected him of malice. Here they came, the long measuring looks he had expected, the crisp, polite questions, so devilishly hard to answer.

"If you found the strap on the scene of the murder, why did you not bring it to us at once?"

"Why did you leave the house this morning, and then come back to bring this charge?"

"Do you not agree that your attitude yesterday indicated rather more than an ordinary interest in Signora Montesanto?"

He discovered, in five horrible minutes, how like a clumsy lie the truth can sound, even in one's own ears. And there was always Olimpia, reproachful but gentle, holding him in the fixed and shining regard of her great eyes; and behind their bewilderment and hurt he caught the irresistible flash of amusement, and worse, of half-affectionate indulgence.

"Silly child," she said to him clearly, without a word, "to think you could ever drive me into a corner. Now see how much trouble and suspicion you've brought on yourself. And I could make it much worse for you, if I chose."

She still liked him, there was no resentment in her at all. She would only scratch if he persisted, and then without malice. Her eyes reminded him of the previous night, of her mouth surrendered to him without reserve, of the stars drowned in her eyes.

"But there is no evidence to suggest that Signora Montesanto had more than a passing acquaintance with Leoni—none that she ever saw him alone."

"I did not—ever. I have only spoken to him among other people, in the dining-room or the hall—"

It was at that moment that the door opened quietly, and Giulia came in.

She had been crying again, though there was little to show it except the brightness of her eyes, and the slight unsteadiness of her lips. She gave one intense glance round at them all, sitting there tensed and wary in their chairs, and then she advanced towards the table, extending a slip of paper in her hand. Halfway across the room she wavered, and presented it instead to Professor Lacey.

"Please—read it first in English. It is best your friend should hear this."

Charming as she was, it had never occurred to Edward until then how much delight and satisfaction there could be in looking at Giulia. A fine little woman—straight! She called a *bagascia* a *bagascia*, and to her face, too, not behind her back. A man would be safe with Giulia. Paolo had been safe with her, if only he'd had the sense to appreciate his luck.

"I find it," said Giulia, her large eyes resting gently upon Edward's face, "in my husband's card-case, in the coat he wears the last morning he lives. At lunch he changes his clothes. Now I am packing his things, and I find *this*." She looked at Olimpia, who had drawn herself back into her chair, and was as still as stone, her eyes flaring greenly in her taut golden face.

"Paolo is not a good husband," said Giulia simply, "and it is not easy to live with him. A long time now I am not in love with him, but I love him like a troublesome child, and I do not let my child be killed."

Professor Lacey read, translating reverently in the midst of a deep and foreboding hush:

Very well, then, at six, but be a little sensible about it. Wait for me well down the slope, and out of sight of the path. If I can get rid of Tonino, I will be earlier, but you know what he is. Be sure no one follows, or knows where you are going, and take care to burn this. You are a fool, but nice. Olimpia.

When he had finished, Giulia repeated it gently in Italian. She had it off by heart. The police officer reached out his hand without a word, and took the paper.

Olimpia's eyes were lowered, but her face was serene again. She had begun to reassemble her powers already. By the time she looked up she would be ready with her parry, and it would be tireless and ingenious, and she would take delight in it still. Silly children, to think they could ever drive her into a corner! But, the world was narrowing.

Limp with relief, Edward was not thinking of her, and that in itself was remarkable. He was thinking first and foremost of his own self-esteem, which had been so unexpectedly reprieved, but close upon that preoccupation pressed the thought of Giulia. She lifted her fine, dark eyes, and gave him a kind, regretful, partisan look. She did not like her children hurt, and any man in trouble had acquired a sort of kinship with Giulia.

"She is very sure of her power with men, you see," she said simply. "But these are the only words Paolo has from her, he cannot bear to burn them. It is perhaps the only thing in the world she can ask of him," said Giulia very softly, "that he will not do for her. But this time she asks too much."

A LIFT INTO COLMAR

As soon as the first sweeping curves of the ascent had raised him clear of the valley of the Meurthe, Jonathan Creagh stopped the car in a lay-by scooped deep into the steep roadside, and looked back towards St. Dié. The terraces of the motor road went herring-boning away from him down into the green valley, steaming gently in the mid-morning mist; and scattered on both sides of the river the tufted heads of the foothills of the Vosges shook their plumes in an air already quivering with heat. Toy mountains, playful as puppies about the solid flanks of the main range, they erupted as far as his eye could see, and the road, threading them at leisure, lay open to view for several miles. No splash of bright red moved on the ribbon of whiteness. A few cars were visible, dark spots trailing faint feathers of dust, but none of them flaunted the unmistakable colour of Hilary's Triumph. He'd shaken her off successfully at last. Either that, or she had deduced correctly that there was nowhere for him to go in this direction except over the Col du Bonhomme and was therefore in no particular hurry to catch up with him. The Triumph could, as he knew only too well, overhaul his old Morris whenever she chose to push it. And with Hilary you never could tell!

The thought of that exasperating minx hunting him thus across France brought the inevitable scowl of displeasure to his thick brown brows; but as he drove on up the long traverses of the mountain road the equally inevitable grin followed the scowl. She was a spoiled little devil, who had never in her life wanted anything without having someone run to buy it and give it to her, and it was no wonder adolescence caught her as unprepared for realities as he had found himself for the reality of her womanhood. He had known her since she was seven years old, and maybe he wasn't entirely innocent of the crime of helping to spoil her, for he had been in and out of her father's house as regularly as an uncle, and preserved an affectionate and indulgent relationship with her through all the mysterious years of her growing up. No wonder the whole affair had caught them both-off-balance. It was the normal ritual of their meetings that she should throw herself into his arms and kiss him, and that he should return the hug and the kiss with enthusiasm. And then, quite suddenly, something in the way she failed to relax in the clinches, a certain deliberation about the new hair-do and the re-styled make-up, and a look in the large guileless eyes that was far from guileless—and he had found himself backing out in consternation from the predatory arms of a totally strange young woman. Unnerving, to say the least of it! He could no longer pull her hair, and tell her to go and play, and she couldn't get used to the idea that there was something nobody was going to be able to buy for her.

But she was certainly game. What nobody could give her she had set out, with disarming candour, to take for herself. He couldn't go to a party but she would be there, he couldn't even take a long holiday and remove himself across the Channel but she would appear suddenly, smiling and demure, and take her seat at his table for dinner on the very first night at Le Touquet, fresh from the air ferry with her wicked little red car that could run circles round his Morris. As often as he gave her the slip, she picked up his trail and followed. This morning he'd eluded her at Raon-l'Étape by getting up and breakfasting at seven, an hour she did not acknowledge as having any legitimate place in her day; but he knew very well that the waiter would tell her which road he had taken, and other hapless bystanders, wherever she turned the battery of her innocent and demoralizing eyes, would rush to give her the latest news of his progress. What chance had a man against a girl like Hilary?

What he loved about her was that she could still laugh about it. It was a matter of life and death to her, but she could still see that it was funny, and conduct herself accordingly. She might be a pestilential little nuisance, and her campaign as indecorous as desperation could make it, but both it and she had style. If he could remain on the run for a few more months, he felt, paying her the compliment of ascribing to her a quite unusual tenacity, she would be over him, as children are over measles when the quarantine ends, and fit for civilized society again. Then he could kiss her, and she wouldn't even remember that she had any reason to blush at the impact.

He drove on up the coils of the easy rise, until the modest saddle of the Col du Bonhomme opened ahead, with its brightly coloured kiosks of postcards and souvenirs, and its hotels, and its Resistance memorial. In Flanders everyone still talked of the battles of the First World War as though they had happened yesterday, but here in the Colmar Pocket they commemorated quite a different warfare, something nearer to present-day reality. Instead of the monstrous cemeteries of Loretto, this stone and handful of flowers, and instead of the anonymous expendable thousands upon thousands, still in uniform under the Pharos at Souchez, these few live and individual names of men who had never worn uniform for their best fighting, and who had chosen their part with a deliberation and independence proper to man. There had been no conscripts in Alsace, at least, not upon their side.

Parked beside the hotel he saw three cars with GB plates, and an unexpected coach from Huddersfield, and before the windows of the restaurant the men of the coach party were drinking beer, while their womenfolk bought postcards at the kiosk opposite. Colmar beers are respectable, at least, and Jonathan would have liked to join them, but this was not, perhaps, the best place to make a halt.

Up to this point she would not even have to enquire after him, there being only one likely road for him to take; beyond, she might hesitate, wondering if he had gone over the saddle and down through the village of Le Bonhomme towards Colmar, or turned right into the long, airy, lonely stretch of the Route des Crêtes, which unrolled along the summits of the range, shrugging off cars variously at the lakes and hotels along its forested sides. So he drove on, over the pass and into the first curving descent. To the motorist this was a land of two or three major roads, with blank country between, but on foot a populated and comfortable mountain district threaded with tracks and paths, where losing a pursuer should present no great difficulty, and before now men's lives had depended on their ability to make good use of its cover.

Le Bonhomme lay about three miles beyond the pass, a quiet village drowsing in a hot bowl of woods and meadows in the noon sun. The scent of sawn wood was heavy and aromatic on the air, and from all the windows of a farmhouse geraniums flashed scarlet as he slid by. Another mile beyond, where the forests opened for a moment into a gentler level of fields, a narrow track turned off to the right. It seemed to him that it was navigable, and on impulse he turned into it. In a few hundred yards it widened a little and became a reasonable road, though it proceeded downhill rather more abruptly than the main road. He had never succeeded in shaking off Hilary yet, and doubted if this manœuvre would do much more than delay her for a time, but at least he might be able to eat his lunch somewhere in peace.

The road, once having detached itself from all its kind, proceeded, like all mountain roads, to create a world of its own, full of vistas which could never be recaptured from any other viewpoint. Sometimes it turned the Vosges into mountains on an Alpine scale, sometimes it sauntered through mere upland meadows. In a little while the lie of the land became clearer, and he saw that he was moving by randomly graded traverses down one slope of a deep valley, while the brook which had cut it out lay lost to sight beneath him, silent under bushes and close-growing grass at the bottom of its miniature gorge. On his left the hillside rose in soft, rounded folds of woodland, darkly coloured and richly scented in the hot sunshine, and scarred here and there in the steeper places by little runnels of stones.

It was on one of these raw slopes that the girl appeared. He was driving peacefully round a left-hand bend, hugging the outer edge of the road dutifully and as the stretch ahead opened before him he saw the reddish-brown *couloir* of stones in perceptible motion, and a flash of alien colouring, blue and white, sliding with it. He braked hard, for he thought for a moment she was going to be carried out into the road, but she came down the slope still on her feet, moving with long, balanced, lunging strides which made it clear that she was no stranger to scree-running, and arrived at the edge of the track with every movement so perfectly under control that there was really no need for him to stop, and he sometimes wondered afterwards why he had done so. It was not that she had yet made any sign to him, or indeed shown herself aware of his presence at all; the initiative, if stopping the Morris accurately beside her could be called an initiative, came from him. Perhaps it was simply that she was so astonishing that she could have been nothing else but the beginning of an adventure.

She was perhaps twenty-four or five, he thought, tall and fair and handsomely built, her colouring not the pale fairness of the Nordic blonde, but a red fairness of the Celt, sunburned and vigorous. The vehemence of this colouring made more remarkable the dignified calm of her movements and her face, which emerged in perfect repose from the exertion of the descent. She lifted her head, and looked at Jonathan with large, speculative and intelligent eyes of a golden hazel colour, fringed with darker brown lashes and arched over with spacious red-brown brows, not at all disconcerted by the suddenness of their encounter or the peculiarities of her arrival on the scene. It was not that such a girl did not belong in such a country, but rather that at this moment she was so plainly not dressed for it. Whatever she had intended to do with her day, she had not foreseen this downhill rush, cutting the corners upon this almost forsaken road. She was wearing all the country-town elegance of France, a short summer jacket and slender skirt of blue silk with a white nylon blouse. A pinch of white straw clipped the back of a head gleaming with red-gold hair, and she carried a large white handbag in one hand. The long legs which had made such easy work of the run down the stones were smooth in sheer nylon, and the dusty sandals, high-heeled and consisting largely of a few twisted strands of plastic, had once been white, too.

What she saw in the course of that mutual inspection, apart from his GB plates, which she certainly did not miss, he always wondered but never asked; but at the end of it, and it lasted only a second, she asked in competent English, in a voice low-pitched, quiet and quite matter-of-fact: "Monsieur is going to Colmar?"

"That's the intention," he said, with equal simplicity, "but I don't know this road. It does bring us there finally, I suppose?"

"Oh yes, the road is all right, it comes out on the main road just beyond Kientzheim, on the other side of Kaysersberg. If Monsieur would be so kind as to give me a lift into Colmar—?"

He had opened the door for her already, but on an impulse he paused and looked up at her again, more intently. "Forgive me, but are you in some trouble? If there's anything more urgent I can do to help—"

The calm eyes regarded him without a smile, though with friendliness, and continued to contain their own disquiet. "Thank you, you are very kind, but all I wish is to get to Colmar."

"Of course, I shall be delighted!"

She installed herself with composure in the front seat beside him, folding her hands in her lap over the white handbag; but he noticed that she looked back as they reached the next curve, and searched the climbing sweeps of road behind them with one alert glance before she settled her shoulders back in the seat and relaxed with a quick, thankful sigh. She could not have said more plainly: "So far, so good!"

All the way down the long coils of the road he watched her and wondered about her, and wanted to ask questions, if only he could have found an opening; but as often as he ventured the first tentative lead she would turn the conversation back upon him.

"You are touring in France? How do you like it here in the Vosges?"

"I am finding it," he said with a deliberate glance, "extremely interesting."

"Colmar is a very beautiful city. And now it is the time of the Wine Fair, too, so most of Alsace will be there."

"You are going to the Wine Fair?" That was a shade too direct; she could not ignore it, but the grave glance of her eyes and the brief, sternly suppressed smile which visited her mouth forgave him his curiosity, even returned, he thought, restrained thanks for it, recognizing its friendly intent.

"No," she said, making what turned out to be a bad guess, "I do not think I shall be visiting the Fair this year."

"You live here in the Vosges?"

This she answered readily, turning to gesture back towards the heights with one gloved hand. "I live in one of the villages up there near the crest. My father has a farm and some forest property up there." She did not pretend to miss the way his glance flickered to her dress and her soiled sandals. "You are right, in this *toilette* one would not milk the cows or take forest walks. One does other things on occasion—some on rather rare occasions."

"I beg your pardon!" said Jonathan, astonished to find himself blushing, a thing which had not happened to him for years. "I've no right even to look questions at you, and you're quite right to snub me."

She was disconcerted for the first time; she laid her hand protestingly upon his arm, conveying in the touch something which deepened his involvement where she had meant rather to absolve him. "Oh no, please! It was not meant so! I was surprised myself, that look you gave me made me think how I must seem to you. Why should we pretend I am anything but strange, dressed for a family gathering and now here on this road, going the quickest way down the mountain? It is not human not to wonder."

"It would be politer to contain the wonder," he said, ashamed. "I'll try, at any rate."

She recovered herself so readily that she encouraged the attempt by making cheerful conversation about the cooking at the Maison des Têtes, and the year she had spent in London, perfecting her English. He began to wish that he had not withdrawn all his claims quite so precipitately, with nothing gained. The girl had such an uncompromising singleness about her that there was no way in; whatever had sent her plunging down towards the valley, she had no intention of sharing it with anyone. He hoped, he was even beginning to believe, that what he felt was not merely curiosity, but concern on her account, an anxious presentiment that what she had on her mind might prove to be more than one person could be expected to carry. But she had declined, gently but firmly, to give him any part of it. What more could he do? Was she running away from actual pursuit, or merely from something she preferred to forget, and which with every mile they drove was left farther and more securely behind her? There was no way of guessing; she sat watching the road unroll before her with such opaque composure that she might have been going down to collect the groceries. Was she even in a hurry, now that they were well launched on their way? He felt an urgency about her, certainly, but could find nothing in her bearing to justify his conviction. When they rounded one more corner and came upon the sudden little sweep of gravel with its two yellow-and-blue-shaded tables, and the unexpected café behind, with its low wooden eaves and its crisp, checked cotton curtains, he seized the cue with eager deliberation.

"Have you had lunch? I suspect you haven't."

She was taken by surprise for a moment, and looked startled out of her composure. Its loss made her look younger, and for an instant he believed he saw a gleam of fear in the golden hazel eyes; it wanted only that tiny jolt to allow it to show through. But before he could even be sure of his own vision she had adjusted the resolute calm of her face, like a dowager straightening a hat to recover her mastery of a situation. A delicious face, he observed now, that could make tranquillity more exciting than vivacity. She looked him squarely in the eye, and said with a smile: "That means, I think, that you haven't, either."

"I asked about you." And he was already wishing that he had not; it was too much like dropping a challenge in her lap, and she was clearly not the girl to refuse a challenge. He wanted to say: "Don't take any notice! Don't humour me! You're desperate to get on into Colmar, and I'm happy to take you, and as fast as you like. Tell me to drive on, and I will, and I'll ask no more questions, and do no more angling, either." But he was not yet on the kind of terms with her which would have allowed so much candour. He'd done it, and he had to abide by it.

"I haven't!" she said. "If you would like to try the lunch here, you won't be disappointed. They will give you as good trout as in Colmar." And she gathered up her bag and put her hand to the handle of the door, ready to alight.

So where did he stand now? She had shown no reluctance, and no hesitation.

Maybe, after all, she was not in haste. Maybe this was already escape from whatever was troubling her. If so, she might just as well eat and enjoy her lunch as go hungry into Colmar. All the same, he was not easy as he drove in and parked the car on the stretch of gravel, and jumped out in haste to help her alight. A futile gesture, she had already slid out with a long, smooth motion, and was shaking her skirts into order, and stamping dust from her sandalled feet. She smiled at him with clear but still unrevealing eyes, and led the way into the restaurant.

After the hot sunlight the little dining-room was cool and dim, with crisp gauze inner curtains and checked cotton table-cloths. It held only four tables, and a narrow bar at the far end, where a swing door led into the back premises. They sat down at one of the inner tables, and a middle-aged waiter, who had observed their entry through the glass panel of the rear door, approached unobtrusively as soon as they were settled. Jonathan could never afterwards remember if the lunch came up to her promises, for the truth was that neither of them was capable at the time of appreciating the trout, or the Sylvaner that went with it. Her mind was certainly upon whatever it was she had left behind her up there among the plumed heads of the hills, and his was absorbed more and more in the contemplation of her, and in wondering incorrigibly what her problem could be.

Since she so clearly preferred not to be the subject of conversation, however, it was of him that they talked.

"Are you on business here in France, or just on a holiday?" she asked, studying him over her coffee-cup.

"Oh, just on holiday. I'm not one of the lucky ones whose work takes them careering about the Continent, but at least I can take my time off when I want it, within reason. It's the chief advantage of working for yourself. The chief disadvantage," he said with a smile, "is that you can indulge the disinclination most of us have got to working at all, ever."

"What is it, this work of yours?" she asked with more genuine curiosity. "You are a writer?"

"Nothing so glamorous! I'm doing experimental work in industrial design— mostly for makers of household equipment. I do a lot of work for makers of electrical gadgets, for instance." He thought for a moment of Hilary Prescott, heiress apparent to the washing-machine king, rolling up the miles of the winding road to the Col du Bonhomme in her bright red Triumph, and smiled, astonished to realize how completely she had slipped out of his mind from the moment that this girl had invaded it. "I also have three little patents of my own, but I don't manufacture, myself. This way I can stop whenever I have enough money saved up—"

"And come and disport yourself in the Vosges," she said, a small and charming smile burning up in the clear eyes.

"With delightful results!"

In the very moment when they had achieved, he thought, a degree of ease and intimacy, she stiffened. He saw her fingers tighten upon the edge of the table, and her head rear itself suddenly in an attitude of intent listening which set him straining his own ears in sympathy. At first he could distinguish in the quiet noon sounds about the inn nothing to disturb her contentment; then he heard, as she had heard, the distant throb of a car, approaching from the direction of the pass. The note was leisured but purposeful. She followed it with strained senses for a few moments, while he watched her anxiously and made no attempt to pretend that he did not observe her disquiet. The car drew steadily nearer, it was turning the last corner now, and the removal of the final barrier caused the note of its engine to leap at them with sudden insistence. The girl snatched her handbag abruptly from the chair where she had laid it, and jumped to her feet; but even now she moved with a controlled grace which forbade him to comment on her flight.

"Will you excuse me, please?" Her calm was the most admirable thing he had ever seen, and left him helpless to match its dignity and independence with any word or action of his own. Before he could even reply she was walking rapidly to the rear door, through which she vanished with a flash of a blue sleeve just as the tyres of the advancing car hissed suddenly upon gravel. She had made no mistake, the newcomer was driving in from the road, with the intention of coming in here. For lunch, or to make enquiries about a runaway girl? Had she known the note of the car, or fought shy of even the mere possibility of being pursued? Now the engine stopped. Neither car lay within Jonathan's range of vision from the windows, which in any case were so gauzily veiled against the sun, and so ringed round with potted geraniums, that the outer world shone in upon them only as a hot brightness, without form.

A glint of white caught his eye, lying upon the floor a yard or so from the table. She had dropped her foolish little nylon-net gloves in her flight. He snatched them up without reflecting how deeply the instinctive action committed him, and thrust them into the pocket of his gaberdine jacket, and looked round to see if she had left any other sign of her presence. Apart from the coffee-cups, the table had already been cleared. He transferred the girl's cup with a hasty movement to the next table and, looking up, caught the waiter's bland, dark, intelligent eye fixed speculatively upon him. He beckoned him over urgently, and slid a folded note out of his wallet.

"Monsieur?"

Jonathan's fingers casually pushed the note to the edge of the table, where the waiter from force of habit was straightening the slightly disarranged folds of the checked cloth. "Mademoiselle was not here. You understand? I arrived alone, no lady has been here."

"I understand perfectly!" The note slid into the capable short fingers as smoothly as cream into a pot. The tolerant black brows did not even rise beyond the fraction of an inch needed to express sympathetic comprehension. "Monsieur himself is not known?" The stranger, whose assured footsteps were already audible as he crossed the gravel to the door of the café, was cast, naturally enough, as the inconvenient husband; but perhaps it was as well not to examine the implications too closely. Jonathan contented himself with a shake of the head, and asked aloud for more coffee. Alone, he had no reason for haste; better to wait, and see what followed. He was sure that if this was the enemy, the girl would not come back. But should the whole incident be a false alarm, and the car belong to some innocent traveller, she would surely reappear, and continue her journey. Thus, no doubt, providing a puzzle over which the waiter could rack his sharp brains for months to come, whenever he was at a loss for occupation. In the meantime, wait, and listen!

The waiter, magnificently imperturbable, turned his head towards the door as he marched away for the coffee and presented the most staidly correct of greetings to the man who was just entering. Probably in his own family life he used the Alsatian patois, but his business language was French, "*Bonjour, monsieur!*" he said with his slight, professional smile and continued his progress to the service door without another glance.

The figure outlined against the sunlight was tall, and in a heavy style athletically built. Until he came into the room fully, and ceased to be a mere blackness, man-shaped, his features could not be distinguished, nor his colouring, nor anything about him except this first impression of a powerful bulk cutting off the light. When he moved, he moved with a youthful ease which was light as a cat's, but also with an aggressive confidence which disdained its own capacity for grace. And when he had crossed the room to lean back against the little bar, and survey the scene at his leisure, so that the light fell upon his face and form instead of obliterating their features, Jonathan found himself looking at a very personable young fellow indeed.

A large, hard, fit body, with country movements and town assurance, in a light-grey summer suit, with the jacket slung round his shoulders over a white silk shirt, open at the throat. The dark russet-gold of his muscular arms and thick, strong neck against that whiteness was startling, and he was probably aware of the artistic value of the contrast. And why not? He had a certain beauty to offer the world. His hair was just too dark to be flaxen, too light to be straw-coloured;

honey, perhaps, came nearest to its shading. He wore it rather long, but without much indication of vanity, for its thick waves clearly took care of themselves rather than owing anything to his tending. And his face was tawny, russett over the hard, wide cheekbones, a strongly marked face with long, arrogant mouth and light blue eyes, which roved slowly and consideringly over the whole room, and dwelt for a long, thoughtful minute upon Jonathan sitting at his table. Their stare was not insolent, but achieved a nice status on the edge of insolence and maintained it, Jonathan thought, with deliberation, calculating minute by minute the effect it would have upon its object.

The waiter came back with the coffee, and, passing by the newcomer in a waft of rapid air, floated back a placid "Immediately, monsieur!" in response to his demand for notice. When he returned to the bar, undisturbed by suggestions of impatience, the stranger ordered *café filtre*.

"You're new here, aren't you? What happened to old Jules?"

It seemed strange that it had not occurred to Jonathan until that moment that the girl might be known here, and his request for the waiter's discretion more than ever an equivocal one. It seemed he was spared that complication. The stranger had expected to find here someone who could recognize him, and would know for whom he was enquiring; instead, he found an Algerian-born Frenchman—that guess about his native tongue had been a long way from the gold—who was willing enough to tell his whole life-story, to explain that old Jules had gone into hospital for an operation and to deplore his own too rash exchange of the comparatively lively scene of Lunéville for this backwoods village. The stranger brushed half the story away with a thrust of his hand and a heave of one wide shoulder.

"My name is Eisinger, I'm from the sawmills up at La Croix. I'm looking for Mademoiselle Becher. You don't know her?" He was perfectly equal to the task of describing her, and did so with so much detail that it was clear he had seen her this very morning, and knew everything about her down to the gilt clasp on the white handbag. The waiter listened with bright-eyed attention, never once letting his gaze stray to Jonathan in his corner, smoking at leisure over his coffee. He shook his head regretfully at the end of the recital.

"I am sorry, monsieur! Mademoiselle has not been here. I opened the restaurant myself, I have been here all the morning. There was a middle-aged lady with her husband here, perhaps an hour ago, but since breakfast no other lady has been in."

"You are sure? And you have not seen Mademoiselle Becher pass by on the road?"

"No, monsieur. It is not impossible that she has passed, but I have not seen her."

"So—very well!" But the light blue eyes, not a little vexed at being thwarted, wandered again about the room as he waited for his coffee, and settled with silent insistence upon Jonathan. It seemed for a moment that he might walk across the room and ask the same questions of the unexpected and somewhat suspect Englishman, but he did not. He sat down with his coffee in such a position that he could without actual rudeness keep his gaze fixed unwaveringly upon the only other occupied table. Like Jonathan, he was waiting. Borne upon the air, in the strongly suggestive manner some personalities have of projecting their thoughts so that they fill a whole room with uneasiness, came impressions of the movements of his mind. The girl had vanished at such-and-such-a-time, he knew when, he knew virtually how, he had by enquiry discovered in what direction. It was hardly possible that she could have gone beyond this point on foot, even by cutting the corners of the road, which was by no means an easy or safe way of hastening her progress. There was no trace of another car having passed this way, therefore it remained unlikely that she was at this moment rolling merrily along towards the valley with some other benefactor. Much more likely that she had been with this man, and that she had removed herself only when she heard the pursuing car arriving. In which case she could not be far away. Perhaps they had some pre-arranged rendezvous. If so, one had only to wait. Either she would come to the Englishman, or the Englishman would go to her.

He was not, after all, Jonathan now perceived, such a very young fellow as he had at first appeared. Such a face remains constant at the same age for years, changing only by a gradual hardening and fixing of the same harsh but handsome outlines. This face was already advanced in this process, the cheekbones teak, the jaw braced rigid as ivory under the stretched skin. He must be over thirty, perhaps round about Jonathan's own age, which was thirty-four. Jonathan was amazed to discover how much relief he derived from the consideration that this fellow had no advantage over him in the matter of years. A completely fruitless consolation, as he realized the next moment; for Eisinger was quite certainly wrong, and the girl, who alone could create a state of rivalry between them, had surely gone. She had left his life when she left this room, as unaccountably as she had entered it just over an hour ago in a shower of stones. They had no secret rendezvous, and he would never see her again. The adventure was over, and she, no doubt, had made use of this interval to put as great a distance as possible between herself and this place.

He realized then, for the first time, what a dismaying weight of regret he was going to carry away with him in the direction of Colmar.

There was no longer any point in lingering; she would not come back. The only service he could hope to do her now was to draw Eisinger after him down the road to Kientzheim, on the off chance of picking up her trail again. So he beckoned the waiter and paid his bill, relinquishing with a raised brow and a significant glance more change than he would normally have abandoned so cheerfully. There might be still more silence to buy after he had gone. To do the waiter justice, he believed he would have maintained in any case the brief he had once accepted, but there was no harm in making sure. Then he patted the little, smooth, cold coil of nylon in his pocket, the sole souvenir of this too-brief adventure, and rose and went out into the sunshine.

In the full bloom of heat on the yellow gravel outside the door, he paused to put on his sun-glasses, and to see if Eisinger would also show signs of leaving. He did. The waiter, on his way to the table, slanted one eloquent look through the doorway and was reassured by his client's saturnine smile. Evidently the situation, whatever its exact definition, was well in hand.

The Morris stood at the far end of the curve of gravel, ready to push on again downhill, and making use, also, of the only fragment of shade before the inn, the attenuated shadow of a birch tree by the road. Its bonnet was still protected, but the rear part of the body lay in full sunlight, and the upholstery was burning hot to the touch. His two cases and his raincoat lay tumbled in the back seat; the metal hasps gave off a reflected heat that quivered on the air.

He took his time over settling himself, adjusting his seat and polishing his glasses before he started the engine, to make it clear to his newly acquired shadow that this was in no sense a flight. It did not occur to him that in playing such an elaborate pantomime of deliberation he was tacitly declaring his belief that the adventure was by no means over, that he was doing his best to draw it after him. Watching his mirror, he saw with satisfaction that Eisinger had come out into the doorway and was sauntering across without haste to where his own car stood, a battered grey Renault, probably an early post-war year. Jonathan let him lay his hand on the door before he started the Morris and slid it gently away down the hill. The next bend was sharp and blind, about a hundred yards away, screened by an outcrop of rock and trees. All the way to that bend he watched, but the Renault had not moved, nor could he hear its engine. Well, he had given Eisinger every inducement to follow him, and every opportunity; now it was up to him. Jonathan's part was to behave normally, and drive crisply away towards Colmar. He did so, and rounding the curve with care, put the incident regretfully behind him beyond the screen of rock, and turned his mind with an effort to the onward journey.

The trouble with this incident was that it would not stay thrust behind him. He was two coils of the road divided from it, and beginning to distinguish a meagre thread of relief among his disappointment, when there was a rustling and sighing in the rear seat, and a breathless voice exclaimed in his ear, with inconsiderable suddenness: "My goodness, but I am so nearly *dead*! I thought you would never leave that place."

The Morris, plunging under his hands, swerved in astonishment towards the river-valley, which lay tangled in bushes fifty feet below them. He wrenched it back on to its course, brought it clear of the next curve and stopped it on the edge of the narrow grass verge. She was kneeling on the back seat, leaning forward with a placating hand on his shoulder, when he turned to stare at her. He had to make the movement with some deliberation, so that, she should not see too clearly how little of his expression was exasperation, and how much was delight.

"I am sorry! I thought you might guess that I was here. I could not leave you like that, could I? And, besides, how was I to get to Colmar without you? I did not realize I should surprise you so much."

She was ruffled and flushed from that stifling wait under his raincoat, her corn-red hair was a bush of tangled curls and the ridiculous wisp of a hat was gone, he never found out where. It had impeded her, and she had jettisoned it. She looked hot and tired, but as collected as ever; and when he opened the door and urgently bade her come in beside him, she said reassuringly:

"Don't worry about him, he will not be following us. There is now no need to be in such a hurry, though of course we should not lose any time."

"You're wrong, he does intend to follow. He came out to his car as soon as I started up mine. Come in here, and let's get on."

She obeyed him placidly, saying not a word more until they were on their way again at the car's best speed, so that he should be satisfied, while he listened to her, that they were doing all that was necessary to deal with the situation. It was nice having her beside him again. He was astonished at the pleasure her presence gave him.

"But he won't follow us," she assured him gently, "at least, not in that car."

"Why? How can you be so sure about it?"

"Because his distributor rotor arm is somewhere down in the brook, and I don't think he will find another one there at the café. When I left you I went round into the kitchen garden until I saw him go into the dining-room, and then I went and arranged his car so that it cannot go and hid myself in here under your coat to wait for you. I was never so hot in my life," she said, sighing happily in the breeze of their progress, "and certainly I never waited so long for a man before. I thought you would never come."

"If I'd known what you meant to do, I could have been a little more of a help. But you had no time to drop me even a hint, and I'd hardly collected enough data to give me much of a chance of guessing, had I?"

She gave him a long, thoughtful look, between compunction and reproach; for she was all woman, and any failures in co-ordination would inevitably be at least half his fault. "I know, but I did not know myself what I would have to do. I was almost sure it was his car, but you know one Renault is like another, and have you seen how many of them there are here? So I had to wait until I saw him, and even then it was necessary to watch what he would do. If he had even put his car where it could be seen from the window, then I could not have managed the affair in this way. But I had great luck, and now we have a good start, for I think there is no car there at the café and very few ever come by this road."

Jonathan suffered one of those sudden remembrances which visited him now regularly whenever he felt too complacently at peace, too sure of his well-being. One car, at least—unless Hilary's normal ingenuity had failed her—might very well be cruising down the traverses of this road at this moment, somewhere between them and the Col du Bonhomme. Worse, a competent and fast car, which might easily provide Eisinger with precisely the speed and power he needed to overhaul his quarry. And, worst of all, driven by a young creature of the most impetuous kind, for whom he, Jonathan, God help him, felt in some degree responsible, and who was perfectly capable of running her hot head into trouble, even without the complication of a passenger who bore all the signs of a potentially dangerous man. However, he said nothing to his companion; what was the use? She had enough on her mind already.

"What happened in the café?" the girl asked practically, leaning back with relaxed shoulders in the seat beside him.

"You dropped your gloves." He saw her stiffen a little in quick concern, and went on hastily: "No, it's all right, they're in my pocket. He didn't see them. Whatever he may think, he can't possibly *know* you were there. I cleared away the traces of you, and bribed the waiter to tell anyone who asked for you that you hadn't been there—though to give him his due I believe he'd have done as much just for the asking. Sure enough, this fellow came in and asked after you and got the answer I'd paid for. The waiter thinks we are runaway lovers."

She smiled. "He is new. We had luck there, too, the old man would have known me and it might not have been so effective. I think he would have done what you asked, but I can imagine with what a bewildered face. He would have known—him—too, you see."

"I think I ought to tell you," said Jonathan scrupulously, "that I heard both your name and his. He mentioned them both."

"But if you had asked me, I would have told you." That, he thought, was just like a woman, too, to turn round and reproach him, however gently, with failing to demand a confidence she had done everything in her power to withhold from him. But her voice was very soft, and the tranquillity of her face had become a little less guarded. Soon the anxiety, the uneasiness which was not quite fear, though he felt that it ought to have been, would begin to show through in all candour, so completely would she be trusting him.

"You have been very good to me," she said in a quiet voice.

"Just by giving you a lift into Colmar?"

"You know quite well that is not what I mean. When you picked up my gloves," she said, "perhaps you fell into deep water."

"I can swim."

"Ah, but it might be as well to swim ashore quickly, otherwise later the distance might be rather far. When you make it so clear that you have trusted me and made my cause yours," she said seriously, "without asking a single question, you make it very hard for me not to tell you everything. And I know that might be a very suitable compliment, but I think, too, it might be a very dangerous one."

"For you, or for me?"

"For both, perhaps."

"If you mean that," he said, "I won't ask you anything. But if you mean simply that it might extend to me a danger which at the moment threatens only you, then I won't be quiet until you tell me everything. Sharing something like that might prove to be halving it, anyhow. Suppose you begin with the name that goes with Becher. And mine," he said, "in fair exchange, is Jonathan Creagh."

"Mine," she said, "is Marianne. I told you my father has a farm back there below the crest road, near La Croix—that is where you must have turned on to this road. Did you see the cross? Only an old broken shaft, really, just a hundred metres or so from the main road, close to a woodland."

"I didn't notice it, but there was a wood there, just off the road, I remember."

"That is the place. By the old cross there is a new rough stone. There would be flowers—there are always flowers."

"A monument to the Resistance?" he asked.

"As always here. One must live as near to the frontier as we do, to remember with so much passion what it means to be French. Seventeen Resistance prisoners were murdered in that wood. My brother was one of them. My young cousin Jean-Marie got away with two broken ribs and a bullet in his shoulder after the shooting began, and went to get help. He was twelve at the time. He is really a third cousin, not Alsatian but from Nancy, his family moved to Colmar only two years ago. But then he was staying with us to be safer, because he was of a nature to look for trouble and his mother was worried. She would have been even more worried if she had known that these hills were so full of people of the same temperament. You see, this incident was the climax of our war. For all of us who live near La Croix life was altered by it."

He saw that she was considering, with gravely levelled brows, how it had altered her own life, not only by the loss of her brother, but in some other way no less drastically.

"You were wondering," she said, looking up at him suddenly, so that he felt the gold of her gaze as an added brightness even in the radiant sunlight of the afternoon, "about my dress, which was so clearly not for walking the mountains. And you were right. It was really for an engagement party, a little ceremonious gathering of the two families. That was what the massacre of La Croix did to me, you see—it engaged me to be married."

"Ten years after the event?" he asked, trying to suppress the somersault his heart had essayed at this announcement, and clutching greedily at certain curious comforts. If she had ever reached that party, she had left it in haste, and if there had ever been an engagement, he doubted if it had survived that flight. His mind went back to the arrogant blond athlete, leaning on the bar at the café. "Eisinger?"

Marianne said, with a distinct note of pleasure in her voice: "How very strange! Now you are angry!"

"I'm not angry!" he said, immediately perceiving that he was, and growing momentarily angrier.

"I had better tell you how this happened, because you must remember I myself was only fifteen in 1945. You understand, it was late, the war was already won and lost, it remained only for the Germans to realize it, and they were just beginning—if not to realize, at least to fear it. So then there was no more point in treading softly to appease local feeling, they were harassed and afraid, and they killed very easily. There was a lot of fighting all round us, some new detachments of German troops were moved here from Strasbourg, all was chaos. Some of the prisoners they held were men of influence; they decided it would be better if they were all dead. They were brought by night to this wood of La Croix—there were five men of La Croix among them. Our Jean-Marie was out that night with a message, and he saw the column entering the wood. He followed, wishing to find out what this was and before he could realize what was happening, he saw the shooting begin, and he ran towards the village to give the alarm. They fired at him, and he was wounded, but he got away and raised a rescue party before he collapsed. Of course they were too late to prevent the murders, but at least they killed the murderers. After the fighting was all finished they found a heap of bodies, and the soil already broken for the digging of their grave. And they found one man alive underneath the dead, shot through the upper arm near the heart, but not vitally wounded. He was the only survivor. He was not one of our local men; he said he came from the Bas Rhin. All his family were dead; he had no ties anywhere to draw him home. When he came out of the hospital after the end of the war, he was taken in as a son by an old friend of my father's, a wealthy old man who has two saw-mills near us, and who lost both his own sons in that one night, as my father lost his only one. They made an agreement between them then. All in good time I was to marry Johann Eisinger, and join up those two properties. It was very practical, as well as satisfactory to them."

"And you," asked Jonathan, with some difficulty and fixedly regarding the road ahead, "you were quite complacent about it?"

She shrugged her shoulders. "We were consulted, it was not an imposed match. Johann was willing, and I—I had no other in my mind and I did not object to him. He is personable, and he is the old man's heir, and I liked him, he was lively and good company—"

"Do you know," said Jonathan, himself astonished, "that you are talking about him as though he were dead?"

"He is very much alive. You have seen him—you said that he mentioned his name, you cannot fail to know who he is. He does not show any sign of that bad shoulder wound now, does he? It is strange what people can survive. Jean-Marie lost so much blood that it took them a month to be sure he would live, and after that he was nearly a year under treatment, and his parents took him back to Nancy straight from the hospital. But when he was old enough for military service he was quite fit, and he has been two years in North Africa without a day's illness. He is just back in France after his service, as strong as an ox. And to look at Johann Eisinger, you would never think he had been shot and left for dead, would you? Human beings are very durable."

She fell silent upon such a sombre note that he waited with held breath for her to continue, afraid to disturb her thoughts too roughly; but minutes passed, and she did not take up her story. Finally he said gently: "You can't leave it there. That's either too much or too little to tell me. I know now how you came to be engaged. I don't know yet why you changed your mind and ran away from the engagement."

"You think I should marry him?" The level brows had risen, she was smiling at him provokingly, but he saw that she had repented of her confidences already. She was in recoil from the first touch of his curiosity; not, he thought, from his indignation. She did not mind his being angry, he was not sure that it did not give her pleasure; she minded only his wanting to know.

"God forbid! But I think you should tell me why you felt you had to get away from him."

She leaned towards him suddenly, and laid her hand upon his arm with a touch so candid and kind that his heart lurched at its intimacy. "Please, bear with me! The less you know, the better for both of us. I should have known better than to tell you even so much. Only take me into the city, and I give you my word everything will be well with me."

He wanted to protest further, but he did not. After all, it was not an affair of seconds; she was there in the car with him, and there were many miles yet to go to Colmar. "Where do you want me to take you," he asked soberly, "when we get there? To the police?"

"No, Jonathan!" her voice, relieved and grateful, gave an odd lilt to his name. "Not the police. I would like it if you will drive me to Number 11 Ruelle des Limaçons, off the Rue Turenne, near the Petite Venise. Do you know it?"

"I can find it. I know the Petite Venise. I'll deliver you to the door."

"Afterwards," she said, "I promise you, if you still wish it, I will tell you the part which I have not told. Afterwards, if I have judged correctly, everything can be told."

Hilary Prescott drove down the by-road from La Croix singing at the top of her voice, the Triumph's obliging and accomplished hum providing a smooth continuo. Jonathan, poor lamb, no doubt thought she was proceeding blamelessly down the twirls of the main road all this time, forgetting, because he himself had never tried trailing someone else over these passes, how many folds of the way below can be seen from a well-chosen viewpoint. She knew he had passed through Le Bonhomme, because she had enquired for him at the crest, and the woman at the kiosk had remembered an old Morris with GB plates, and been quite sure that he had passed the narrow, mysterious opening of the Route des Crêtes. Below Le Bonhomme, however, she had made enquiries again here and there and been unable to find anyone who remembered having seen him. So she had found herself a high point from which, with glasses, she could keep watch on an open stretch of the road, several miles below. She was reasonably sure he could not have passed that spot earlier; she watched it for nearly twenty minutes, and still he did not pass it. She turned the Triumph into the first lay-by she found, and raced back up the hill, keeping a sharp look-out for a turning on the left, that being the descending side, and the only probable direction in which he could have left the main road. And it had not taken her long to discover the modest little turning past the wood of La Croix.

It was lonely, and hot, and still, and very beautiful. The folded forests in the niches of the hills, the rounded, plumy crests, blue with heat-haze, throbbed softly in the mid-afternoon drowsiness. Hilary sang because she was nineteen, and in love, and felt no doubts at all that she would get her own way in the end. Her mind, while she trilled suitable lines about the blue Alsatian mountains, carried on a tender conversation with the absent and obstinate darling. She told him that she loved him, that in the end he would realize the force of her love, that she would always love him, that there would never be anyone else in the world for her. This was by no means the manner of her address when she was with him, but sometimes she was afraid that he knew only too well how to make the necessary translation. But he couldn't spend his life on the run, could he? And certainly she was never going to give up, so he would have to surrender in the end. Meantime, perhaps because of the excitement, perhaps because of the weather, she found herself quite surprisingly happy.

She rounded one more bend, and the road opened out a little to make room for a sweep of yellow gravel, and a little wooden café with two outdoor tables shadowed by umbrellas, the yellow paint on the legs of the chairs blistering in the heat. The windows had checked cotton curtains drawn back straight, and, within those, draped curtains of gauze, and a ring of geraniums in pots; and there was a solitary car standing upon the gravel, a long grey Renault with a dented wing. Opposite the café, on the side of the road overhanging the descent to the invisible stream in the bottom of the valley, a shoulder of ground rose sharply, cutting off the view below. At the top of this hillock grew two or three trees; and in the crotch of the largest tree, side-saddle and apparently at ease, sat a big young man in grey slacks and an open-necked white shirt, calmly scanning the world below him through impressive field-glasses. The duplication of her own performance of a half-hour ago caused Hilary to sit staring at him for a few moments in rapturous astonishment after she had stopped the car, and the splash of assertive red seemed to draw his eye, so that he abandoned the glasses for an instant to inspect the intruder. The impact of his eyes afforded her a distinct shock; she found their assurance, and the authority with which they studied her, pleasant but daunting. Disappointing, but not new, that he should appear to find the car so much more interesting than its driver. She was used to having the Triumph admired.

She went into the café, and the waiter at the bar, at any rate, opened his eyes wider with pleasure at the sight of her. It was probably in spite of the deplorable modern hair-cut and the absurd up-to-the-minute clothes, rather than because of them, that Hilary had that effect on middle-aged men. Sloppy wide necklines exposing her emaciated little bones, and sawn-off ends of hair like those of a child dragged into court as being in need of care and attention, could not obscure the vigour and liveliness and innocence of her face. Thin, vivid and bold, she looked the admiring waiter straight in the eye, and assembled the erratic school French which always deserted her when she got excited, but otherwise stood by her well enough, considering how little attention she had ever paid to the subject at school.

Had a car with GB plates passed that way, driven by a tall, distinguished man with dark hair? She found her vocabulary unequal to a more detailed description, but gave the number of the car, and its make, and smiled trustingly at the waiter, wondering why he should gaze back at her for such a long and bewildering moment in silence, as though she had somehow placed him in a rather awkward situation. It took him almost a minute to answer her at all, and then his reply had an odd note of baffled regret about it.

"No, mademoiselle, I have not seen this car."

She was a little dismayed. Was it possible that there was another turning from the main road, nearer to Le Bonhomme? Must she turn back yet again, or acknowledge defeat and go on into Colmar alone?

"Could he have gone by, do you think, without your seeing him?"

The look of helpless and extremely puzzled protest on the waiter's face grew every moment more pained. He was no longer even sure of what his client would have required of him in this situation. The man Eisinger was one problem, but this charming black kitten with the sharp little face and the large, soft eyes was quite another. However, there was undeniably already a lady in possession in the Englishman's car, and a lady no less delightful than this one. Odd, he thought, that the Frenchwoman should be a heroic red-blonde, and the English girl a glittering little dark creature who could, once cured of her tiresome and unbecoming modernity, have passed for French.

"No, mademoiselle, I do not think it likely. I have seen no car go by since mid-morning. One hears them long before they pass, they do not often go unremarked."

Her face fell distressingly. She thanked him in a small voice, and went out with her chin on her flat little chest, frowning at the ground.

The young man had come down from the tree, and was leaning negligently against the sun-baked wall beside the open door. He watched her cross slowly to her car, and linger in miserable indecision with her hand on the door. He was smiling; meeting his eyes, she was held fast by the frankness with which they confronted her, and in a moment he lifted his weight lazily from the wall and came towards her. She saw the thick, flat, powerful brown wrist ripple with smooth muscles under the watch strap as he turned the screw that closed the glasses. He was so big that she had to tilt back her head to look up at him when he drew near, and perhaps it was because he was aware of this that he drew so dauntingly near. It made her feel very young, yet she found it pleasant.

"I think you are looking for someone," he said directly, looking down at her with a challenging smile. "I think you were asking about a certain car. Please believe I am not merely being impertinent, I have a reason for this intervention. Will you not repeat your enquiry to me?"

His English was correct, though sometimes strangely pronounced, academic English out of the book. She liked his directness, it was the way she approached situations herself.

"Yes, I was looking for someone." She repeated her description of Jonathan and his car, relieved to be able to do it this time in English. "But the waiter already told me he hasn't been here."

"The waiter, for quite respectable reasons, is lying. Your friend was indeed here, perhaps a quarter of an hour ago, or a little more. I saw him myself. And I have just seen him again, passing on the road below there."

Hilary opened her mouth in indignant astonishment; she had not expected Jonathan to go as far as this, it seemed to her a negation of all the rules. "You mean that—that he bribed him not to tell me—?"

"Not at all—nothing so ungracious! He bribed him, I think, not to tell *me* something. Look, I shall tell you what you will think perhaps a very funny story. I have a fiancée with red hair, and a temperament of the same colour. We are very fond of each other, but let us be honest, we fight. Today we fought once too often, and she ran away from me in a rage. I was sure she took this road, and I came here looking for her. Your friend was then here finishing lunch, and it seemed to me that he had not *quite* the look of a man who has lunched alone. But after all, I do not know him, I can hardly accuse him of hiding my fiancée from me. I ask the waiter, but no, Mademoiselle Becher has not been here. I wait. Finally your friend leaves, and I, feeling that I have misjudged him, since to all appearances he drives away alone, also go to my car. Ah, but my car refuses now to start, and it is hardly surprising, for after five minutes of trying this and that I find that the rotor arm is gone. So then, you see, I climb a tree, to see if the car which left here with only one person in it will appear below with two. And it does. And the second has red hair, and, I think, my rotor arm in her handbag." He laughed at the distrustful tremors of Hilary's face. "Don't be afraid, it is not so bad as that. Marianne has asked him for a lift into Colmar, perhaps, but nothing more. All she wants is to elude me. And all I want is to overtake her and be forgiven for not losing the last argument. Your friend is at a disadvantage—what can he do but play the chivalrous knight? But if you and I should appear, in a fiery chariot but not from heaven, I think they would perhaps both be secretly pleased to see us."

His laugh was audacious, but not offensive, and he had been careful not to align her situation too frankly with his own. All the same, she made haste to account for herself, stoutly reflecting back the laughter, and already excited to the first genuine sparkle of pleasure in the encounter. "With me it's even crazier, and much too long to tell. It began with the cars, and ended in a bet. I've got to take the same road he uses, and still get to Colmar before him."

"You have the power to do it, but easily. Is it permitted to me to do as Marianne has done and ask you for a lift?"

Her dark eyes had begun to dance with amusement. She unfastened the tonneau cover and whipped it back impetuously from the passenger seat. "Get in! We'll catch them before they get to the main road below!"

They overtook the Morris towards the end of the steepest stretches of the mountain gradient. Hilary, excited by the chase and in love with her own driving, shouted that round the next bend they would be able to pass them. Her black hair, short as a boy's, stood erect in the wind of their going, and she was laughing gleefully. "I'll whip by on the straight, shall I, and then pull across and force them to stop. There'll be no other traffic—what does it matter if I block the road?"

She looked for an instant at her companion. He was staring ahead, braced forward in the passenger seat, one hand behind him gripping the flapping edge of the tonneau cover, which she had pushed back out of the way but not removed. He was waiting for the moment when they would sweep round the curve and be close upon the heels of the Morris. His eyes were narrowed and bright, his mouth was smiling. And here came the curve.

He slid suddenly from the seat to the floor, and with a heave of his arm drew the tonneau cover over him. Startled, she clutched hard at the wheel to correct a swerve, and opened her lips in alarm to demand of him what was wrong, when something small, circular and hard pressed abruptly into her left side. She put a hand down to it, foolishly incredulous, and then as sharply snatched it back because there was no need to touch in order to know. It was not really happening, it was some monstrous joke! If only she had not missed some essential clue there would be nothing frightening about it. Afterwards she would be able to laugh at herself for being such a fool. But the gun remained a gun, and at her instinctive gesture it had ground sharply into her ribs, warning her again of its invincible reality. She felt nothing at all for a moment, only an opaque incredulity through which the man's voice, hard, confident and alertly calm, spoke like a voice in a nightmare.

"Drive past, and don't stop! You have a bet with him—you are winning it. Wave to him, laugh at him, make sure that he knows all is well with you. Then drive on, and lose them quickly. You understand? It would be wise to be convincing. I think you like this man? So put his mind at rest about you. And don't forget, because he must think I am not here, that indeed I *am* here, and *this* with me!"

The bend was passed, she was on top of the Morris almost before she realized it, so numbed was her mind with shock. Not merely the shock of fright, but the horrible shock of having been taken in, made use of, the humiliation of her own fallibility. If she had not had the car in her hands, and her responses to that need had not been so instinctive, she would have been trembling with that sudden rush of self-disgust. But she never doubted that the man beside her was dangerous. It was something about the gun, the way it seemed not something alien, but a part of his body, as though he were not complete without it. The use of it came as readily to him as the use of foot and hand.

"Have you understood me?" The barrel of the gun bored at her ribs deliberately.

She said through her teeth: "Yes." Her throat and tongue were so stiff that she could hardly speak at all, so strongly did her mind object to surrender. But that girl, the red-gold head now turning to stare wide-eyed as the Triumph swept down upon her, she was at the centre of this affair, and she had as much immediate need of Hilary's submission and self-control as Hilary herself had. You can gamble with your own life, but not with other people's, not even to salve your self-respect.

"Your horn. You are winning a bet, let him know it!" the gun directed her, laughing from its hiding-place. It was the gun speaking, the gun laughing, not the man. Without the gun, she thought, the man would hardly exist, it had been the gun directing the operation all along.

She sounded the horn loudly and long. Jonathan, watching her in the mirror, drew well over to the rim of the road, and between curve and curve, in the straight stretch of road shaded here by a thin screen of young firs, the Triumph forged by. Hilary saw the red-haired girl's face strained and wondering, and caught a flash of Jonathan's broad grin. Evidently it looked all right to him. Whatever glimpse of the man and the gun the cover might have allowed them was screened by her body. Nothing to be done now but make a good job of it. She gave him two short blasts of the horn, and waved a hand as she swept by.

"Good! You are a wise little girl, you will do well," approved the gun, still laughing. She was becoming more alive to details now, less obsessed by disgust at her own failure of judgement; she could hear that the laughter held no amusement, and never had held any. "Now leave them behind! Let us have more speed!"

She put a sharp spur of hillside between herself and the Morris. Jonathan was still grinning when she lost the last glimpse of him in the mirror. More speed! She put her foot down savagely, and began to roll out behind them the curling miles of road.

"What now?"

He had put back the cover from over him, and was lolling back in the seat, the gun still lazy but alert in his hand, his eyes in the hard, handsome brown face still laughing up at her thoughtfully. It was the gun thinking, too. She felt now a faint, wondering disgust which was not directed against herself, a desire to giggle at the spectacle of this man, crouching under a rainproof sheet in order to be able to compel and actions of others without being himself in any danger. It seemed to her a curious and revealing inversion of all the values of integrity and dignity. It gave her a feeling of her own strength in the middle of this galling weakness, this infuriating obedience.

"Now you drive on until I tell you to turn aside. And you drive as fast as this car will go—and do not forget that I know how fast it will go."

She shut her lips then, and drove in silence, furiously. He could be frightened. Not, she thought, by speed, but he could be frightened. There would be a time for her, if she watched for it with sufficient devotion. For her, and for Jonathan, and for the red-haired girl. In the meantime, she drove as she had been told to drive, at top speed, along the now levelling road to Colmar, in the hush and the vibrating heat of the summer afternoon.

The café-bar À L'Étoile lay off the main road at a corner where it was joined by a small field-track, about two miles out of Colmar. It was not the kind of place where Hilary's escorts ever took her, and she felt that even her indulgent father would not have approved if he could have seen her drive in through the peeling rear gate into the bare and dusty yard, and there stop the car and shut off the engine. She had even thought of ignoring the order to turn in, and putting her foot down harder than ever on the accelerator, but the gun had a way of pricking up its barrel like a cobra in her companion's hand, and there was not even another car on the road just then, to provide a witness. She was not going to wreck the car without some sort of guarantee that there was something to be achieved by it. Moreover, the man beside her was large, active and physically extremely capable, whatever his possible weaknesses of character might be. He could drag her out of the seat with one hand and steer the car with the other, she suspected, if she tried any tricks. And most persuasive of all, she felt a formidable disinclination to humiliate herself by attempting an attack foredoomed to failure. Better to save herself and her powers unextended until a real opportunity offered.

The house was two-storeyed, of brick covered with a peeling ochre plaster, with a jumble of outhouses huddling behind it, and a parched kitchen-garden extending beyond these. A high wall hid the yard from the road; the car could lie here out of sight for days, just as an unwilling guest could disappear into the house and never be heard of again. Wild thoughts of kidnapping and ransom demands passed for a moment through Hilary's head, not unreasonably, for there was certainly an inordinate amount of money in the family. But she put them away impatiently. Not she, but the other girl, was at the centre of this tangle. Hilary Prescott was nothing but a way of getting at Marianne Becher, a hostage for the good behaviour of Jonathan Creagh, who had inadvertently plunged himself into the inexplicable adventure by giving Marianne a lift. None of it made any sense yet, because she had not the necessary clues to make it cohere, but that was essentially the shape of it.

"Into the house!" said her companion, sliding out of the car as soon as it came to a halt, and lunging round it to grip her arm before she could so much as reach for the door. "Don't be afraid, nothing bad will happen to you if you behave sensibly."

She doubted if he would have heard her furious questions or expostulations, even if she had condescended to utter them. She was sure he would not have answered them. But it was rather out of a politic desire to continue incalculable that she maintained her stoical silence as he dragged her by the wrist through the peeling brown door, along a dark and odorous passage, and halted her for a moment at the open door of a crowded and untidy little living-room behind the bar. There was a short middle-aged man there, sitting over a newspaper spread out on the oilcloth-covered table, a squat, square man in a navy-blue singlet, canvas trousers and dirty grey tennis shoes, who looked up at them at the sharp sound of her companion's voice, and with indifference examined Hilary from head to foot while he listened to a flood of French far too rapid for her to follow. She hoped it disturbed them that the extraordinary girl listened throughout with a grim composure, and did not plead or cry, or even ask questions; but that was the only comfort she had.

The small man did the listening, the big man the ordering, that was evident enough. After a minute or two of the unequal exchange, the café proprietor shrugged his shoulders and jerked a hand resignedly towards the dark stairway beside which they stood. Then, with a deliberate rejection of curiosity which she found more frightening than hatred, he went back to his paper, spreading his compact and muscular forearms across the table. The man with the gun turned her towards the stairs.

"Go up! Don't be afraid, no one is going to hurt you. I merely need your retirement for a little while, after that you shall go on to Colmar as fast as you wish."

Along the linoleum-covered landing, echoing and bare, he drew her after him, and into a small room with little in it but a bed and a wash-stand and a rickety chair, and a couple of daguerreotypes of ancestors on the walls, faded to such a vague and apologetic brown that their features had almost disappeared.

"Not a palace, I am sorry! But for an hour perhaps you will excuse it." He was smiling at her the contented, amused smile of a man for whom things are going well. "I regret I can't stay and talk to you, but I have work to do. I should not bother to shout, or otherwise disturb yourself, my dear, for no one will hear you except Georges, and he will pay no attention. In a little while I promise you shall go. An enforced rest in the late afternoon—no other injury—it will be hardly worth going to the police to complain of that, will it? But you must decide that for yourself, it will occupy your mind while I am gone."

He gave her a push forward by the shoulders into the room, not ungently. She turned in time to catch the last glimpse of his amused face as he closed the door between them. Then she heard the key turn in the lock, and his retreating footsteps, light and in haste, darting back down the stairs.

She sat down on the bed for a little while, and thought carefully exactly how much she had to complain of in him. Very little for which she had any witness, very little which, when considered coolly, provided much of a hold on him. It would be his word against hers on the only points which amounted to anything. He had threatened her with a gun; very well, but of course he would not have a gun when she brought down the police upon him. He had confined her against her will: well and good, but he would swear he had not, and the phlegmatic Georges would swear whatever the other man told him to swear. In short, unless she could find someone else to confirm a part at least of her rather odd story, it was hardly worth her while going to the police at all, though she was willing to try it. No, the best way would be if she could actually be found here, locked in, something Georges would hardly be able to deny, no matter what other method he might find of accounting for it.

She had been assured that it was no use shouting, for no one would hear her. The idea, in any case, did not appeal to her, for to stand alone in an empty room and shout, in cold blood, is something considerably easier to suggest than to do. There might, however, be other ways of calling attention to herself. In addition to the indignation she felt on her own account, it was nagging at her mind that time was vital, that something was about to happen which involved nothing worse than this indignity for her, but must mean something far more serious to Marianne Becher, and all too possibly to Jonathan, too. She must get out of here. She must at least try.

The lock on the door was not of the old-fashioned kind for which one might reasonably have hoped in a room like this; there was no open catch to which she could get her fingers. She spent ten minutes feeling her way about the lock with a nail-file, and after that five more with a hair-grip, but she could get no promising contact. When she turned her attention to the window, she saw that it looked out on the back premises, so that she had no hope of being seen or heard from the road. Even the yard was hemmed in with sheds and outhouses, setting the rest of the world far from her. She remembered the field-path, and considered thoughtfully where it must run, behind the sheds to the left. She was not sure that she could throw so far, though in her schooldays the strength of her wrist-action had been admired. It was worth trying. She tried to open the window, but it was nailed shut, and beneath it there seemed to be a sheer drop to the yard. Nothing for her there unless she got rid of the glass.

No fear of Georges restrained her, though afterwards she could never think why. A sort of academic coolness possessed her, so that she could see only one problem at a time. She picked up the chair and, holding it by the back, jabbed the legs through both lower panes of the window and, after the startling shower of icy sound had ceased, carefully went round the frames stabbing out the protruding slivers from every inch. She could not get play for her arm if she leaned out, and to throw from within hampered her; but she tried it. She wrote a demand for help—it had not the tone of an appeal, somehow—on the blank half-sheet of her father's last letter, and shut it into her powder-case, which was of a convenient shape and weight for throwing, compactly small and thin. She took up her position somewhat dubiously, aimed over the crest of the shed's sagging roof and let fly with all her small weight and the added weight of her indignation behind the throw. The powder-case took the air magnificently, in a slightly curving line, but struck the roof a few inches below the crest, and bounced and slithered helplessly back into the yard, spilling powder as it fell.

She tried again with the envelope of the letter, weighted inside, this time, with several lowly but ponderous French coins. It struck somewhat lower and, slithering down, lodged in an uneven place and remained aloft.

She rummaged in her bag, feverishly, insistent that she was not beaten yet, looking for more paper where she knew she had none. She was not the kind of girl who carries notebooks or keeps a diary. And all the time she knew that she was swimming against the tide, that she was in any case tiring too quickly now to be able to surmount that roof, that time was running out, and somewhere something was happening which she was powerless to prevent.

"Well, at any rate," said Jonathan, as the Morris emerged into the main road beyond Kientzheim, "we know Hilary's all right!"

"Yes," said Marianne gently, "it must be a weight off your mind. At the speed she was going she ought to be in the city by now."

He was not altogether sure how successful he had been in explaining Hilary. When she had flashed by them with that derisive wave, and the characteristic solo on the horn, he had felt, in the middle of his relief at seeing her flourishing and alone, a curious embarrassment, too. Almost as though he had committed a breach of contract in knowing her, and being on such familiar terms with her, and would be required to account for it to his companion. And then he had turned and stolen a wary glance at Marianne, and found her looking at him with a sly little smile on her lips, and a very thoughtful expression in her eyes. Not at all like a wife, or a fiancée, or a woman in possession. Marianne had perfectly understood, she said, that he should have been in anxiety about a girl so young, and for whom he felt almost a relative's responsibility. Naturally he was relieved to see her heading safely for the town; Marianne was relieved herself, when she thought of what so easily might have happened.

"If she had picked him up, and been a little too confiding, as a young girl like that easily might, he would have realized at once that she could be used against you, to strike a bargain. I don't like to think of it! Why didn't you tell me she might be following, when I was being much too sure that scarcely any cars came this way?"

"What could you have done about it? Except worry? And I thought you already had enough worrying to do. Besides, it was only an off-chance. She might more probably have missed me and gone on by the main road."

"But I didn't know what I was doing in asking you for help. It seems so simple, and then one finds one has involved so many innocent people." She stared ahead along the widening, levelled-out road and her voice was very sombre.

"But you haven't. Never mind what might have been; you saw her go by, at the top of her form and in danger from nobody but herself. We can both relax and be thankful now, and inside twenty minutes we shall be in Colmar."

"And you will be relieved of me, too," she said, with a small and resigned sigh.

He was by no means pleased at the thought, but it did not seem the right time to go into it. First he had to deliver her intact to Number 11 Ruelle des Limaçons, and then he would be in a position to remind her that she had promised to tell him the rest of the story afterwards. But for the moment he contained his thoughts, and began to search the stretches of the road ahead.

"I must pull in somewhere for petrol as soon as possible. I hadn't bargained for quite such a long spell without the amenities. Tell me if you see a garage before I do."

In less than a kilometre they came to one, and drove in from the road on to an oil-spotted concrete expanse beside the pumps, in front of open garage doors that yawned into blackness, retiring into a surprising depth. No one appeared at once to serve them. From somewhere behind a wooden yard fence they could hear the motor of a heavy lorry turning over in an experimental fashion.

"Sound the horn," advised Marianne.

"No, never mind, they've got a big job on there, I expect. And I want to get some change, too, so I may as well go in and find someone, if you don't mind waiting a moment."

He disappeared cheerfully into the cavern of the garage, and she saw him hesitate between two doors, and choose the more distant, aiming at a way through into the rear yard. She sat back with a sigh, and waited. The sound of a car coming up at speed from behind did not disturb her; they were on the main road now, there had been a regular stream of other cars.

This one, however, swung abruptly in from the road and bore down upon the Morris, its sudden inward rush causing her to spring round in astonishment and alarm. The brilliant red of the body assaulted her eyes like a blow, and the man in the driving-seat, pulling up sharply alongside, leaned out and laid his hand on the door beside her. He was laughing, but the laughter had no amusement and little sound. He watched recognition, of the car, of him, of the terrible implications of their simultaneous appearance, blaze up in her eyes and drain the colour from her face in an instant. The meeting was a masterpiece of economy, hardly needing any time for its accomplishment, or any words. It did not need the gun at all, though she felt its presence, persuasive in the background.

"Where is she?" she demanded fiercely, plunging to the heart of the matter.

"Safe, if you're prepared to put down the price for her." His voice was a hard thread of sound between his smiling lips. He saw through Marianne's fixed eyes the frantic motions of her mind, trying to divine how this had come about, trying not to believe in it, or to determine how it could have been accomplished by some trick, without necessarily placing the English girl in his power. "Don't be a fool!" he said. "You know I have her. You know I'll keep her if you make it necessary, and kill her if you leave me no alternative. And you know that if you exchange yourself for her I shall keep a bargain that's all to my advantage. If you want him to see her again, come with me and let her out. If you don't—scream now, and bring him running."

He knew she would not scream. She believed too shrewdly in the lightness with which he would carry out his threats, even without advantage to himself, once his stake was lost.

"You'll let her go? You *will* let her go?" Yes, she saw that he would have no interest in keeping the girl, once she had served his purpose. She drew a deep breath, as if before lifting a burden. It had been unfair from the beginning to let any part of that weight light on these pleasant passers-by, it was she who must carry it. She stretched out her hand to the handle of the door. Less than half a minute had passed since Jonathan had vanished into the rear premises of the garage; it seemed impossible that so much could be changed in so short a time.

"No, lift your hands—let me see that you touch nothing and leave nothing behind. That handbag, please!" The gun, as she had expected, was ready to his hand, he swung it upward from his waist as she held out the white handbag. "Now, come! Quickly!"

She stepped from the Morris and, with the barrel of the gun following her like an inquisitive eye, went quickly round the Triumph and got in beside him. The impetuous leap the car made in starting threw her back hard against his shoulder, and she heard him laugh softly, pleased to have disturbed even her physical balance. They shot away from the side of the Morris and soared into top speed within thirty yards.

She did not look back, she could not bear to. Eisinger, who was watching the mirror narrowly, saw a figure emerge and cross to the Morris, but because it clearly was not the Englishman he paid no great attention. A garage boy coming to fill up the tank of one car would hardly find anything curious in the spectacle of another one just vanishing along the road in the direction of Colmar. He underestimated, as it happened, this garage boy's interest in his job. The French garage attendant can be an enthusiast of the most devoted kind. The flash of scarlet that attracted the young, sharp eyes blossomed into such a car as he would have loved to possess, a shining new example of a make he had studied lovingly in motor magazines. He stood with the nozzle of the pump motionless in his hands, looking after it wistfully until it vanished round the slow curve of the road, and in those few seconds he noted its GB plates and registration number, and because he was just of an age to deflect one thoughtful glance, almost grudgingly, from a handsome red car to a girl's equally beautiful red hair, he also observed Marianne in the passenger seat, and spared the fraction of an approving smile for her. He turned back with disfavour to the ancient Morris.

Jonathan came out of the office and through the garage with a handful of change, stuffing the notes into his wallet as he came and moving smartly, for he was in high spirits. He saw the boy just withdrawing the nozzle, and the car standing empty, and stopped in mid-stride, his heart leaping forebodingly.

"Where is Mademoiselle Becher? Was she here when you came out? Have you spoken to her?"

The boy turned upon him an alert and intelligent look, quick to recognize the note of alarm. "No, monsieur, no one was here. I did not know that monsieur had anyone with him. I—"

"You haven't seen a lady? A very pretty girl in blue and white? Beautiful red-gold hair, you couldn't help noticing that, if you saw her at all—"

The young, bright eyes rounded into wonder and concern, almost into embarrassment. "Oh, monsieur! But she was in the other car! Such hair, I could not be mistaken!"

"The other car? What other car?" But he knew already, his instincts were several leaps ahead of his reason, his memory was belatedly pointing out grounds of misgiving which had escaped him before. Something wrong about Hilary's flight past him, something wrong about her incurious passage, which had accepted the provocative presence of Marianne without troubling to stop and tease him about it—"Not a bright red car? A red Triumph with GB plates? She didn't go off in that?"

"But yes, monsieur, she did. I saw it disappear there, towards the town."

Jonathan, stuffing the half-closed wallet into his pocket, caught the boy by the shoulder. "Who was with her in the car? Another girl? A small, dark English girl?" But it was a forlorn hope, he could have answered the question for himself.

"No, monsieur, no girl. The car was already some way past when I saw it, but there was no other girl. Driving it was a man, a fair man—I did not see more than his hair, and his white shirt."

No more was needed. Who could it have been but Eisinger, who else would have dragged Marianne away? Eisinger, lurking in some narrow turning with Hilary's car, waiting for them to pass, then following them patiently, just out of sight, until an opportunity presented itself of approaching Marianne, or both of them if need be, on his own terms—with Hilary as a lever to prise them apart. What had he done with her? How was she to be recovered? And Marianne—

He had no chance whatever of catching them in the Morris, he knew that; but at least he knew that they were still heading towards Colmar, and he had a straightforward reason at last for dragging the police into the affair, without committing Marianne to confiding in them. He seized the boy by the arm urgently.

"Where can I telephone? Quickly! I want to call the police."

The boy was entering thoroughly into the spirit of the thing now. He set off at a run, with Jonathan in tow, back into the small crowded office, and himself snatched up the telephone and demanded a quick connection, in an adolescent squeak of excitement. He was as effective with telephone operators as with engines, and in a matter of seconds he thrust the receiver into Jonathan's hands.

"They are on the line, monsieur. I told them from what place we are calling."

He stood by in breathless eagerness while Jonathan identified himself and plunged into his message. Nothing quite so satisfactory had happened at the garage in the two years the boy had worked there; it dismayed him to think that the denouement would have to take place, in all probability, far out of his orbit, and he would never know what had really happened.

"I want to report a stolen car," said Jonathan, his name established with some difficulty. "It left here a few minutes ago, travelling in the direction of Colmar, a bright red Triumph TR2, carrying GB plates and the number POZ153. The car is the property of a friend of mine, Miss Hilary Prescott, but when it was seen a few minutes ago she was not in it. It was driven by a fair-haired man, who had a girl with him as passenger. No, definitely not Miss Prescott, she is dark and small, this girl had striking red-gold hair—" He caught a glimpse of the boy's amazed eyes above the receiver, growing rounder and rounder with wonder, because this very curious lover complained of the theft of a car which was not his, but made no charge regarding the theft of a lady who presumably was his, since she had, on his own statement, been with him. Jonathan was grateful for even the momentary sensation of amusement. When he had hung up, after promising heartily to report to the police immediately on arrival in Colmar, he pushed an extra note into the boy's hand, and gave him a brief and tormented smile.

"Don't look so staggered! Would *you* admit she'd left you flat? But she didn't do it willingly, believe me, and the car is really stolen."

He ran out to the Morris, leaving the boy staring helplessly after him, and drove away furiously in the direction of Colmar.

It was extraordinary, thought Marianne, how greatly she was encumbered by her empty hands now that she had no handbag to grip in her lap, and how difficult

it was to keep her fingers from straying to the pocket of her skirt, that unobtrusive left-hand pocket shielded from his observant eyes only imperfectly by her
body. If she allowed him to see her so much as touching it with any secrecy or
concern, he would know she carried something in it. She had to get rid of it now,
before they came to whatever safe place he had chosen for her interrogation.
Under his eyes, sitting shoulder to shoulder with him, she had to dispose of it
quickly and cleanly. If he intended to turn the English girl loose he would certainly return her car; and she felt sure that he would be glad to get rid of both of
them, for they were too noticeable for his comfort, and to involve a foreigner in
desperate business is always dangerous. Yes, the girl would get both her car and
her freedom, in exchange for Marianne. Well, Marianne had contracted to deliver her own person on that understanding. She had made no promise about the
thing she carried.

"How much have you told the Englishman?" asked Eisinger abruptly, staring
with narrowed eyes along the road ahead.

"Nothing. I do not involve other people in my problems."

"Knowing you," he said, with a thin smile, "I might have believed that, if he had
not played your hand so well up there."

"He was playing it blind, on the simple assumption that I did not want to see
you. You have nothing to fear from him. I asked him to take me into Colmar,
that's all."

She said it with so little emphasis, and with so indifferent a calm, that he
considered carefully whether to believe her. Probably his wish was to believe,
since he did not want to have to deal with others potentially as dangerous as
Marianne herself.

"So all the while," she said thoughtfully, "you were in the car with her. One
must have to sink very low indeed to get out of sight in such a car. It must have
been very uncomfortable."

"Yes, I was in the car. You made it necessary, you should not complain that I
took steps to recover you."

She had let her left hand slip down gently beside her to the corded edge of the
seat cover. Hilary's furnishings were all of the most dashing, but not well kept
for very long after their newness wore off. There was a little place under the
cord, towards the back of the seat, where some stitches had given way, and she
could insert her fingertips into the slit. It was not long enough for her purpose, but
with her nails she picked carefully at the threads, prising the seam apart stitch by
stitch, with extreme care not to let these feverish movements agitate her arm
above the wrist, where he might observe the curious tensions convulsing her.
While she worked at it she turned her head, and with deliberation kept her eyes
fixed unwaveringly upon him, so that he might feel the intensity with which she

concentrated upon him, and not sense in his blood the passionate activity of her fingers.

"Why didn't you make her stop the car up there, when you overtook us? Did you not like the odds? Not even with a gun on your side?"

He was not moved, but at least his disdainful smile indicated that he really believed she was trying to provoke him.

"You are wasting breath. I am not concerned with your subtleties, they do not convince me that losing is winning. Nor do they convince you, or you would not need to express them. The girl has been talkative and very useful; if you behave yourself he shall have her back."

"I am here, am I not? What more do you want?"

"You know what more I want. I would not have run after you for your own bright eyes."

"I am glad to know," she said, "that I have never meant anything to you. You reconcile me to my situation. Where did you find her, this young girl?"

He was in such content with himself that he did not mind answering her questions. "She came to the café asking for him, and the waiter told her he had not been there. It was a predicament so like mine that it seemed an obvious move for us to join forces. It occurred to me that though she did not have, perhaps, quite such a value for him as she would have liked, yet he would not let her come to any harm, and that she might be exchanged for you. So I put her in a place of safety, and drove back in her car, and lay in wait for you off the road. It was a pity she had to choose so bright a colour, we are a little conspicuous, but we have not far to go, and I think we shall not be intercepted on the way."

She had her fingertips in the opening of her pocket now, the edge of the thick card gripped tremulously between her first and second fingers and was drawing it steadily, steadily out. To cover the movement she kept her face turned and fixed upon him with a calm bitterness which gained its conviction from its very desperation. She even leaned towards him a little, staring with wide golden eyes, her breast almost touching his arm, so that the curve of her body afforded a little more cover for that vulnerable hand. Her palm felt sticky with sweat. If she dropped the card now, she could not regain it. And supposing the slit in the seat-cover was still not long enough to admit it? Or that her fingers, incredibly tired from that stealthy parody of activity, should fail to negotiate the remaining movements, and betray her now?

"Where have you taken her? How have you accounted to her for all this? I might be easily explained away, but if you used the gun to intimidate her and if she recognized it as a serious threat—and it seems she did, for it was effective, was it not?—how are you going to explain away the gun? You swore to set her free, you owe it to me at least to be convincing."

"You are very anxious," he said, his lips curling, "that they should all leave you to your fate."

The end of the card passed between the unpicked stitches very gently and slowly, sliding between seat and cover. It fitted tightly; she imagined she could hear the infinitesimal protest of frayed thread, and a fine sweat broke out upon her forehead and lip. Her hand, smoothing together the parted edges, rearranging the cord accurately over the slit, shook with reaction, but it was done, and something might yet be saved.

"I am only anxious that they shall not be dragged into trouble on account of me. I wish this child to go away believing this to be nothing more than a private quarrel, and to forget every part of it. You owe it to me to make it possible for her to forget even the gun."

He swung the car in abruptly from the road, towards the solitary café by the field-track. The swerve made it possible for her to reclaim, as though from a long journey, her left hand; she clutched with it at the edge of the door, displaying the innocence and emptiness of her fingers joyfully.

"It is to my interest, too," he pointed out reasonably, "that she should be satisfied. Don't be afraid, she shall see for herself that the gun is not loaded." He turned his head, and met her unbelieving eyes. "Of course it is, but that can be arranged! She will go away convinced that I am a little eccentric, perhaps—nothing worse. We are here, Marianne! Be so kind, let me see your hands as you alight. It would be a pity if you left anything behind."

"You have my bag, and even my handkerchief," she said bitterly. "What should I leave behind—my shoes, perhaps?" But she held her breath as he looked quickly round the car when she had quitted it, his long left hand closed round her wrist. The white piping cord on the red-and-black seat-cover hid all but one dangling end of black thread, and this he did not observe. Her white handbag was tucked under his arm, and he was smiling at the touch of the cool plastic, sure of what he carried.

"Very well, let us go in!" He was drawing her peremptorily towards the peeling brown door, when his foot rang upon broken glass. Fragments lay sparkling like ice in the sunshine, under the wall and upon the groundfloor window-sills. Without tilting back his head he shot one calculating glance upward towards the first-floor window, and caught the rapid retreating movement of Hilary's head. He stepped back suddenly, and drew Marianne into his arm, holding her hard against his body.

"You want to set her mind at rest?" he said in a rapid whisper into her ear, as she braced flattened hands against his chest. "Then do one thing for her! For her, not for me! Kiss me! She will need nothing more."

She was silent and rigid for a moment in his arm, staring with fascinated helplessness at his grinning face, which drew near to hers with the languidly powerful movement of a hawk circling once before the plunge. "You wanted her to be convinced," he said, in a laughing whisper, enjoying her loathing. "Can't you play one little scene of reconciliation for her sake? You look as though you'd rather kill me than kiss me."

She lifted her arm with a shuddering effort, and encircled his neck and offered him her mouth coldly and violently. He kissed her lengthily and with enjoyment, well aware of the interested eyes watching them from above, round the empty window-frame of Hilary's prison. He took pains to satisfy the watcher that however curious the means by which it had been achieved, and however unsuitable the place where it was staged, this must be a genuine reconciliation. After that, the girl was hardly liable to go running to the police with the complaint that her car had been borrowed, and she, in some incomprehensible manner, turned to use in adjusting a lovers' quarrel. A few hours and a little bewilderment were not much to pay without complaint in such a cause. He tightened his arms about Marianne deliberately, and drew her towards the doorway in his embrace, until they passed out of the sunlight and Hilary's sight.

Marianne went before him into the passage, her cheeks burning and her eyes lowered, and withdrew herself vigorously from the insultingly solicitous arm as soon as they were within. Georges leaned out from the living-room, and looked her over with no comprehension and little curiosity, lifting one expressive shoulder as he caught his master's eye.

"She is a bitch, that other one, you do well to exchange her. If she had not been English I would have paid her for the window, but I want no complications with foreigners here. For all that glass you owe me. And if you are wise you will get her out of here quickly, before she thinks of something worse."

"Don't be afraid, she will be going at once. You are ungrateful," said Eisinger in great good humour, "not to thank me for providing you with so entertaining a guest. Do not agitate yourself about your window, it shall be paid for. Give me five minutes more, and she is already out of the house."

He was laughing softly to himself as he thrust Marianne before him up the staircase. "In here—I will let you satisfy yourself that I have kept my word, you shall see her go. Don't, I beg, try to outdo our little friend in destruction, Georges will go mad if you do, but it won't help you. There, watch from the window, and in a few minutes you shall have your wish for her." He turned the key upon her carefully, she heard its decisive click and smiled wryly as she looked round the room. It was an old-fashioned bedroom, with a high brass bedstead and a profusion of pictures and photographs on the green-papered walls. Marianne crossed to the window and stood looking down into the enclosed yard, where the car stood waiting.

Her eyes dwelt anxiously on the spot where she had hidden her treasure. Everything now depended on his being so sure of himself and his success that he would send Hilary away before he explored the contents of the handbag; if he looked for what he wanted first, and failed to find it, neither of his guests would get out of here easily, and perhaps neither would get out alive. She waited for what seemed a long time, her heart beating painfully as the suspense grew. Then she heard voices in the yard beneath. The note of content and pleasure was still in Eisinger's assured tones, though she could not distinguish his words.

A moment more, and they came into sight. The girl Hilary walked rapidly to her car, and laid her thin little hand on it protectively, as if to soothe and reassure a misused horse rather than assert her rights in a machine. Eisinger was at her elbow, and leaned to open the door for her. Marianne could not see his face, but the arrogant ease of his head and shoulders told her all she needed to know. He was still at peace with himself, he had not yet examined his booty; and he was speeding Hilary on her way with the easy and cheap expenditure of a little male charm, elaborating that picture he had staged for her beneath the window.

When the girl turned and allowed her hand to be captured for a moment, her small face looked blank and wary. It was impossible to tell what she was thinking, though she certainly smiled and did not draw back when Eisinger raised her hand to his lips, with a gallantry playful rather than fulsome. Children often baffle adults with just such faces, unresponsive, self-contained, aloof, the eyes withholding criticism in a manner highly critical; but most people have lost the uncomfortable faculty at nineteen. Hilary had not; she kept the disconcerting evenness of regard, the considering stare, the unreadable eye, in perfection. Whatever he had pretended to her, she was not entirely convinced; but no doubt she would be glad to go away and forget the whole incident, which, after all, was what Marianne had demanded for her.

Georges came out, his eyebrows resignedly raised, to open the doors of the yard for Hilary's exit. She reclaimed her hand firmly, got into the car and started the engine, and without a backward glance drove out of the yard and turned once again on to the road. Marianne saw her go with so much relief that her knees gave under her in the reaction, and she had to retreat to the high bed and sit down there. With her forehead in her hand and her eyes closed she listened to the hum of the Triumph, soft, high and contended, as it receded rapidly in the direction of the town.

Less than a minute later she heard the key turned briskly in the lock, and Eisinger came in, swinging her handbag lightly in his hand, and whistling a sprightly little tune. Without a word he came to her side, and opening the clasps of the bag, tumbled its contents out on to the bed beside her.

He ran his hands carelessly over the small pile of Marianne's intimate possessions, distributing them at large about the quilt, and quite suddenly the whistling stopped. Looking on with a kind of fatalistic interest, she saw his fingers crook and claw among her powder compact, comb, handkerchief and diary, rapidly sorting and discarding. One or two letters which she carried offered him a lingering hope that what he sought might be hidden inside them, and he tore them out of their envelopes and crumpled them and flung them aside, the tempo of his movements always accelerating. He went through everything a second time, more thoroughly, then a third, his hands shaking; and then he took up the bag and, grasping the pearl-grey silk of its lining, he dragged and tore it out upon the bed, but nothing whatever was concealed behind it.

He flung the wreckage from him in a movement of fury, all the more frightening because it was deliberate, and, turning, took her by the arm and wrenched her round to face him.

"Where is it? If you have it hidden on you, I advise you to give it up now. It would be kinder to yourself."

"I have not," she said, watching steadily the pale glitter of his blue eyes. "But you had better convince yourself, had you not?" The only way to take the sting from his touch was to anticipate it. She stood up and kicked off her sandals, and shrugged her arms out of the short, wide sleeves of her silk jacket. She stepped towards him, spreading out her arms compliantly and her face was resigned and calm. "It is not an easy thing to hide in thin summer clothes—it has obtrusive corners. But see for yourself."

The device of going to meet the contact she dreaded was surprisingly successful, or perhaps it was rather that his interest at this moment was so single and professional that submission to his touch was no longer distasteful. He wanted one thing only, he could think of nothing else until he had it. Only when he had assured himself that it was nowhere upon her did he allow himself to be angry. He had her by the forearm with one hand, he struck her in the face with the other, releasing in the blow only the superficial exasperation which covered his real indifference to her. When he made use of his whole anger it would not be in light, uncalculated blows of that kind. She closed her eyes for a moment, shook her hair back into order and stood looking at him with the shadow of a smile curving the corners of her mouth.

"Yes, of course, there is that possibility. But I don't think it would get you your real objective."

"You underestimate my powers of persuasion," he said grimly. "If you are wise, you will tell me at once what you have done with it. If you are less wise, you will tell me all the same, a little later on."

"I think it is very doubtful. I don't guarantee my heroism," she said with a disdainful smile, "I merely doubt if you will have as much time at your disposal as you think—and I doubt if you will be prepared to go too far in persuasion. It is apt to leave too many marks—but I need not tell *you* that. And I think you would prefer to be able to send me home again without marks, once you have got what you want out of me."

He thrust her back by the arm until she was forced to sit down again upon the edge of the bed. It helped him, and no doubt he hoped it might demoralize her, to have his strength demonstrated.

"What makes you think I will hesitate to maim you, or to kill you if I have to?" demanded Eisinger.

"Nothing, I assure you, I know you too well now for that. But I think you still entertain the hope that you will not have to. Marianne Becher missing, or dead, or damaged would be a serious embarrassment to you, and probably stir up the very suspicions you want to avoid. You want to stay where you are, to go on living a very comfortable and profitable life. You can only do that if I can go home again intact, and without evidence to bear out any stories I may tell about you—so completely without evidence, in fact, that the stories will never be told, for fear of being disbelieved. Isn't that so? Isn't that the whole point of this pursuit?"

"You argue excellently," he said, leaning over her and speaking in a hard whisper, close to her face. "In short, if I can recover from you what you stole from me, it will be your word against mine and so little worth your while to begin the quarrel that I think you would hesitate too long, and find your moment in any case lost. An excellent reason why I should treat you gently, my dear Marianne, as long as I have a reasonable hope of getting back my property by that means. But time, as you reminded me, is not without its limits for me, and does it not occur to you that these are also vital reasons why I should take the risk of disposing of you finally, if I once give up that hope of getting back what you took? Wherever you have put it, I think no one but you has at this moment the knowledge to find it again. Does it not occur to you that if you persist in your silence, the only alternative I have is to kill you? Make no mistake, it could be done without any danger to myself; my alibi could be arranged. My position would be a little delicate for a time, no doubt, but I could handle it. Think of it so, Marianne—I am prepared to release you in exchange for the evidence, and risk what you may venture against me without it—or I will accept the risk of the evidence turning up again, and be prepared to deal with it when it does, but in order to be ready for that situation I must relieve myself of *you*. Permanently. The choice is yours, not mine. I should think about it carefully."

"The evidence," she said, "will be just as eloquent without me, and just as unmistakable."

"I don't think so. You forget there will be no one left then to allege that it was ever in my possession, and no one to show where it came from, or how it got to the place where it will be found. As for its own peculiar eloquence, I have a tongue, too—and you will not be there to cast doubts on my story. And have you not considered the possibility that it may be found by someone to whom it will mean absolutely nothing, and merely dropped into the fire? Or that it may never be found at all?" She gazed back at him all the while with an unmoved face, but the probability he had suggested lay heavily in her mind. "It would be short-sighted, would it not, to choose martyrdom without even knowing that you are sure of the spiritual triumph? You are not such a fool!"

She thought of the red car being driven aboard the air ferry to England, and merrily home again at the other end of the journey, and of the bewildered young owner some day stripping off the loose covers for laundering, and finding an oblong of pasteboard which would convey little or nothing to her; and it did indeed seem to her that she would be mad to risk her life for so barren an ending, even though she could not quite believe that he was yet ready to take such a desperate measure as her murder. He had so much to lose. Only when it seemed to him that it was already as good as lost would he accept that final gamble.

"What have you done with it?" he asked, quite softly.

"I shall not tell you."

"You gave it to him! Is that it?"

"No!" she said sharply. "I gave him nothing. I told him nothing about—what I carried. If you require it, I will swear that. But I'll tell you nothing more."

"Very well!" He turned to the door, looking at his watch. "It is a quarter to six. I have no time to waste on you—you have until six o'clock to make up your mind whether you will give it up to me or throw your life away. Think it over, Marianne! You shall have quiet while you decide what to do." He went out with long, quiet steps, locking the door behind him. She heard him walk with resolute calm along the landing and down the stairs.

In a few minutes she rose and went to the window. He had left the house by the back door, and was crossing the yard, lighting a cigarette as he went. She watched him pass through a gate at the end of the kitchen garden and stroll up the field beyond, his head raised to contemplate the folded blue forests of the hills. She had not been afraid of his anger, but of this sudden assured placidity she found herself very much afraid; it meant that he had made up his mind, that he knew exactly what he intended to do, and was prepared to carry it through to a successful conclusion.

She was still looking out from the window five minutes later, and Eisinger had passed from her sight into the rim of the copse which bordered the field. She was thinking of Jonathan; an unprofitable subject for thought, since she had left him without a word, and was never likely to see him again. Nevertheless, she let her tired mind dwell upon him with gratitude and regret, remembering the large, lean, practical hands on the wheel of the Morris, and the thin saturnine face. From the first moment of their encounter his eyes had with equal candour welcomed and respected her; coming like coolness after the heat of her shocked self-disgust, that gaze had reconciled her to the world and her own fallibility. And now she would never even be able to thank him.

She heard the key turn suddenly in the lock, and turned to face the doorway with a gasp of protest; even if she was going to throw her life away at the end of it, he had promised her fifteen minutes of solitude, and she had had only six. She watched the door begin to move, with infinite stealth, and remembered with wonder that it was only a minute since she had watched Eisinger stroll into the shadow of the trees and vanish there. A narrow sliver of an olive cheek, blue-shadowed with stubble, appeared in the chink, the white of an uneasy eye, the fingers of a thick, short hand easing the door open. Georges leaned inward from the threshold, and with a motion of his hand warned her to be silent. He was breathing hoarsely in his disquiet, and moved past her to stare out cautiously from the window.

"He went out there, towards the wood. Come now—and be quick!"

She could not believe it, she stood staring at him round-eyed. "Do you mean you'll let me go? But you—you and he—"

"I don't want you here. I don't trust him, I don't want murder done. What do you think I am? He thinks he has only to say: 'Do this, do that, come here!' and I shall always do it. Not this time! This I don't like in my house. Now, quickly, while he is in the wood, you must go."

"Oh, if I can— But what about you?" She followed him eagerly to the door, and slid after him with breathless quietness down the stairs.

"Leave me to take care of that. I am not a murderer, that is where I can't follow him." He listened to her soft, heartfelt murmur of thanks with a sour and secret smile. "Wait here a moment, I must look from the back door."

He was back in a moment, padding silently on his rubber soles. "All right, he is still out of sight. Now go, here by the front. And listen to me! Leave the road— from that field he may see you if you stay on the road. There is a path from the corner opposite, it will bring you into Colmar finally by the Rue de Strasbourg. There, run!"

She felt the evening air on her face, the softly stirring coolness at the end of the afternoon's glowing heat. The few people who were drinking in the bar looked at her through the open door as she passed, with incurious appraisal. She went quickly down the three steps to the road, crossed it and hurried to where the field-path opened on the opposite side, shaded for a little way with trees and folded into a seam of the ground. The feeling of numbed astonishment had not worn off yet. Who would have thought that that fellow drew so firm a line between sins he could and could not contemplate? Who knew where grace was to be found? She began to feel the joy of being free. A pity she had not thought to pick up the contents of her handbag when she took it from the bed, but she had thought only of getting away. Now she had no money, no cosmetics, not even a handkerchief or a comb. It did not matter, she was free and Colmar only some two or three kilometres away. She began to run, partly from a sensation of urgency still driving her, partly from sheer pleasure in being at large to run, and with every step nearer to the end of her solitary journey.

Within the shelter of the trees, about fifty metres from the track, Johann Eisinger rose and stretched himself largely as she passed by, and stepping lightly from shadow to shadow, moved serenely after her. Evidently Georges had done his part with conviction; he must have unsuspected abilities. And all the guessing he had done must have been accurate. She had been taken completely by surprise at the garage, and had had no time to dispose of anything. Also he thought she was telling the truth when she said that she had not confided her dangerous possession to the Englishman. There was therefore only one place where she could have hidden it, and that was in the girl's car; she must have had it on her person, instead of in her handbag, and under his very nose she had disposed of it temporarily. Witness now this haste to get to Colmar; probably Marianne knew, from her English friend, where both he and the girl would be staying, and if she knew that, she knew where to reclaim her hidden treasure. For, of course, once at liberty her first thought would be to recover it. She would have died rather than tell him where to find it, but it had only been necessary to approach by an indirect route and she was willing enough to show him. However many miles she led him before she laid her hand again upon his stolen property, he would be at her shoulder when she reached it. She was out of her class at this game, it would give him no trouble to follow her all the evening, if necessary. And it would be well worth it, he thought, smiling as he strolled silently from tree to tree after her, just to see her face when he reached out gently and took the evidence out of her hand.

Jonathan drove the old Morris to a rattling and protesting seventy on the best stretches of the road into Colmar, and held it as near to that speed as he could for the remainder of the way. The approach to the town by the Rue d'Ingersheim slowed him down to a more orthodox speed, shutting him in almost suddenly between its hot white houses and apartment blocks and shops, shuttered against the sun. He had to stop by the Musée and ask his way to the main police station, and then to puzzle out his instructions in a town by no means well-known to him. For the moment its Gothic beauties made no impression upon his eye or his mind; he wanted only to get to the police and find out if the Triumph had been picked up yet, and most of all, if Marianne had been picked up intact with it. Compared with that urgency, he found it hard even to care whether Eisinger had been captured with her.

He had no more than mentioned his name when he was whisked immediately through the big charge-room and away down a corridor to an inner office, and the presence of a middle-aged inspector who was at that moment conversing with two of his subordinates, in high satisfaction, apparently, about the stolen car. They welcomed him with pleasure, so that his heart leaped with excitement and he imagined himself again face to face with Marianne in a matter of moments.

"Ah, Monsieur Creagh, in good time! Your friend's car has been reported only a few minutes ago. It was picked up at one of the crossings on the Avenue de la Republique, after ignoring orders to stop at two previous points. They are bringing it in now. If you will take a seat, we should have something of interest for you."

"And the girl?" asked Jonathan, drawing a great breath of relief and joy.

"The girl would seem now to be driving it, and she has no passenger."

"There was no one with her in the car?" He was surprised and uneasy, it did not fit in with any of his ideas. Could Eisinger have obtained from her so quickly whatever satisfaction it was he wanted? And abandoned her to answer whatever questions might be asked about Hilary? It grew more and more complicated the more he thought about it. He sat down dubiously, watching the Inspector's face with anxiety.

"No one. About this girl, Monsieur Creagh, you were not informative—perhaps you could not be. Had you any reason to think she is not known to Miss Prescott? Or perhaps the man, her companion? It was, of course, correct to notify the matter, but—"

Explanations were precisely what Jonathan did not want to give until he had seen Marianne again; but he was saved from having to decide how much or how little to know by the arrival of a young and ingenuous policeman who came bustling in to announce, with modest triumph, the arrival of the disputed car and its driver.

"She is in the charge-room? No matter as yet for the forms, it is not yet clear if there will be any charge. Bring her in here."

And in a moment there entered, in a royal rage and a sparkle of fiery tears, Miss Hilary Prescott. The tears were of purest fury, and every word of her school French had treacherously deserted her. She erupted in English, like an overtuned fountain, but in the middle of her explosion she saw Jonathan standing by the desk, staring at her with eyes and mouth wide open in such a confusion of consternation, relief and bitter disappointment that even English abandoned her. She gave a tearful squeak of: "Jonathan!" and flung herself into his arms, hanging round his neck and sobbing with fury.

"Hilary! How did you get here? I thought—we saw him, that fellow, driving your car, and no sign of you. I reported it stolen, I was afraid something had happened to you—"

"It *did* happen! All kinds of things have happened. I've been threatened with a gun, and locked up, and the wretched car taken away, and—and now these silly idiots tried to say I'd stolen it myself! I tried to tell him," she said, trembling with frustration, "that I was coming to the police myself, but I couldn't remember a single word, and he doesn't know English, either—" She looked from the Inspector, who was concealing something suspiciously like a smile, to the young officer, who was scarlet to the hair, and stammering excuses. "We lost any amount of time because he had to wait for a relief before we came here, and if he'd let me I should have come straight to the police, anyway, but he wouldn't believe me!"

"You didn't think to tell him your name?" asked Jonathan. "Or show your passport?"

"I didn't think my name would mean anything to him, why should it? I never thought about my passport. All he kept saying was that it was a stolen car, and I couldn't make him understand—"

"Forgive me!" said the Inspector. "I have a little English, enough to have concluded by now that this is indeed Miss Prescott herself, driving her own car in all innocence. It is very certain this lady has not red hair—it is evident that I should have sent out my general warning in more detail, but I was in some haste. Miss Prescott, I much regret that you have been subjected to such annoyance, but I beg you won't hold it against Clément, who was only doing his duty. It was a matter of urgency; we circulated immediately the number and description of the car, with orders to pick it up on sight. And the interval, you will allow," he said, seeing the first unwilling spark of a smile moderate the indignation of her small, flushed face, "has been short for such a reversal. More than ever, Miss Prescott, we want and need you, for it's plain you must know more of what has been going on than any of the rest of us, and it seems to me that there is more in it than the temporary misappropriation of a car. Come, now, sit down here and tell us all about it."

"I'll go out and get you a drink," offered Jonathan as she sat down.

"No need to disturb yourself, you should hear what has happened. Clément, be so kind! You would like coffee, Miss Prescott?"

Her eye gleamed at the thought. "Do you know, I haven't had any lunch? I had some beer and a snack at the pass, but I never stopped again, because of meeting that man. Could I have some sandwiches, too?" She had forgiven Clément for accusing her of stealing her own car, because of his youth and his blushing unhappiness. She smiled at him, paying for her coffee in advance. Then with fierce composure she launched into her story.

"I was supposed to be driving after Jonathan over the pass, and I missed him at Le Bonhomme. We used to duck each other by taking odd roads, and the game was to beat each other to the next point—which in this case was Colmar." She cast a deprecating glance at Jonathan, pleading indulgence for this single piece of deception, and blushed faintly. But the rest of the story was direct enough, and told with remarkable vigour and economy.

"Then he came and let me out," she concluded, frowning at the memory over her coffee, "and apologized very prettily, and couldn't have been more pleasant and plausible. He was very keen to give the impression that everything was all right, and they'd just been making use of me as an extra in a highly personal comedy. He showed me the gun was empty, and went out of his way *not* to ask me not to come to the police, not even to seem anxious about it, but that was what he wanted, all the same. And after all, I *did* see her kiss him." She looked up suddenly at Jonathan. He was frowning down at his fingers, which drummed softly and rather feverishly upon the table, as though trying to provide a slight counter-irritant to some very painful speculation within his mind. She remembered the kiss again, and watched the beating fingers trying to fend off his own too vivid imaginative reconstruction of the scene; and for a moment she was convulsed with the first terrible pang of a totally unforeseen jealousy.

"Yet you have come to us. You were not satisfied that this reconciliation of lovers was genuine?" prompted the Inspector gently.

"No, I—" She swallowed the unevenness which impeded her voice, and said with deliberation: "I didn't believe in the kiss."

She was no longer looking at Jonathan, but she felt the quick, hopeful lift of his head, and the brightness of his eyes upon her.

"You see, it would have looked all right if I hadn't heard something already that didn't go with it. He didn't think of me at once when they drove into the yard, because, of course, he hadn't noticed yet that the glass was out of the window, so he couldn't know how well I could hear. And you know how you have to raise your voice to talk to someone in a car, even a good, quiet car. Just as he switched the engine off I heard him saying something to her, and it was still in this slightly raised voice, so it reached me easily. Then he got himself adjusted, of course, and even before he kissed her I didn't catch any more words. But what I did hear was enough to make the whole set-up look phoney. He said: 'Let me see your hands as you alight. It would be a pity if you left anything behind.' So afterwards, even when on the face of it it looked all right, I began to see all kinds of things that were wrong. And I didn't believe in any of it. I'm sure she doesn't love him—I think she dislikes him, and is afraid of him, and I'm almost sure she never wanted to be there with him. So hadn't we better go back there quickly, and get her out?"

"We shall do exactly that," agreed the Inspector briskly. "But I think Monsieur Creagh will also have something to add to this story, for it seems to me you have been sharing the events of this curious affair equally between you and are now for the first time in a position to put them together and make a little sense. Please!" He looked across at the young policeman significantly, and raised an eyebrow. "In five minutes, perhaps—we shall need two cars. Yes, Monsieur Creagh?"

There was no longer any question of keeping anything back. Jonathan told the whole story as it had happened to him, the improbable meeting, the eccentricities of the journey, and the abrupt and unexplained departure of Marianne. "It doesn't take much understanding, does it? He locked Hilary up for safe keeping, realizing she was a trump card, because one of the first things one would find out about Marianne is that she wouldn't let anyone else carry her troubles for her. He had only to slide up to her while I was out of the way, and point out that he held Hilary, and that she was going to suffer for it if Marianne didn't do as she was told, and she'd go with him without any hesitation. The first essential to her would be to get Hilary safely out of it. She'd even—" He shied away from the reported kiss, with all its implications, and looked up suddenly at Hilary with the warmest, most unwary smile he'd ever given her since she'd sprung suddenly to maturity in his arms and frightened him out of England; and all because she reassured him that Marianne Becher was not really in love with the man Eisinger! There was no justice in the world, thought Hilary bitterly.

"It appears, then, that there is something this man wants from Mademoiselle Becher and also that she is of a temperament not to give up easily whatever it is she is holding out against him. Mademoiselle Prescott, you can find this café again?"

Hilary demolished the last sandwich with unseemly haste, and was on her feet and ready for action. "Yes, of course I can!"

"Then you shall be the guide. No, the cars this time shall be ours. Your machine is a little noticeable for such a call, don't you agree?"

Hilary sat by the police driver in the first car, with the Inspector and Jonathan behind them, the second car following with two more policemen in addition to the driver. They covered the two miles to the café at high speed, and separated to approach by both doors. In the yard, now half in shade as the sun declined gently westward behind the roofs of the sheds, the fragments of glass crunched underfoot, and tinkled as they were kicked aside. In the bar half-a-dozen men, local people from nearby farms or transport drivers dropping in from the road, were drinking and talking, and Georges was leaning on the bar, freshly shaved, in the middle of an argument about wine. He grinned at the sight of the police, and with complete self-possession looked clean through Hilary. Clearly the visit did not surprise him, and he had no particular reason to recoil from it.

"This is the man you saw, Miss Prescott?"

"Yes," said Hilary, "that's Georges. He never touched me, you know, not even when I smashed his windows. But he was here, and he talked to the other man and can't have helped knowing I was locked in upstairs. I think this one just does what he's told. The other one did the telling."

"This lady has been walking a long time in the sun today?" enquired Georges solicitously. "It has very curious effects, one should be careful in such weather. I have never seen her before—with regret I say it. There are many cafés not unlike mine, and one must admit with modesty I am not even of a strikingly distinguished appearance myself. I think she makes a mistake."

Unnecessarily, perhaps, but with considerable aplomb, Hilary launched into a detailed description of the upper floor of the house, the drab corridor, the bare room with the daguerreotypes and the smashed windows. The Inspector laughed, patting her on the shoulder approvingly. His men were already up there, moving methodically from room to room.

"Be easy!" he said in English. "We rely on your identification, and we shall take him in with us. But unless something further comes to light I think he will not be greatly concerned about his little holiday. No very serious charges can be made against him, and no doubt for accepting the matter philosophically he will be well paid. Let us go up, then!"

But nowhere in the house, or the sheds, or the yard, was there any sign of Marianne Becher or Johann Eisinger. There was not even a thread of the grey lining of Marianne's bag in the bedroom where she had been confined.

Jonathan, with increasing desperation, quartered every corner of the place after the police had already searched thoroughly, but there was nothing to indicate where Marianne had been taken, and nothing but Hilary's testimony to prove that she had ever been there. All they had to show for their visit was one compliant and somewhat amused prisoner, who blandly answered all questions still with a sweeping denial, and expressed resigned concern that so charming a creature as Hilary should be subject to delusions. He was still grinning when they stowed him under escort into the second car, and left his customers to the care of an old woman, apparently his mother, unearthed from the kitchen to take charge of the bar.

"So now we are without any lead," said the Inspector, "and do not know where to begin looking for Mademoiselle Becher. No doubt this Georges could tell us something of Eisinger's associates and habits, if he would, but I think he knows too well he himself has little to fear. He is not, I think, a stranger to us, his record may suggest something. In the meantime, Monsieur Creagh, you had better go once again through everything that passed with her. It may be that we have missed something."

"I've been doing that," said Jonathan, gnawing his knuckles in the back of the car. "I can think of only one thing, and it doesn't lead on from here at all, it simply starts afresh somewhere else. Probably it's useless, since as far as we know she's still a prisoner and can't strike out for herself at all—but at least we do know where she originally intended to go in Colmar. I don't know what it was all about, or what she wanted there, but she asked me to drive her to a private house near the Petite Venise—Number 11 Ruelle des Limaçons."

"Good!" said the Inspector, instantly recovering his animation and closing his hand upon the phrase in mid-air, as on a clue of thread that would eventually bring them out of the labyrinth. "We shall see who is at home there, and what they know of Mademoiselle Becher. Pérard, you heard? Drive to the Rue Turenne end of the Ruelle des Limaçons, and hurry!"

At the end of the Grand' Rue the canal bridge carried the narrowing street leftward towards the Rue Turenne, and laid open for a moment, on either side, glimpses of the enclosed world of the Petite Venise. In the clear saffron light of the evening, under a sun already declining, all the tender greens of water and fern and willow shone with a heightened delicacy, distinct from one another, as if seen through a filter. Marianne cast a quick glance along the canal from the crest of the little bridge; the backs of the houses crowded in over the scummy and odorous water in a jumble of windows, and walls, and gables; of tiny landing-stages and boats green themselves with age and neglect, of miniature balconies and disintegrating fences, ferns and mosses and lilies, tottering Gothic roofs, sleepy dormer windows. A secret world, hidden from the streets every way except by this narrow window, draped with willows, decaying, insanitary, silently beautiful. On the other side of the bridge the houses stood back for a few yards, leaving a little open quay, then folded closely and jealously once more upon their green waterway. Beyond the bridge, the road shook its cramped sides free and widened into the Rue Turenne, spacious and quiet, lined with its pollarded trees, round and bushy as the trees with which children embellish their drawings of landscape. And from half-way along the Rue Turenne, on the left, opened the narrow little Ruelle des Limaçons, already in its own deep dusk.

She came to the turning and leaned against the wall for a moment, trembling

already, trembling too soon, with a sense of arrival. She was very tired, rather
with nervous tension than actual exertion and sick to death of the attractive
sandals she would never want to see again after today. Pretty to look at, agreeable
to wear for strolling about the streets of a town or the lawns of a garden, but not
meant for walking on field-paths or mountain tracks. She was oppressed also by
a quite unexpected loneliness. It was not even dusk yet, except in the Ruelle des
Limaçons, and yet she felt as if she were groping her way in superstitious fear
through the obscurities of a moonless night. Colmar was so empty, so silent;
everywhere this silence, in the Grand' Rue, by the old Douane and the Gothic
houses with their overhanging storeys, the footsteps of the few strollers resounded
hollowly, throwing into relief the appalling stillness. Only from somewhere unseen,
borne in soft waves from a distance, there was music floating on the air. She
was too tired to connect, she could only feel, and what she felt was a terrifying
isolation, as though humanity, seeing her in flight from a private nemesis, had
withdrawn even from the city, and refused to enclose and cover her. As often as
she approached a refuge, it would dissolve like this and leave her naked.

She entered the narrow street, and felt the shadows filled with warmth, reflected
back upon her from the stone walls which had stored up the sun all day. No one
moved between wall and wall except herself. She came to the deep-set door of
Number 11, and knocked. There was no sound within, none in the outer evening
except a sudden surge of distant music that swelled and died away in a moment
in a current of wind. She waited, holding her breath, but no one answered the
door. She knocked again, more peremptorily, feeling that she could not bear to be
much longer alone. No one came, nothing moved. It seemed to her that she had
been there a long time, hammering at the door of an empty house and that the
evening was closing in upon her like silently grasping hands.

From high above her a sudden thick, elderly voice said reasonably: "You'll get
no answer there. They're all out."

She looked up with a leaping heart, ready to start at her own shadow. At a
second-floor window on the opposite side of the lane a fat middle-aged woman
was leaning on a pillow placed on the sill, her bare arms folded under her bulging
bosom, her frizzy grey hair bright in the last sunlight, which was withdrawing
inch by inch from her window, and had already left her face in shadow. This was
evidently her regular evening relaxation, the most active excitement her bulk
allowed her after the exertion of the day.

"Monsieur Jean-Marie is out, too?" asked Marianne, relieved to have awakened
another human creature.

"They are all at the Fair. Didn't you know? Everybody in Colmar will be on the
fairground by now. Yes, Monsieur Jean-Marie, too."

Relief and enlightenment flooded Marianne's heart. How could she have forgotten, or failed to understand the silence and emptiness of the town? The whole life of Colmar had removed itself for the evening to the covered Market Halls, and the open ground adjoining; and where else would a young man choose to spend his first evenings of freedom?

"Ah, of course, I understand! Thank you, Madame! I will go and look for him there."

The encounter had heartened her. She went on along the street with a lightened step, and the woman, leaning solidly on her stout arms, watched her go. There was so little happening within her view tonight that she could not afford to miss any movement or sound. She saw the girl vanish into the shadows at the end of the lane, and instantly upon that disappearance she saw a man materialize out of a deep doorway near the Rue Turenne, and stroll softly, calmly, purposefully after the girl. It was too methodical to be disconnected, his movements followed hers at a considered distance, as in a smooth mechanical toy. With silent interest the old woman watched him go by, grow shadowy at the lane's end, vanish. She measured with an impartial eye the wide shoulders, the powerful body, the still, hard, handsome proportions of the face. She even looked at the time, because the double progress was of a kind which has curious echoes. It was twenty minutes to seven.

Another half-hour had passed, and she had taken her pillow in from the window-sill, when the expected echoes came. From within her room she heard the knocker rattling again at Number 11, and went and leaned out again to see who this might be. The affair was becoming seriously interesting; here were several people now, a young man and a girl standing at the centre of the street and looking up at the house together, an older man plying the knocker, two more looking on expectantly and straining their ears after a movement within. The young couple looked like foreigners to her, but all the others were police officers. She called down to them:

"There's nobody in, all the family are at the Fair." And when all their startled eyes had flashed upward to where she hung vast and curious in the upper window, she went on with relish: "You're not the first to come asking for the Lesouliers tonight. There was a girl here after them only half-an-hour ago, and she had no luck, either."

"A girl?" The Inspector exchanged a rapid glance with Jonathan, and his voice sharpened into eagerness. "What was she like, this girl? Did you know her?"

"No, but she knows them, all right. A tall young woman, in a blue skirt and a white blouse. You'd call her good-looking—hair like red wheat—"

"That's Marianne!" said Jonathan, leaping at the identifying glory. "Half-an-hour ago? And you told her they were at the Fair, as you've told us? Was she alone?"

"Alone and not alone," she said, and looked along the street to the doorway out of which the shadower had emerged so silently. "She thought she was alone, but there was a man following her. When she went off towards the fairground, *he* appeared from back there and went after her. He was keeping a safe distance between them—if he'd wanted, he could have overtaken her at any time. But it was her he was following. She didn't know it, but I knew it."

"And this man? Describe him, if you please!"

She did so, with exactness and appreciation. She had an eye for a fine figure of a man, and preferred them blond; by the time she had detailed his physical beauties, there was no mistaking Johann Eisinger.

"So she was clear of him," said Jonathan, with excitement, "or thought she was. And he was still keeping her under observation. You heard how he was holding back from her—it means he must have connived at her being free, so that she—" He subsided at the Inspector's slight warning frown, and blushed to find himself exclaiming aloud like an adolescent boy.

"A moment! Madame, for whom did she ask, this girl? For which member of the Lesoulier family?"

"She wanted the son, Monsieur Jean-Marie. What did she think, that a boy of twenty-two is going to come out of the army and spend his first evenings sitting quietly at home while the Wine Fair is on? Go there, I told her, you'll find him on the fairground."

The name echoed and re-echoed like the tone of a bell in Jonathan's memory, and added upon the instant a new shape to the whole confused problem. Somewhere at the back of his mind he was beginning to construct from these several broken images an understandable picture. He looked up at the woman in the window, for it seemed to him that an urgent question remained to be asked.

"Madame, how far away was the man when you spoke with her about Jean-Marie? Could he possibly have overheard the name?" For it might not even mean anything to him if he did hear it, but there was a terrible possibility that it would mean all too much, the end of complacency, the beginning of desperation.

"No, Monsieur, I do not think so. Sound carries here, it is true, but with confusing echoes; and he was only just within the street at that time, in a doorway there, not three yards from the Rue Turenne. The street is too straight to permit him to enter openly until she had left it at the other end."

"It seems we also must make for the fairground," said the Inspector, setting off purposefully along the darkening street. "Come, we shall make our dispositions, there is no time to lose."

The old woman watched them go with detachment. She was used to seeing the beginnings of dramas which would be played out far from her knowledge, and too wise to let the flavour of what she had be ruined by regrets for what she could not have.

They plunged into a short street close to the old Douane, and the music came out in a great gust of brass and met them like a civic reception. Only a few yards behind them the Grand' Rue lay quiet and deserted, and the inn Au Fer Rouge inclined its lovely Gothic head over an empty city, but here they were suddenly enfolded in light and glitter and sound, and engulfed in a stream of people. The Inspector led them briskly in through the turnstiles by the pay-box, and there on their right lay the market halls, now the wine-tasting halls, and before them stretched the open fairground, wide and clamorous and thronging with people, a glitter of lighted booths, displays of machinery, furniture, electrical equipment, every conceivable article to do with the home or the farm or the vineyard. The charm of lights made the sky seem suddenly cobalt, and the hour deepest night, though it was scarcely dusk; and the din of voices and music was bewildering after the outer silence. But the Inspector, drawing them after him, made straight for the entrance of the wine-halls and button-holed the middle-aged woman, who sat in a booth just within with a tray of tasting-glasses before her.

The first great room was divided into booths, ringed round with wooden counters and stacked with bottles and casks, where the various wines of Alsace might be tasted in turn: Sylvaners, Traminers, Zwickers, Muscats, Pinots, Reislings, all served by young girls in Alsatian dress; and in the centre was a flower-ringed fountain playing into a wide circular bowl, where a few industrious tasters were rinsing their glasses between assays. Beyond opened a vista of restaurant tables, trellised round with flowers, and somewhere out of sight a band was playing lustily, fine galloping waltz tunes and marches, full of bass thunder. Hilary looked round her with wonder and delight, forgetting for a moment the urgency of the need which had brought them here.

"What happens? You come in here and get a glass from that box by the door—and then what? What are those tickets they have there in rolls?"

"You buy as many tickets as you like at ten francs a time, and give whatever the fixed rate is for the particular wine you want to taste—two tickets a glass, or three, or four if you want the *vins de réserve*—"

"Observe it, if you please," said the Inspector, coming up suddenly at her shoulder, "from within the booth. Will you do this for us? You know both Mademoiselle Becher and Eisinger, I would like you to become for this evening a seller of those tickets—or if you prefer you shall retail the glasses, that will be easier for you—and to watch for either of these people. I shall leave one of my men here in the hall, always with an eye upon you. Whenever you see either of our hares, you will signal to him by taking off your kerchief."

"My kerchief?"

"Madame here will dress you. Please! Everyone who comes to the Wine Fair must at some time come in here, probably will come repeatedly, therefore Mademoiselle Becher, if she has not already found Monsieur Lesoulier, will certainly seek him here. And where she comes, Eisinger will come. My men do not know them by sight, but you do and we have need of you."

He had need, too, thought Jonathan, of a relatively safe place to which this volatile child might be confined without wasting her enthusiasm or hurting her feelings; and in one of those booths among the glasses she could hardly come to any harm. She went away delightedly with the smiling woman, and reappeared in a few minutes in a long red skirt banded with black, a wide-sleeved blouse of white, and a tightly laced little black bodice over it, with a handkerchief knotted round her neck and a winged red cap on her head; so transformed in this graceful dress, and, he thought, so instinctively modulating her own manner to match it, that he wondered if Eisinger would recognize her even if he bought a glass from her.

"So, that is well!" said the Inspector, approving her. "Remain here in the booth with Madame, she will take care of you. If you see either of the people we want, make your signal. Do not trouble to try and see where my man is, it will be for him to have his eye always upon you."

He waited only a moment, to see her installed, wonderfully dignified, serious and demure behind her tray of tasting-glasses; then he took Jonathan by the arm, and drew him back quietly towards the open air, where the soft, greenish-blue darkness was falling tenderly.

"I have the entrance covered, and all unofficial ways in and out will be watched. Eisinger was somewhat of a local celebrity at the time of the La Croix affair, his face will be known vaguely to some of my men from a few old newspaper pictures, perhaps. But you are the only other person who will know both of them at sight. I wish you to make this whole fairground your beat, Monsieur Creagh. Go through it carefully, and if you find either of them, use your discretion. If you can be sure that for the moment she is safe from attack, blow this whistle and bring us running. If not—"

"He has a gun," said Jonathan, thinking with extreme anxiety of the possible effects of desperation upon Johann Eisinger. "If he thinks everything's up with him in any case, I'm sure he'll use it. At least, I'm afraid—"

"I, too, am afraid. But remember, he will not be right on her heels, because he does not wish her to know she is followed until she brings him to whatever it is he wants of her. Therefore he will keep what distance he can without losing her. Go and look for them. We shall be looking, too. And it will be necessary to be guided by the particular circumstances when you find them."

He was springing away, with that remarkably speedy gait of his, when Jonathan caught him by the arm for a moment. "I must tell you—it's the reason why I'm afraid he'll start shooting when the crisis comes—this Jean-Marie—"

The Inspector's shrewd, mild, uncommunicative eyes widened into candour for one revealing instant. "Monsieur Creagh, I am well aware of the possible significance of Jean-Marie Lesoulier. He, too, is somewhat of a local celebrity, that boy. It has not escaped me how curious is the coincidence, that one who runs away from Johann Eisinger should so urgently run straight to Jean-Marie.

"Be assured I have it only too well in mind what the results of such a meeting could be—if we are right in our surmises. It is why I say, use your judgement. None of us can do more. I already have two men who do know him, but well, hunting through this crowd for Jean-Marie himself, since the crisis will not come until she also finds him. By which time, I hope, we shall already be at hand. Therefore, if you can find and separate her from her shadow, do it. And we, if God is good, will do the rest."

Marianne left the blare of the band and the perambulating wine-tasters of the covered hall behind her, and moved on through the noisy, shouting, glittering arcades of the trade stands, threading her way with watchful eyes through the elbowing crowds, looking for one face. Thousands of people, gaily coloured, dressed for holiday, swirling and circling endlessly like the eddies of a river, nowhere still, nowhere waiting to be identified.

Young men turning towards her delicate quarter-views of a lean young cheek and long lashes, or the back of a head of neat black hair and drawing her after them for a few steps before they turned and showed her a face as different from the fierce, gay, self-willed face of Jean-Marie as milk from wine. Movements which deceived the eye for a moment, only to be lost for ever in the moving crowd. She moved through the array of agricultural and viticultural machinery, hydraulic and electric presses, bottling machines, atomizers, cultivators; monstrous, brightly coloured, fleshless shapes in their comparatively quiet corner, critically admired by a gently flowing stream of middle-aged professionals.

In one corner of the grounds, the crowd had gathered even more thickly before a draped backcloth of black, on a large stage, where artists of Radio Strasbourg were giving a variety concert before a shifting audience, who came to rest for a while on the graded benches until their weary feet were again ready for movement, and then walked on and made room for new audiences. Marianne walked slowly along the gangways on the soft, cool turf, under the rainbow lights, searching the rows of faces for Jean-Marie's face, and failing to find it. He would certainly not be in need of rest before morning, nor would the pretty blonde singer be likely to hold his attention, but there was always the possibility that he had already

encountered some more attractive girl who was also more attainable, and who
wanted to sit for a while and listen to sentimental *chansons*. But she could not
find him, he was not there.

In the *Foire Gastronomique* the salesgirls leaned out from their pavilions,
offering samples of chocolate, sweets, local cakes, biscuits, prepared cheeses.
Marianne walked along the turf lane between them, watching everyone who
lingered, everyone who passed. In the distant corner, lighted booths showed
displays of furniture, ornate and expensive, radios, radiograms, electrical
equipment, kitchen gadgets. Every space between these various components of
the fair was filled with flower-decked wine-restaurants. She studied the faces at
every table, but still she could not find him.

Somewhere behind the tall stands of garden furniture there resounded curious
wooden sounds, heard clearly through the conflicting music of the variety show
and the Alsatian band, and punctuating the uproar of chatter and laughter.
Marianne recognized the knacking of the heavy bowls in the skittle alley, and the
long rumble as the small boy in attendance rolled each ball back down the wooden
trough to the players. She thrust forward through the crowd and, circling the
booths, came to the more open space where the alley was set up, the long, rising
wooden ramp with the pins at the upper end, the boards to keep the shots in, the
trough on one side like a primitive aerial railway. Four young men were playing.
She could hear their shouts of applause and derision, and the provocative jokes
with which they sought to upset one another; but she could not see them, except
in rapid glimpses as they moved and threw, because of the gallery of grinning
admirers they had drawn about them. On both barriers of the alley watchers
were leaning, and others crowding at their shoulders. It seemed to her that one
of the voices, the clearest and most hilarious, the one with the sharpest turn of
phrase, was hopefully familiar.

She moved round the group, quickening her pace, to reach a spot where she
could see and be seen. The man who followed her, and who had walked at ease
through the fair after her with a bare three yards between his hand and her
oblivious shoulder, since cover was plentiful and anonymity perfect in such a
crowd, shortened his distance instinctively, his hand flying to the gun in his pocket.
It was not the voice which had given him warning, but only the sudden quickening
haste of her step, the eager tension of her body and head as she craned to see
over the heads of others. He had followed her thus far in increasing doubt, even
wondering sometimes if she had detected his presence and was deliberately
leading him astray; but there was nothing in her behaviour to justify such fears,
and everything to convince him that she was without any suspicions. He saw
anxiety, and weariness, and excitement in her and knew that they were genuine.

He could not have miscalculated; she must be looking for her evidence and he should be there when she located it; and if she could not find it again, then in any case it no longer constituted a threat to him. He saw her shoulders thrust forward urgently between the strolling women who barred her way, and quickened his own pace.

She did not feel his nearness; here one moved in constant contact with some other human body, and all her senses were concentrated upon the players. Between burly shoulders she caught a glimpse of the man who was about to bowl, a dark young face, a flashing grin; then he stepped back, swinging his bowl, measuring the distance, and lunged forward the few crouching steps to the mark.

For one instant Marianne forgot that her loneliness was hemmed about with so many witnesses. She darted forward, crying out his name in a gasp of joy: "Jean-Marie!"

The eyes of the players sprang to her face; they fell back a step from Jean-Marie's run, and left him balanced on the edge of the ramp, the ball swinging back weightily in his hand, his eyes staring astonished at the girl who launched herself towards him through the crowd. He saw and recognized the red-gold hair, the familiar and welcome face and gaped at the pallor of her cheeks and her look of strain, and the excessive note of joyful relief in her voice. And over her shoulder, closely and clearly, he saw another face, one which after so many years he might have passed by without recognition but for that startling cry of hers. A handsome, large-boned face, brown and strongly moulded, with light blue eyes flaring pallidly in it, and a mouth drawn long and thin, tensed for action. The pale eyes followed the girl's gaze, and found there no meaning for her cry, but knew that there was indeed a meaning, and that it was life and death to divine it quickly.

Jean-Marie halted, rocking on his forward foot, tensing his fingers in the shaped holds to sustain the weight of his bowl. His vivid face flamed into knowledge and triumph. He yelled: "Reutte!"

Then everything happened at once. Agonized intelligence leaped up in the pale eyes, and despair and rage after it. He did not know this boy, but this boy knew him, and became in that instant a thousand times more dangerous than Marianne Becher, who only suspected. He sprang forward and caught her in his left arm, pinning her arms to her body and dragging her against him with such violence that the breath was crushed out of her; and behind this shield he dragged out the gun and took aim at Jean-Marie.

Marianne hacked backward at his ankle with the heel of one sandal, and he splayed out his foot at the very moment of firing to avoid the threat to his balance. She gave a short, angry cry of warning, and grief, and despair, because it was she who had unwittingly brought this danger upon her cousin, and now there was nothing for Eisinger to do but shoot his way out, and nothing either she or the unarmed boy could do to stop him.

All round them people started back with alarmed shouts from the sudden violence and the sight of the gun. But Jean-Marie, his hair erect and his eyes glittering, sprang not back but forward, launching his bowl before him along the ground between them, and hurling himself after it. The bowl struck Eisinger's braced left foot, swept it from under him and brought him down in a heavy fall, dragging Marianne with him, just as he fired. The bullet tore a furrow across the outer side of Jean-Marie's arm on a level with the heart, ripping the rolled-up sleeve of his pearl-grey shirt to ribbons, but he did not even feel the graze. He made a long spring, and kicked at the right hand which was struggling to bring the gun to bear for a second shot; and to protect himself Eisinger was forced to relax his grip of Marianne. Jean-Marie caught her by the arm and waist, and dragged her clear, and with all his weight fell upon his enemy.

They rolled over and over upon the ground, the boy levering the other man's gun-hand strongly away from him, frightened women scattering with screams from its threshing motions. With the released flow of blood numbness surged down to Jean-Marie's thin whalebone wrist, and when the blood reached his fingers he lost his grip in the slippery struggle, and Eisinger drew up a foot suddenly, kicked him off viciously and sprang clear. The boy's head struck loudly against the corner of the skittle alley, and he rolled over in the grass and lay dazed for a few minutes, hugging his body in rocking arms and smearing himself with blood.

Taking advantage of the moment when all eyes were on his opponent, and half-a-dozen people were running forward to pick him up, Eisinger darted swiftly round the skittle alley and plunged into the the crowd. When they turned to secure him, fighting their way through the clawing arms of those who had only just come pouring on to the scene, he had already vanished, and no one knew in which direction.

Jean-Marie put his head in through the doorway of the small retiring-room reserved for the use of the girl attendants, and cast a glittering eye over the little group gathered round Marianne. She lay in a deck-chair borrowed from the garden exhibits, and Jonathan, Hilary and the Inspector were all bending solicitously over her.

"She is not hurt?" demanded Jean-Marie, tensed as though he had just alighted in the doorway from flight and in an instant would soar away again. "She will be all right? I am sorry I had to be rough, but the matter was urgent."

"Yes, she'll be all right now, there's no damage." The Inspector attempted to arrest the impending flight by means of an authority which scarcely held good with wild creatures like this one. "Monsieur Lesoulier, we need your statement—"

"We need Reutte far more," said Jean-Marie insubordinately, and turned in one violent and graceful movement to return to his hunt. The left sleeve of his shirt dangled from the slit of his wound, heavy with blood. Hilary cried protestingly after him:

"But your arm!"

He halted for an instant, astonished, his black eyes fastening with pleased surprise upon her indignant face. He had never seen her before, and what she was doing in this affair, with her local dress and her English voice, and her purposeful excitement the mirror of his own, was more than he could guess. He had not even time just now to take pleasure in her, though the momentary glimpse promised him future pleasure. "It is nothing!" he said contemptuously, glancing in derision at his wound; and incontinently vanished before anyone could interfere.

Hilary gazed after him with shining eyes. Such singleness of purpose she could understand and appreciate. He was right, what mattered now was to capture Eisinger—Eisinger, Reutte, whatever his name might be. There would be time enough for tidying up the details of the story afterwards. Her part was already done; they no longer needed her, surely she could go and join in the hunt?

By the time Jonathan remembered and looked round for her, a few minutes later, she was already following with excited joy the strategic dispositions of Jean-Marie, who was directing a party of his friends, recruited apparently in one flashing glance, in the quartering of the auditorium. The din of the fair continued with mounting gaiety; only a handful of all those gathered here in the glittering, noisy night even knew that the police were combing the fairground for a killer with a gun. Hilary watched the hunters moving methodically between the benches, searching every face that turned towards them as they passed. She forgot that she had left Jonathan bending over Marianne's chair with a glass of wine in his hand and a lover's anxiety in his face. She had probably never been quite so happy in her life.

"She wishes," said the Inspector, marking the defection of one of his helpers, "to be in at the death. To her we have already become a little dull, the action is more than the motives. Well, she at least is of no interest to Eisinger, now, and young Lesoulier is by no means a fool, and can, I hope, look after himself. Do you feel strong enough now to tell me how all this began? For I think, Mademoiselle Becher, it began with you."

"Yes, I am all right now, I want to tell you." She put away Jonathan's ministering hand, very gently, letting her fingers rest with a warm pressure upon his wrist. "Thank you, I am really quite well, I was only shaken. Jonathan, will you stay, I would like you to listen."

"Of course! Unless they need me—"

"We have men all round the ground," said the Inspector. "He cannot get away, it is only a matter of time. Sit down, I think you may be needed here rather than with them."

"I must say again," began Marianne in a calm voice, "that it was intended I should marry this man. It was the wish of my father, and of his adopted father, and I think it was as much for a memorial to their sons as for a practical joining of their properties. I grew up knowing him, and having that idea always before me. He seemed to me a pleasant person—you see he was good to look at, older than I, but not by too many years—why should I not accept such a match? Today I went with my parents to his home, where the engagement was to be formally announced.

"Nothing would have happened if the day had been wet—that's strange, isn't it?—for then we should all have been together indoors, but today everyone sat in the garden, and so it was that when I found I had no cigarettes I went alone into the house to get some. There was a box on his desk in the sittingroom. It is out of sight from the lawn, and I was in there alone for the first time—I wonder if you can understand? I opened his desk, and began to look what he had in it, and also to consider carefully the photographs he kept upon it. I knew so little about him, although I had known him so long, and I was curious. It was not that I found his life in any way suspicious—it was only, somehow, too empty of women. And now, since I was entering into a real engagement—

"He had a photograph of his father—I mean his adopted father—in one of those chromium frames on his desk. You know the kind, two side holders contain the card and glass, the top is free. It was a thick card. I don't know why I looked at it so carefully, but I saw that this thick card was divided by a hair-line, as though two cards had been stuck together. I drew it out, and it seemed to me by a mere shade thicker within than at the edges. I took a penknife, and separated the two cards along the bottom edge. Between then there was another photograph."

She raised her eyes and looked at Jonathan. "I thought it would be a woman. You understand? It did not matter to me, I wished only to know, to feel that I had gained some knowledge of him which could give me confidence. I was sure it would be a woman. The only rather important thing was that I should be right in my judgement. But I was not right. Please, is Mademoiselle Prescott's car here? It would be good if you saw this thing I found."

Jonathan looked at the Inspector. "We left it at the station. Shall I go and fetch it?"

"No need, I have already had it brought here to the parking ground. Bricquot, a moment! Will you go to the English lady's car and bring from it—Mademoiselle Becher will tell you what, and where to look for it."

"The edge of the cover on the passenger seat," she said, "is unstitched for perhaps three inches, towards the back. Underneath the cover there you will find a photograph—it was just of a size to go through, though it fitted tightly. He was sitting beside me when I put it there, I could use only one hand, and could not look what I did. It was not a nice moment."

"Bring it!" said the Inspector, and the young sergeant departed at a run.

"So you found that because of this photograph everything was changed. And you ran from this party, taking with you the discovery which rendered marriage impossible."

"You know, I think, what it was. So, then, you can understand why I ran, why I did not go back to my mother and father and that poor old man, and say: 'Look what I have found in Johann's possession!' I had been about to marry myself to this man. I wished not to see, not to speak with, anyone who knew me, until I had cleaned myself of him. And also, though I did not reason about this until I was already running from that house, you will see that even this could be explained away, that it was his word against mine. The men of the Maquis often played very unusual parts in the course of their work, and a harmless souvenir—And he was, of course, a man of the Maquis, as everyone knew. Either that, or—"

"It is well seen," agreed the Inspector gently, "that there were only two kinds of people in the wood of La Croix that night."

Her cheeks were burning with a bitter, angry colour, she closed her eyes and was silent until the sergeant came back with his find, and handed it in silent excitement to his superior. It was more eloquent than she knew how to be. The Inspector placed it quietly in Jonathan's hand. A small but excellent studio portrait, head and shoulders, cut down, perhaps, from a larger size, for it bore no trade name or mark; Johann Eisinger's arrogant, handsome face and disdainful smile stared out directly, the German uniform smooth across his broad shoulders, the upright collar with its unmistakable insignia hugging his powerful neck, the cap at the approved angle and with its front pushed up into the approved shape. Seeing it, Jonathan felt its final appropriateness upon this head. He had seen half-naked German prisoners in England, working in the heat of sugar-beet factories, whose blond heads, like this one, constantly implied this missing part of their personality, and troubled him indefinably with a sensation of incompleteness.

"So you set out," said the Inspector quietly, "for Colmar, to find Jean-Marie. Who had seen a part of what happened that night, and who might have seen this man clearly enough to recognize him—"

"And who, if you remember, had never seen Johann Eisinger. Jean-Marie was very ill for two months, and for over a year not yet well. His parents took him back with them to Nancy as soon as he could travel. It is true they moved here to Colmar nearly two years ago, but he was then already in Africa, and has only just come home. Consider it, all these years one meeting between those two people could have brought to light all this deception, but because Eisinger never heard any more about the boy, he felt no anxiety. He felt quite safe. And then this! While I had the photograph safely, I knew I could at least accuse him with a hope of making good my accusation; but if I could confront him with Jean-Marie, and Jean-Marie recognized him, then our case would be unanswerable. And as for him, when he found that I had stolen his photograph he realized at once that if he could get it back from me and destroy it, then it would not be difficult to cast doubts on anything I might say. A woman changing her mind about a marriage may use very odd arguments to justify herself. He thought the only real danger to him was that photograph. He did not know about Jean-Marie."

"You think," said Jonathan, "that he was one of the Germans who did the shooting in the wood at La Croix that night?"

"It seemed to me there could be no other explanation. There were fresh troops moved in only recently from Strasbourg, his face would not be known here. I think that when the men of the Maquis arrived, too late for a rescue but in time for their revenge, he knew that there could be no escape. Not only from the wood, but from the logical end of the war, from defeat, no escape ever. I think he knew the end was very near, and preferred to cut his losses and become a Frenchman in order to survive. I think he changed clothes with one of the murdered men, and wounded himself, and crawled into the heap of the dead. The effect of this undressing and dressing in the dark and in haste would not be neat—but, Jonathan, have you ever seen a heap of bodies shovelled together for common burial? The pits of the concentration camps, you remember them? I think a little carelessness in the arrangement of his dress would not be noticed."

Her voice was quiet and calm, as if she felt it incumbent upon her not to shock him by any display of bitterness. He owed it to her to be equally practical.

"And where, then, did he hide this? And why did he keep it? It was lunatic."

"He kept it because it was his religion. It still is. I do not know, but I think he hid it somewhere in the wood, and reclaimed it long afterwards. I think there must have been one of those waterproof wallets soldiers carry for their personal papers, since it is not stained. The papers he left on his victim, but this he obviously could not leave to be found, and would not sacrifice unless he had to. I think he acted only to preserve his life at the time, but afterwards, such love, such luck, such comfort falling into his lap quite unasked, why should he refuse them? But his real allegiance was to this—why else should he keep it? I think soon he might even have been tempted to change countries again, unless the sawmills proved very profitable. There is again a future in this religion of his, it seems."

"It is perfectly evident," said the Inspector, "that Lesoulier knows not only his face but his name, and that he recognized him immediately as an enemy. But how did you get away from Eisinger when he had you?"

She told, briefly and almost cheerfully now, the story of her release by Georges. "I did not realize that it was the only quick way he knew of locating what he wanted. He reasoned that I should make straight for where I had hidden the photograph. He did not know about Jean-Marie, a much more lively danger to him. When I recovered this picture, he meant to be there. And he had a gun, and with a gun it is not difficult to get one's way. As for Georges, there must be something that makes him consent to be Eisinger's creature in little jobs of that kind."

The Inspector pocketed the photograph and turned to the door, where the sergeant had reappeared and was beckoning urgently. "I hoped for a capture before now, I must go and direct my hunt. Remain here, Mademoiselle Becher, you will be safe now that your secret is no longer a secret. If you want anything, call, the girls will hear you. Or perhaps Monsieur Creagh will remain with you—"

Marianne looked up into Jonathan's eyes, and said with a smile: "No, go with him, Jonathan, you know you wish to. I am quite safe now, it is almost over."

False rumours of Eisinger came flowing in from every corner of the fairground, complicating the search unreasonably. People who did not know him, and had only just grasped that a man was being hunted among them, nevertheless claimed to have seen him among the dancers in the Wine Hall restaurant. So far he had fired only one more shot, but the fact that he had brought down a policeman with it convinced them that he was merely conserving his ammunition, not avoiding its use out of prudence or despair. The policeman had been the only person within touch of him when he broke cover, and his survival with nothing worse than a flesh wound along his ribs was a matter of luck. It was all the more necessary, in view of the hundreds of harmless people who might get in the way of the next bullet, to approach the gun, if not the man, with respect.

Marianne lay stretched out in her deck-chair in the little retiring-room, her eyes closed, no longer thinking, no longer even feeling. When she heard the quick, light step in the doorway she did not at first open her eyes, supposing that this must be Jonathan come back to reassure himself that all was well with her. Then she heard the laboured, noisy breathing of exhaustion and fear, and opened her eyes in sudden understanding upon the apparition of Johann Eisinger. He had slid through the doorway quietly, and closed the door behind him, and was moving towards her across the bare wooden floor with lurching steps, the gun in his hand.

She fixed her eyes upon his and waited for him to speak. What she felt first of all was a surprised and alert interest, a critical wonder at seeing him so changed.

He had made shift to alter his appearance by discarding, somewhere, his well-fitting light grey coat, and had put on instead a dinner jacket, borrowed, no doubt, from somewhere behind the variety stage. It was too small for him, his broad brown wrists thrust out from the sleeves ludicrously, and a soft black hat perched foolishly on top of the blond waves. He moved stiffly, his large, catlike gait cramped by the strain of the cloth across his shoulders. He was sweating profusely, and his face was a teak mask of rage and despair and hatred, all for her. She sat staring at him with lively wonder as he raised the gun and pointed it shakily at her. She could not be afraid of a creature so diminished, so ridiculous. Fear was no longer appropriate. All she could find within her was a slight distaste, and an incredulous amusement. She watched him point the gun at her, and involuntarily she laughed, a loud, fresh, astonished sound that seemed to fill the whole space of air between them with incalculable vibrations.

He began to shake, then, all over, and to shout at her in hoarse German, his voice rising to a scream. His hand was shaking so wildly with the intensity of his hate that she found herself doubting if he would succeed with one shot, even at this range.

A flying shoulder, with all the weight of a determined body behind it, thumped the door. Feet pounded across the hall outside, a distant voice cried out: "In there—" Eisinger sprang round, firing blindly towards the door. The bullet splintered the edge of the door-post and buried itself deeply into the wood, missing Jonathan by more than a foot, and before Eisinger could fire again Jonathan plunged upon him in a shoulder-charge which would have got him sent off any football field. Eisinger was flung across the room; then, regaining his balance, he swerved without hesitation towards the open door, intent only on escape. Jonathan went after him in a flying tackle, but secured only a tenuous hold on one ankle, and Eisinger kicked viciously backward at his face, and broke away into the Wine Hall.

Jonathan had flung up his arm over his face, and the heel of the solid walking shoe hacked into the muscles of his upper arm and spread an explosion of pain and numbness down to his finger-ends; but he had rolled back in time to lighten the shock, and now he went on rolling, clean over with spread elbows and hunched shoulders. Marianne had sprung out of her strange lethargy, her inability to feel fear, the moment the gun had swung towards the doorway. She uttered a fierce cry of "Jonathan!" and darted forward, falling on her knees beside him, gathering him into her arms as he came up wry-faced and gasping. "Jonathan, has he hurt you?" She felt at his bruised cheek with tremulous fingers, her lips suddenly shaking uncontrollably. "Are you all right? Oh, Jonathan—"

He came to his feet in a quick spring, flinging a reassuring arm about her. "I'm fine! Hardly touched me! But you—"

"No, I am all right. Oh, he must not get away now, he will fire at anyone, kill anyone—"

He put her gently behind him, and ran out into the Wine Hall, which resounded with the shrieks of women as the girls scattered from the gun, crouching behind their counters and the piled barrels of wine. Eisinger had almost reached the outer doorway when Jean-Marie and the Inspector burst in, the boy running like a hound on a trail. His very speed saved him. He saw his enemy halt and swerve, saw the gun rising, and lowered his head, plunging onward, reaching forward with a long, hacking blow of his left hand that swept the gun downward before it could find its level. The bullet went into the floor, and the two men were swept on the wings of Jean-Marie's headlong rush clean into the fountain, with a rending of flowers and a surge of water that spattered the floor for yards around.

The Inspector, advancing at a run upon the locked and thrashing bodies, found Hilary under his feet and, taking her unceremoniously by the shoulders, pushed her into the Traminer booth out of harm's way. Eisinger was struggling to bring the gun again into play, but Jean-Marie had him by the wrist. The older man had the advantage in weight and strength, however, and wrenched himself aside, swinging his opponent round with a crash into the stone rim of the bowl, and sprang back until he had the solid wood of the wine-booth behind him. He was shaken and breathless, but he spread his left arm backward upon the counter to sustain his weight, and raised the gun.

Hilary, dancing in agonized excitement, recoiled for an instant from the counter as Eisinger's big body fell against it with a heavy impact. She saw the gun flung up, selecting its target in Jean-Marie's defenceless young body. She snatched up the bottle of Traminer that stood almost full upon the counter, and brought it down two-handed upon Eisinger's head with all her might. The gun did not go off. She waited in anguish, the endless fraction of a second while the reflexes of that tightening finger hung in doubt, and then she began, unreasonably, to cry.

The gun fell tamely out of the relaxing hand while Eisinger was still upright, then he slid slowly down the counter, and reached the floor with a dull, soft thump.

"His name," said Jean-Marie, "is Reutte. I saw him plainly in the light of a torch, that night at La Croix, and I heard him called by that name. He was in charge of the party that began the shooting. It was a very private killing, that, each man was led away from the group singly, and shot alone. They botched the first one. I saw this man walk up to him as he lay on the ground, and shoot him again in the back of the head. I will swear to it whenever you choose to put him in court."

"You are sure there can be no mistake?" The Inspector sat gazing at the big body of the man who had been known as Johann Eisinger, whose ten-year dream of security lay in pieces about him. "It is a long time ago."

"There is no mistake." Jean-Marie also looked down at his enemy, and his face tightened. "It may be ten years, but I have not forgotten anything about that night. There were nights when I dreamed of this man."

The soft fingers sponging the drying blood from his arm lingered coaxingly, drawing his eyes and his mind away from the memories that darkened both. He looked at Hilary's radiant, astonished face, still smudged with tears, at her hands which approached the bandaging of his grazed arm with the same dedicated vehemence with which they had wielded the bottle of Traminer only a few minutes ago. They were back in the small room, and outside the closed door, incredibly, tickets were already passing over the wine counters, and the band had resumed playing.

"I am hurting you," said Hilary tenderly, and flushed to her delicate cheekbones. "I've almost finished now. I'm sorry, I'm not frightfully good at this."

"You could hurt me much more," said Jean-Marie, enchanted, "and I should still love you. I am alive, am I not?"

She paled at the thought that he so easily might not have been, and her hands trembled so much that she nearly dropped the roll of bandage, and he had to shut his own good hand over hers to save it.

"Well, perhaps you are better with bottles than bandages, but no one can be perfect at everything," he said mischievously, delighted with the embarrassed butterfly touch caressing his arm, and the rapid fluctuations of her colour. He had never met anyone like her. She, for her part, was going about her self-chosen task in a daze of admiration and wonder at his uniqueness, for it seemed to her that there could never have been any young man so quick in decision, so admirable in movement, so crazily brave.

"He's beginning to come round," said the sergeant, who was kneeling beside Reutte's body.

"What will happen to him?" asked Jonathan in a low voice, watching the lolling head begin to stir uneasily, the mouth to move in painful grimaces.

"He will be put on trial as a war criminal. In the meantime, we have enough minor charges on which to hold him."

They had all drawn closer, staring down at the unconscious man as he returned slowly to life. He opened his eyes a fraction, then screwed them up again in protest against the light. In a moment he opened them again and stared round him at the array of watchful faces. He moved his head and groaned, and memory and comprehension came gradually into the light eyes. He drew himself slowly upward into a sitting position, looking round desperately for a way out, but there was no loophole left anywhere. His face seemed suddenly to have lost its form, to have wilted and run like wax under heat.

"I didn't kill anyone," he said in a rapid, eager, insinuating voice. "The policeman—it was a mistake, I never meant to hit him. I wouldn't have touched you, Marianne—you know I wouldn't. I wanted to marry you! I only wanted you to give me a chance, I wouldn't really have hurt you. I never touched the other girl, did I? And I turned Frenchman. I never wanted to be a Nazi, I was glad to have a chance to get out of it. Just a chance to begin a new life—I haven't done anything except try to keep that!"

They had stepped back a little from him in fascinated repulsion, staring with wide eyes. Only the Inspector and his men held their ground, smiling grim smiles of professional disillusionment. They had heard all this many times before.

"Perhaps you should not have taken Georges Martel so far into your confidence," said the Inspector maliciously, dropping the gun gently into his pocket.

"That frontier rat, has he been blackening me? You know what he is, he will lie to get himself out of trouble, you know better than to believe anything he has told you. He has plenty to cover up, you know only a very little about Georges Martel. But I can tell you—I know how many people he sold to us that last winter and spring! If he can grow talkative, so can I!"

The Inspector said: "Get on your feet! You are making a little journey with us."

The right hand which looked so incomplete now without its gun moved imploringly towards Marianne. "Can't you understand? It wasn't only the new life I had to fight for, it was you! Marianne, we have been good friends! You should have let me talk to you, there was no need for all this! You should have given me a chance to explain to you! I loved you! Haven't I lived quietly and decently all these years, does that count for nothing? It was you who drove me back. Marianne, for pity's sake—!"

With the smallest most fastidious of gestures she drew back the hem of her skirt from his touch. She was otherwise quite still, her face a mask of silent and controlled disgust.

The Inspector said: "Bring him away! All the wine will be turning sour!"

When the door had closed finally upon him, but not before, she began to shudder uncontrollably. Jonathan put his arms round her, and held her gently, and she relaxed with a great sigh and laid her cheek upon his willing shoulder. And after a moment, forgetting that they were not alone, he bent his head and kissed her. But it did not matter; Hilary's cure was complete, she had neither eyes nor ears for anyone but Jean-Marie.

They had caught, when the door was opened, the full brazen ebullience of the band, and the boy had already turned, with the singleness which was so essentially a part of him, and which she was so well equipped to understand, from what was over to what was only beginning. "Look, it is early yet, and the dance will go on all night. What do you say if we go home, so that I can change my clothes, and then we shall have dinner here in the restaurant, and then we shall dance. Who has better reason than we?"

Her eyes had begun to gleam, and her tiredness was gone, but she made a faint protest. "But you should rest—your arm!"

"I do not dance on my hands," said Jean-Marie witheringly. "At least, not until after the third bottle. Come, we shall go quickly to the Ruelle des Limaçons, so that I can make my dress proper, and afterwards at dinner I will buy you a whole bottle of Traminer, so you can see how potent is the inside of the bottle, as well as the outside."

He took her by the hand, and towed her to the door, and she went with him like a child in a dream, forgetting her discarded English clothes, forgetting, in the abundance of Jean-Marie's life, how near death had been to them, forgetting Jonathan.

Marianne said in a low voice: "You see, do you not, why I ran away? I must telephone to my parents—they will have to break this news to the old man. And he will feel defiled, as I did, to think he had allied his life voluntarily to such a creature."

"But you delivered yourself and, I think, the old man, too. And Alsace."

"And all this," she said, her voice relaxing into tired wonder, "in one day! I feel as if I had known you and relied on you for a lifetime. This was to have been an important day for me, a turning point in my life—I was to become engaged to be married!"

He glanced at his wrist-watch over her quiet head, which fitted so snugly into his shoulder. It was a little after ten o'clock. He stooped, his lips to her ear, to whisper: "If you feel like carrying out the programme, Marianne, there's still time." But after all he did not say it; she was tired, and hungry, and trembling still in reaction, and since he had no longer any intention of leaving Colmar the following day, or indeed for many days to come, there was no hurry. He had to get to know her family, behave with becoming orthodoxy, overcome the slight handicap of being merely the young man who had given her a lift into Colmar. He had no doubts of being able to manage it all, if she helped him, and he was pretty sure she would. At any rate, when, finding her cheek so near, he stooped his lips to it instead of whispering in her ear, she raised her face suddenly and received the kiss warmly and willingly upon her mouth.

AT THE HOUSE OF THE GENTLE WIND

Geoffrey Danesbury was a young archaeologist. He got his first sight of Aurae Phiala from the highest point of the raised causeway which marched Roman fashion, dead straight, across the fields from the bus-stop on the main road. He stood upon the rim of a great saucer of fields, threaded bewilderingly by the intricate coils of the river, which lay at its summer level, four feet beneath its Devon-red banks.

Midway between his vantage-point and the languid curves of the river, the ground-pattern of something like a small village lay outspread in neat turf and low, broken stone walls; and this was all that was to be seen of the Roman city of Aurae Phiala, the Bowl of the Gentle Wind. Beside it stood one unobtrusive modern house in a garden populous with trees, and a fistful of cottages and outbuildings.

At just this time of year, thought Geoffrey, surveying the goal of his pilgrimage, the tribesmen must have crossed the river from Wales and sacked the town. The legions were already gone, Silcaster retained only a decrepit remnant, Rome itself was beginning to totter. What was there to prevent the raiders from plundering this soft luxury city isolated in the fields? Only the shadow of the camp at Silcaster had ever kept it inviolate.

And he had been right about it, he told himself with approval as he followed the track down the gentle slope. It was no wayside station on the road to anywhere, but a summer resort for the wealthy families of officers and officials bored with garrison life. And there must be more of it than had ever come to light yet, in spite of old Winterton's excavations last year.

Probably the old idiot had only found a fraction of what was here to find. Geoffrey was young enough to consider it natural that the old should also be a little idiotic at times.

A white gate admitted him to the enclosed area of Aurae Phiala, two acres of a green and sunlit desolation mapped with red gravel paths and spaces of tessellated pavement preserved within fragments of walls. He turned his face towards the copse in which the curator's house lay and, passing by the long, shallow depression in which the broken bases of pillars stood like burned-down candles, entered the walled garden.

The house was pleasant, its white walls greenly shadowed by trees, a space of grass before its front windows. Its name was neatly printed in white letters on black: Aurae Domus—The House of the Gentle Wind. The name suited it, thought Geoffrey, not only because of its obvious association with the Roman city, but because it somehow epitomized the silence and seclusion of this lonely house.

Geoffrey approached the door and rang the bell, feeling in his pocket for the letters which were to introduce him to Austin Close.

A disinterested maid opened the door to him, and received his name and his letters with equal indifference. He was left to kick his heels for five minutes in a cool grey and blue room.

He heard a quick, light step descending the stairs, and Austin Close came into the room, the opened letters in his hand. He was of Winterton's generation, certainly, Geoffrey thought dubiously; fifty-five if he was a day. But he had a handsome vigour about him. He was not above medium height, but looked taller because he was built with such delicate attention to proportion. His hair was thick, close and crisply grey, but only a few grey hairs sprinkled the black of his trim moustache. In the lined and thoughtful face the eyes were large, brilliant and serious, and weighed up Geoffrey's youth as accurately as Geoffrey could possibly have assessed their owner's age. Austin Close smiled warmly. "My dear fellow, it's nice to find someone taking an interest in us. We're out of the world here. Come into my study upstairs."

He swept his visitor up the staircase and into a brown and cluttered room, pleasantly smelling of tobacco.

"Smoke? You're at Bamford with Lewis-Jones, I see! No one of his calibre's been round here for years. I'm glad to hear of him again. I only wish we had more to offer you. What is it exactly you're planning, Danesbury? You're covering the whole chain of border cities, I understand—it's a lot of ground!"

Geoffrey became eloquent on the subject of his projected book on the Roman civilization in the Welsh marcher country. Close listened thoughtfully, but finally shook his head ruefully.

"My dear boy, I'm sorry to dash your hopes, but we've been wrung dry already. Everything we have to show is already documented. I'm not surprised you didn't encounter Winterton's book, he's by no means a major name—but sound, in his dull way. He spent six weeks here last August and September, taking up pretty well the whole site, and he came to the conclusion—we've all been forced to it—that there's no hope of making any new finds here of any significance."

"But I don't agree, sir. I've read Winterton's book. It's been puzzling me ever since I got hold of a set of air survey photographs that were made over here about two years ago. I took it for granted they were the reason Winterton came here on last year's dig."

He took fire at the very thought of them, and hauled out his wallet to spread his copies over the littered table. "You see the terracing so plainly from the air. Look at the levels! I still can't reconcile Winterton's statements with these pictures— and, personally, I prefer the evidence of the pictures. That's why I want to open some of the ground myself, with your permission, sir.

"I know it's too late to do anything big this year. I only want to survey the ground and see if it bears me out, in preparation for a proper dig next year."

Close was smiling. "I tell you what, we might go down and discuss it over some tea."

It was going smoothly, after all. Geoffrey followed him blithely down to the grey and blue room, warmed now with the full touch of the sun.

At a low table near the window a girl was rearranging teacups. Her hair, catching the sunlight, gleamed smoothly blue-black. Her intent profile was delicate and pale, and when she heard them enter she raised startled eyes of so profound a purple, fringed with thick lashes of so sooty a black, that Geoffrey found himself frankly staring.

He thought in astonishment: Who'd have expected him to have a dazzling daughter like that? And how in the world does he keep her in a backwater like this, with her amazing looks?

He heard Close saying pleasantly, "Celia, my dear, do you think we could find another cup for Professor Danesbury? He has designs on our antiquities, but we'll be magnanimous and give him tea." The smiling eyes, shrewdly observant, rested upon his slightly flushed face. The clear deep voice said deliberately, "Danesbury, this is my wife!"

As they drank tea, Close said, "Well, if you insist on wasting your time and labour, there's nothing I can do to prevent you. You already have *carte blanche* from Lord Silcaster. My concurrence is only a matter of form."

"Not to me, sir!" This sounded so insincere that Geoffrey felt ashamed of it. Perhaps it was knowing that the wild violet eyes of Celia Close were resting upon him with such intent and silent consideration that had upset his balance.

"Not to me, sir!" Geoffrey repeated firmly. "I'm absolutely relying on having your advice and help."

He stole a glance at the girl. She had not spoken more than three or four times. Her voice was low-pitched, and very soft and clear. "I'm afraid this must be a little boring for you, Mrs. Close," he said apologetically. He offered his cigarette case. "You smoke?"

"I do, but I won't now, thank you!" She was wildly shy and drew back from him instinctively. "But do light your own, please—I like it!" He had only to move a hand towards her, and those amazing eyes flared wide, warning him off; and yet she smiled, too, with quick pleasure. It was like being in a room with a beautiful half-tamed cat that enjoys being near humans, but won't be touched.

Close accepted a cigarette, and groped for his lighter. "You'll want to start work at once, of course. By the way, where are you putting up?"

"I've taken a room at the Black Bull," said Geoffrey.

"That's what I thought! It's quite impracticable, of course. You'll lose half your time running backwards and forwards. Move in here with us, my dear fellow, for as long as you like."

"That's uncommonly kind of you, sir! It would certainly help me—"

He broke off there, in astonishment and dismay. He had caught the warning gestures of the girl too late. She had stepped to the desk to fetch an ashtray, and now, turning with it in her hand, the light of the sun bright on her face, she was shaking her head fiercely at the visitor.

Confounded, he felt the colour rise in his cheeks. She did not want him there; he had done the wrong thing, and for the life of him could think of no possible way to undo it. She had abandoned her desperate signals with a sigh, and was leaning over her husband's shoulder to place the ashtray on the table between them.

"Then that's settled! Bring your luggage over before dinner, and we'll have everything ready for you. Yes, you'll join us for dinner, of course!"

It was far too late to reverse the arrangements, now, but he made an attempt. "I don't want to upset the household, sir. I'm making enough trouble for you as it is."

Close rode over his diffident excuses with confidence. "Nonsense, of course you'll stay with us. You won't be any trouble. Besides, it does Celia good to see a visitor occasionally. It's a dull life for her here at times." He looked up with a smile at his wife. "Persuade him, Celia!" She looked into Geoffrey's eyes with a perfectly blank face, and said compliantly, "You won't be the least trouble, Professor Danesbury. We shall be very happy to have you." Her beautiful expressive voice was as cold and flat as stone.

It was with distinct reluctance that he approached The House of the Gentle Wind for the second time that day, in the bright hush of the evening, his suitcase in his hand. If he could have slid out of the whole enterprise he would have done it. True, it should have been pure pleasure to meet Celia Close again, and so it would have been if he could have faced her without blushing; but after what had happened he foresaw nothing but embarrassment.

Yet, when he drew near to the high garden wall, and looked down into the hollow to see the grey-blue of her skirts spread over one of the broken forum pillars like a great periwinkle flower, his dominant feeling was, after all, one of pleasure.

He halted on the path above her and set down his suitcase: and she, who had clearly been waiting for him, rose and looked up into his face with such an urgent and serious invitation that he jumped down to her side in haste, as though she had called to him.

They began to speak in the same instant. "Mrs. Close, I do want—"

"Professor Danesbury, I should like to apologize."

"Oh, *no!*" he protested. "You have nothing to apologize for. It's I who was too stupid to realize. Please don't worry, I'll take the first opportunity of disappearing."

It was warm in the hollow, and the turf about the broken columns smelled of wild thyme and sunlight. His covert and fleeting glances at her over the tea-table had all floundered in the huge purple eyes, but at this range he could hardly fail to observe the soft, suave lines of the oval face, the plaintive, but richly-shaped mouth, the broad ivory forehead, the nobly impetuous chin.

She did not look at all a timid woman; and yet the eyes still fended him off, even as she drew her black brows together in vexation at having to explain herself in so difficult a situation.

"But I'm so ashamed of having to make such signals to you! And it wasn't that I didn't want you. You don't understand!"

He said gently, "There's no reason why I should. I know that you must have had good reasons, and I don't need to know anything more."

"You're very kind, but I *want* to explain myself. It's necessary. It doesn't seem to you," she said, with a gesture of her hand about the place in which they stood, "rather odd that I should lie in wait for you out here, instead of talking to you at the house, if I had anything to say?"

He looked at her doubtfully, trying to reconcile the composure of her face with the desperation of her eyes, but every moment she became more complex and more mysterious.

"It's very simple," she said bitterly. "My husband is insanely jealous of any man who comes near me. It's something to do with our ages, and he can't help it. I'd like to be glad when someone comes to stay here—I could be very glad, if everything was normal—but as it is I can't do anything except keep away from all men, and keep all men away from me.

"I'm sorry to embarrass you like this," she said, in the same desperately calm tone, "but it's best that you should know the hazards."

"But—" He was confounded, yet he could not let well alone. "But why, then, should he himself ask me to stay here? It wasn't necessary. Why did he do it?"

"I don't know! I think it's a kind of masochism. And he's an archaeologist, too. I daresay he really does want to help you, in his way. But that won't stop him suspecting us of heaven knows what if he ever leaves us alone together. That's why I had to warn you."

She fixed her eyes unwaveringly upon his. "I realize how unlikely all this sounds," she said, her lips curling. "You're not compelled to believe me. I'm merely asking you to realize my position as it seems to me, and to understand if I take care to keep as far away from you as possible."

She was an extraordinary creature. How could he so lightly believe Close to be a man obsessed by jealousy, when he had the scene at tea so clearly in his memory? Close had invited him there, brushed aside his protests, appealed to his wife to second his invitation. All along it was she who had recoiled from him, she who had watched him silently from under her long lashes, at once aloof and curious.

He said uncomfortably, "You must realize that I had no intention of precipitating a situation like this. Please believe that I'll do anything I can to put things right again."

She was not far from tears of frustration and shame; she lowered her eyes to hide them, and turned her head away.

"I'm sorry to be so difficult. Please don't think of leaving, now that you've accepted. It would only make Austin more suspicious. I only wanted to explain to you why I shall have to stay as far away from you as possible."

Geoffrey had taken an instinctive step towards her, but dared not touch her. He asked distractedly, "You want me to stay? Is that really the best thing I can do for you now?"

"Yes, please do stay and do the job you came for. And now, would you mind very much waiting here about ten minutes before you come up to the house? That will give me time to go round the other way, through the orchard, and be in before you ring the bell."

He watched her until she rounded the corner of the garden wall. Then he sat down upon the broken column and lit a cigarette to while away the ten minutes.

He wondered why his heart seemed to have accentuated its beat, and why the fingers that struck the match were not quite steady.

The weather held, and Geoffrey's compact with Celia Close held with it. And if, by the end of the first week, Geoffrey had contracted certain suspicions of Austin Close, they had nothing to do with his attitude to his wife. No, what he shrewdly suspected was that Close was keeping very quiet about the most promising sites in the city, and trying to deflect him into the less interesting places, in order to reserve the best of the dig.

Some day, when he could get the necessary money and labour out of an indifferent patron, no doubt he meant to try for the kudos himself.

It was on the tenth day of his stay that Geoffrey came in late and grimy in the evening, washed hurriedly, and came down to dinner looking tired but elated. He said nothing to disturb the peace until dinner was over.

Celia had withdrawn, as she always did, into the depths of her chair and was languidly reading, her cheek in her hand. When she sat like this, present yet absent, Geoffrey wondered if Close felt, as he did, how intently she still listened, and how acutely sensitive she was to every shade of meaning in the long professional conversations between them.

"With your permission," said Geoffrey, suddenly throwing down his mild challenge, "I'm going to take up part of the baths site."

Close looked up quickly, with a flash of his shrewd eyes, half amused, half wary. "But it's been up, only last year. Why on earth do you want to go over the old ground again?"

"I don't. I want to have up about fifty yards of the terrace that carries on from the fence there, outside the enclosure. I'm convinced that the baths were about three times as big as the part you've documented and enclosed, and I want to have a look for myself."

"But man, that's a tremendous job. Not that I agree with you about the place, of course." Close added vigorously. "You're drawing quite unwarrantable conclusions from a few vague shadows on a photograph. And on the ground there's nothing to justify you."

"I think there is. I know you don't attach the same importance to that photograph as I do, but for me it's conclusive. I want to open the ground in just one or two small areas, jobs I can handle with a couple of men to help me, just to prove my point. The real job will have to wait, but next year we can have an army of students on the site."

"I'm afraid it's impossible," said Close briskly. "It means going outside the enclosure to work, and we've no authority to do that."

"I understand it's been done before, and the turf replaced afterwards. That's all I want to do."

"In any case, my authority to give you facilities can't extend outside our own ground."

"The farm is Lord Silcaster's property, too."

They were sitting forward in their chairs now, facing each other with kindling eyes.

"It is, but there's a new tenant arrived during the last few months. I don't think for a moment he'll give us permission to dig up his ground, even supposing we had authority to ask him, and we haven't."

"That's too bad," said Geoffrey, "because I had him up there with me all this afternoon, and he lent a hand with the digging himself. What's more, we didn't come away empty-handed."

He rose quickly from his chair then and went out, to return in a few minutes with three large shards of pottery in his hands. They had been carefully cleaned of earth, but not washed. They showed the full round curves of large jars, and they were all of different glazes, and highly finished. Geoffrey laid them upon the table. He was aware that Celia was watching from behind her book, her eyes wide and dark with excitement.

"Do you know what those are? They still smell of good border soil, but can you detect anything else? I make it verbena in the only one I can really pretend to identify. There's a whole layer of broken pottery there. I say that what you have within the enclosure is only *part* of the baths."

Close was on his feet, facing him with suffused eyes.

"You began this work without consulting me? You had no right! I shall get in touch with Lord Silcaster at once! I'll see Tilleston, too—he shouldn't have let you break the turf without asking us about it first. Winterton worked on that site last year, the ground is covered, and the few accidental finds you may make there don't alter the facts of his survey. You may know your subject, Danesbury, but Winterton had ten times your experience, and he was satisfied to record facts. Facts, not romances! You'll oblige me by letting the work of older and abler men than yourself alone."

"I can't, sir! I'm sorry! The thing's there to be seen, if only you'll come and look at the place tomorrow, you'll agree. . . ."

"Damn your impudence!" cried Close, trembling with anger. "You will not continue with this work, I assure you—I'll settle that with Lord Silcaster, at once!"

He turned with the compact and splendid movements of controlled rage, and strode out of the room, and the door slammed behind him. They heard him mounting the stairs, and suddenly they looked helplessly at each other.

"It isn't the credit he wants," said Celia agitatedly, clasping her hands about the fragments of pottery with a nervous pressure. "You're quite wrong, I'm sure you are, if you think that. I don't know what it is, but it isn't that. If he'd wanted to open the site himself, he could have got the money out of Lord Silcaster long ago. No, he wants it to stay closed."

She had forgotten her fears of being left alone with him, or else at this moment she was even more afraid of leaving him, and being entirely alone.

"What *did* happen when Winterton was here?" Geoffrey asked quietly.

"They were supposed to be friends—neither of them prominent names, but able men in their own line. They were even going out to a site in Syria together last year, only it fell through. Their air passages were booked as far as Paris, even—they were stopping to consult some library there before they went on.

"Winterton closed up his town flat when he came down here, five weeks or so before they were due to leave, and they were working on the baths site together. But even that old man, obscure and grey and ordinary—not really as impressive as Austin himself—oh, it doesn't matter how old they are, if they're too civil to me!

"It wasn't the first time it's happened, you know," she said defensively, looking up over her tightly clasped hands. "I'm not imagining things. The professor was too gallant—there was a terrible scene, in the evening, just three days before they were due to leave. Austin ordered him out of the house, and rang up the airline, on the spot, and cancelled his own booking to Paris.

"When I got up next morning, the professor had already packed and left by the early train. He's still somewhere in Syria, I suppose—anyhow, he posted his manuscript to the publishers from Egypt, on his way out, about a month after he left here. But you see, even an old man can't come near me without something like that happening. And you're not old—or ugly, either. . . ."

He looked diffidently at Celia, and blurted out the one question he had meant never to ask her.

"Why did you marry him?"

She flashed upward one wild, startled glance, and then the black and glossy lashes came down upon her cheeks.

"On the rebound from someone else. I was eighteen, and the someone else was everything that was wonderful and irreplaceable. And when he was no longer amused, he dropped me! Austin was a friend of my family, and he'd always been very kind to me, and while I was having a breakdown they began to think I should never get over, he—went on being kind.

"When he asked me to marry him it was like being able to go into a closed room, and turn the key, and be safe. I suppose I married him for security, for companionship, for a home that wouldn't be kicked over as soon as the other partner got tired of it—because that was all I expected of young men then. It wasn't as dishonest as it sounds, because he knew the whole story. I married him for safety and peace of mind—and I've never enjoyed either since."

She was turning the shards of pottery in her hands, her eyes fixed on them gravely. She raised them to her face, and sniffed delicately. "Is it really verbena? It's certainly something lemony and sweet. You think this scent has been lying in the ground in its broken jar for about sixteen hundred years?"

He did not answer, because her voice had broken, and she was shedding heavy tears into the lap of her dress, her glossy black head drooping forward until the light laid a soft blue shadow on the tender nape of her neck. He dropped to his knees beside her chair, and gathered her into his arms. She was shaking violently, but he was aware only of the clumsiness of his own movements, and the thunderous beating of his heart as he held her.

"I never loved him," she whispered, "but he knew that. It didn't seem to matter then—I thought I was done with love. How was I to know …?"

She raised her face, stained by tears. He kissed her, and though she drew breath in astonishment at his touch, her lips responded suddenly, ardently, clinging with a desperate eagerness.

There had been no sound, nothing to startle her into turning her head, nothing to make him open his eyes from his crazy, impossible dream of loving and being loved by her. Yet he did open his eyes, suddenly but warily, conscious in his heart of danger and, staring sharply over her shoulder, beheld the door reclosing with infinite care upon the sombre face of Austin Close.

He said nothing to her of the interruption. It was between Close and himself if there was anything to be said. He only released her softly, and went and sat on the other side of the room from her. Neither of them spoke again until Close came in.

Geoffrey rose as the older man turned to shut the door behind him. Close was looking at him with a very slight, a very sad smile. Hadn't he seen the kiss, after all? But he had, he had been gazing full at them.

"I'm sorry, Danesbury!" said Austin Close quietly. "I'd no right whatever to try and scare you off the work you've been sent to do. I'm afraid I must ask you to make allowances now for a very undistinguished scholar's dream of making a noise in the world at last. The fact is, I've been waiting ten years for the chance of doing this job myself, and was too self-centred to call attention to the need and bring other men—better equipped than I—to take over the work.

"I'm glad, now that I've had time to think it over, that you've put it out of my power to go on being a dog-in-the-manger any longer. It's high time the job was done. Go ahead, and I'll lend you a hand with it!"

By the end of the tenth day they had uncovered arched courses of masonry, a first flue and part of a second, which was enough for their present purpose. They dug carefully down and reached the paved floor of the first flue, though the passage was silted up with earth, and some of the outer courses of the arch showed signs of crumbling. The air passage was more than two feet six high.

No one could have behaved better than Close had done. In an effort to repay the generosity which had been shown to him, Geoffrey had kept fiercely out of Celia's way.

But she came to call him in to lunch on this particular day and she was holding two letters for him in her hand.

"*He* suggested they might be important," she said. "I don't know why he should want me to come here to you, but it was his suggestion, so I didn't argue."

It was difficult being alone with her again, her eyes were at once so despairing and so expectant.

"What room was this, then?" she asked, looking out over the trodden earth and the carefully-placed tiles.

His eyes avoiding hers, he answered, "The hot room—dry heat. They sat here chatting until they broke into a sweat, and then they were scraped down by the attendants, and some of them went on to the hot water bath, as well. You saw those brick arches we've uncovered these last few days? Air chambers like those run under this whole floor in a grid."

"And what is that hole in the corner there?" It was a broken stone rim like the casing of a well.

"Did he never tell you all about this set-up? That's the laconicum. It would be built up into a stone pillar, about so high, when it was intact, and it simply gives into what they called the hypocaust underneath.

"They had a removable cover for it, so that if they should want to raise the temperature quickly they could just unseal the laconicum, and admit the hot air directly into the caldarium—even the flames, if they wanted to. But the cover doesn't seem to be here. We've found no trace yet."

She came a few steps nearer to him, her eyes lingering wonderingly upon his face. "Geoffrey ..." she said, with a faintly questioning intonation.

"It's the biggest thing of its kind I've seen," he said, out of his anguish. "Look at the area!"

"Geoffrey ...!"

"Oh, my God!" he said with a groan, turning away from her. "What can I say to you?"

She followed, taking him by the shoulders, forcing him to look at her. He put his arms round her with an enormous sigh of despair, and laid his cheek against hers; and beyond her, coming slowly along the line of the fence and up the meadow towards them, he saw her husband, walking with hands thoughtfully clasped behind him, and his eyes fixed upon the ground.

Geoffrey took his arms from her, and led the way back from the field.

In the decline of the afternoon, when they were sifting some of the moved earth for small fragments of tile, Close said suddenly but very gently, "Danesbury, I feel I must talk to you frankly about my wife. I don't think I shall surprise you very much, and I very much hope I'm not going to hurt you."

Geoffrey was silent.

"The truth is, my dear boy, Celia, though a charming and intelligent girl in every other way, is in one respect—well, not quite perfectly balanced. I'm quite sure she has told you her own story by now, so I'll spare you a repetition. That early shock in love damaged her permanently. She was very ill for some time, and on that one subject she will never again be entirely well.

"She cherishes an illusion, a very pathetic one, that I am pathologically jealous of every man who so much as comes near her, and she has a temperamental disposition to repeat her ruinous love affair with every unwary male who enters her life.

"I married her because I love her, and because I knew she needed someone like me, willing to spend all the years of his marriage protecting her from doing harm to herself and others."

As Geoffrey was still silent, he let fall the crumbled loam out of his hands, and looked across at him with a grave smile.

"I'm quite sure she's told you long ago that I'm a dangerous monomaniac on the subject of her relations with other men—hasn't she? Well, have I behaved like one? Do you really think I didn't see that kiss the other night?"

"I know you did," said Geoffrey in a low voice. "And this morning, too, you saw my arms round her. I've always known it. She said—you sent her here."

"I did not. She plays this pathetic game with herself, and with whatever partner she can find. That's why I have always to watch and guard her."

"I don't understand," said Geoffrey, moulding earth in his hands, "why you ever asked me to stay here in the first place, if you knew how it would be."

"The thing about knowing how it will be, my boy, is that one is given to the incurable hope that this time it will be different. You can surely understand that if only she could get over tormenting herself in this way, I'd fill the house with boys and girls of her own age."

Geoffrey looked up over his mudlark dabbling with a pale and rigid face. "After tomorrow you can put your mind at rest about me. I'll make some excuse tonight, and get out tomorrow by the first train."

Before dinner he packed. He went down with one of the letters Celia herself had brought to him open in his hand, and said across the table, as he sat down, "Mrs. Close, I'm afraid something has happened that makes it necessary for me to drop my work here. Professor Lewis-Jones wants me to take a group abroad for him, and I have to go and talk the job over with him at once. I shall have to leave here tomorrow, by the first train."

He thought with horror that he could hardly have been more brutal if he had spent the past hour selecting the means of hurting her, rather than trying to find ways of preserving her from suffering. She shrank as though the bald words had been missiles thrown in her face, and all the colour drained slowly from her cheeks. It was Close who broke into gentle, regretful, loyal exclamations, filling the terrible quietness with a soothing sound.

"Oh, no, must you run off so soon? Is it absolutely necessary? We shall miss you!"

Geoffrey said, his lips feeling stiff and cold, "I know I can safely leave everything here to you, that's the main thing."

Celia's quietness was frightening. She looked down into her plate, and the plaintive lines around her mouth trembled.

"It's a very sudden call on you—isn't it?" The low-pitched voice was only just audible. "I'm sorry!" And that was all.

She sat through dinner under their concerned eyes, playing distractedly with her food, eating nothing, her face expressionless.

When she had got up and given them their coffee, which she did like a well-made machine, she suddenly raised upon them both the full, fixed stare of her stricken eyes, and said clearly, "Will you excuse me if I leave you alone tonight? I feel rather tired, and I have a headache. I should like to go to bed early."

They rose as one man with a mutual murmur of concern.

"I hope you'll have a good journey. And a successful trip!"

"Thank you!" he muttered miserably.

She did not give him her hand. She went very quickly up the stairs away from him.

He wondered if Close knew just how serious it had become. The long glances, shrewdly compassionate, seemed to indicate that he did; and Geoffrey was confirmed in thinking so when the older man suggested gently, "I tell you what, it would be better for you if I walked up with you to the pub by the bus-stop tonight, and you stayed overnight there. Wouldn't you prefer it? I'm so afraid she'll be up and waiting for you in the morning. Much better for her, too, I think, to find you already gone."

"But will they have a bed for me, at such short notice?"

"I'll go and give them a ring now."

He came back in a few minutes with the reassurance. "They'll have a room for you. Finish your cigarette, and we'll go up by way of the dig, and take one more look at what remains to be done."

Geoffrey was almost glad to hoist his suitcase and walk out of that house, but he felt the click of the closing door as a wrench at the roots of his heart.

There was no moon, but the sky was so lofty and so clear as to shed a dark blue radiance of its own. He dared not look back at the house, to see if Celia's room was in darkness. Every step lightened by an infinitesimal shade the weight of his self-reproach. There was no cure for the ache, however.

"I should like to say, sir, that you've been uncommonly kind," he said, as they passed by the hollow of the forum. "It was my own fault. I suppose, apart from things one digs out of the ground, I'm a pretty inexperienced person. It doesn't matter, if you're sure—*she'll* be all right."

"She'll be all right. It's my job to ensure that."

They passed through the gate of the enclosure of Aurae Phiala, which shone ghostly in the glossy dark, the dull black well of the laconicum opening ominously in the pale stones. Large as a ball-room, the terrace of this one great room stretched away from this spot, twenty yards or more to the subtle dip in the ground and the excavated pit where the choked tunnels of the hypocaust burrowed into the earth.

"I seem to be leaving quite a job on your hands," said Geoffrey, looking miserably at the relics of his ambitions. "Next year, they'll send you the students, if you can use them, but I shan't come back."

"No—I think you're right." Close seemed to be smiling. "It's queer that I should inherit it in the end—after deferring to Winterton's greater experience last year."

Geoffrey put down his suitcase, and went close to the gaping hole of the laconicum, and dropped a small stone into the darkness, leaning over to catch the sound of its fall. "Not deep, of course, but enormous of its kind, all the same. You'll make headline professional news when you do open it up."

Close did not answer him. Dazed with staring into this circle of darkness, from which an earthy chill rose into his face, Geoffrey turned his head, languidly.

It was mere chance that he looked round when he did. Nothing had warned him, not the rustle of a quick step, not the disturbed air of a rapid and violent movement; there was nothing but some very subtle and indefinite shifting of the shadows and the deeper shadows.

The stone that should have struck him squarely, with the full swing of a long arm behind it, achieved only a glancing blow upon his temple.

The contours of earth and the complexities of starlight whirled and dissolved about him. An arm took him about the thighs, heaving him from the ground. He fell, cold, dank air rushing upward past his face for what seemed an infinite time, and dropped heavily upon some uneven and loosely shifting stuff that rolled, and bore him helplessly with it.

Something rebounded from the wall of the shaft above him, and scraped a corner of the opposite wall. The light, the only light, was the faint circle of sky now beginning to glow almost with the radiance of day by contrast with this incredible dead blackness. Then, in the panic of shock, he prised himself upward to run, and struck his head sickeningly against the arched ceiling of the flue. All over his body the delayed protests of other pains began, outraged and insistent. They helped him, too. They made him aware that he was alive.

The second object tipped down the shaft had simply been his suitcase, the only evidence left of him; his camera, with the undeveloped rolls of films which might have provided a clue to his whereabouts, his clothes, all lay underground here with him.

He put his head in his arms, and felt horribly sick. As he lay gathering his damaged faculties, the thump and reverberations of falling earth and stones began in the shaft and disturbed dust silted down over him acridly, choking him. He dragged himself forward to escape from it, holding by the rough bricks of the floor.

Then he knew that Austin Close was filling in the shaft. He heard the thudding of the great fallen stones from the column, hurled down to lodge awkwardly in the loose rubble and pile up until they began to climb the walls.

For a long time then there came a staccato rattle of brick and tile, and after that there was already so much matter between him and the outer air that the continuing softer fall of earth over all made only a slight, dulled sound, receding until he could hardly distinguish it.

The circle of starlight was quenched: nothing broke the solid perfection of the dark. He was buried in the old Roman hot-air chambers, some ten feet beneath the innocent green surface of the meadow, which in a few days would hardly even show a scar to mark the place where he lay.

He was mad, of course. Austin Close was mad. Everything Celia had said of him was true, only Celia hadn't known the half. All that plausible and kindly demeanour had been a calculated deception, as purposeful as it was expert. How could a man with so much hate in him contain and belie it so patiently? How could he watch his wife and another man kiss, and then go softly away to revise his plans for them to include the only penalty now appropriate—the death of the lover?

His head was clear now, though it ached horribly. He lay couched in his pillowing arms, thinking frenziedly back along the past days. Up to that moment, he was sure, Close had indeed intended merely to enlist the prejudices of his patron by some means, and kick out the intruder who wanted to steal his city. It was the kiss that had altered everything. After that, Close had wished his visitor to stay—to stay, in fact, permanently.

To ensure his staying, Close had pretended surrender, given him the baths as a lavish present, helped him to open the site and dig his own tomb. And when he was ready he had organized, with crazy delicacy, those confidences about Celia which caused Geoffrey to blush painfully now under his multiple mask of darkness and sweat and grime. He was a redoubtable organizer; he had ensured that Geoffrey should announce his own departure, that his total disappearance should be taken for granted even by Celia, that only one person in the world should know how short his final journey proved to be, and where it ended.

His hair rose at the thought, but he admitted it, and lay trying to digest it. Not a soul but Close knew where he was, no one could come to his rescue. His luggage had gone with him, his work was already handed over to Close, who would duly superintend the refilling of the site until another season. No, there was no chink there at all by which doubt could get in. By the time his people began to wonder about his nonappearance at the opening of term, the traces would be clean and cold.

So there was only one person whose exertions could get him out of his nightmare alive, and that was himself. He thought with despair: *But there's no way out!* and felt the sweat running down his grimy cheeks and trickling into his mouth. There was not the slightest possibility of his being able to dig his way vertically upwards through the settling mass of earth. And what other way out was there?

The full realization of his horrible situation fell on him at that moment with a shattering shock, obliterating the last traces of the comfortable haze of concussion. He was buried alive! He was going to die the most frightful of deaths, conscious for days of every facet of his own hunger and terror and loneliness before the air mercifully gave out on him, and stupefied his last agonies.

He felt his inside knot itself into a hard, hot tangle of fear, and for a moment he lost control of himself, clawing desperately backward at the shifting pile of rubble, burying his hand to the wrist, shouting wildly in the forlorn hope that his murderer would hear and relent.

But his own hoarse cries sounded grotesque and hollow to him, and the dust he dragged into his throat soon strangled every other utterance in a paroxysm of coughing and retching, doubling him up again until he was sobbing into his folded arms. He hadn't cried since he was a very small boy, but he was crying unashamedly now.

To die in the dark, in an elaborate brick coffin, cut off even from his own generation, covered in with the dark ages of British history! And, above all, to have to think of Celia in the hands of that madman—!

He sobbed angrily, shuddering at the slight trickling sounds of earth still settling behind him, shocking his own ears with an unnerved shriek when a sudden small thing scuttled by him in the blackness, trampling his sleeve. All the same, the rat was his salvation. It was alive, it breathed, it must have some means of going in and out.

His mind had began to work again. The field under which he was buried sloped downward to the river. And, in that slope, he himself had uncovered the masonry of one flue of the same hypocaust.

His heart clutched incredulously at the tenuous hope. That tunnel was stopped with earth, true, but the brickwork seemed to be sound, and surely the barrier of soil could not be very thick. There might be broken and blocked places on the way to it, but at least he could attempt the passage. If only he could get his bearings in this horrible darkness! He had not even the minute flame of his lighter to give him comfort; it had run dry early in the evening and he had meant to buy matches when he reached the inn. More than anything else, the darkness oppressed him.

Which way had he been facing? How had he fallen? He had no sensation of having turned, he had simply clawed his way forward when the suitcase clanged in the shaft. Therefore he must be facing up the slope of the field so now he must turn and move as far as possible to the right as he went forward.

But he could not turn; the flue fitted him too tightly here. And, even if he could, the passage behind him was blocked impassably. On the other hand, he must be near the limit of the floor, and the network of flues must link up along the wall. Go on to the end, turn left, proceed on that line until it, too, closed in a blank wall, then left again, and he would be on the right course. If the air held out! If the final barrier did not prove so thick that he would die miserably digging his way through it with his fingernails! If there was really access from flue to flue clean through the whole maze—.

He thought desperately: *I can't!* and all the closed centuries of this terrible place weighed down like lead upon his bruised body. Then he remembered Celia, and all the complexities of thought left him; he dragged himself to his hands and knees, and began to crawl forward, feeling his way through the crowding, palpable dark, inch by inch along the cold filth of the floor.

In only a few seconds his extended hand met with a solid facing wall, just as he had estimated. Groping right and left, he found the connecting flue open in both directions, and turned almost hopefully into the left-hand one.

But his senses were beginning to wilt in the earthy, smothering air; he lost the sensitivity of his fingers at moments, and the silted dust under him felt like marble, cold and smooth, and then like boulders, hurting his flesh as he crept forward. The worst thing of all was thrusting his way bodily through the clinging darkness, that hung on him stiflingly, and resisted him as fiercely as if there had been a malevolent will in it.

Once, before he reached the second turning, he met with a mound of intruding earth; the outer wall of the flue was caved inward, but there was space enough left to crawl through, with some difficulty. The tug of the soil and stones at his shoulders brought the sweat pouring down into his eyes again, but he shuffled on, found the corner, turned it. Now, if his mind had not failed him altogether, he was in the very passage which led to his pit in the meadow.

A few yards more, and he was brought up short by a block which could not be passed. He felt from floor to roof, and all was closed to him. There was nothing to be done but inch his way painfully backwards to the nearest connecting passage, turn into it, and by-pass the obstruction in the parallel flue. But this one, too, was blocked, and he had to repeat the diversion. He was growing a little confused with weariness and concussion, and kept reminding himself feverishly: *Don't forget to bear right again—two moves to the right!*

The air was giving out, or else it was he who was weakening. His head was swimming with the sickening, earthy smell. But there was the first turning to the right, and with luck he could return to his course. He felt round the corner cautiously, and it seemed open and almost clean.

As he was turning thankfully into it his left hand encountered something lying in the tunnel he was about to leave; something queer, not earth or stone or brickwork, but soft, yielding, dank. The odour of the vault had become the more terrible odour of actual physical death. A rag of fabric, lying in dirty folds along the floor, something long, rounded, swathed in cloth, something upright at the end of it, and hard, and of a shape his fingers recognized ... a leather sole—a foot!

He was too tired, and had gone too far towards desperation already, to be anything but calm. Antique tragedies marched through his mind. But the next moment his inquiring hand, unquenchably curious, had explored beyond, and found a hard, rectangular corner of a case, shod with metal, a long edge closed with metal, and furnished with a leather handle; then, separate, oval, a deep furrow still cleaving its damp and filthy crown, an unmistakably twentieth-century trilby hat. . . .

Celia slipped out of bed quietly at dawn, dressed, and went out softly, retreating with infinite care from the room where her husband lay sleeping. She crept to Geoffrey's room, opened the door cautiously, and looked in.

Through the uncurtained brightness of the room, she stared at the bed. It was smooth and untouched. She looked round wildly; the dressing-table was emptied of its brushes, there was no sign of his suitcase or coat. He was gone, without waiting to speak to her, without even a word of goodbye.

She could not believe it; she stood searching pathetically for some sign that he had not forgotten her. Perhaps he had got up already, packed, and made his own bed before going down. Knowing that she had only one daily maid, he had often done little things like that for himself.

It wouldn't occur to a man that, since he was to leave, his bed would promptly be stripped again. But he was not downstairs.

She ran down the drive, and through the spectral city of the Bowl of the Gentle Wind, but she could see no tall figure striding ahead of her up the striped green track through the meadow.

After a while she turned sadly, and walked down the meadow again, her feet dragging in the grass.

She paused above the crumbling archway of the exposed flue. As though some tremor of the earth troubled the stability of the whole field, little trickles of soil were starting down out of the choked mouth, and running downhill with a tiny sibilant sound. The disturbed dead were trying to get out! If they could remember what it was like to be alive, she thought, they would let well alone.

She went down into the pit, and looked at the rustling, restless puffs of dust that moved downward over the baked surface of soil. When the pool of Betheseda was troubled it did miracles. She badly needed a miracle, but doubted if this narrow well into the depths of history, for all its disquiet, could provide one. She closed her eyes and the first tears gathered slowly within her eyelids, burning bitterly.

"Are you looking for Danesbury?" asked the voice of her husband mockingly at her shoulder. "You won't find him, you know."

She sprang round upon him wildly. He had come up quietly and was standing only a yard from her, rooted in the scarred ground, his hands in his pockets, a soft smile upon his distinguished face. He was pleased with her tears, satisfied with her morning flight after an illusion. The whole bright aspect of the day pleased him.

"He left last night, my dear. He thought it better that he should. And he gave me his word," he said gently, the smile deepening, "that he wouldn't come back. I'm sure he'll prove a man of his word."

Something prophetic, a small flame of wondering and waiting, had already kindled in her mind, though she did not know why, even before she heard the stones begin to roll. They were only small stones, too little to change her world, but they ran, and rolled, and jumped, and the troubling of the well was every moment more urgent with the promise of a miracle.

With an effort she kept her eyes fixed upon her husband's face, and only out of the edges of vision did she see the sudden small, dark hole appear in the mask of earth, high up under the brick archway. It grew, this hole, its rim crumbled away steadily. She saw something pale that moved within, scraping at the soil. She saw a hand emerge, a dirty hand caked with grime, a real, human hand that felt through into the light with feeble exultation.

Then she heard her own voice asking, dryly and mechanically because of the necessity not to scream: "What did you tell him about me? What did you say, to make him leave me?"

"Does it matter now? He's gone. You won't see him again, he promised me that."

Soon, very soon now, her knees would collapse under her, and she would let herself fall into the kind, blind darkness. But not yet, not until she had avenged herself in one appalling moment for all the hell of her married life. She stepped a little aside, so that she could the more easily see beyond her husband's oblivious shoulder the act of resurrection. Her face was fixed in a slight and dreadful smile.

"I shouldn't be too sure," she said softly, "if I were you. If I call him, he'll come back."

Close threw back his head and laughed. "From where he is now? You'd have to call very loudly, my dear Celia! And you'd be a very long time in getting an answer!"

Just beyond the hollow of his cheek, vibrating with laughter, the earth delivered an arm, a shoulder, a head. Briefly, in the only glance she dared deflect towards him, she saw Geoffrey thrust at the thinning barrier of soil, and send its ruptured fringes scattering. In a moment the noise of slithering stones would reach her husband's ears even through his own delighted laughter, and make him turn his head.

She said, "There's nowhere you could send him, that I couldn't call him back."

"Call him, then! Try! Let me see you conjure him!"

Out of the opened cavern in the flue a second arm emerged, both hands pressed downward, hoisting his body forth.

She cried out, her face flashing into vengeful triumph: "Geoffrey! Geoffrey!" And then, stretching out her arm to point beyond him: "Look, Austin! Look behind you!"

He swung round, drawing in a sharp, derisive breath, just as the heaving body, with a strong lunge, erupted out of its grave, and with a staggering jerk stood erect.

Louder than her own exultant laughter, Celia heard her husband shriek. He put his hands up between himself and the lurching figure that confronted him, and made an ineffectual gesture of pushing the apparition away; and then, as if he had felt his hands pass through its impalpable substance, plucked them back with a moan and, turning blindly, ran at full speed down the slope of the meadow towards the bank of the river, leaping and stumbling as he went.

Celia's knees gave way under her; she sank forward. Geoffrey, who had taken one step after his enemy, heard the soft, sobbing gasp she gave and, abandoning all thought of pursuit, came blundering back and gathered her into his exhausted and grimy arms. She breathed shallowly and broke into a passion of silent weeping, until they were both stained and spotted with his filth and her tears.

He lifted her unsteadily, and carried her towards the house. Neither of them looked back to see the running figure, black and grotesque in the innocent morning, leaping along the river bank towards the rim of the copse.

She would not let him out of her sight now; she clung to his side as he telephoned and he kept one arm about her, as afraid to let go of her as she to take her eyes off him.

"Hallo, police? My name is Danesbury. I'm speaking from the Roman city at Aurae Phiala—from the curator's house. Could you send someone out here? We've got plenty of trouble for you. Murder and attempted murder!"

He remembered that one of these charges would come as shocking news to Celia, and he tightened his arm about her reassuringly. "Yes, there's the body of a man in one of the flues here— What? Oh, the heating chamber under the floor of the baths. I found him myself; there's no false alarm about it.

"No, he's not a left-over Roman skeleton, I can assure you. He has three large suitcases with him, and he wore a trilby hat. In fact, I can tell you now who he is. He's a certain Professor Winterton, who is supposed to be excavating somewhere in Syria at this moment. Only he isn't," said Geoffrey succinctly. "He's here, and he's very dead."

"Up to that point," said Geoffrey later, thinking back with a strained frown to the moment of discovery, "I thought I had the answer to everything in Close's plans for my disposal. But after I found the Professor I realized I'd never found a strong enough reason for his inviting me to stay with him in the first place. Everything else fitted in, but not that. Naturally he tried to frighten me off when I suggested taking up the baths site again. And with his sort of mind it was just as natural to decide to keep me here and kill me, after he'd seen me, after he believed he had evidence—"

"Yes, Professor Danesbury!" The Inspector made a soothing and helpful murmur. They were sitting facing him, side by side on the blue and grey settee, with their hands unobtrusively linked between the cushions, the young man red-eyed and battered, with scarred and swollen cheek and bandaged hands, the girl very pale, with the blank look of shock still in her eyes. "Yes, I quite understand."

"Well, there was still the puzzle of why he'd invited me to stay in the first place. There was no need for him to offer me hospitality. I could perfectly well have worked from the hotel. Celia suggested that it was a kind of masochism. But after I found that Winterton was down there with all his luggage, I realized that from the start I was a bigger threat to him than I'd thought.

"If I started to take up the baths, sooner or later I should find the body. But he couldn't simply refuse to let me dig, because Lord Silcaster had already given me his permission. So the best thing he could do was have me here under his eye day and night, where he could hope to persuade me away from the dangerous places and—deal with me if he couldn't."

He rubbed a sore palm wearily over his eyes. "Stop me if I'm talking too much. It's your pigeon now, thank God, not mine!"

"We're interested in everything you've thought about it, Professor. Just go on talking."

"Well, I had time to do a lot of thinking while I was scratching my way out of the flue. It seemed to me that when Close refused to go with Winterton to Syria, cancelling his air reservation to Paris on the spot, and ordering Winterton out of the house, he was setting the scene for Winterton's disappearance just as he did for mine.

"I thought then, it must have been Close who claimed that single reservation to Paris, since it was undoubtedly claimed, and certainly not by Winterton. You've seen the body—I was only in the dark with it, but I've asked Mrs. Close what Winterton was like, and it seems to me it could be done."

"He wasn't really like my husband," Celia said. "But he was about the same age and build, they both had moustaches, and both were about equally grey. It would be a slight gamble, but if he put on Winterton's glasses and a suit of Winterton's clothes, I doubt if the passport photograph would ever be questioned, unless it's a better photograph than most."

"And was your husband away from home on the date of this flight to Paris?" asked the Inspector.

"Yes, he was. He went north—that is, he *said* he was going north—two days after Professor Winterton left—after I *thought* he left—" She was exhausted, too. "I'm not being very lucid, excuse me! He said he was going to a conference in Edinburgh. I knew about the invitation; he'd expected to be out of England at the time, of course, but when the plans were changed it seemed natural he should attend, after all. I think he was away three or four days."

The Inspector said, "It's your theory, then, that he risked presenting himself as Winterton, and got away with it, to establish that Winterton had really left on this trip, so that no one would wonder about him for months, perhaps years. Then he came back from Paris, presumably on his own passport. It makes sense, all right."

"And then, you see," pointed out Geoffrey eagerly, "this would account for Winterton's very odd book about Aurae Phiala, which made out that there was really nothing here of any interest, nothing worth investigating any further. Of course it wasn't Winterton who wrote it; it was Close. The manuscript was posted from Egypt to the publishers, some time after he vanished from here. I bet Close was abroad some time last autumn or winter, if only for a few days again."

"Can you tell us anything about that, Mrs. Close?"

She frowned, thinking arduously.

"He did go to Malta, I think it was in late October. He was doing some work there on one of the palaeolithic temples. But I'm sure he never went to Egypt."

"I wouldn't be too sure, Mrs. Close. From Malta to Egypt isn't far. It wouldn't be at all difficult to pop across and post a parcel on a one-night stay. Well, you've given us enough angles to keep us busy. No doubt about the identity of the body, at any rate, seeing the amount of personal stuff we found down there with him." The Inspector rose, looking down at them with an almost paternal eye. "Try to get some rest. We haven't picked Close up yet, but you can be sure we shall before long."

It was in the declining light of the afternoon sun that the Inspector came back with the last news of Austin Close.

"He slipped through our fingers, after all. Two of my constables spotted him in the wood down there. He made a run for it, straight down to the river and, when they got him cornered on the spit of land by the island, he jumped in. He was swimming strongly, and he'd have got across and vanished into the trees on the other side with a fair start, but one of my fellows blew his whistle, and brought up the other lads who were combing the spinney on the far side, and they came down to cut him off.

"When he saw them waiting for him—well, he just stopped swimming, and deliberately let himself go down. You won't be troubled more than we can help about any of the formalities, Mrs. Close, though of course there'll have to be inquests on them both. We'll make things as easy as we can."

Geoffrey asked, from the couch where he had dozed uneasily all the afternoon, "If you should find any notes or papers about Aurae Phiala in Professor Winterton's things, when you go through them, would it be in order for me to have them? I could get in touch with his executors about them, as soon as we know who they are."

"We haven't examined his cases yet, but if there's anything of that nature I should think you could see it. We'll go into that."

When he had left them alone again in the quiet house, Geoffrey explained almost diffidently, "If Winterton was an honest man and a decent scholar, then the book he meant to write was a very different affair from the blanket book that appeared in his name. If any of his notes do survive, in his cases or here in the house, I shan't be writing my own book, after all—I shall be editing his. We can at least do justice to his memory, if we can't give him back his life."

"Then, after all," said Celia regretfully, "you won't be getting anything at all out of it."

They were sitting together in front of the fire, their hands peacefully linked on the arm of her chair, in a clasp which had not been broken all day for more than a few minutes at a time, so deeply did they need the reassurance of life and love, even now that the nightmare was over.

He knew very well what he was getting out of it, and it was much more than reputation; but he did not intend to speak of it too clearly yet, for marriage was a word with terrible connotations for her. So he only smiled, and said gently, "You think not? I'm going to do the job properly next year, have the whole place up, foot by foot, let the light right into it. After that I shall be able to forget the dark. And I'm going to make it my business to see that you forget it, too. Oh, yes," he said softly, remembering the brash young man who had come looking for honours to the Bowl of the Gentle Wind, only three weeks ago, "I shall be getting something out of it, all right More than I expected. More than I deserve!"

BREATHLESS BEAUTY

If it had happened on any other day of the week but Sunday, Randall Wilkes, who acted as police photographer when one was required locally at short notice, would have been in his studio, and the commission would never have found its way, by any obscure chance, into the hands of the junior partner in the firm of Wilkes & Grandison. But Miles Avery was new in his job as police superintendent, and a stranger to the rising little community of Whitcliff-on-Sea. A native would have known all the parties by name, and would never have made the mistake that Miles made.

It was about half-past ten when the small boy entered the park which, at that hour on a Sunday, was quite deserted. He was supposed to be at Sunday school, but instead he was on his way to the lake to try out the new boat he had smuggled out of the house under his coat. It was a morning of stormy autumnal sunshine, with thunder clouds piling up already in half of the too-blue sky, and squally drifts of leaves dancing uneasily about the gravel paths, to emphasize the fact that the summer season at Whitcliff had closed the previous evening. On the promenade the blue shutters were folded upon its little booths and coffee-stands and side-shows; the concert party had given its last gala show to a thinning audience; the eerie sea-noises of solitude invaded the pier on the echoes of the departed voices of children. And by the long, green, oily lake in the park, faintly quivering with the whip-lashes of wind before the storm, leaves rained down on gold hair and smoky dark-blue nylon, and settled in the delicately pleated folds of a bodice sprinkled with gilt stars.

The small boy stood and stared for several minutes, with wonder but without disquiet, and then, aware of the need to direct adult attention to this puzzling phenomenon, went off to find someone who might be able to relate sleeping princesses to normality. He happened to find Police Constable Barrett in Park Street, and approached him confidingly.

"Please, sir," he said, "there's a lady asleep on the grass in the park."

"Is there now, son?" said Police Constable Barrett, alert but unperturbed. "Well, maybe she stayed out a bit late to wind up the season and got locked out of her digs. Suppose we go and see if we can wake her up." But he didn't expect anything of much interest. "Some old Biddy on the gin, I suppose," he thought resignedly to himself as he made for the park gates with the boy trotting hard at his heels.

They rounded the shrubbery which screened the narrow end of the pool, and looked down into the green bowl of turf. The radiant creature was still there, a swirl of blue draperies, a sparkle of gilt embroidery between the folds of soft, dark fur, a cascade of yellow hair. The constable's mouth fell open in ludicrous astonishment.

The lady was indeed fast asleep. She was never going to wake up again, at least not in this world. In the smooth, pale temple, ivory under the shining hair, there was a very small dark hole, with a crusted rim.

The thunder clouds had covered more than half the sky and rumblings like distant gunfire were rolling round the landward horizon when Miles Avery answered the telephone and was informed that he had a murder case on his hands.

"West Park, sir, the end gate's quickest. Right by the boating lake. Shot through the head, small calibre, no mess at all. But no gun, of course. The bullet's lodged inside somewhere, though."

"I'll be there in ten minutes," said Miles, and cast a quick look out from the window at the thickening clouds. "We're going to have to rush it, or we'll have the whole scene drowned out on us. I'll call the photographer and have him drive out from his place at once and try to get a record. Sounds as if the layout may be important. Know her?"

"Never seen her before, as far as I remember—and believe me, you couldn't see her and forget it!" His voice was reverent and still faintly astonished. The last thing he had expected of a corpse was beauty.

"Right, we'll be over." Miles reached for the second telephone and called the home number of Randall Wilkes.

A woman's voice answered the telephone, a disillusioned and indifferent local voice which he rightly judged to belong to a maid or a housekeeper.

"Superintendent Avery here. Can I speak to Mr. Wilkes, please?"

"Sorry!" said the voice, without perceptible sorrow. "He's away for the week-end. Won't be back till late tonight."

"Confound it," said Miles. "What about his partner—what's the name, Grandison?"

"Oh, yes, I could take a message there, if you like—it's next door. Will that do?"

"Oh yes! That's fine. Tell him to come immediately, as fast as he can, to the West Park boating lake and bring his equipment. It's an official job, and it's urgent!"

"Okay!" she said, almost impressed, and slammed home the receiver without waiting to explain or argue the niceties of personal pronouns. And Miles lingered only to put through one more call to the police doctor before collecting Sergeant Rhodes and tumbling out to the waiting car.

The Sunday morning had grown leaden and ominous now under the pewter-coloured cloud-bank driving seaward, and the pealing of church bells for the eleven o'clock service echoed heavily through the charged air, like a tocsin. Miles watched the sky anxiously as the gates of the West Park came into sight beneath the quivering trees. He wondered if the photographer would be in time, or whether they would have to move the body and cover the site with tarpaulins against the inevitable rain, which could hardly be much longer delayed.

Barrett was standing guard over the body, and another young constable was parading the gravel path above the pool, to ward off the curious, although the impending storm had effectively done that for him. In the distance among the flower-beds a few church-goers hurried by the short-cut towards All Saints, and a few fathers wheeled prams desultorily on their Sunday tour of duty, but no one else had yet discovered the sleeping princess. Barrett looked from the sagging sky to his chief's purposeful approaching walk, and came up the slope of the grass to meet them.

"Hope I did right, sir—I sent the kid home, the one who found her. I've got his name and address, and we can lay a hand on him whenever you want him."

"He's much better out of this," agreed Miles, running down the decline to the place where the deep blue draperies were spilled in the grass. There she was, indeed, gracefully half-curled into the shallow green bowl of turf not a yard from the water, which just at this spot had no open beach, but a sharp bank of grass not quite two feet high. A willow trailed silvery, thinning leaves not far from her feet, arching one thick bough outward over the pool. Beyond, the long, dark mirror-surface of water coiled away into shores of greensward, and shrubbery, and trees.

The girl lay almost on her right side, but with her shoulders pressed back into the cradling shape of the turf. Her knees were bent, gracefully outlined under the soft folds of her long skirt, which covered her to the insteps, and spilled out on either side of her in a foam of deep blue. Her right arm was flung out from under her, the wide sleeve of her short fur coat fallen back into the curve of her elbow, her hand half-open in the grass. The left lay peacefully tumbled upon her body, as though she had turned over in her sleep. The coat had fallen open over her breast to show the pleated swathes of her tight bodice, cut low over milk-white flesh, and glistening with its gilt stars. Her head was turned so that the right cheek was pressed closely against its pillow of turf, and its features were as calm and severe as a classic face in marble, long russet lashes lying tranquilly upon spare cheekbones, bright gold hair outspread behind and above the shapely head. With her floating blue draperies and her floating yellow hair, and her wonderfully delicate and slender body, she looked like Ophelia.

Miles uttered an exclamation.

Barrett said: "When we do get a murder we certainly get a classy one. Almost looks as if the fellow who killed her didn't want to spoil the picture, doesn't it?"

The small, dark hole in the uplifted temple, with its black encrustation at the rim, was so unobtrusive that it was almost possible to believe she had chosen to wear a patch there to call attention to the brilliance of her eyes. Miles knelt in the grass beside her, and looked closely at the wound.

"One of those toy jobs," said Rhodes, at his shoulder. "Don't know that I ever saw one as small as that before."

"Effective enough at point-blank range, like this," said Miles. "I shall be surprised if we don't find powder-burns there."

"And you see what she's got in her hand?"

The long fingers of her right hand had relaxed, and lay half-curled over a battered rose-bud, the edges of its yellow petals dashed with red, its single leaf bruised and bent. Leaning down, Miles saw that the short stem peeled off in a long, tapering sliver of bark, and that the two thorns on it had pierced her palm, for it was marked with two infinitesimal flecks of blood. She held her souvenir lightly enough now, but for one moment at least she had closed her hand upon it in a grip of desperation, wounding both herself and the rose. An odd little rose to be running round the world alone, not sufficiently blown to be chosen as a buttonhole, too short in the stem to have come from a bouquet.

"Torn off from another stem," said an unexpected voice from the slope of grass just behind them. Footsteps made no sound at all in that end-of-summer lushness, and the remark fell so suddenly and so appositely into their silence that they both jumped, whirling round abruptly upon the inexplicable newcomer. How had a girl been allowed to get past the constable's watchful patrol? He could hardly have helped noticing her, for she was not the kind of girl you could miss.

"How on earth did you get here?" demanded Miles with irritation, jumping up to make himself as large as possible between the dead girl and the live one. His eyes took in with mingled consternation and pleasure her fresh, composed youth, the wide, direct, somewhat startled brown eyes, the resolute mouth. He also noticed and related, with a distinct shock, the large and businesslike camera she carried slung over one shoulder. "You mustn't stay here," he said firmly.

"But you sent for me," said the girl indignantly. "You *are* Superintendent Avery, I suppose? You wanted a photographer, didn't you?"

"But I didn't realize that—" He slid one furtive glance down at the delicate blue sandal protruding from beneath the frothing nylon so close to his feet. "This is not a job for you, and I can't let you—"

The girl interrupted him mildly. "It's too late now to do much about it, isn't it? I've seen her, and I'm still on my feet. And you'll forgive me for calling your attention to it, but if you really want photographs you haven't time to be squeamish. In about ten minutes it'll be pouring with rain. Hadn't you better let me get on with it? I assure you I shall be far too busy to faint." And she added rather belatedly, but with a propitiatory smile: "I'm Olivia Grandison. Mr. Wilkes is my uncle, you know. And I'm quite a good photographer; he wouldn't have me if I wasn't competent."

In the face of her admirable composure Miles was aware that his instinctive resistance to her entry into the case had already become somewhat presumptuous. In the face of the encroaching thunder and the first heavy, isolated drops of rain upon his sleeve it now became absurd.

"All right!" he said, stepping aside. "If that's how you feel about it, go ahead! Get some complete shots from every angle. Then I'll tell you what details I want."

And as she unslung the heavy camera and went to work, he paced out the bank of the pool slowly, studying the ground but it was virgin. The dry weather had hardened the soil beneath the turf. No gun, of course! They'd have to drag the lake, but she odds were that it had been carried away and jettisoned somewhere else.

The girl worked like a devoted fury, her intelligent young face sharpened into an intent mask of concentration. A few stray curls of brown hair showed beneath the brim of her little cloche rain-hat. Her hands were deft and thin, the nails unpainted.

"You'll want the wound in close-up—and that hand with the rosebud?"

The ambulance had drawn up inconspicuously in the alley of trees off the main road, and the doctor was coming striding over the grass from the gates, outstripping the stretcher-men. The girl cast calculating glances at the sky, and said, without again deflecting her attention from the work in hand: "We shall just about make it!" The rain was beginning to fall more heavily, great leaden drops spattering the surface of the pool.

"You know who she is, don't you?" she said, relaxing a little as she drew the waterproof cover over her camera, and felt down to the depths of an inside pocket to stow away a filter.

"No, not yet. Why, do you?"

"She's half of a dance act from the show that's just finished at the Winter Garden. Sylvie and Roberto, they call themselves. I saw the show once, but I didn't recognize her at first," she owned with a thoughtful frown. "Somehow I didn't remember her as being quite so lovely as this. But that's who she is, all right."

"Hold up that tarpaulin a moment," said the doctor, hunching his shoulders against the drops that fell singly, loudly, like blows. "Been dead some hours—I'd say offhand she was dead by midnight. Tell you better when I've got her indoors. Don't need me to tell you what killed her, do you? The bullet's there; you can have it and welcome in a couple of hours. All right, cover her up. As far as I'm concerned, we can move her."

When they lifted her, covered the stretcher and ran with her, the rain suddenly tore the sky apart in a sheer fall of water, slashing upward in fountains again from the lake's boiling surface.

"Run for the car!" Miles, shouting against the crashing thunder, folded an arm about Olivia and her camera to help her along. Rhodes had the rear door held wide open for them when they reached it, and they went to earth gasping in the back seat. Water poured and streamed down the windows, sealing them off from the outer world.

"My own car's only just round the corner in Parkway Drive," she said breathlessly. "I ought to go and start work on these at once."

"Wait a few minutes, until it eases up a little. You can't run about in this."

They sat looking at each other mutely, faintly awed by this monstrous demonstration of nature's contempt for them and their minute preoccupations. Olivia pulled off her hat, and shook out her short hair.

"You're an odd girl," he said. It was not at all what he had intended to say, but it was out before he could restrain himself.

"For not fainting, or screaming, or anything? I don't find that so odd," she said simply. "She looked beautiful, and beautifully composed, like a work of art. There was nothing there to shock anyone, or to haunt anyone, either—except, perhaps, someone who had been in love with her. Or someone who had killed her."

"You're certain of the identification?"

"Yes. She's Sylvie, all right—whoever Sylvie may be." She looked down at her hands with a puzzled frown. "You know, on the stage she was good-looking, of course, but not remarkable. When I came over that ridge and saw her just now, she took my breath away for a moment. And it does seem the wrong way round, doesn't it? Or maybe death sometimes does that for people—makes them memorable for ever to anyone who sees them. I shall know better," she said seriously, "when I've developed these plates. Sometimes I can see things with the camera that I shouldn't see with my own eyes."

"You might try seeing who killed her," suggested Miles, with a wry smile. "That's what I've got to find out."

Olivia said, with daunting gravity: "I'll try."

The Winter Garden Theatre had the closed, neglected, dilapidated, end-of-the-season look, its posters old and fading, its photographs in their glass cases faded. Yet the pictured Sylvie, with her public smile and her sequinned splendour, was clearly the same sleeping princess of the West Park, if in a distinctly cheapened version. The partner who swung her in the circle of a long arm was young, probably much younger than she, and very handsome in a facile way, tall and slim and athletic. His smile was less accomplished than hers, the uncertainty and sullenness showed through. But probably his particular public would find that attractive, too.

The rest of the *Footlight Follies* were there beside them in the frames; Miles matched them up critically with the list he had collected from the manager. That young man with the lopsided grin and the lugubrious eyes, wearing an Anthony Eden hat several sizes too small for him, must be Fred Brayne, the comedian. The small, dark, lean lady with the roguish expression, working hard at being young and energetic, looked like the soubrette, Loretta Selver, born plain Laura Sykes. And the disillusioned couple cheek-to-cheek in a romantic duet which exposed their tonsils, these could be none other than the singing duo, Dan and Daphne Florian, in private life Mr. and Mrs. Sidney Prout. Their various lodgings were scattered along the back streets of Whitcliff, and the remainder of his day would probably be spent in darting from one to another to check up on the entire company. But the first port of call was Sylvie Fryer's temporary home in Laud Street.

Mrs. Collinson was a thin, grey woman with narrow, suspicious features and quick, shrewd eyes. When she heard that her lodger was dead, she drew in her lips angrily, affronted that anyone should show such bad taste as to drag her house into a police case. When she realized that the death might prove to be murder, she sat down suddenly, and looked for one gratifying moment faintly disconcerted. She told what she knew about Sylvie readily, almost vindictively, but it did not amount to much.

"She came here with a young man, beginning of the season, her partner she *said* he was, but I had only the one room free, so he had to go elsewhere. To tell the truth, I wouldn't have cared to have them both on the premises in any case. This is a respectable house, and there was more between those two, if you ask me, than just a dance partnership. But I will say she's been a very quiet lodger while in my house. Temperamental sometimes, like all these theatricals, but kept herself to herself. It was their last performance of the season last night. She never told me if she had a new engagement to go to, but she did say she'd probably be leaving on Monday. All her things is upstairs, packed. No, I suppose she can't have come home last night, but she had a key and I go to bed early. You'll want to see her room, I suppose?"

"Was she wearing an evening dress when she left here?" asked Miles, as she led him resignedly up the stairs. He described, as he looked thoughtfully round the faded, anonymous room, the blue gown. Mrs. Collinson's brows went up into her hair.

"Oh, dear me, no, nothing like that. She left here in a sensible grey coat and skirt, a bit earlier than usual, just after tea. I never saw her in a frock like that."

The bed was neat and frigid under its pastel cover, the packed cases stood patiently by the wall. In the wardrobe hung a raincoat, a red duffle, a black woollen cap.

"No handbag," said Miles thoughtfully. There had been no handbag in the park, either. "Did she usually carry one?"

"Oh, yes, a big pigskin affair, crammed full of stuff."

"And she had it last night? When she left here?"

"Can't say I noticed particularly—but I think I'd have been sure to notice if she hadn't."

Miles thanked her, and went away to telephone Rhodes at the theatre. The grey coat and skirt, it seemed, were on a hanger in the little dressing-room she had shared with Loretta. The handbag was nowhere to be found.

Miles went next to Roberto's lodgings in Vine Street. There was this to be said for Sylvie and Roberto; they had stuck to their own names, apart from that Latin-American touch the boy had given to his stage version of plain Robert Gregg. He had been luckier in his landlady than his partner had, Miles thought, when Mrs. Soames opened the door to him. She was a pleasant, plump woman with mild eyes and a ready smile, and she welcomed him in with puzzled politeness.

"Why, yes, Mr. Gregg has been living here, but I'm afraid you've missed him. He left for London after the show last night. I've got his address there, though, if you want to reach him. Is it urgent? Miss Selver and Mr. Brayne are still here, if it's any use seeing them?"

For some reason which had more to do with instinct than with rational thought, he accepted this offer without telling her, as yet, anything more about the occasion of his visit. Miss Selver was busy packing, kneeling on the rug in her bedroom in the middle of the debris of her summer season, a cigarette dropping from her lip. She looked older than in the publicity photographs, and her eyes, relieved of the necessity for looking roguish, had a certain cynical liveliness which Miles found preferable. With indifferent readiness, she swept a pile of underclothes from a chair to allow him to sit down.

"Did you really say *Superintendent* Avery? What's happened? Somebody pinched Mrs. Soames's front gate this time?" She laughed at Miles's wary glance of enquiry. "The weight that closes it disappeared off the chain two days ago. I thought maybe the kids had come back for the gate. I can't think of any other likely crimes round here. What's wrong?"

"I'd like to know anything you can tell me about Sylvie Fryer, especially her movements last night," said Miles.

"Why?" The intent eyes became serious in a second. "What's happened to Sylvie?"

He told her. She took it with alert and intense calm, watching him narrowly at every word.

"Well, that's the last thing on earth I expected to happen to *her*! Last night she walks out of the theatre alive and blooming, and this morning— No, I don't get it! She— Listen, you ask the questions, it'll be quicker."

"What was her relationship with her partner? Her landlady scented an affair, but landladies can be wrong."

"Not wrong—just behind the times. Sylvie picked up Roberto somewhere in very small-time business, and brought him on with her this far—if you can see much advance in that! He's about five years younger than she is—was—and there was an affair, all right, only it had worn thin long before they joined this show. But she had him tight under her thumb. If the poor kid could have raised the pluck he'd have broken up the partnership long ago and got away. But—you know how it is! He was grateful, and he was fond of her, in an awful, tired sort of way, and he was short of a spine, anyhow—and every time he tried to break away there were terrible scenes, and he gave in. They've worn each other to shadows the last few weeks. And then Bob went and found somebody who put the backbone he'd needed into him, and this time he's gone!"

"Yes," said Miles, "I gather he's gone. When? He appeared as usual last night with her?"

"Sure he did! He left with her, too. She was lying in wait for him, in a brand-new dress, a beauty—aimed at him, of course. She looked good, too—she could when she made a special effort. That's the last I saw of either of them."

"What time did they leave the theatre?"

"Oh, say about half-past ten."

"Did he look as if he knew there was another scene brewing? Did he go with her willingly, or couldn't he get out of it?"

"Oddly enough," said Loretta, with her grudging smile, "that seemed to be one time he wasn't dodging. He looked as if he knew he was for it, and was ready to stand his ground at last. And he did, didn't he? He got away!"

"People get away by running rather than standing their ground, don't they? People like Roberto?"

"Ah, but you don't know our Peggy! She could put pluck into a half-dead rabbit. Maybe she even managed to put a grain or two into Bob."

"I gather," said Miles, "that Peggy is Roberto's newest girl-friend. A local girl?"

"Couldn't be more so. She's Mrs. Soames's daughter. And she's gone to London with him."

"Last night? Are you telling me they've run away together? Or was this all open and above-board?"

She gave him a long, level look, her eyes suddenly measuring him with new awareness of what might be involved in her answers. "If you mean, did Sylvie know, judging by the tension they were both generating last night, I'd say yes. Knew, and meant to prevent it if she could. If you mean, did Mrs. Soames know, why don't you ask her?"

"I will. Meantime I'd also like a word with Mr. Brayne."

"Fred's next door," said Miss Selver. "I heard him come in a few minutes ago." And she leaned over the bed and banged on the wall with goodwill.

"Fred, come in here! You don't know what you're missing. We've got detectives!"

The door opened upon the large, lightly moving form and merry-melancholy face of the light comedian, whose mobile eyebrows ascended into his hair at the sight of Miles sitting among the scattered intimacies of Miss Selver's packing. "No! She's pulling my leg! You don't look the part."

"I apologize for the inadequacy," said Miles gravely. "My name's Avery. I'm making enquiries in connection with the death of Sylvie Fryer. When did you last see her, Mr. Brayne?"

The comedian propped himself by one lean shoulder in the doorway, and smiled a calm, sad smile. "Last night after the show, probably about two minutes after she left Loretta, here. I'm sorry, but it's too late to try any shock tactics on me. The grapevine's got hold of the tale of the body in the park."

"Tell me more about this last glimpse of Sylvie. Was it at the theatre?"

"It was. I shared dressing-rooms with Bob, and he'd told me he was off to London last night. He told me, too, not to wait for him after the show as he'd promised to walk home this last time with Sylvie, seeing it really was going to be the last time. I could tell from the way he said it he knew as well as the rest of us did that *she* didn't intend it should be the last. But he was evidently braced up to stick it out, so I left him to it. And just as I was having a word with Jeff at the stage door, out they came together, he with a face like a new matador just going into the bullring, she hanging on his arm and gazing up into his eyes. Poor girl, she was so desperate to keep on the right side of him that she wouldn't even let him carry her handbag when he offered to take it from her—it was one of those outsize ones men are allowed to carry as a rule. They walked off down Dean Street, and that's the last I saw of either of them. Funny, isn't it," he said reflectively, "how love goes round in circles and never completes any of them. There's Dora Prout dotes on her husband, Sid prowls round after Sylvie in a thundercloud, Sylvie can't see any man on earth but Bob Gregg, and Bob's a bad case for little Peggy Soames. Only that circle does seem to stand a chance of closing, if all I hear is true."

"You didn't hear Roberto come in, when he came back from escorting Sylvie?"

"No," said Fred Brayne, and: "No!" said Loretta flatly in the same instant. He understood their unanimity. They might even be telling the truth. Yet it was a pity they should both disclaim all knowledge, for if by any chance they *were* lying it could mean only one thing—that Roberto had come back to the house to collect his luggage and his Peggy at an unreasonably late hour, late enough, perhaps, to have allowed him time to dispose of a great deal of dangerous and secret business.

However, he did not question their reticence, took his leave, and went down to talk to Mrs. Soames.

She countered questions about her lodger with a thoughtful and considered quietness which gave Miles enormous confidence in her truthfulness. Either she had implicit faith in the infallibility of the law, Miles thought, or in the innocence of Roberto.

"Yes," she said, "my daughter went with him. No, we didn't object, her father and me. Peggy's of age, and she's a good, responsible girl, who doesn't do things for flimsy reasons. They went in his little car, late last night. There was a chorus engagement he was hoping to get in a new show, and she was going to stay with my sister up in town, and try to get a job up there, so as to be with him. They'd told us all their plans. They're going to be married as soon as they're settled in steady jobs, and have got a bit saved up towards the home."

"Were you happy about that arrangement? Did you know," he asked gently, "that there had been much more than just a partnership between Sylvie Fryer and Gregg? Did your daughter know it?"

"Yes, she knew. He told her," said Mrs. Soames, looking him straight in the eye, "and she told me. I don't say it's what we'd have wished for her, or what she'd have wished for herself, come to that, but it's what had happened."

"Tell me, did your daughter know that Gregg intended to accept the risk of a showdown with Miss Fryer on the way home last night?"

"She didn't say anything to me about that, but I'm sure, if that was what he intended, it was not without Peggy's encouragement that he did it. It wasn't the sort of thing he'd have taken on by himself," said Mrs. Soames, quite simply. "And, of course, if they were going to start on a life together, it would have to be on an honest foundation."

He was ready to believe that to the daughter of this woman that really would be a necessity.

"Miss Soames must have been waiting for him to come in and collect her. At what time did he come home after the show?"

"He was a bit late, but it was only to be expected that he should be. It was just turned half-past eleven when he came in. I can't believe he— You didn't know him! The only thing I ever had against him was that he was too soft— He let people push him around too much. You couldn't imagine him hurting anyone."

Miles said very gently and slowly, watching the distressful tightening of her clasped hands: "Mrs. Soames, I want you to give me the address in London where your daughter can be found. There's nothing whatever against her, you know that, and about the boy you can be sure I have an open mind. But you must understand that it will be infinitely better for both of them if they come back here and tell us everything they know about this matter. Tell me where I can locate them, and you shall have your daughter with you by tonight."

She relaxed gratefully into the ease of her own helplessness, and told him what he wanted to know.

Olivia brought the blown-up photographs to Miles's office late that evening, insisting on bringing him the fruits of her labours with her own hands.

"I want to see what you think of them. They worry me. I thought we might get somewhere if we looked at them together."

In the event, however, it was Miles who had done the talking. There was something about this direct and capable girl that loosened his tongue in a manner which might have been alarming, if he had not been so enormously sure of her discretion. It was like talking to a fresh and unwearied adjunct of his own mind, so secret and serious was she.

"Everything points to the probability that he went into the park with her intending to have a final show-down, as peaceably as possible—that she overwhelmed him with reproaches and emotional blackmail, as apparently she's done a hundred times before, and in desperation he freed himself of her by the only way he could see. Loretta saw them leaving the theatre together, Brayne saw them walk away down Dean Street. We've found a courting couple who met them in the gateway of the park. The girl is prepared to swear to them both, the boy can't be absolutely sure of Roberto, but thinks it was. That was at about ten to eleven. And according to the doctor Sylvie died before midnight. Every circumstance points to Roberto.

"There are a few other strands. According to Brayne, this man Prout was mad about Sylvie and she couldn't be bothered with him. And his wife could have been jealous, only they give each other an alibi. They went back to their digs together, and went to bed, so they say!"

"I agree the whole thing points too obviously at Roberto," Olivia said, "but it's all circumstantial."

"You haven't yet heard all the circumstances," said Miles grimly. "Roberto came home in a state of nervous emotion just after half-past eleven, collected his luggage and Peggy, stowed them in his little car, and set out for London. That allows him adequate time to have shot Sylvie and rushed home afterwards. This afternoon we've dragged the lake. In the shallows round the side we fetched up her handbag. Everything in it was intact, purse, wallet, some letters, including some of Roberto's old love-letters, keys—and there was one item we hadn't bargained for."

He fished it out of a drawer of his desk and stood it on the blotter between them, an old-fashioned, bullet-shaped weight with a ring at the top, standing about six inches high. "You wouldn't recognize it, but Mrs. Soames did. It used to hang by a chain on her garden gate, to make it swing to if people left it open. It vanished from the chain two days ago—you remember? It was one of the accidentally pregnant things Loretta said. That's rather a gift of hers, saying more than she knows."

"But from a garden gate," objected Olivia, "anyone could take it."

"So they could—but none more easily than the young man who was practically a son of the house. Sylvie's handbag had to disappear so that it might look like an impersonal case of robbery. But it wasn't, of course, because nothing's been taken. Impersonal's the last thing this murder could be called."

"You're saying," said Olivia, frowning fiercely, "that he made certain preparations two days ago. That means the murder was premeditated. If you're right, he must have come ready primed with weight and gun."

"For use if the worst came to the worst, as a last desperate resort. He'd been through this business of trying to get loose from Sylvie so often, he knew how it might end. But I don't suppose he meant to kill her if he could get his freedom any other way."

"He wasn't very efficient in getting rid of the bag, was he? I'd have thought if he could take care to bring a weight, he could show enough forethought to sink it in deeper water. Why didn't he throw it in from where he was? It's the deepest part of the whole pool off that point."

"A man in a panic doesn't reason, he just throws the thing into whatever hiding-place comes handiest."

"But that's exactly what he didn't do. And what about the gun? You didn't find that?"

"No, we haven't found that. The doctor recovered the bullet for us, and I've got a preliminary report on it. It was fired from a .21 automatic pistol."

Olivia's brown eyes opened wide in a startled stare. "But that's only about four point something millimetres. They don't come so small."

"4.25 millimetres, actually, is about the smallest effective calibre in automatics. The only one I know of that size is the German-made Lilliput, and that's what this one was. Roberto and Sid Prout have both served in Germany. Prout was there during the last year of the war. Roberto was too young for that, but he served in the B.A.O.R. The Prouts swear they have not and never did have a gun of any kind, but both Brayne and Sid Prout are prepared to swear that Roberto had a very small gun among his baggage, and ammunition for it, too. So I simply can't afford to ignore the size of the case that's building up against that young man. I'm bringing them both back from London. Rhodes has gone to fetch them—they should be here almost any time now."

"Are you going to charge him?" asked Olivia.

"That will depend partly on the story he tells. A few more circumstances falling into place like that, and I should have no option. In our job the obvious is so often true."

"And what happens when the obvious comes into conflict with the obvious?" she asked thoughtfully. "Take these, for instance. The most obvious thing about them, the thing everybody noticed about Sylvie when she was dead, is her beauty— her quite unmistakable beauty. And yet it doesn't square with one single word that anyone can find to say about her while she was living. She was just good-looking—what was it Loretta said? 'She looked good—she could when she made a special effort.' Yes, I know she *was* making a special effort that night, but wouldn't you think it would end when she got a bullet through her head? There's something wrong about this whole affair. The camera knows it. I've been looking at these for hours now, and I *know* there's something wrong, something that doesn't square with the obvious picture of Roberto shooting his mistress to get rid of her. Only I can't see how to make sense of it."

She spread the pictures out upon the desk, and he came round and looked at them again, closely and uneasily, over her shoulder. Her restlessness did not seem to him merely "feminine intuition"—an unfair argument put forward for the rejection of the only reasonable view. It was rather the sensitivity of a craftsman to the unexpected response of his tools, and he had, somehow, developed so considerable a respect for her that it troubled him. He argued against it as one arguing with himself.

"Death, in itself, is not necessarily ugly. It's only the disorder, the indiscipline that offends. Death, when that has been arranged out of it, can be both beautiful and elegant—more so, sometimes, than life."

She had raised her head listening to him alertly, as though he had made an unexpected communication with some buried idea in her mind. But before she could answer, a knock came at the door, and Miles jerked upright.

"That must be Rhodes—they're here."

Olivia swept the photographs together into a pile upon his blotter, and turned them face-down as she rose quickly. "Shall I go? I wanted to ask you something— you've just given me an idea. But I'll ring you in the morning."

"No, stay—unless you'd really rather not? Today you're an official. Come in, Rhodes!"

The sergeant came in and closed the door quietly behind him.

"They're both here, sir. Found them both at her aunt's place—acting very normal, to all appearances, polite but mystified. I couldn't get either of them to say anything to give away that they knew Fryer was dead. When I did ask him about how he left her last night, still not letting on that we'd found her dead this morning, he made a statement saying he just walked most of the way to her lodgings with her, and said good-bye at the corner of the street. I admit the questions must have indicated that something sticky had happened to her—but still, it's interesting that he began to lie at that stage, isn't it?"

"Hm! Yes—still, anyone could go cagey after a hint like that. And when you told them what had really happened?"

"To all appearances they were both absolutely knocked over. If it was acting, it was good. And when I invited them to come back and give us all the help they could, they came without any fuss. But if ever I saw a frightened man, he's one. So stiff with fright he's clean overlooked one little thing I think you'll notice for yourself, sir, when he comes in. I don't suppose he'd had his coat on, of course, since they arrived at her aunt's house this morning—when I asked them to come back with me he just picked it up and dropped it in the back of the car. But it was chilly walking up from the garage, and he's slipped it on now. Shall I bring them both in together, or just him?"

"Both," said Miles, drawing up chairs towards the desk.

They came in hand in hand, the girl leading the way. She was of medium height, tall enough to look well beside his elegant length, and her face was oval and grave and touchingly young, with wide, scared, roused eyes, and points of hectic colour on her smooth brown cheekbones. She kept her hand hidden between their bodies as she came forward, but the rigidity of her slight shoulder and upper arm made perfectly plain the passionate, protective grip she had upon the young man's fingers. He, for his part, was somehow at once more ordinary and more pleasing than his publicity photographs had suggested. All the sullenness and dissatisfaction had been shocked clean out of the nicely chiselled face to make way for a far more urgent passion of pure fright. He contained it, but he was grey with the effort, his lips dry and pallid, his dark eyes enormous in their sunken settings. He wore a light grey coat loose about his shoulders. Miles inspected it in one swift glance.

There was no mistaking the little thing Rhodes had seen—a very little thing, but big enough to put a man behind bars for life. In the lapel of the grey coat was a withered yellow rose, flushed with red at the tips of the petals, and on the russet stem could be seen, even across the room, the long, pale scar where a younger bud had been torn away.

Olivia thought she had never watched anyone sit and suffer so acutely, so silently, as Peggy Soames suffered, as she sat and listened to Roberto lying his way from extremity to extremity among the pitfalls Miles Avery dug for him. But she held herself rigid and mute throughout his interrogation, only her eyes agonizing over him silently. A remarkable girl! She had chosen an ordinary mortal, but she had chosen him, and now she had to resist the temptation to try and change him. If there was any changing to be done, he must do it himself.

So she let him lie, as ninety-nine out of a hundred men would have lied in the circumstances, sitting in silence while he reiterated strenuously that he had had no special arrangement to walk home with Sylvie the previous night, that he had gone with her as far as the corner of the street, said a final good-bye, and left her there. He hadn't seen her again, and had had no idea that she was dead until the sergeant came and told them so. No, there had been no scene between them. They'd split up the partnership by mutual consent.

"I think I should tell you," said Miles, "that two young people who happened to be in West Park last night are prepared to identify you as the man they saw with Miss Fryer at about ten minutes to eleven. We also know that you did not reach your lodgings until just after half-past eleven. If I were you, I should reconsider that story of yours, and make it the truth this time. Believe me, it's the best thing you can do."

Roberto did not avert his eyes from his questioner when his lies collapsed about him; he was not ashamed. Desperation has its own dignity, and to put up a fight for life with whatever comes to hand, lawful or otherwise, may, in extremity, become a duty. But he did turn his head away from Peggy with a tired gasp that sounded like a sob, and then, with a better appreciation of the quality of her anguished stare, as abruptly turned it back again, and smiled at her. It was unexpected, and touching.

"I'm no good at this," he said, "I knew I wouldn't be."

It was an odd moment for him to achieve so decided a leap upward in Olivia's regard. She thought it was because he had really wanted rather to put his head in his hands and howl, or burst into unhelpful swearing, and instead had gone to the trouble to smile at his girl, and ease the fearful intensity of her anxiety for him. "I believe he'd die for her," thought Olivia, astonished and attracted, "just as much as she would for him."

"Do you own a pistol, Mr. Gregg?" asked Miles casually.

"No." He was getting better at it, that exchange of glances had revived him; he did not feel moved to embroider the flat, indifferent negative, but let it stand alone.

"Can you use one?"

"I have done, when I was in the Army."

"Did you ever happen to pick up a Lilliput, while you were in Germany?"

This time he did not answer at once. He sat thinking for a long moment, his lower lip caught between his teeth, sweat drying slowly on his forehead.

"Was that what she was killed with?"

"At a range of an inch or so," said Miles. "She'd hardly be likely to let a perfect stranger get as near to her as that, would she? But—forgive me, Miss Soames—you were a privileged person, Mr. Gregg, were you not?"

The sweat broke out again on Roberto's forehead and lip. He felt helplessly for a handkerchief, couldn't find one, and for a moment looked as though he were going to faint. Peggy leaned over and put a clean handkerchief from her handbag into his hand. Their fingers clung for an aching instant, and they were both eased. The boy wiped his face shakily, and looked at the lace-edged trifle in his fist with a sudden tremulous smile at its incongruity.

"I feel like hell, and I'm sure Peggy must, too. Couldn't she have some coffee, or something? You don't have to grill her; she hasn't done anything."

They were both given coffee and sandwiches, which Barrett conjured up from somewhere with admirable efficiency, considering the hour. They regained something of their normal colour, and though they did not exchange a word during this respite, their eyes communicated fluently. Olivia, acting on impulse, slid a hand forward and turned over the pile of photographs on the desk, so that, when he leaned forward to lay down his cup, Roberto found himself staring down at the delicately disposed body of Sylvie, curved gently within the swirl of her out-spread draperies. He froze into stillness, his hand hovering over the picture, his face motionless and wary.

"May I look at them?" He looked up at Miles across the desk, and his handsome, irresolute chin quivered for an instant.

"Do. They'll interest you."

He went through them slowly, his eyes dilated and blank with shock. "Poor Sylvie! I never meant her any harm, never consciously did her any." He said it only to himself, or perhaps to Peggy, too. He reached the close-up of the half-open right hand, cradling the rosebud. His body gave a convulsive jerk, his chin drove down into his shoulder, he stared with horror at his own faded buttonhole, the unmistakable parent of this fragmentary rose. Then, with fingers shaking uncontrollably, he fumbled the rose from its anchorage and laid it on the desk beside the photograph.

"So that's it! But I didn't! I never touched her! She asked me for it! 'Divide it with me,' she said—'the last thing to remember you by,' she said, 'when you've gone.' But how can I prove a thing like that? What am I to do?"

Peggy Soames got up and crossed to the table where the coffee-pot stood, and brought it over and refilled his empty cup. She laid her arm round his shoulders with a beautifully delicate calm, and set down the cup beside his hand, touching him remindingly with a fingertip only, as though he had been an absent-minded husband who must be prodded gently into finishing a meal before it got cold. He took up the cup docilely, accepting the role. The coffee quivered, and the cup chattered for an instant against his teeth, but he was calmed already with her touch and her nearness, and his hand was almost steady as he sat back wearily in his chair.

"I'll tell you the truth. I'll tell you everything just as it happened. I did have a gun, and it was a Lilliput. I've had the thing ever since I was in the Army. I hadn't thought about it for months; it lay around with some of my stuff at the theatre most of the time, but when I came to pack up two days ago, I couldn't find it, and don't know where it went to. If that's what killed her, somebody else was holding it at the time, not me.

"And as for Sylvie and me—"

He told them what they already knew, the story of that disintegrating partnership, of his last heroic resolve to set himself free to aspire to a new life with Peggy, and how he'd agreed to that last walk and talk, determined that it should indeed be the last, but leave no ill-feeling behind if he could help it. They'd gone into the park and down towards the lake at Sylvie's suggestion. At that hour they'd had the place to themselves. She had given him every kind of hell and he'd let her, because he felt that he owed her that. But at the end, when she'd seen that she couldn't turn him, she'd given in with unexpected grace, asked him to forgive her and remember her with kindness, and begged the bud from the rose he happened to be wearing in his coat. And then she'd said, "Go now, don't say any more, just kiss me and go," and he'd done it, only too thankful to have got out of it so lightly. He'd gone straight home to fetch Peggy, and they'd set out for London. And that was the last time he'd even given a thought to Sylvie until Sergeant Rhodes had come asking to see them.

"And her handbag—what did you do with her handbag?" asked Miles casually at the end of the recital.

"It was on her arm when I left her. She stayed there, not moving."

"And the weight from Mrs. Soames' garden gate—can you tell us anything about that?"

"I don't know what you're talking about. What's a weight got to do with it?"

Peggy said, with the ghost of a smile: "He never closes gates. Or doors, either."

Miles sat drumming his finger-tips softly on the desk, and thought what he was going to do with them. The girl could go home, of course. As for the boy, he must either charge him or let him go. The case against him was so strong that he took a decided risk by letting him out of his hands, even for one night. And yet he found himself curiously reluctant to take decisive action tonight. Roberto was too sick with exhaustion to do himself justice, and Miles was prepared to stake heavily that, if Peggy Soames stayed in Whitcliff, her lover would not attempt to get away. There was also the little matter of Olivia's disbelief. He knew of no reason why it should infect him with so much uneasiness, but he knew that it did.

"All right, Mr. Gregg!" he said, making up his mind. "I'm letting you go home with Miss Soames for tonight. I don't intend to take any formal statement from you until you've had a night's sleep. I'll expect you here, tomorrow morning at half-past ten, and if I were you I'd come prepared to make a full statement then. Believe me, the best thing you can do for yourself is to tell us the whole truth."

They couldn't believe it. They looked incredulously from him to each other, their eyes puzzled but hopeful, their hands groping out a little to meet between the chairs. "You mean you're not going to charge me?" asked Roberto faintly.

"You're free to go, but I ask you to stay in town until I give you permission to leave."

"I won't run," said Roberto in a voice of stunned relief. "I'll be here tomorrow."

"Good! See to it! You'll be in better case to think straight tomorrow. Matson can drive you home."

Roberto put his arm round Peggy, and shepherded her tenderly through the door, his face still blank with disbelief in this unforeseen respite.

When they were gone, Miles and Olivia looked at each other for a long minute of silence across the desk, where the withered rose lay forlornly beside the sheaf of photographs.

"I didn't expect that," she said at last.

"I didn't myself. But in the morning it may come to the same thing, you know. And he won't leave her. He won't run."

"No," said Olivia with a smile. "Roberto's running days are over, if you ask me. She's the kind that stays with things—and he's become the kind that stays with her. I'm glad you sent them home. By tomorrow morning at ten-thirty you may have found it needn't be the same thing, after all."

"You wanted something of me," he said. "You still do. What is it?"

"I want you to come down to the pool with me, early in the morning. There's something I want to look for there, something you put into my head. If I find it," she said, "you won't have to charge Roberto."

Under the willow tree, in the early morning light, the grass was wet from the night's soft rain, and the bowl where Sylvie had lain cradled was as lush and green as though no weight had stained its turf for many months. The steep bank of the lake heeled over and plunged under water, grass to the very rim. The bough that leaned out over the pool trailed long, yellowing fingers in the surface, but most of its leaves were already fallen, and the shapely skeleton of the tree stood in filigree against the pale sky.

"You see," said Olivia, leaning over the rim of the water, "how the ground falls away. No weed, no sight of the bottom. There's a natural hollow under here, the deepest part of the pool—probably a bottom of smooth mud. Why should anyone, even in a panic, stand here with something he wanted to hide, all ready weighted as it was, and do anything more elaborate than simply toss it in? Why should he run off down there, a quarter of the way round the pool, to throw it into the shallows?"

"You suggest," said Miles respectfully, "your own answer:—unless, of course, he wanted it to be found."

"That's what I think, anyhow. And supposing he also had something that he wanted hidden—hidden for keeps, that is—never to be found. . . ."

"But we dragged the lake, you know. It isn't infallible, but it's reasonably effective. To make absolutely sure, we should have to drain it."

"I think you'll have to. But we can easily make sure. Are you good at climbing trees, or shall we borrow the park-keeper's boat, do you think?" She was looking keenly along the length of the overhanging bough, but it jutted out too far for her to be able to examine it for more than a yard or two of its compass.

They walked down to where the boat was moored beside the wired enclosures where the park-keeper stocked his fish, and rowed themselves across until they lay off the steep green bank by Sylvie's willow. Standing on the seat, while Miles held the boat steady, Olivia could just run her hands and her eye along the smooth, silvery-green bark.

"Yes, it's here!" she said, with a sigh of achievement. "Climb up and look for yourself. I'll steady the boat."

And when he was on his feet, she knew by the intent sharpening of his face that he had found and recognized what she wanted him to see.

"It's new," he said, running a finger-tip along the narrow scar which crossed the bough obliquely on its upper side. "New and clean, not even discoloured yet from the rain. Yes, call that a couple of days old, and you wouldn't be far wrong. Yes—that alters things. It looks as if we shall have to drain the lake, after all."

He stood for a moment steadying himself by the bough, and with a long, sweeping glance measured the angle from the spot where Sylvie's body had been found to this minute scar on the willow-bough, and continued the trajectory beyond, into the deep, green water.

"Yes, there—just about there," he said thoughtfully, and turned and gave Olivia a long, wondering, admiring look. "Do you know you're a very remarkable person, Olivia Grandison.

Without another word they went to moor the boat at the park-keeper's hut, and made their way out to the gate where the car was waiting. He had to telephone the park superintendent at once. She had calls to make in the town, for a few hours of Sylvie's last day still remained to be filled in. According to Mrs. Collinson, she had left her lodgings immediately after tea. She had arrived at the theatre about seven, as usual. The interlude held, perhaps, only an academic interest, but Olivia preferred that the gap should be filled in. It was, after all, a matter of professional pride now to complete the case she had begun.

By noon the outflow had lowered the surface of the lake by a couple of feet, and left the smooth black folds of mud uncovered round the shores, draped in the more remote shallows with strands of vivid green weed. By early evening the water was almost gone, only the deep pockets left still gleaming dully under the sunset light. The daylight was beginning to fail as a thin cordon of police began working their way in gingerly towards the hollow beyond the willow tree, slithering in their waders in the oily mud. In the black waste, raking carefully as they went, they looked like cockle-gatherers on some desolate shore.

Olivia, coming back after a snatched tea, and flattered by the complacency with which Constable Matson let her pass the cordon, saw that two other unofficial people had received the same privilege. On the green shelf by the willow, near the spot from which Miles directed operations, Peggy Soames and Robert Gregg stood watching, in frowning and slightly apprehensive puzzlement.

Sergeant Rhodes, raking delicately but deeply in the waste of slime, raised a sudden short bark of triumph. One end of the wooden rake tilted upward, with a festoon of cord taut about two of its teeth. Miles let himself down from the shelf of grass and waded across to him.

"Looks like it! Take it easy, there'll be a weight of some sort on the deeper end. Is it cord, or elastic?"

It was thick, round elastic, under the coating of slime; several yards of it came slowly oozing out of the mud round the teeth of the rake. The two ends, still buried, moved steadily apart. Miles pursued one towards the centre of the lake, while Rhodes followed his a little nearer to the willow and the shore. They had to plunge their hands and forearms into the mud to excavate the ends. Miles had the lighter burden, so tiny that it flew into the light at last with a muddy plop like a sodden cork being drawn. A small, compact black shape, it lay snugly in the palm of his hand, and when he twisted his fingers about the barrel and wrung the mud from it, the hard gleam of metal came to the surface in a recognizable shape. He had no doubt that it was the Lilliput which had killed Sylvie Fryer.

Rhodes had reached the limit of the elastic at his end. It stretched and sucked in the ooze when he pulled at it, and would not rise another inch. He probed disgustedly in the mud, heaved and stood gazing in astonishment at the thing that sucked and groaned its way into the air in his two hands. It was an old-fashioned flat-iron.

"That's it," said Miles, wading shoreward, "and that's all. Come on, we've finished here. Let's get the sluices working again, and go and clean ourselves up."

He brought the curious treasure trove to land, and scrubbed it clean of the worst of its slime in the turf. They stood round staring at a dull metal object wrapped in a coil of strong elastic. Peggy and Roberto had drawn nearer, arm in arm, pressed together as though they felt the chill of the evening. The young man's face was motionless, and guarded his thoughts, but it seemed to Olivia that in a large measure he had already understood.

"Not much use asking you, at this stage," said Miles, "whether you recognize it. It's barely recognizable as a gun at all, yet, let alone as a .21 German automatic."

"It looks the right kind," said Roberto, without any expression at all in his voice or face. "It could be mine."

Clinging to his arm, Peggy asked anxiously: "But what does it mean? I don't understand!"

"All you need understand for the moment, Miss Soames, is that it's all over, and you have neither of you anything more to worry about. But if you want the details, I think you're entitled to hear them. Shall we say in an hour's time, in my office? I have just one more call to make before the case is closed."

The last call did not take long. Mrs. Collinson, surprised and suspicious at such an apparently irrelevant question, said at once: "Yes, I've got a set of three irons that used to belong to my mother, and her mother before her. I never use them now, of course, as I've got an electric. But they're all here, somewhere at the back of the top cupboard ..." Her confident voice trailed away into consternation and offence as she reached into the darkest recesses. "There are only two here! The smallest one's gone!"

"When did you last see it?" asked Miles, opening his case.

"Oh, I haven't *seen* it for months ... or, wait a minute, yes I have, I turned out that cupboard about three weeks ago to find a pair of tongs. All three irons were there then. I'd have noticed if they hadn't been."

"Is this the missing one?" He laid it, cleaned of its mud and corrosion, on the table, and she seized it instantly in an indignant hand.

"That's it! That's mine. I can tell it by this nick in the handle. Where did you find it? Who's had it?"

The distrustful stare of the outraged property-owner followed him from the house when he left. He could sense that to Mrs. Collinson the most discreditable aspect of the whole terrible affair was the theft of her flat-iron.

"Properly speaking," said Miles, offering cigarettes across the desk in his office nearly an hour later, "this isn't my story at all. It's Miss Grandison's. She was the one who felt from the beginning that one inconsistent factor was misleading us into investigating the wrong crime. So you can tell it," he said, smiling at Olivia, "and I'll listen. There are still things I need to know myself."

Olivia looked at the two young people sitting side by side in their office chairs, still a little stiff and on the defensive, still maintaining the watchful quietness of those who have been in acute danger, and cannot believe even now that the peril is really past.

"It was just that the photographs worried me so much," she said. "She looked so *beautiful!* It seemed to me that *unforeseen* death ought not to be like that … or perhaps it ought to be, but never is. She looked as if she'd been brought there in a band-box and lifted out on to the grass. But the picture set up by all the circumstantial evidence, the unconsciously significant things people said, was totally different from the picture recorded by my camera. The evidence said, here's a woman who has been shot in desperation by her lover, and left lying where she fell. The photographs said, a triumph of stage décor, carefully assembled, equally effective from any angle, unmistakably a work of art.

"And then these echoes began, in everything people said. There was Loretta, with her verdict on Sylvie: 'She looked good . . . she could, *when she made a special effort.*' And again: 'She knew she was up against it this time … she'd gone to so much trouble she must have known.' And Fred Brayne noticed something that fitted in afterwards—that Sylvie insisted on carrying her own handbag, when she left the theatre with you. . . ."

"She did, too!" agreed Roberto, raising for a moment the hollow eyes he had so steadily averted since this recital began. "Was that important? I thought she was just playing extra sweet."

"So did Fred, but it was important, all right. And then Superintendent Avery here said the thing that really opened my eyes. He said: 'Death, when the disorder has been arranged out of it, can be both beautiful and elegant.' When *the disorder has been arranged out of it!* That was what I'd had at the back of my mind, and then, looking at those pictures, I realized they were telling a bigger truth than all the rest put together. Here was death without disorder, an arranged, a dignified, an artistic death. What interest could a murderer possibly have in making his victim look beautiful? No, only one person could have cared to turn Sylvie into a legend of loveliness. . . ."

"*Sylvie!*" said Peggy, in a shocked whisper, closing her hand convulsively upon Roberto's hand.

"Sylvie. Suicide never occurred to anyone as a possibility because there was no gun. But once it became clear that she had killed herself, the absence of the gun had somehow to be part of the pattern. If she had organized its disappearance, there could be only one reason for that … to make her suicide appear murder, and to saddle someone else with the responsibility for it. You, Roberto."

Peggy said on an almost soundless breath: "Oh, *no*! Nobody could be so wicked! She must have been mad!"

"No, I don't think she was mad … just vengeful. People do cut off their noses to spite their faces. Sylvie isn't the first. Her preparations began two days ago, when she took the weight from your mother's garden gate. It had to be something from your house, because that was where Roberto lived. She also took the smallest of Mrs. Collinson's flat-irons, which hadn't been used or thought of for years. The one weight was to be easily missed, and readily identified when found; the other had to be something that wouldn't be missed for months, or years, or indeed ever. I should think that the agreement to meet after the last show and have things out was also made two days before, and at her suggestion."

"Yes," said Roberto in a low voice, "it was. She asked me … and she was so sweet and reasonable that I felt I owed her that much."

"At what stage she took your pistol I don't know, but I imagine it wasn't difficult. As your partner, she was well acquainted with your possessions. When she left the theatre with you that night, she had in her bag your Lilliput, the two weights and the coil of elastic. That was why she wouldn't let you take the bag. You'd certainly have noticed the excess weight.

"I've checked on her movements between tea and the show that evening, just as a matter of curiosity. She bought the dress she intended to die in. It cost her more, I expect than she'd ever paid for a frock in her life. Then she bought the sandals. Then she had her hair done, and a facial, and a manicure. It was a special effort, all right."

Roberto stared fixedly at the cigarette in his fingers. "Poor devil!" he said, in an almost inaudible voice.

"I don't think you need feel pity for her. Let's face it, it wasn't an agony of love. It was an agony of spite. She was determined to destroy you, even if she had to do it by destroying herself.

"Well, once I'd made up my mind that she must have disposed of the gun herself, the next thing was to determine how. The scene itself made that pretty clear. There, under the willow-tree, was the deep water. But how could she have got the gun into it? Of course, all she had to do was to attach it to a weight heavier than itself, and then find a fulcrum overhanging the water. The willow branch served perfectly. With such a weight on the other end of the elastic, she could be pretty sure that, as soon as she let go of the gun, the weight would fall and pull gun and cord down after it. Of course, there were hazards, but the tree was already losing its leaves, and willows are so pliant that there wasn't much likelihood of a tangle with twigs or foliage. And in the event, you see, it did work.

"The method had another advantage. The weight she chose was enough to plunge itself and its tow so deep into the bottom mud that dragging would be very unlikely to dislodge it. But once we'd found the scar the elastic left on the branch as it was pulled over, then we knew we were on the right track, and it was well worth emptying the lake."

"Judging by the use she made of the handbag," Miles put in thoughtfully, "Sylvie had gone over every inch of this ground very carefully. There was nothing left to chance that could possibly be calculated."

"I agree. And once in the park she led the way to the place she'd chosen, and made her last fling. It didn't work—she'd never really believed it would—so now she'd arrived at the alternative. She begged the rose from you as a last souvenir, and sent you away. The rose was her masterpiece. She couldn't have known beforehand that you'd be wearing it—that was something fate put right into her hands, and it was the most damning thing of all.

"When you'd left her, she threw the handbag into the shallows, where it was sure to be found. Then she came back to her stage set and prepared the last scene. She tied the elastic to flat-iron and gun, threw the flat-iron out over the willow branch, and hung on tightly to the gun while she lay down in her green hollow, recreating an act she'd probably rehearsed a dozen times before, spreading out her beautiful new dress, tossing out the beautiful new waves of her hair, manipulating even the edge of her skirt into the right pathetic draping, her toes just peeping from under it. She did all this, knowing her body would be photographed, hoping you'd be shown the pictures, hoping you'd be haunted for ever by the vision of what you'd thrown away. She went to endless pains to perfect her work of art, all the time with the pistol dragging heavily at her left hand. And when she felt that it was perfect, she held the pistol to her temple and pulled the trigger.

"The recoil did its part very well for her. The wrench of the weight as her muscles relaxed pulled her arm down, and left it lying rather gracefully over her body; and the gun flew out of her slackened fingers, over the branch and into the water, just as she'd planned. And circumstances began to close in round you, just as she'd planned."

"As a matter of merely academic interest," said Miles, looking up at Roberto, "*was* she left-handed?"

"No. She could use both pretty well equally, but she was right-handed by nature."

"So even that was calculated! It would have been nice to find just one point she'd overlooked! The only error of judgment she made was in being too thorough. But you see now what I meant by saying we were investigating the wrong crime. Instead of wasting our time enquiring into the murder of Sylvie, we should have been concentrating on the attempted murder of Robert Gregg."

"You won't hear any complaints from me," said Roberto fervently. He turned his head, with the burning, angry colour still scorching his cheeks, and looked at Peggy, and found her near to him, within touch, with no walls in between them, and no Sylvie, either. "And it could have come off!" he said, shivering. "We owe you a lot! We owe you everything! When I think what she intended to happen to me ..."

"On the contrary, we owed you the full measure of justice, and I'm grateful that, thanks to Miss Grandison, we've been able to pay it so promptly. I don't know what your plans will be, but I'd like to wish you both happiness and good luck in whatever you do decide to do."

The change of emphasis was timely, and nicely calculated. They drew together shyly, blushing this time without distress, and murmured slightly incoherent thanks. It was wonderful how even the thought of Sylvie had faded, leaving upon the air only a faint, dry bitterness, like the dryness in the mouth upon waking out of a hectic dream.

"I'm thinking of getting a job here," said Roberto, kindling into eagerness. "Peggy's father thinks there may be an opening in the Corporation Transport, where he works. I'm game to do anything, and I can at least drive. I'm through with this dancing racket ... we're going to settle down."

When they had taken their leave, the two who were left behind heard them break step in the corridor, and halt for one soft, confused instant. It was not quite silence, but something like a murmur and a sigh, an infinitely brief, infinitely quiet mutual cry of relief and rapture before they kissed each other. Then they went on softly and quickly, and escaped into the cool, autumnal evening with their suddenly enormous happiness, for which buildings had not room enough.

"I hate to think," said Miles soberly, "what would have happened to those two if I hadn't accidentally called you into consultation. Providence was certainly on the job when I made that 'phone call."

"You did your level best to get rid of me when I did come," she reminded him.

"But, you see, I'd only just been promoted then to the privilege of a guardian angel, though I *did* have a divine premonition of good ...

Oh, when mine eyes did see Olivia first,
Methought she purged the air of pestilence!"

Her mind, still busy with Peggy and Roberto, let the quotation pass her by, but she heard her name. It sounded so new and significant and delightful on his tongue that she looked round with a startled smile. "What was that? Sorry, I wasn't listening."

"Nothing! Just a prophetic utterance by a chap named Shakespeare."

A PRESENT FOR IVO

If Sara Boyne had not taken her duties as the secretary of the Shelvedon Teachers' Christmas Committee so seriously, the curious affair at Shelvedon would probably have remained a mystery, a rankling reproach to the local police, to this day. But Sara, in addition to being very young and earnestly pretty, was conscientious, and new to the responsibilities of office.

The committee was collectively responsible for the organization of the great Shelvedon Christmas party, held annually in the castle on Christmas Eve for all the school children of the little borough; but in practice the onus fell fairly and squarely upon the secretary. And if Sara took on a job, she did it thoroughly.

The night before the party she lay awake half the night, checking over everything in her mind. Was there a present for each child, duly selected and wrapped by his or her class teacher? Did the tree look pretty enough?

In some towns it would have been unthinkable to hang all the parcels on the tree overnight, and stand the tree in the open courtyard of the castle, which was also the town hall and civic offices, at the mercy of any passer-by, and protected only by the occasional perambulations of a constable on his beat. But in Shelvedon it was part of a proud tradition, and nothing had ever been stolen, and no one entertained any fears that anything ever would be.

And the food for the party tea—was there really enough of it? Were Tom Fielding's decorations too adult to please? Roger Brecon had been sweet about the fairy lights, too—fancy a solicitor being so knowledgeable about electricity! Sara, who wasn't vain but knew that she was attractive, could not help wondering whether Roger's interest in the party was on her account.

She awoke with the first hint of dawn to the conviction that the carol sheets had been forgotten. Shelvedon parents, coming at half past six to fetch their children home, liked to stay for a final half-hour of carol singing. She must go along very early to the castle and bring down the leaflets from the cupboard upstairs, in case they should be overlooked later.

That was how she came to leave home immediately after lunch, though the party was not due to start until half past three.

On her way to the castle she bought an evening paper—the first edition was on the streets at noon—to see what it had to say about the junior school nativity play, in which some of her own hopeful pupils had starred. Not until she had sunned herself in the praise of her charges did she suddenly register the shock of the staring headlines which had the place of honour on the front page.

SHELVEDON CHRONICLE STOLEN
Daring midnight raid on town museum

During the night the town museum, housed in one ward of the castle, has been broken into by means of the removal of a pane of glass from which the burglar alarm could be reached and switched off. An expert job, arguing a preliminary reconnaissance, and considerable experience of all kinds of safety devices. By chance the constable on his beat made a round of the buildings, found the window unfastened, and observed the vacant pane, whereupon he immediately gave the alarm, and kept close watch on the building until the arrival of reinforcements who could cover all exits from the castle.

The report went on to say that the museum had then been searched, but the thief must already have vacated this wing, and the search had to be extended to all the civic offices and the arcades of the castle, before a man was run to earth in the open undercroft of the rear gatehouse.

He was sitting on one of the benches, apparently asleep, and claimed that he had no recollection of how he had got there, though he admitted earlier he had been drinking in the Black Bull. The man had been detained and it was understood that he was well known to the police. However, nothing incriminating was found on him.

Examination of the museum premises had revealed that only one item was missing: the world-famous *Shelvedon Chronicle*, the most perfect fourteenth-century manuscript of its kind in existence, a local history written by the monk Anselmus of Shelvedon Priory, and particularly renowned for its beautiful illuminations.

The manuscript of the *Chronicle* had not been recovered. Enquiries were being pursued both in Shelvedon and elsewhere, as this was the latest of many such thefts of extremely valuable antiques and works of art during the last six months, and the police suspected what must be an organization of a national scale for their acquisition and consequent disposition.

Sara stood gaping at the improbable paragraphs with all the consternation and disbelief of a Londoner reading of the theft of the Crown Jewels. *The Shelvedon Chronicle* lay alone in a black velvet-lined case in the museum, with a small strip-light shining upon its exquisite, jewel-like initial letters and minute pictures.

A steel frame closed down over the glass case at night. How could it be stolen? Only an expert could have done it. A national scale? International, more likely, thought Sara, impervious for the moment to the frosty sharpness of the air and to a rapid ring of footsteps crossing the glazed cobbles.

A tall young man in a duffle coat was reaching up into the branches of the tree, setting the chains of lights tinkling.

"Hallo!" said Sara, embarrassed and delighted to recognize her helpful amateur electrician. "Have you got this affair on your mind as badly as that, too?"

Roger Brecon swung round, the needles showering down over him as he turned his head. "Oh, hallo, Sara! My goodness, you startled me!" But his surprise struck her as slightly overdone. "Where did you spring from?"

"I didn't spring. I was here. I was reading the paper."

"Whatever brings you here so early, anyhow?"

"I just couldn't rest. I wanted to make sure everything was all right. I forgot to bring down the carol sheets yesterday. Anyhow, what about you? It isn't even your headache, really."

He laughed, twitching a bright red parcel into a better position, and stepped back to observe the general effect. "I just wanted to make sure they really light up. After all, I was the one who fixed them up. I'd look a fine fool if they didn't work."

But they did work; the whole tree leaped into brilliance and colour at a flick of his finger. He stared up at it delightedly, and then bestowed upon Sara the most radiant and intimate of smiles.

They were silent, looking at each other with slightly flushed faces and slightly dazzled eyes, when Tom Fielding came slithering across the cobbles with casual skating strides of his long legs, a newspaper crumpled up under his arm. His black forelock bobbed over the broad brown forehead, and his lean cheeks were red from scurrying through the frost after Sara.

"Hi!" said Tom, pulling up in a long glissade, Roger still hidden from him by the tree. "Your sense of duty will be the death of you. Did you remember to eat any lunch, or were you too worried about the ice-cream for the kids? Seen the news? Crime marches on!"

"I was just reading it. Isn't it terrible? Somehow you never expect that sort of thing to happen in your own town."

She was annoyed with herself for sounding embarrassed, and her rising colour caused Tom to scowl suddenly in suspicion. He took a couple of steps to the right, and his line of vision embraced Roger Brecon.

"Oh, it's you!" Tom remarked, with no enthusiasm at all. His lowering brows added: It would be!

"Hallo, Fielding," said Roger, with more civility but no more warmth. "A bad business, this museum affair!"

"Oh, I don't know, might be quite good business for you. I heard you'd just stalked out of the police station—don't tell me you're turning the client down? Think of the capital there must be behind an organization big enough to market stuff like the *Shelvedon Chronicle*!"

"Did this man you're talking about really want you to be his solicitor?" asked Sara, fascinated.

"They charged him, and he asked for a solicitor." It was clear from his flush of annoyance that Roger had no wish to talk about it. "He didn't seem to care who it was—said a local man would do, and picked me out at random. I didn't know anything about the case until they notified me he was asking me to act for him."

"And are you going to?" Sara couldn't help asking.

"No, of course not, how can I? You'd have thought the police would have seen that for themselves. I'm a councillor, and the *Chronicle* is municipal property. I'm even on the museum sub-committee. It wouldn't be proper for me to involve myself in the case legally." He was red with irritation now. "Hadn't we better get those carol sheets down, Sara?"

"Didn't you take a good look at him?" asked Tom, happily pursuing what he saw to be an unwelcome subject. "Surely you wanted at least to *see* the one that got away?"

"I didn't even know what it was all about until I was there. It was only decent to see him, and explain why I couldn't act for him. Sara, I'm just going to straighten that one chain—you go ahead, I'll follow you in a moment."

"I'll hold the steps for you," volunteered Tom, maliciously obliging. Even willing to let me out of his sight, thought Sara, as she scurried indoors and through the entrance hall, rather than stop baiting Roger. Well, let him get on with it. Roger could hold his own.

The decorations leaped into beauty as she switched on the lights, and the laden tables shone with jellies and trifles and cakes. She ran up to the small committee-room in the gate tower, unlocked the cupboard, and brought down her carol leaflets. There was really nothing else to be done.

Surprised that the two young men had not yet followed her indoors, she took an apple from the bowl of fruit on the nearest table, and went out, peacefully munching it, to see what they were up to.

"Well, well!" said Tom, observing the apple. "Eve in person! Now which of us two, Brecon, old boy, would you say was cast for the serpent?"

"Which of us," snapped Roger bitterly, "looks more like a snake in the grass?" And he strode away from the tree and took Sara by the arm, turning her back towards the hall. "Come on, Sara, let's get inside. Here come the others."

Paul Hartland and two of his juniors from the Modern School were just unloading a car on the pavement outside the gatehouse, and little Miss Price from the infants department was trotting across the courtyard with her arms full of sheet music.

Then, quite suddenly, came the first of the children, with dazzled eyes fixed on the tree. And the tenth great Annual Joint Christmas Party for the schoolchildren of Shelvedon began.

Everybody agreed the party was the most complete success so far, and the best organized. They played games first—active games and quiet games alternately—then they ate an enormous tea, and after it came the puppet show, the conjurer, and the ventriloquist, to keep the guests reasonably still and engrossed while the tea settled; while the helpers snatched a brief rest, too, and Tom Fielding sneaked away and clambered into his beard and his scarlet gown, ready for the climax.

Then out they all trooped, already warmly packed into their outdoor clothes, to cluster round the lighted tree. Tom's assistants climbed about the tree handing down parcels, while he called up eager owners to receive them. He was a voluble and effective Father Christmas. The one real consolation, he claimed, was that inside all that red flannel he didn't feel the cold.

Then the parents came, and the town band, and the time-honoured half-hour of carol singing began, under the coloured lights and the floating balloons; and before anyone was really ready for it—which was the right time for it to happen—the party was over. With a noise like the descent of the evening starlings upon Trafalgar Square the children of Shelvedon were on their way home.

Sara stood under the ravaged tree, speeding the departing guests as they withdrew.

"Goodnight, Jimmy! Happy Christmas! Goodnight, Alison! Goodnight, Pat! Did you have a good time? A happy Christmas. . . ."

"You seem to know every kid in Shelvedon personally," said Roger, grinning from behind her shoulder.

An under-sized boy in a navy flannel duffle beamed up at her demurely over his large, flat parcel and gave the string an extra twist round his wrist. "Miss Boyne, I got a book!"

"You haven't opened it yet," she said, smiling. "How do you know it's a book?"

"Oh, yes, Miss Boyne, I have. I did it up again carefully, so it won't get wet even if it snows. The man on the wireless said it would snow."

Plainly he hoped for the prophecy to be fulfilled. "And do you like your present, Ivo?"

Large eyes, black-fringed, shone in the shadow of his hood. "Miss Boyne, it's *beautiful*! It's a *beautiful* book!"

"Funny little thing," said Roger as the small figure trotted away over the scintillating cobbles. "Who is he?"

"He's an orphan, in the county's care—name's Ivo Jenkins. He's boarded out with old Mrs. Freeman—you know, at Cross Farm Cottage. She's very good to him, but she's rather old. I wish he had more young, stimulating company, he's such a reserved, serious child."

"One of yours, I see," said Roger, gently laughing at her. He stretched and sighed, looking after the last stragglers as they withdrew under a barrage of dancing balloons, leaving the courtyard suddenly quiet and desolate. "I should have liked to stay and help you tidy up, Sara, but I've got to go to a dinner tonight, and I promised I'd go home first."

"You've done enough," said Sara. "You've been most helpful. Thanks for everything!"

She had almost hoped that he would make some tentative reference to the New Year's Eve dance, but he didn't. He simply smiled, wished her a happy Christmas, and fled.

She turned away with a sigh, and went to join her weary fellow-workers who were clearing up the debris. Just then Tom emerged, scarlet and perspiring, from his beard. He stripped off his robes, and began to gather up the coloured heaps of tinsel and wrappings under the tree. "Hallo, what's this? There's something buried in the soil here!"

Sara went to his side. The earth in the tub had certainly been disturbed, and Tom's vigorous gesture had swept aside the fallen needles and exposed a corner of brown paper.

"It's a box—no, a book!" He tugged it clear and brushed away the needles that clung to it. An oblong package wrapped loosely in a single fold of stiff paper, which fell away as he turned it in his hands, revealed the vividly coloured dustjacket of a book. "*Boys Gigantic Adventure Annual!* Oh, lord!" said Tom blankly. "Has somebody been forgotten? One of the absentees?"

"No, I'm positive! Besides, this was for one of my boys. I remember it perfectly. But how on earth did it get there do you suppose?"

"Sara!" Tom stared at her reproachfully. "*You* didn't choose this for some poor kid, did you?" Just because he taught art at the Secondary Modern and the Technical College, she thought indignantly, he didn't have to be so damned superior about other people's taste.

"Yes, I did! What's the matter with it? But—" She gaped helplessly towards the gateway, through which young Ivo Jenkins had vanished some ten minutes ago. "But he *had* his book! He just told me he'd looked at it, and it was beautiful."

"Couldn't have meant this," said Tom, averting his eyes from it. "Anyhow, he buried it decently. Probably disapproved of the art work—and who could blame him? Obviously he was just being nice to you—thought you didn't know any better."

Sara experienced an urge, by no means new to her where Tom Fielding was concerned, to box his ears. "I tell you he *liked* it! A beautiful book, he said!" She heard him saying it again, and knew that he had meant it; and quite suddenly the confusion in her mind was all blown away by a staggering thought.

This annual was undoubtedly the book she'd chosen for him; what, then, had he been clutching so tightly under his arm as he took leave of her? What was the beautiful book that had caused his serious eyes to shine so brilliantly in the shadow of his hood?

She clutched at Tom's arm, forgetting all her irritation with him. "Tom!—*how big* is the *Shelvedon Chronicle?*"

Tom turned a face stricken into ludicrous consternation, and stared at her wildly, making the same mental leap she had just made. *"Just about as big as this thing!"*

They stood gaping at each other, trying to grasp the monstrous implications. "It couldn't be! Things like that don't happen!"

"But they have happened! It disappeared from the museum, didn't it? And the police closed all the ways out of the castle, and then made a thorough search for the thief, didn't they? And found a man with a criminal record in just that line—"

"Right here inside the courtyard!"

"But without the *Chronicle*," said Tom. "You realize what that means? They had him penned inside here, unable to get clean away with the goods, but with a few minutes respite while they combed out the museum buildings.

"Long enough for him to swop his loot for a similar-sized parcel on the Christmas-tree, wrap it and leave it to be collected later—by himself or someone else. Without it, he stood a chance of getting off. He'd only to hang the *Chronicle* on the tree, and hide it, and let himself be picked up. What else could he do?"

"But how could he get a message through to anyone else?" protested Sara breathlessly, swept away by this reconstruction.

"I don't know. There are ways; maybe he had a confederate outside the enclave, maybe he managed to get some sort of signal through."

"Then one thing's certain," said Sara. "He'd let them know the name on the parcel, otherwise they could hunt all day. And if he did manage to get word through, why haven't they collected it?"

"Maybe they have. Maybe that's some fresh substitute young Ivo's carrying home now. Or perhaps they simply didn't get here in time. The precincts would be rather popular this morning, while the offices were open. And this afternoon conscience brought us along so early—"

"Then they'll be looking for Ivo now," said Sara with fierce finality, and grew pale at what she herself had said. It wasn't the *Shelvedon Chronicle* she was thinking of, it was that funny, old-fashioned little boy with the quiet manners and the impenetrable reserve, trotting home through the frosty evening with thousands of pounds worth of skill and beauty and devotion under his arm.

"A beautiful book!" said Tom with awe. "My God, he was right!"

They exchanged one bemused, incredulous glance.

"Come on!" said Tom, seizing her by the arm. "At least, we've got to make sure. See him safely home, and beg a look at his book, just in case."

"And take him this!" Sara grabbed up the *Boys Gigantic Adventure Annual* as she was towed away at the end of Tom's long arm.

"*That!*" Tom snorted as he slid into the car and reached for the starter. "A boy who falls for the *Chronicle* won't think the *Gigantic Adventure Annual* a fair exchange."

"This is entirely appropriate for his age group," said Sara indignantly, slamming the door on her side as the engine obediently hiccupped into life.

"Only unfortunately he doesn't seem to be entirely appropriate to it himself."

"You don't know him! I do! I chose it specially for him, because he's far too prim and quiet. I want to encourage him to think adventurously," she said, all the more aggressively because Tom always made her feel self-conscious about her beliefs.

Tom swung the car out through the gateway. They threaded their way rapidly through the late Christmas shoppers and the lighted windows fell behind them. Through the archway in the town wall the black sky lowered at them, heavy with cloud. The first desultory flakes of the promised snow were already falling.

"Perhaps there's no one to collect," said Sara. "Perhaps there wasn't any message. Maybe he's just been hoping they couldn't hold him, so that he could pick it up himself. It may be just a one-man job, after all."

"Not a chance! He can't be any more than a very small cog in a very large system of wheels. What would an ordinary thug want with a thing like the *Chronicle*? No, this is no one-man job. It ties in with all those other thefts of works of art, just as the newspaper said."

"Isn't it queer," she said, "to think there are people willing to spend a fortune on a thing they'll never be able to show off to anyone? What do they get out of gloating over them in secret?"

"If I had the chance to gloat over the *Chronicle* in secret, and feel I owned it, I might be able to tell you. They exist, all right. Plenty of them, if you know where to look."

He put his foot down hard as soon as they were well out of the shopping streets and through the gate. The high, windy road, fringed with semi-detached houses at first, soon fell into darkness between the occasional older cottages. Not three miles away to the right, keen in the strong salt scent of the wind, was the sea.

"Wouldn't Ivo be with some of the other children? The little Grettons have to come out this way, nearly as far as Cross Farn."

"They left well ahead of him. No, I'm afraid he'll be alone." He was so often alone, partly from habit, partly from choice.

She wished he lived with some large, cheerful family in the town, where he'd be jockeyed into mixing with other children whether he liked it or not. But foster-homes are where you can find them. And the old lady was very good to him. Sara found herself thinking of Ivo with an indignant, anxious affection, as though she had only become aware of his deprivations when danger was added to them.

The road ran between hedges and fields now, and the street lighting was all left behind, but it was only a quarter of a mile to Cross Farm. And suddenly Sara gave a breathless laugh of sheer relief, and pointed ahead. "There he is! He's all right!"

The small figure, bent purposefully forward in an old man's trotting walk, scurried along the footpath with his parcel tucked under his arm.

Tom heaved an audible sigh, and relaxed the pressure of his foot on the accelerator. The next moment he had to jam it hard upon the brake, for out of a side road on the right a large, old, dark-bodied car drove suddenly across his path, and turned into the road ahead of him, cutting off his view of the child trotting briskly into the distance.

It all happened in an instant. The big car drew alongside the hurrying child, and slowed there smoothly, and an arm and shoulder, no more than a vague black movement in the murky dusk, leaned out and plucked the parcel from under his arm.

Ivo's scared squeal sounded thinly through the moan of the snow-laden wind, and sharpened into a yell of pain as the strong cord dragged sharply at his wrist. Sara, remembering how tightly he had wound the string round to anchor his treasure, gasped in sympathy. It must have been the sound of Tom accelerating furiously that decided what happened next. If only the string had broken Ivo would have been safe, but the string did not break, and delay was impossible.

The man in the passenger seat transferred his grip suddenly from the book to the boy's arm, and hoisted him bodily into the car, which shot away into the night with a roar of a powerful engine, Tom's old Morris throbbing on its tail.

Sara heard herself repeating the car number breathlessly, memorizing it because she had no opportunity of writing it down.

Tom said nothing at all. His jaw was set, and his foot had the accelerator pedal flattened to the floor of the car, and every ounce of energy he possessed was devoted to hurling them along after the kidnappers. Sara hooked an arm over the back of the seat to steady herself as they rocked round the corner into the Westensea road, and met the squalls of thin, sharp snow head-on.

The rear light ahead winked at them through the murk, and seemed if anything a shade nearer. The speedometer needle was wobbling furiously around sixty-five; it crept up towards seventy, in a flash of desperation lunged above seventy, and lurched back shuddering at its own temerity.

Past the Mitre Inn now, and round the long curve, turning with the curve of the coastline. Two miles or so more, and they'd be entering the suburbs of Westensea, and the big fellow would be forced to slow down. They'd get him there, if they had to ram him to do it. If he kept up this speed the police would join in the chase, and he wouldn't risk that, with what he had on board.

"He's stopping!" panted Sara. The big car seemed to have drawn into the hedge and slowed considerably, if not stopped. The driver opened his door, and seemed to be getting out, though he clung close to the body of the car.

Tom didn't lift his foot until the first tiny flash against the blackness of the night and the deeper blackness of the car warned him. The report was lost in the protests of his own sorely tried motor, but he recognized the signs, and slowed for an instant, then, realizing that if he stopped he would merely present a sitting target, he gritted his teeth, trod hard down again, and wrenched the wheel round to drive full at the enemy. Head-on he'd have a better chance of upsetting the marksman's aim.

The second shot, by luck or skill, got their right front tyre, and brought them round with a horrible, lurching plunge towards the ditch.

Tom, wrestling frantically with the wheel, wrenched the Morris back on to the road, and somehow managed to pull it up without disaster on a front tyre slashed to ribbons; but by the time they had tumbled, panting and trembling, out into the snow the big car was pulling away at speed, and before they had breath enough to speak it had vanished completely in the direction of Westensea.

Tom caught Sara by the shoulders, and held her for a moment against his heart. "Sara, you're all right? You're not hurt?" The alarm and ardour in his voice hardly registered until later, she was so intent upon the chase.

"I'm all right! A bit shaken, that's all. Now what do we do? We *can't* let them get away!"

"We're not going to. I've got to change this wheel. Thank God the spare's all right! I can manage alone—only a twenty-minute job! Sara, darling, could you run on alone? You're not afraid? We can't be far out of the town, there must be a call-box soon, or a house with a phone.

"Call the police, tell them the car number, and where it's headed. As soon as I've changed the wheel I'll come on after you and pick you up, and we'll go on together and report, see if we can help at all. After you've called them, walk back towards me. Or if the snow gets bad stay in shelter somewhere by the side of the road and watch out for me. Can you do that?"

"Yes, of course!" She was glad to have something active to do, glad to be still in the hunt. She set off at a rapid run, head-down into the snow. Not until she had left Tom and the Morris well behind did she realize that she was still clutching the *Gigantic Adventure Annual* under her arm. She tucked it inside her coat to keep it dry, and ran on.

The first larger house, after several isolated cottages, lay back from the road behind a screen of trees and shrubberies. There was a wide carriage-gate, and a small wicket beside it, and the overhead wires, thrumming angrily in the wind, turned inward with the drive towards the house.

As she pushed open the wicket gate she thought it might be wise to leave Tom an indication of where she had halted, in case he came along before she was back on the road. No use leaving boy scout's signs in this obliterating blizzard. She detached the gaudy cover of the *Gigantic Adventure Annual* and impaled it firmly on one of the top spikes of the iron gate, so that it stood up and faced the road like a professional sign.

Then she ran up the drive, and rang the bell at the front door of a large, complacent Victorian house in two-coloured brick.

There was what seemed a long interval before a light came on inside the porch, and high heels tapped up to the door. The woman who opened it was dressed in a smart black suit, and had the cool, noncommittal manner of a housekeeper or a secretary.

At Sara's request to use the telephone she raised her eyebrows very slightly, but waved the intruder civilly into the porch out of the snow.

"It's urgent," Sara found herself saying, "or I wouldn't trouble you." Possibly the eyebrows had intimidated her a little. "I want to call the police," she added breathlessly.

"Not an accident?" the woman in black asked, with quick sympathy.

"Well, no, but—"

"I'm sorry, of course you mustn't lose any time. One moment, I'll tell Professor Brayburn." And she left Sara standing in the hall, and vanished through one of a bewildering array of doors.

After a few minutes the same door opened once again, and out bustled a small, benevolent, grey-haired man, peering kindly at Sara over the rims of bifocals.

His face was rosy and elderly, and instantly familiar, though it took her a moment or two to relate both face and name to her memories of three or four summers ago, when she had last seen him.

It had been at a rally of adult educationalists, at the University of Westchester, and the Professor of English Literature had moved benignly among guests at tea. She felt herself suddenly back among known, safe, comforting things; the lurking car and the gunman on the lonely road seemed as remote as the moon.

"My dear young lady, of course, of course, come into my study, you'll be more comfortable at the extension in there. Such a night! Terrible!" He waved her before him into a brown, book-lined room full of deep leather chairs, and indicated the telephone.

Sara lifted the receiver. The line was quite dead. She tried dialling the operator, joggled the rest, waited, tried again. But nothing happened. The heavy, dead silence closed on her hearing like a vice.

Professor Brayburn, surprised by the delay, looked in from the next room. "Dear, dear, is there some trouble on the line? It was all right an hour or so ago."

"It seems to be dead. No response at all."

He bustled across with a concerned face to try it for himself, and had to admit defeat. "That's extraordinary—surely there's not been enough snow to bring down wires? My dear child, I'm so sorry! Can I—"

"Oh, I can't put you out any more. You've been most kind. My friend will soon be along to pick me up, and we can go on into the town."

"But my dear, you can't possibly go out again in this, it's still snowing heavily. Won't you at least let me give you a warm drink, and wait a little, and see if it stops?"

"It's most kind of you, but I can't. My friend might miss me if I don't go to the road. He won't know where I am, you see—"

She was moving steadily towards the door as she spoke, preparing to bow herself out as gracefully as she could, when she stepped upon something that felt sharp and hard in the pile of the Persian carpet, something that stabbed through the sole of her shoe. She withdrew her foot and looked down, quite involuntarily, to see what she had trodden on. A button. A wooden toggle button from a duffle coat, with a girdle of red string still circling its middle.

The thick, strong cord by which it had been attached to the coat had torn loose, bringing with it a few threads of dark blue flannel; and the button was not big enough to have come from a man's coat. A child's, then; a navy blue one—*Ivo's*!

She tore her eyes from it instantly, but she was too late. Across three yards of charged air they encountered Professor Brayburn's old, faded, benevolent blue eyes, and she knew that he had followed her glance, and understood all its implications.

She made a gallant attempt. She took another tentative step towards the door, and said, "Goodnight, and thank you very much. I'm sorry I've troubled you for nothing."

But with that the door opened, and the black-clad secretary slid through it, and after her, circling gently, one to the left and the other to the right, like dancers, two large and silent men in dark overcoats.

They drew into a tight semicircle between Sara and the door.

"What a pity!" said the Professor sadly. "Such a nice young lady, too! But we can hardly let you go running off into the night now, knowing what you know—can we?"

The door closed behind her, and she heard the key turn in the lock. The soft footsteps of the man with the gun receded down the staircase.

The room, heavily furnished but with that impersonal look of a bedroom which is seldom slept in, was dimly lit by one inadequate electric bulb under a fringed shade. On the big bed, draped with a dark tapestry cover, Ivo sat staring at her in astonishment and uncertainty through the tears he had just hurriedly scrubbed away.

"Miss Boyne, you mustn't be scared. I'll look after you! Was it you, Miss Boyne, in the car with Mr. Fielding, following them? They haven't got him, too, have they?" He slid off the tall bed and stood in front of her, quivering gently like a terrier on a scent. "Was he hurt when they fired the gun? What happened?"

She told him. Putting the whole crazy sequence into words somehow clarified it for her, too, and she found in it more to reassure her than she had expected. "So you see, he's sure to come, as soon as he's changed the wheel. Even if he misses seeing my sign as he comes by, he'll go straight to the police when he doesn't find me. And once they start looking for us properly, they're sure to start from where the car was halted, so they'll soon be here. They can't miss us, really Ivo."

"But suppose Mr. Fielding sees it the first time, and comes here by himself?" asked the all too-knowing child, staring at her with those unblinking eyes of his. "There's at least *four* of them. I think there may be more."

"Mr. Fielding will almost certainly call the police first," said Sara, all the more firmly because of the sinking feeling he'd given her. "Why, *all* your buttons are gone!" she said, surveying the duffle coat that hung open over Ivo's Sunday suit.

"I pulled them off. I left one in the car, in case we ever have to identify it," he explained simply, "because there might be a lot of big black cars like it, and they could change the number-plates, couldn't they? And one in the garden here—"

Somewhat staggered, Sara sat down on the bed, and drew him down beside her. "Ivo, I want to ask you about the book you had from the Christmas tree."

His face burned up into indignation. "They took it away from me! They can't do that, it's stealing. It's *my* book!"

"Ivo, dear, I'm afraid it may not be. You see, I think it was stolen already, from the town museum, and put in the place of the book that was meant for you. Tell me what it was like."

He gave her one dismayed glance, and then obeyed, shutting his eyes the better to see it again. "It was in a folding leather case, without any fastener. Inside it had a beautiful leather cover, and the paper was funny, but nice to feel. I couldn't read the letters, they were funny, too, but they made lovely patterns, and the big ones were done with colours, with birds, and animals, and people. And there were lots of little pictures, with people with queer dresses like in the history books."

"It is a history book, Ivo, a wonderful one, made hundreds of years ago. Somebody stole it from the museum, and then he wanted to hide it because the police were after him, and he hid it in the parcel meant for you."

"What will they do with us?" asked Ivo.

That was what Sara was wondering, too. She hoped he had not realized the full implications of their position, but she was afraid he had.

"Oh, take us and leave us somewhere miles from home, while they make their getaway. Or leave us locked up here—that would give them time to vanish, too, before anyone finds us."

"But if that old man who lives here has got to vanish," said the disconcerting child after a moment's thought, "that means he'll lose his house, and his job, and everything. And then he wouldn't be any use to them again, would he? I mean, if the police knew who he is, and are looking for him, and all that? I don't think he'll like that. And the people he's working for—they won't like it, either, will they?"

They would not, and she knew it. There was too much at stake. To leave Ivo and herself to tell what they knew, however much later, meant to sacrifice at least all this local part of a carefully-built organization. No, the game was far too big. They would be quietly disposed of. Not here, though! This house was too close to the scene of the latest theft.

Furthermore, it would be very much easier and safer to remove them to some more discreet place for disposal alive. They would be taken away from here, she felt sure. In this blizzard? There was too great a chance of a car getting stuck in the drifts. No, nothing would happen until the snow stopped. Tom and the police had a little grace in which to find them, and she and Ivo a short respite in which to help themselves.

She was uncomfortably aware that Ivo was adding up the probabilities no less accurately than she, and it was largely to distract him if she could, and avoid confirming his conclusions at all costs, that she jumped up briskly, and began to look round their prison.

First of all she crossed over to the window, pulled back the thick, dusty curtains, and hoisted the heavy lower sash. Its weight was greater than she had expected, and as soon as she relaxed her upward pressure she saw why, for instantly it surged down again, and she had only just time to catch it before it crashed.

Both sash-cords were broken so she let it slide down the last few inches, quietly, and looked round for something with which to prop it open.

There was an enormous book on the old-fashioned table in the corner, a family Bible. She propped it under one end of the sash, and through the opening the snow blew in thinning eddies.

Sara hoisted the sash of the heavy window cautiously higher, inserting her shoulder under it, and stacking the *Boys Gigantic Adventure Annual* on top of the Bible. When she gently lowered the weight upon this precarious erection it settled and held fast, giving her reasonable room to lean out and inspect their position.

"We're on the garden side," said Ivo apologetically. "I looked. We couldn't signal to the road from here."

Sara looked down upon a depressingly blank wall. "We're only on the first floor," she said strenuously.

"The bed isn't made up," said the practical child, even more sadly. "No sheets or blankets, only that big cover. And the curtains!"

The curtains were old brocade, far too thick to knot successfully without losing half their length. And even if curtains and bedcover could be joined together, how were they to be anchored? The furniture offered no help, the bed had no posts, only a solid footboard.

Then, looking round with more optimism than she felt, she perceived for the first time in her life the true beauty and utility of Victorian furnishing. Instead of a neat little track and plastic runners, the curtains were slung by metal rings from an enormous mahogany pole, as long as a tilting lance and as thick as her wrist.

This pole, she discovered, was at least three feet longer than the width of the window frame, and the very pins by which the rings were secured to the fabric of the curtains were of solid brass, and thick as skewers.

She began almost to believe in what she was doing. She hoisted a chair across to the window, and piled several volumes of a discarded encyclopaedia on top of the chair, and climbed precariously to the swaying crest. Large curved brackets supported the curtain pole.

She had to exert all her strength, thus straining upward, to lift clear one end, and then the sudden shifting of weight sent all the rings rattling and chiming down the pole in a fine shower of dust and almost toppled her from her perch. Ivo flew to prop her up, and stretched up his puny arms to nurse the weight while she climbed down and moved her ladder to the other end. There was no need to explain anything to him, he was already ahead of her in spirit, his eyes glittering with excitement.

The pole, braced across the open window to take the weight upon those huge, solid rings, was the safest anchorage they could have found anywhere. Sara stripped off one of the heavy curtains, rings and all, and with the brass pin attached to the rings secured it firmly to the curtain which still dangled in place. She pulled at the join, first gingerly, then more confidently. A few threads strained warningly, but nothing gave.

Then Ivo dragged the tapestry cover from the bed.

Attaching that was not so easy. There were no more spare pins, and after one attempt she gave up the idea of tying it on. There remained only the two looped curtain cords. She used them to bind the thick fabrics together as tightly as she could, and hoped they wouldn't slip. The thickness of the hems would certainly help to hold them fast.

By that time she really believed in the machinery of escape. She had the awkward bundle coiled in her arms on the snowy window-sill when she checked for a moment to say: "Turn out the light!"

When it was out, the whole face of the house below her lay black and unpeopled. The Professor and his henchmen were all at the front, there was no one to observe the dangling curtains snaking down the wall and past the ground-floor window.

Past it? She was afraid that even when the whole length was paid out the end still swung only just level with the upper panes of the downstairs window. From above it was difficult to tell by how many feet it hung clear of the ground, but she was afraid it must be almost six feet.

"All right, Ivo, put the light on again. It looks a long way to drop. Do you think you can manage? Are you good at climbing?"

The snort he gave was the most contemptuous sound she had ever heard! He leaned out and peered down the wall. "Do it on my head! Plenty of snow to drop in!" He was already balanced on his stomach with both legs waving out of the window, and both hands locked fast on the pole, when he checked. "Sorry, Miss Boyne," he said, abashed. "Ladies first!"

Sara looked at the distant ground, and the absurd rope, and shut her eyes. "I'm not sure it will bear me. You go, quickly! When you get down, get into cover at once, and go down the drive to the road. You must go into the town, to the police, and tell them everything, do you understand?"

"But what about you?" His solemn eyes stared anxiously across the window-sill.

"Never mind me, I shall be all right until the police come. Go on down, quickly!"

She was so intent on seeing him safely down that she never heard the door of the room open behind her. The first she knew of it was the sudden pull of the ice-cold wind surging more strongly into the room, and a bellow of alarm and indignation that made her leap round wildly to face the doorway. One of the two gunmen, the taller, came plunging across to the window in three great strides. She saw the dark-blue gleam of the revolver barrel in his right hand, and screamed, "Quickly, Ivo!" Then the man swung his left arm and struck her out of his way, and she was flung against the wall, and slid to her knees, shaken and dazed.

It took her a moment to realize what he meant to do. In her world such things had never happened before. It took time to adjust herself to them. He was leaning well out from the open window, looking down the still jerking rope. He took hold of it for an instant as if he meant to try and haul it up again with its burden, then abandoned the idea, for Ivo was now so near to the end of it that he had only to slither down the last foot or so and let go. Instead, the right hand that held the gun steadied deliberately, pointed the barrel downwards and took aim.

She flung herself forward on her knees, gripped the spine of the *Boys Gigantic Adventure Annual* in both hands, and wrenched it from its place. The family Bible, pulled askew with it, toppled majestically to the floor, just before the falling window could strike it. Instead, it struck the leaning man across the small of the back with a crunch like that of a tree falling, just as he fired. Shot and scream, and the awful, crushed sound of the sash thudding into his ribs, all came together. Where the shot went nobody knew, but the gun flew out of his paralysed hand and dropped into the snow and one muted yell of triumph from the invisible garden eased Sara's heart once for all of any terror that Ivo had been hit.

His movements were so implicit in that joyful shout that she almost saw him drop like a hunting cat upon the fallen gun, and dive with it into the snowy shrubberies, that threshed for one moment after his vanishing, and then were still.

She stood petrified in the middle of the room, clutching the battered annual, and staring at the trapped man in fascinated horror.

He had left the door wide open. Sara turned and darted through it. Instinctively she turned towards the staircase, and scurried down it. At the foot she suffered a moment of terror, because the woman in black was standing by the hall door, peering out into the drive. No quick way out there. She drew back hastily, and backed through the nearest doorway in the shadow of the stairs, into an unlighted room. Somewhere she could hear the humming of a car.

The curtains of the room were not drawn, and her eyes, aided by the reflected glow from the snow outside, gradually grew accustomed to the darkness. The place seemed to be a little rear parlour, looking on to the same silent, bushy garden she had seen from above. She felt her way to the window, and put down the *Boys Gigantic Adventure Annual* while she quietly eased back the catch and freed the lower sash. Before she could raise it there were rapid footsteps at the door, and the rattle of the knob turning.

She had no time to think or plan. She dropped to the carpet and crept under the chenille-covered table, just as the door opened and the light was snapped on.

The neatly-shod elderly feet entering could belong to no one but Professor Brayburn. Sara cowered in her hiding-place, and watched him approach her across the room; and for one awful moment she believed he had seen her, and was coming to coax her out of cover with his gentle, regretful, almost apologetic voice.

But she saw he was only making for the window, just as she had done. When he reached it she was even able to peep from under the chenille folds, and watch him. He had a leather case under his arm, something like a flat briefcase. Her heart gave a lurch as she realized what it must be.

A folding case minus fastener, Ivo had said. Was the Professor just in the act of putting his plunder safely away somewhere in this room? It didn't look like that. He had laid it down on the edge of the table—she heard the tiny, dull sound it made on the chenille pile.

Now he had left the table and gone back to the door for a moment. He opened it a crack, and curious sounds came in. Wasn't that a car again? More a roar than a purr this time, surely, in the drive. It sounded like more than one car. Then suddenly a shot, or at least something that sounded like a shot.

She no longer understood anything that was happening, it was all a terrifying confusion. The Professor was quietly closing and locking the door.

Now he had turned his back on her, and was bending over the drawers of a writing-desk across the room. Sara reached up a timid hand, and groped along the edge of the table until she found the leather case. She lifted it gently down, and drew it into the shelter of the tablecloth with her.

The flap opened quietly, the vellum, supple as velvet, slid softly out upon the floor. She slipped the battered annual into the case, and gingerly hoisted it back on to the table. They'd reckoned it a fair exchange once, so why not a second time?

The Professor had not turned. He was busy stuffing his pockets with small, rustling bundles from the drawers of the desk. Sara retired undetected into the darkest corner under the table, hugging *The Shelvedon Chronicle* to her heart. Now it only remained to get safely out of here!

But that, it appeared, was just what the Professor was doing. She ought to have known. Why else should he be wearing a long black overcoat and a scarf? And why else should he be methodically filling his pockets with money, and quietly withdrawing into a locked back room with the *Chronicle*?

The cars, then, and of course the shot—these were wonderfully relevant. They must mean that Tom had got through to the police, that the hunt was up, and this house written off—at least by the Professor.

His underlings, apparently, were expendable. For now he was hoisting the creaking lower sash of the window, and picking up his precious leather folder, and sliding, with an agility surprising in one of his sober years and appearance, out into the snowy garden.

Sara crept from under the table, and clambered resolutely over the sill in his wake. She waded through the deep snow under the window, and followed his track into the thick darkness of some fir-trees.

Behind them, from somewhere on the other side of the house, came a few brief, staccato shouts, a shot, a confusion of sounds.

Then there were other sounds, much nearer, the snapping of a twig, trodden inadvertently under the snow, a soft, slithering fall from other branches, behind her now. She was following the Professor, but someone else was following her.

Frightened of what this might mean, she began to hurry and then, remembering how precious and how dangerous was the thing she carried, she took off the scarf, wrapped it about the unprotected leather cover, and halted for a moment to thrust it into the middle of a big, round hollybush at the side of the path.

She was not ten yards past the hollybush, and hesitating in momentary panic, unsure of her direction, when hands reached out of the obscurity behind and grasped her by the shoulders. She opened her lips to scream and her captor clapped one palm over them and hissed frantically, "Sara, darling, don't! It's me, Roger! Don't make a noise!" He withdrew his hand and she gasped in a quavering sob of relief, "Roger, thank goodness! I thought it was *them*!"

Sara clung to him, trembling with reaction, looking up at his strained and anxious face, so close to her own. "How did you get here? How did you know where we were? Where's Tom?"

"Later!" he whispered back urgently. "No time now to tell you. Come on, this way, quickly!" And he folded his arm round her, and dragged her on through the bushes, away from the house. She hung back for a moment. "But the police—I heard cars—"

"Not police cars! It's more of the gang. They're in trouble, but so are we if we run into them before the police arrive. Come on! Let's get out of here, quick!"

"And Ivo—" panted Sara, almost swept off her feet by the masterful and most reassuring arm about her waist. "He got out safely—I told him to get to the road and go on into the town—"

"I know! We'll take care of Ivo. Let's get you safely out of here first. Come on, run for it! My car's down here."

She had neither breath nor time to say a word more, or she would probably have told him what she had done with the *Chronicle*.

Round the curve of the path, shrouded in trees, there was a long, low, creosote-brown shed. Open garage doors had scooped new arcs out of the piled snow, and someone was hurriedly shovelling away the remains of the drift which had formed in front of them. With a sudden sickening downward lurch of her heart she recognized Professor Brayburn. The old man had imposed upon Roger!

He possibly thought they were all escaping from the same alien danger, carrying the rescued *Chronicle* with them. She tried to halt, but Roger dragged her onward.

"Roger, stop! The Professor—he was with them—he's in it! Don't let him—"

He must have heard, he must have understood, but he didn't stop. His grip tightened upon her arm, he drew her into the shed, and held her hard against the side of his familiar grey Jaguar. He looked over her shoulder at the Professor with a white, strained grin and said, "Insurance! The kid's evidence won't be worth much."

"Admirable!" said Professor Brayburn, giving her a brief glance bereft now of all benignity. "She'll come in handy if there's any bargaining to be done, too—but I hope it won't come to that." And he opened the rear door of the car, and slid rapidly into it, fastening a hand on her wrist to draw her after him.

She hung back, trembling, too dazed to understand what was happening.

"Roger, what are you doing? Roger, you can't—"

"Get in!" he said peremptorily, and thrust her bodily into the car. She fell against the Professor, and he took her by the arms and held her fast as she fought to reach the handle of the door. Roger got into the car, and started the engine.

Bitterly through all her rage and hurt she remembered how she had admired and envied the car's rapid getaway and breathless acceleration when he had driven her home from the Hallowe'en dance.

They lunged forward out of the garage, and crunched into the snow, turning away from the house. Down the steps, down the path, shouts echoed distantly, and small black figures came running, too late. The nearest of them, tall, long-legged, running like a hare and shouting like a maniac, was already recognizable. She screamed, "Tom!" "Tom!" But he couldn't possibly reach them—she might never see him again.

The car heeled round the curve of the narrow drive, gathering speed. Far behind, another car roared into action. Close at hand, Tom Fielding took a flying leap at the rear door, and was flung off and sent sprawling into the snow by the wing. Nothing could intercept the Jaguar now.

Between the enclosing trees the shot was flung back and forth in a loud, stammering repetition. The car swerved violently to the left, plunging like a wild horse under Roger's startled hands. Sara heard the squeal of the front tyre, the horrid scraping of wings against branches; then with a shattering crash the Jaguar flattened its nose against a tree, and settled sideways into the snow.

By the time Sara had got the door open and tumbled out into Tom's arms the police were all round them, and everything was under control. The Professor emerged unhurt into the welcoming hands of constables. From the driving seat they lifted out Roger Brecon, stunned, shaken and bruised, but without more serious injuries. And then, as though by common consent, everyone looked round for the source of the shot.

Ivo Jenkins came swaggering out of the bushes, glowing with excitement and pride, and brandishing his captured revolver in a manner which caused the policeman to exclaim in horror.

"Give that to me!" Tom said.

Ivo looked mutinous for one moment, but he was resigned to the fact that the scales are loaded against the young. "Sorry!" said Tom. "Very hard, I know, but the law's the law." And discreetly ignoring a muttered comment which had sounded to him like: "Just like a bloomin' teacher!" he added generously, "Jolly good shot, all the same, had you been practising Ivo? Congratulations!"

"I *am* a good shot," said the marksman, expanding into good-humour again. "Did you find my book? Did they have it in the car with them, Miss Boyne?"

Sara had almost forgotten the *Chronicle*. She smiled for the first time, rather wryly, as she saw the sergeant lift the leather case triumphantly out of the car, and laughed aloud at his dumbfounded face as Tom drew from it the *Boys Gigantic Adventure Annual*.

"It's all right," she said, suddenly, ceasing to laugh because of the childlike disappointment in Tom's face. "It's all right, I know where the real *Chronicle* is. I hid it myself."

Her only regret, and for personal reasons it was admittedly a vindictive one, was that Roger Brecon wasn't present to see her draw the precious bundle from its refuge and put it safely into the hands of the police.

"They wouldn't use Brecon's car or him for the snatch job, naturally," said the police sergeant as they stood in the main garage a little later. "It was far too conspicuous, and he was too well known in the district. He had to rush out here and send someone else to get the book back from the kid. An old, unobtrusive job like this of Brayburn's was much more the mark. Once the London registration was whipped off again, a big, dark, elderly car could be any one of hundreds.

"I know one thing, if it hadn't been for Buster here, with his toggle buttons, we couldn't have proved this was the right car without digging up the number plates— unless the other two or the girl choose to talk. I don't imagine they will. Organizations as big as this take care of their pensioners, as a matter of business, and besides, selling them out would be suicide. On the other hand, they're not likely to hold out anything that can shop the Professor for years, once they know he was leaving them to rot. Well, one centre of the organization's wiped out anyhow, and one of their experts immobilized, and we've got *The Shelvedon Chronicle* back.

"Well, young man, we'd better see about that telephone extension that so conveniently wouldn't work. I bet it will for us. The sooner we get in touch with your folks, and send you safely home, the better."

"I'm not tired, thank you very much," said Ivo politely, if not very truthfully. But he climbed contentedly into the back seat of Tom's car when he was told, and curled up in the corner with his marvellous memories.

"I tell you what," said the sergeant in a low voice, looking warily after him, "that one may have pulled off all his buttons in a good cause, but take it from me, I never saw a kid who more certainly had his buttons *on!*"

Ivo fell asleep on the drive home, and only opened his eyes again when Tom lifted him gently out of the car and carried him into the cottage, where Mrs. Freeman was waiting to fuss over him and put him to bed. "I shall have something for Christmas instead of the beautiful book, shan't I? Something just as nice? But I wanted that!" And his mouth drooped for a moment.

"You'll have two somethings. And you shall choose any book you like, or anything else within reason."

"Can I have a gun?" asked Ivo, waking up fully for a moment.

"No, you certainly can't!" said Tom very firmly indeed. "You've cost me ten years of my life tonight with the one you borrowed. Suppose Miss Boyne had been hurt badly when the car crashed?" But remembering what might well have happened to Sara if the car had not crashed, he was not disposed to dwell upon that.

"All right," conceded Ivo, recognizing one of those blank walls in which the young cannot yet hope to find a convenient door, "I'll have a book, if I can pick my own."

They were silent as they drove on towards Sara's home. Too much had happened too suddenly. They sat side by side in the car, and couldn't think of the right things to say.

"*Boys Gigantic Adventure Annual*, indeed!" said Tom abruptly. "I told you he didn't need any stimulants, he's an adventurer born. Took to it like a duck to water."

"Yes," said Sara in a low voice. "I was wrong about a lot of things, wasn't I?"

"I'm sorry!" Tom said hastily, "I didn't mean to say *I told you so*—really I didn't." And he added hesitantly: "Sara, I *am* sorry! I never thought Roger could be crooked. They think he must have been the one who provided all the necessary information about the burglar alarms, you know—he's on the museum committee. And the burglar got his message out by asking for a local solicitor, and then choosing him, of course. That's why he came rushing to the castle as soon as he got away from the police station. But you were earlier still, and he never had a chance to pick up the loot."

"You know what I thought, don't you?" said Sara, turning her brown, honest eyes upon him and blushing to the roots of her hair. "I thought he'd followed me because he—liked me. I was nearly as wild with you for butting in as he was. And all the time he was only exasperated with both of us for getting in the way."

"We did it jolly effectively, anyhow," said Tom, scarlet in his turn. He coasted to a stop outside Sara's front door, and the quiet, snowy darkness of the street folded round their mutual embarrassment. "Sara," said Tom huskily, "*He* may not have been following you because he—liked you—but *I* was! I've been doing it for months!"

By that time she was in his arms, without any clear idea of how she had got there, without any clear idea of anything, except that the castle clock had just begun to strike midnight, and all the bells of Shelvedon had burst into a triumphant and entirely appropriate peal of exultation. In the clamour his words were lost. He gave up the attempt to talk, and kissed her instead.

Some time later, between the loud reverberations of the bells, she heard him mumble happily, "Bless that kid! We'll adopt him for this!" Not that he was expressing a serious intention at that stage, of course. Still, Mrs. Freeman was old, and Ivo was very young, and it was at least the germ of an idea. She put it away somewhere at the back of her mind, to be pondered over later.

"Happy Christmas, dear Tom! Happy Christmas!" she murmured, and settled her check more comfortably upon his shoulder.

GUIDE TO DOOM

This way down, please. Mind your heads in the doorway, and take care on the stairs, the treads are very worn. And here we are in the courtyard again.

That concludes our tour, ladies and gentlemen. Thank you for your attention. Please keep to the paths as you cross to the gatehouse.

Yes, madam, it *is* a very little castle. Properly speaking, it's a fortified manorhouse. But it's the finest of its kind extant, and in a unique state of repair. That's what comes of being in the hands of the same family for six centuries. Yes, madam, that's how long the Chastelays have been here. And in these very walls until they built the Grace House at the far end of the grounds a hundred and fifty years ago.

The well, sir? You'll see the well as you cross the courtyard there. What was that sir? I didn't quite catch—

Not that well? The *other* one?

Now I wonder, sir, what should put it into your head that a small household like this—

The one where Mary Purcell drowned herself!

Hush, sir, please! Keep your voice down. Mr. Chastelay doesn't like that affair remembered. Yes, sir, I know, but we don't show the well-chamber. He wants it forgotten. No, I can't make exceptions, it's as much as my job's worth. Well, sir—very handsome of you, I'm sure. Were you, indeed? I can understand your being interested, of course, if you were one of the reporters who covered the case. You did say *Mary Purcell?*

Oh, no, sir, I wasn't in this job then. But I read the papers, like everybody else. Look, sir, if you'll wait just a moment, till I see this lot out—

That's better, now we can talk. I'm always glad to get the last party of the day through this old door, and drop the latch on 'em. Nice to hear the cars driving away down the avenue. Notice how the sound vanishes when they reach the turn where the wall begins. Quiet, isn't it? Soon we shall begin to hear the owls.

Now, sir, you want to see the well. The *other* well. The one where the tragedy occurred. I shouldn't do it, really. Mr. Chastelay would be very annoyed if he knew. No, sir, that's right, of course, he never need know.

Very well, sir, it's through here—through the great hall. After you, sir! There, fancy you turning in the right direction without being told! Mind your step, the floor's very uneven in places.

179

You mustn't be surprised at Mr. Chastelay not wanting that old affair dragged up again. It very nearly wrecked his life. Everybody had him down for the lover, the fellow who drove her to it. Her being his farm foreman's wife, you see, and him having been noticeably took with her, and on familiar terms with the two of them. I daresay it was only natural people should think it was him. If he could have run the rumors to their source he'd have sued, but he never could. For a year it was touch and go whether his wife divorced him, but they're over it now. After all, it's ten years and more. Nobody wants to start the tongues wagging again. No, sir, I'm sure *you* don't, or I wouldn't be doing this.

She was very beautiful, they say, this Mrs. Purcell. Very young, only twenty-one, and fair. They say the photographs didn't do justice to her coloring. Wonderful blue eyes, I believe. *Green*, were they, you say? Not blue? Well, I wouldn't argue with you, sir, you were reporting the affair, you should know. Watch out for the bottom step here, it's worn very hollow. *Green* eyes!

Oh, no, sir, I wouldn't dispute it. Wonderful trained memory you have.

Well, at any rate she was young and very pretty, and I daresay a bit simple and innocent, too, brought up country-style as she was. She was the daughter of one of the gardeners. I don't suppose you ever met him? No, he wouldn't have anything to say to the press, would he? He had a stroke afterwards, and Mr. Chastelay pensioned him off with a light job around the place. But that's neither here nor there. Mind the step into the stone gallery. Here, let me put on the lights.

Yes, gives you quite a turn, doesn't he, that halberdier standing there, with his funny-shaped knife on a stick? I keep him all burnished up like that specially, it gives the kids a thrill. Tell you the truth, when I've been going round here at night, looking up and seeing all's fast after the folks have gone, I've often borrowed his halberd and carried it round with me, just for company, like. It gets pretty eerie here after dark. Makes me feel like one of the ghosts myself, trailing this thing. If it's all the same to you, sir, I'll take it along with us now.

They put a heavy cover on the well after that fatality. There's a ring in the middle, and the haft of the halberd makes a very handy lever. You'd like to look inside, I dare say. There are iron rungs down the shaft like a ladder. Her husband went down, you know, and got her out. More than most of us would like to do, but then, he felt responsible, I suppose, poor soul.

Where's her husband now? Did you never hear, sir? He cracked up, poor lad, and they had to put him away. He's still locked up.

The way I heard it, this affair of hers had been going on some time, and when she found she was expecting a child it fairly knocked her over. Made her turn and look again at what she'd let this fellow persuade her into. She went to him, and asked what to do.

And he told her not to be a fool, why should she want to do anything? She'd got a husband, hadn't she? All she had to do was hold her tongue. But he could see she didn't see it that way; she felt bad about her husband and couldn't let him father the child with his eyes shut. She was hating herself, and wanting to be honest, and wanting her lover to stand by her even in that. And wanting her husband back on the old terms, too, because I don't suppose she ever really stopped loving him, she only lost sight of him in the excitement. So this fellow put her off and said they'd talk about it again, after they'd considered it.

And he lit out the next day for I don't know where, and left her.

No, sir, you're right, of course, I wasn't in this job then, how would I know? Just reconstructing in my own mind. Maybe it wasn't like that. No, as you say, if it was Mr. Chastelay he didn't light out for anywhere; he stayed right here and got the muck thrown at him. But a lot of people think now it wasn't him, after all.

Anyhow, she went to her husband and told him the truth. All but the name, she never told anyone that. Very nearly killed him. I shouldn't wonder, if he was daft about her, as they say. He didn't rave or anything, just turned his back on her and went away. And when she followed him, crying, he couldn't bear it; he turned round and hit her.

Yes, sir, a very vivid imagination I've got, I don't deny it. So would you have if you lived in this place alone. I fairly see 'em walking, nights.

And the way I see it, she was too young and inexperienced to understand that you don't hit out at somebody who means nothing to you. She thought he was finished with her. And if he was gone, everything was gone. She didn't know enough to wait, and bear it, and hope. She ran along here, crying, and jumped into the well.

Five minutes, and he was running after her. By that time it was too late. When he got her out she was dead. Her fair hair all smeared with scum, and slime in her beautiful green eyes.

Right here, where we're standing. There's the cover they've put over it, since. Good and heavy, so's nobody can shift it easily. But if you'll stand back, sir, and let me get some leverage on this halberd—

There you are. Nobody knows quite how deep. Let's have a little more light, shall we? There, now you can see better. A girl would have to be at the end of her tether, wouldn't she, to go that way?

My sweet Mary, my little lamb!

No, sir, I didn't say anything. I thought *you* were about to speak.

What am I doing, sir? Just turning the key in the lock. Just seeing how smoothly it works. A lot of keys and wards to look after, you know, and Mr. Chastelay is very particular about this room being kept closed. No one's been here for more than three years, except me. Not until tonight. I don't suppose there'll be anyone else for the next three years, either, and if they did they wouldn't lift the well-cover. I do all the cleaning myself, you see. I'm a great one for keeping things in perfect order. Look at this halberd, now. Sharp as a butcher's knife. Here, look.

Oh, sorry, sir, did I prick you?

Mad, sir? No, sir, not me. That was her husband, remember? They put him away. All that happened to me was a stroke, and it didn't affect my co-ordination. Pensioned off with a light job I may be, but you'd be surprised how strong I still am. So I shouldn't try to rush me, if I were you, sir. It wouldn't do you any good.

It's always a mistake to know too much, sir. *Mary* Purcell, you said. Alice was her first name, the one all the papers used, did you know that? It was only her family and her intimates who called her Mary. And then, *how did you know her eyes were green?* They were shut fast enough before ever the press got near her. But her lover knew.

Yes, sir, I know you now, you were the young man who was staying with the Lovells at the farm that summer. We must have a talk about Mary. Sorry poor Tim Purcell couldn't be here to make up the party; it might have done him a power of good. But we'll spare him a thought, won't we? Now, while there's time.

Funny, isn't it? Providential, when you come to think, you walking out here from the farm, without a car or anything. And I'd stake this key and this halberd—I don't have to tell you how much I value them, do I?—that you never told a soul where you were going.

But you couldn't keep away, could you?

And I don't suppose either you or I will ever really know why you came—never dreaming you'd meet Mary's father. So I can believe it was because I've wanted you so much—*so much!*

Oh, I shouldn't scream like that, if I was you, sir, you'll only do yourself an injury. And nobody'll hear you, you know. There's nobody within half a mile but you and me. And the walls are very thick. Very thick.

THE GOLDEN GIRL

"Shakespeare," said the Purser moodily, over his second beer after the theater, "everything's Shakespeare this year, of course. He did his share of pinching, though. That 'my ducats and my daughter' stuff—there was another fellow did that better, I remember seeing the play once. *The Jew of Malta*, it was called, and Marlowe was the author's name. 'O gold, O girl! Oh, beauty! Oh, my bliss!' Seeing *The Merchant* tonight made me think of it again. And of a real-life case I once knew—only she wasn't his daughter. Not that one.

"I was a raw junior then, under old McLean on the *Aurea*, oh, ten years ago it would be. I dream about it sometimes, but not so often, now. We were sailing from Liverpool for Bombay, my third trip, and this couple came aboard right in the rush before we sailed, and still you couldn't miss seeing them. It was this girl. She was so blindingly pretty, for one thing, corn-gold hair, smoky eyes. And then, so touchingly pregnant. You know, these loose smocks, and then the very slender arms on the ponderous body. And the careful, faintly clumsy gait, balancing the weight. She went slowly on the companionways, and held on fast to the rail. You could feel every male in sight holding himself back from rushing to help her.

"They were booked through to Bombay, probably going out to some expert advisory job. The husband, he was older, probably forty to the girl's twenty-two or so, but he had something, too. The women got their heads together over him before we were an hour out. Big, good-looking fellow, dark and quiet and experienced-looking, hovering round his missus with such solicitude all the other wives on board turned green with envy. A reformed rake, they had him down for. Don Juan after he met the one girl. Try and get him away from her! Plenty of them did try before we neared Bombay. But no, as far as he was concerned there was no woman aboard but his wife. He hung over her with that broody look, every day of the seventeen.

"Two days out we had a boat drill. We always did, though we never expected more than half of 'em to show up, not at that time of year, with the sea acting the way it so often does act. I was the officer on their boat, and I took care to show up near their cabin when the first siren sounded. He wasn't there, he'd gone to get her some library books. I had the pleasure of helping her on with her life-jacket. Like most women, she hadn't a clue how to put the thing on, instructions or no instructions.

"She didn't seem so big, under that loose tunic of hers. Just a bit of a thing she must have been, normal times, I thought. And the way she thanked me, I'd have jumped overboard for her. Yes, she felt fine, yes, she'd go up on deck and report properly, like the others. And she did, too. Like a kid playing a game, the gayest person around. Her husband soon came on the run, wild to snatch her away from the rest of us and look after her himself. There wasn't a man who didn't grudge him his rights.

"Like that, all the way. At our film-shows they held hands in a quiet corner. The women reckoned they hadn't been married all that long, and he hadn't got over the happy shock of getting her, and couldn't quite believe in his luck.

"We dropped about half our passengers off at Karachi, and made across for Bombay a bit subdued and quiet, as usual. And that night, round about midnight, the fire broke out.

"There was a ball going on at the time, we usually staged something gay to cushion the partings. So we never did find out how it started. All I know is, suddenly there were alarm sirens below decks, and unaccountably none up in the saloons and bars, and the music went on, and up on the boat-deck there were still people in the pool long after there was near-panic below. Communications went west because the whole loud-speaker system collapsed. And before you could say 'knife' there was smoke everywhere, and in ten minutes more, chaos. Nobody could give orders beyond the reach of his own voice. And once people got frightened, the range of a voice wasn't much.

"It wasn't a panic. They were a pretty decent lot, they'd have been all right if there'd been any way of telling 'em all just what to do. But there wasn't, except in small groups, and there weren't enough of us to go round the groups. And sometimes confusion and bewilderment can produce just the same results as panic. The best of 'em, the ones who're game and try to do something, do the wrong things for want of instructions. And the others get in their way and ours. What can you do? Thank God it was dead calm, and two or three ships had got our calls, and were moving in to pick up the pieces.

"It had to come to that. The fire spread like mad, and she began to list. We shoved everybody up on deck, got 'em into their life-jackets, and started getting the boats lowered. The din was something I'll never forget. Nobody was screaming, but everybody was shouting.

"I was clawing my way along B Deck in the smoke, opening cabin doors and fielding the stragglers, with one of the women on one arm, and a Goanese steward towing two more behind me. I shoved open the door of 56, and there was our golden girl, clinging to her husband, her eyes like big gray lakes of stupefied terror. They were fumbling her life-jacket awkwardly between them. His lay on the lower berth. I bellowed at him furiously to get the thing on her, quick, and got hold of her with my free hand as soon as he'd bundled her into it. She toiled up the companionways after me, panting, her gait as laboured and painful as an old woman's. I even had time to bleed a little, inwardly, at the thought of hustling her, but man, we were in a hurry. The *Aurea* was lurching under us, shuddering on the dead-calm sea. She wasn't going to last all that much longer.

"Well, I got them up to their boat, into that pandemonium on deck. There was a westbound tanker standing off by then, with boats out for us, searchlights quivering along the black water. And then the deck heeled under us and started to stand erect, sliding us down towards the rail. The women screamed and clung to whatever was nearest. I thought we were going, so did we all, but she partly righted herself again. But the boat slid down by the stern, and jammed, and I knew we were never going to launch that one. Some of the others were safely away already, standing well off and waiting to salvage what they could when we foundered. Other boats were moving in from the tanker off in the dark there. One had come close, and was hailing us. I bellowed back at them, and they nosed in nearer. I grabbed hold of the golden girl. Two lives—you know how it is!

"Her husband yelled at me like a fury, and held on to her like grim death, screaming hoarsely something I couldn't even distinguish in the general hell. There wasn't time for convincing anybody of anything. I hooked my palm under his chin and shoved him off hard, and his grip of her broke. I picked her up in my arms and swung her over the rail, and dropped her gently and carefully into what I knew was the safest place for her, into the sea a few yards from the bows of the hovering boat. The officer I'd hailed was already leaning over to reach for her.

"And two things happened that I still dream about now and then, when I'm out of sorts. Her husband let out a shriek like a damned soul, a sound I'll never forget, and tore his way screaming to the rail, and hurled himself over it. And the girl, the golden girl—my God, she hit the water and she sank like a stone!

"Her face was turned up, mute, staring at me with those lost, terrified eyes, right to the second when the water closed over it. She vanished, and she didn't reappear.

"I was a whole minute grasping it. Can you imagine that? Then I dived after her, down and down, hunting for her, time after time after time, until they hauled me aboard the boat by force. I didn't find her. But once, I think, I glimpsed him, deep down there plunging as I was plunging. I seem to remember a face with hair torn erect, frantic eyes, mouth howling soundlessly. Her name? It would be nice to think I only imagined it. Better still to forget it. I can't do either.

"There was nothing left of him, either, by that time, except his life-jacket washing about aimlessly, where he'd torn it off and discarded it to dive for her. We never should have found either of them, if the vortex as the *Aurea* finally went under hadn't churned up everything from the depths and flung it to the rim of the area. The tanker still had boats out, and one of them fielded the girl's body, by a sheer fluke, as it showed for an instant before plunging again. We never did find him.

"It was finding her, and what we found on her, that brought Interpol into the story.

"She wasn't his wife, of course. She was a photographer's model and small-part actress he'd picked up at some club. She wasn't pregnant, either. Only the way he felt about her, I'll swear, was no fake. He'd never used her before. All his previous cargoes had been smuggled in by air, with other carriers, and this last one was to have been an easy stake, a pleasure cruise with a nice pay-off at the end of it. It was very profitable business. I think they weren't coming back.

"All the stuff she'd brought aboard in the padded bodice under her maternity smock they'd hidden, once the initial boat-drill was safely over, in that life-jacket of hers. A daft place? Well, look, I'll tell you something. Nobody ever believes they're going to need those damn' life-jackets in earnest—nobody. It wasn't so daft a place. And she could make herself comfortable until she had to resume the burden at Bombay, and carry it tenderly ashore and through the Customs. Only they left the job of transferring it again until the last night, and the fire caught them unprepared.

"Of course, he could have worn the thing himself and given her the other. Maybe he would have, if I hadn't barged in on them and forced his hand. Or maybe he wouldn't. She was, after all, a professional doing a job for him. Once in the boat she'd have been safe enough. And whatever followed, it was she, with her disarming beauty and her interesting condition, who would have had the special V.I.P. treatment, and the best chance of retrieving their stake, and getting it safely into India.

"I still wonder which he was really diving for, the girl, or the thirty pounds' weight of thin bar gold that drowned her."

HOSTILE WITNESS

Halloran found her huddled in one of the deep chairs near the refreshment bar of London Airport, gazing with the immense calm of desperation at the dirty yellow drop-cloths of fog sealing the vast windows. As he crossed the glossy floor he marked again the translucent clarity of her abrupt cheekbones under the falling light, the lovely, pallid brow defaced by those urchin fringes of black hair, the soft, dispirited mouth drooping in resignation; and again he suffered that stab of recollection never quite recaptured, as though life and death hung upon remembering where he had seen her before, or what other face this sad little face recalled.

She looked up when he halted in front of her, but she did not speak.

"Mrs. Foyle—"

It was not her name, and she knew that he knew it. The focus of her eyes shortened, fixing in hopeless acceptance upon him.

"Who told you?"

"No one, this time. You've been watched ever since the subpoena was served on you. I felt you might try to run. Believe me, it wouldn't have done him or you any good."

"No," she said, in the same dead voice, "I don't suppose it would. I don't suppose anything could, now."

"I'm taking you home. You heard the announcement—there'll be no more flying tonight. Better give me your ticket—I'll see to it for you."

She surrendered it mutely, the flimsy folder that should have taken her east to Vienna, eight hundred miles from the court where this man proposed to put Danny Foyle in the dock on a charge of murder, and her into the witness-box to clinch his conviction. She walked by Halloran's side like a sleepwalker, his hand at her elbow, out into the pale, smothering, darkness.

"Who told you I wasn't his wife?" Her voice came to him muffled by the fog. "Lois? It must have been! I never told anyone else. And he wouldn't. She claimed to be my friend! She was the only one who ever broke me down."

"She wanted to do what was right," Halloran said, holding open the door of the car.

"She wanted to hurt me. And to kill him, if she couldn't have him. What has all this to do with right and wrong?"

"A man was killed," he reminded her, "at Campiano's."

187

"Not by Danny." And she added, with a sort of distant wonder, "Do you call Campiano a man?"

"Legally, I have to."

The fog-lights burned yellowly overhead like floating sun-flowers, the car's fog-lamp groped gingerly along the tarmac, painful yard by yard.

She sat silent and still beside him. He dared not take his straining eyes from the yellow finger of the fog-lamp for an instant to cast a glance at her, yet he saw her clearly every moment of the time. Professional name, Jenny Black. Age, about twenty-four. Singer with Danny Foyle's band at Campiano's Club. In private life Mrs. Danny Foyle. Only she wasn't. She wore a wedding ring, they lived together in exemplary respectability, but alas, they weren't married. And just once in her life she'd allowed an intimate friend to learn her secret.

It would never have occurred to Halloran to investigate that alleged marriage, not even for the purpose of a murder case, so permanent, so domestic did their association appear. He had been resigned to being unable to put Jenny Black in the witness box to testify, willing or unwilling, against the man who was regarded as her husband; and that had meant being resigned to the fact that he wouldn't get a conviction. Without the gun, and without an opportunity of extracting from her what she certainly knew, the case was bound to fail.

And in a way he hadn't really minded. Campiano was no loss, his removal from the world had made it safer for a great many people, and sweeter for all, while Danny Foyle was an inoffensive soul who wouldn't have harmed anyone if his hand hadn't been forced. All the same, Halloran's professional pride hated an inconclusive case, and his career was dear to him. So what he had felt, when Lois Bell telephoned him with the tip to check up on the marriage, had been 90 per cent excitement and hope, and only ten per cent pity and regret for these two hapless people.

"Why couldn't you leave me alone?" she said. But she expected no answer. And in a moment: "You can't convict him."

"Without you, no, the charge would never stick. That's honest."

"If you can't hang him without my help," she said, "you'll certainly never hang him with it."

"But he did it. Didn't he?"

"No," she said, too tired even to be emphatic about it any more.

"Why did you two never marry? Has Danny a wife living? Or have you a husband?"

No answer.

"Listen to me. I'm not trying to persecute either of you. I'd prefer to help you. On the face of it this is capital murder, but if the circumstances are as I think they are the charge might very well be reduced. We know what Campiano was, even if he did manage to stay out of our hands. We know all about Campiano's profitable sidelines. He specialized in drugs and girls and he required every one of his employees to be safely tied into one of those rackets. And I'm willing to tell you exactly what I think happened that night. You and Danny haven't had a successful season, the competition's tough in the dance-band world unless you're outstanding, and Danny wasn't more than a competent performer. You couldn't afford to turn down the engagement at the club. But you wouldn't fall into line with Campiano. Danny wouldn't peddle either dope or you.

"Campiano didn't like that. So he began to hunt round for a hold over Danny. And unluckily he found one. Everybody at the club said how pleased he was with himself that night. As he clapped Danny on the shoulder between numbers, and told him to come along to his back room in the break. He had something to talk over with him, something very funny. And Danny went.

"When the head waiter went in to take Campiano a personal message, ten minutes later, Campiano was dead on the carpet, with a bullet through him at point-blank range, and Danny was rummaging among the papers of his desk, to make sure he'd left no record in writing."

"Danny told you the truth," said the tired voice beside his shoulder. "He was lying there dead when Danny went into the room. Someone else got there before him."

"So Danny says. But no one else was seen to enter the room, from the time that Campiano went back there after his tour of the tables."

"If Danny shot him, what became of the gun? Why wasn't it still in the room somewhere? Or outside the window, or somewhere—not far—it could have been thrown?"

"That's what I should be asking you," said Halloran. He stole a glance at her pale profile. "You do see, don't you, that if Campiano was trying to blackmail Danny into joining his rackets, and Danny shot him on the spur of the moment with his own gun, then the more fully you tell your story the better chance he'll have?

"You'd much better tell me everything, Jenny. You know, because you were uneasy, and you followed Danny to the door, and listened. Maybe you even looked inside. Maybe you saw the shot fired. Almost certainly you heard what passed and heard Campiano fall. Lois saw you standing hesitating outside the door. She says you hurried away when you saw her."

Her lashes lay on her cheeks, curiously light and golden to go with such black hair. "Tell me everything, and I'll do what I can to help."

"Where are you taking me?" she asked. "To the police station?"

"No, no one but myself knows anything about this. If you care to talk to me tonight, alone, it will be off the record. If you want to make an official statement afterwards, you can. I want you to have time to consider what you're doing."

"I have considered," she said. "Take me somewhere quiet, somewhere I can't be seen."

He threaded slow, cautious traffic toward his own bachelor flat. "Here, through the alley. We'll have to walk the last bit. Hullo, it's turning to rain."

She fished out a pale square of chiffon from her bag, and twisted it about her head, knotting it loosely upon her neck. She walked beside him silently through the silent alley and up the narrow, cream-colored stairway into his flat. He gave her a drink, but she only sat back in the wing chair, nursing it in her slender hands, not looking anywhere except inwardly at the misery of her life.

"What did Danny do with the gun?"

"He never had a gun," she said.

"Very well, let's begin somewhere else. What was it Campiano had discovered? What was it he proposed holding over you two?"

The question was hardly out of his mouth before he saw the answer. He saw it as a sudden explosion of pale golden light, as she turned her head away from him with a movement of inexpressible pain, and the pale brow, its unbecoming black bangs all thrust away under the yellow scarf, shone in the lamplight clear as pearl, and the knotted ends of primrose-colored chiffon coiled softly on her neck, like a knot of fair silken hair. Like the hair she had dyed and mangled into that waif's coiffure of hers.

He felt his heart contract, remembering at last. One photograph full-face, one in profile. The sad, reserved eyes, the straight, shining hair, long and fine, the tired, lofty brow. Now he knew her! Simone Périchon, age twenty-three, vanished from Lille in France eighteen months ago. Wanted on suspicion of murdering her husband, Antoine Périchon, an unpleasant brute who made his living out of girls. Where had Danny Foyle's band been on tour that summer? Was Lille on his route? How had he got her into England? Not that it mattered. Everything was clear now. Why those two had never dared to marry, what Campiano had discovered and flourished over Danny's head like a whip!

"I see!" he said, on a long, sighing breath. "Simone Périchon!"

She showed no surprise, no alarm; she had expected nothing but discovery in the end, he felt sure.

"I didn't kill Antoine," she said wearily. Her hands looked so unaware of the glass they held that he got up and gently took it. He went back to his chair and waited. She was feeling brokenly in her handbag, groping for a handkerchief.

"Why couldn't you all have left me alone? I didn't kill Antoine. Not Antoine. If

only you'd all let me alone I should never have killed anyone—I never wanted
to—"

He started incredulously forward out of his chair. Not a handkerchief. A gun.
Campiano's gun! The long hand that leveled it was not trembling now.

"Jenny—!"

"—not even Campiano—certainly not you—I *liked* you!"

Springing toward her, far too late, he saw with the glittering clarity of all final
things how the frozen mask of despair wept great, silent tears upon the delicate
hand as she pulled the trigger.

WITH REGRETS

He arrived in Delhi in a millionaire's tantrum and a blacksmith's muck-sweat. If you insist on seeing cherry-blossom time in Japan you must expect to find India already uncomfortably hot afterward, but he hadn't expected it. Worse, the travel agency had booked him in at the Victoria, though he had expressly asked (far too late) for the Ashoka, which, as everyone knows, is *the* hotel. Balked of a room there, he took a perverse pleasure in making the Ashoka his first port of call at tea time to see what he was missing.

He didn't, however, miss the girl. In spite of the air-conditioning, she was the only cool-looking creature in sight, an English blonde, tall and willowy and whimsical. English blondes are of two kinds, the dehydrated and the luminous. She was the luminous kind. Great blue-gray eyes took in the not unpresentable newcomer who was taking her in, recognized him as her own sort in a strange land and demonstrated gratitude for him. She was drinking tea alone. That shouldn't happen to a luminous blonde anywhere. He put that right with his customary *savoir-faire*.

"I hope you're feeling kind. I'm new, hot and desperate. For God's sake, talk to me! I'm harmless, I promise!"

That was the last thing a lot of husbands would have called him, but she couldn't know that. She laughed, and she talked to him. He'd got her number first time.

"You're not staying here, are you? I should have noticed—"

"No such luck!" he said.

"Oh, don't sound like that," she protested. "I'm really not this rich, either."

He, in point of fact, was quite disgustingly rich, but he took care not to say so. She was more likely to confide if he didn't.

"It's just that my husband's firm thinks a first-class façade advisable. After all, it isn't for long." Engineering goods, she explained, especially machine-tool plants. Supposing the Ashoka to be necessary, the firm also felt their representative should work about twenty hours a day and get out a few days earlier.

So that was why she was alone. This might add up to something. He settled down to make the figures come out his way. She was the best thing in sight, and she'd be well worth it.

"Why shouldn't we see Delhi together? I bet the firm doesn't allow for the entertainment of wives."

The firm didn't. And when he pressed a little, she looked right back at him, thoughtfully, and said, "Mr. Lansdowne, maybe I should say right away that I love my husband."

"Sure!" he said, wide-eyed. "I've got a wife in California, and I love her, too. I'm proving it. I've brought her six very nice sapphires from Ceylon, worth a packet. But I'd still be grateful for a friend's company round the town tomorrow, if you're free."

She smiled, almost unwillingly, and then frowned. "Sapphires? You can't have declared them, surely? You can't import them into India, you know. They'd make you turn them in to the authorities until you leave, and all manner of fuss and red tape."

"I know, I was warned. Don't worry, they're in my keeping, and there they stay."

"If they find out, they'll raise hell. Most likely they'll confiscate the things, or make you pay twice the value. Keep them on you, whatever you do."

"Uh-uh! Not after what I've heard about the pickpockets in these parts. They lift the gold out of your teeth. Don't worry, I've got a safe place; nobody's going to knock off those beauties. Now, how about tomorrow?"

She hesitated. "Well—" He knew he'd hooked her. "But don't call for me here. He—I'd rather he thought I was with a woman. He can be—rather jealous."

They met, as they did throughout, at a little café in Connaught Place and did the town together. Belinda was fun. Husband Bill, it gradually emerged, was no fun at all. But at least, in his preoccupied way, he was rather pleased that some mythical Indian acquaintance, contacted under the driers at Roy and James', should be keeping his wife company. He worried about leaving her alone so much. A harassed type he sounded, heading for ulcers.

It turned out, about the third day, that she had a dream of seeing Agra.

"But you have to see the Taj Mahal by moonlight," he said insinuatingly. He was making pretty smooth running by then, not rushing it."

"Sorry, no dice! It would have to be a day trip. But even for the Taj by daylight I'd give—"

"Go on! What would you give? We might make a deal."

They were together in his room at the Victoria, for the first time, and soon she would almost certainly decide she had to go, because Bill would be home soon. Still, discretion is a virtue; he didn't want any trouble, either.

"Tell me more. Any other dreams?"

"Well—now that you've shown me those sapphires, I admit I do dream of owning just one good stone, some day." She smiled at him out of the cushions of the couch, her eyes closed.

"You dream it, we arrange it. I'll have one mounted for you, if you're good."
Her eyes opened wide. "Now look here, I didn't mean that. I'm *not*—"
He kissed her, with just the right impulsive lightness.

"I know! Forget it! Agra tomorrow—it's only a hundred thirty miles or so.
Eight o'clock? Will he be out by then?"

"Yes, he's got an early appointment somewhere. And a business lunch, too.
Do you think we honestly could? Could we be back by six? I'd give almost
anything to see it. But look, Bernie, this is on the level. I told you, I—"

"I know! You love your husband. I love my wife, too. Eight o'clock, honey,
usual place."

He took her to Agra. The hired car wasn't at all bad, the road was surprisingly
good on the whole, the monkeys were fun, and things were going his way. The
temple spires of Mathura winked at them distantly between the bumps as they
crossed the many railway sidings. Twice they were flung abruptly off the road
into the dusty furrows of the fields for some hundred yards or so to by-pass road
works, and on emerging were saluted by a charming sign in English, saying
blushingly: INCONVENIENCE REGRETTED. Belinda loved that. The second time it
happened she remarked that all that was wanting was yet another modest sign
some twenty yards on, saying: THANK YOU! And the very next minute, there it was
beside the road, in meek, small letters: THANK YOU!

It happened twice more after that, and became their special joke. They laughed
all the way to Agra. They were still laughing as they passed through the shadow
of the pink and white gatehouse, until the sudden planned, devastating vision of
the Taj, a disembodied pearl afloat in a pale and radiant sky, took their breath
away.

It was a good day. One more like it, he thought contentedly as he drove her
back in the afternoon, and he was home and dry. The Taj is calculated to open
even the most adamant heart to love. A pity they couldn't go to Fatehpur Sikri,
but she insisted nervously that she must be back ahead of Bill, and he couldn't
afford to have anything go wrong now.

"About tomorrow? What time shall we meet?"

"I don't know yet. After this business today he may have a lot of paper work
in the morning. Leave it to me. I'll get in touch with you."

"You won't forget, will you?"

She smiled, and said, how could she? Her voice was soft and content. "You'll
hear from me, I promise. Maybe even tonight."

"Time's getting a little short. How about it, if I drop you off in the Diplomatic
Enclave, just behind the hotel? Nobody'll notice us there."

So she slipped into the Ashoka from her rear, and he drove off to the Victoria in high spirits, pondering the excellence of his own technique. I love my husband! So what, my dear? She hadn't even been very hard to get.

When he had bathed and dressed he unlocked the smallest of his three hide cases to take a quick look at his treasures. Partly for pure pleasure, partly because he just might have one mounted in a clip for Belinda.

One of the blocks that strengthened the corners of the case was made to slide out. He withdrew the stopper from its under end, and tipped the little triangular phial over his palm.

Nothing happened. Nothing slid, nothing rolled, nothing appeared. Furiously, he shook the container. It was empty, the sapphires gone.

He let out a howl of muted rage and dismay, and with the property owner's simple instinct leaped upon the telephone. His mouth was wide open, his lungs filled to capacity, to bellow his loss into the desk clerk's ears, when he knew he was trapped.

He couldn't report it! He couldn't yell for help, he couldn't demand any heads on platters. He hadn't declared those stones, and it's illegal to import them. Most likely they'll confiscate the things, if they find out, she'd said. They might even charge him with smuggling them.

The lovely Belinda, of course! Who else even knew he'd got them, let alone where he kept them? To whom else had he been fool enough to show them? And he'd let her lure him away from here for a whole day, while the invisible, the accommodating Bill—

And he couldn't do a thing about it! All that money down the drain, and he had to keep his mouth shut. Sapphires, Mr. Lansdowne? Don't you know that's an offense? Why didn't you declare them? Whatever he said, he wouldn't be believed. Too many people were smuggling too much of everything valuable into India.

"Did you wish something, sar? Can I help you?" The clerk chanted patiently in his ear.

He swallowed the bitterest outburst of his life, and spat out instead: "Tell room service to send me up some beer, and make it snappy."

"Beer? Sar, I regret it is impossible! On Tuesdays and Fridays no alcohol is served in Delhi. Sar, today is Tuesday. I am sorry!"

Not even a drink! He loosed all his frustration in one blistering oath, and slammed down the telephone. Well, if he couldn't call the police, at least he could take action himself. He charged out of the Victoria and drove straight to the Ashoka, storming up to the reception desk.

"Allardyce? We've no one of that name staying here, sir, I'm sorry. No, certainly not during the last few weeks. *Quite* sure, sir!"

"A very pretty English lady—Did an English couple check out this evening? *Any* name?"

No English couple had. And what could be easier than to walk in one door, pass through the crowded lounge and walk out the main entrance, where taxis are always on hand? Bill's mythical jealousy had been enough to warn him off from ever trying to pick her up here, after that first accidental meeting. No use looking for them through the machine-tool firms, either. That was moonshine, like the rest. Every road closed before him. He'd been taken, and that's that.

It dawned upon him, as he slunk miserably back to his own hotel, that she had gone out of her way to give him fair warning. She *did* love that husband of hers! Hadn't she just helped him to a modest fortune?

She kept her promises, too, he found. When he retrieved his key the clerk handed him a note.

"A lady left it for you, sir, by hand, only about five minutes after you went out."

The pale blue envelope contained only a plain white card. On one side of it, in thick black capitals, it read:

INCONVENIENCE REGRETTED.

On the other, in smaller letters:

THANK YOU!

MAIDEN GARLAND

I never wanted to tell this story, and I hope nobody ever reads it, but I know only one way of getting rid of it, and this is it. I used to write a bit, even poetry sometimes, before I married Molly and came and settled in here as the local copper. She didn't want to leave these parts—for some reason those who stick it here until past twenty-five never do—and I wanted her. And here we still are, and shall be, world without end. But there are worse places. And anything I write that isn't an official report can always be burned. There are a lot of ways of exorcising the past, all effective, given the goodwill.

The thing is, they never should have sent a girl like Kirsten to a village like this. It's like giving barbaric children a nuclear warhead to play with. Maybe you don't know what sort of place a twentieth-century village can be. All up the western fringes you'll find us, very much in the modern world but not of it, sometimes in contact, sometimes isolated, every house complete with refrigerator and television, up to the minute with Bingo and pop and everything that's going, a mini-skirt on every girl, winter or summer, and the back-log of the pre-Christian calendar still setting light to the spring and autumn equinoxes for us, whatever time we observe. You think such places can't survive? You haven't been following the activities of British Rail, have you? They closed the only line that came within trekking distance of us seven years ago, ripping up the rails and selling off the stations, blasting the bridges and tarring over the level crossings, so that nobody should even be able to shove a wheelbarrow along the tracks to us when things got rough. The very winter they sealed us off, things did get rough. Every winter since we've been cut off for days at a time, sometimes as long as a week.

We back on to the Welsh hills, a moderate snow-fall and we're on our own. Only helicopters can reach us. Twice since then they've had to use them to drop supplies. In a small country! But the TV still brings us the Eurovision song contest! We know what's going on, we never miss a trick. We receive but we can't transmit. That's the world we've got, God help us, sophisticated to the nth degree, and half the time forgotten of God and man.

But they gave us a couple of small factories, so that we could keep a handful of the young. The rest leave us as soon as they finish school, and never come back. We inter-marry because we haven't much choice. We develop a very distinct type, square brown men and thick-hipped, thick-legged, spry dark women, sharp-eyed, sharp-tongued, prolific and self-contained, of strong character and intolerant habit.

But we do also develop various new ties with the world. The antiques business spreads like a disease, picking off our scattered country houses. The thing is to buy a small period place to live in, deploy your wares around the reception rooms among your own furniture, and wait for the weekend wanderers to find their way in. We had a couple called Landon who had taken Cleave Court, stuck a flamboyant notice at the gate, and filled the place with fashionable Victorian junk. They came from town, and fitted in nowhere; and because they had a two-year-old infant they brought with them a Norwegian *au pair* girl. They were no sensation to us, not even the foreign girl, we'd seen everything.

Everything except Kirsten Sivertsen.

We'd seen exotics, too, of course, the summer migrants came through in all shapes and sizes and kinds, but they only came and passed. This one stayed. Even if we'd had one or two leggy blondes of our own she might have been less obtrusive. But I doubt it. It wasn't the fairness or the length of her, or the sea-blue eyes or the straight, wide stare and the open smile that made her dynamite. It was something inside that wore all these as a dress.

Kirsten was nineteen, and ripe as the ripe apricot she resembled when she arrived in the summer, all golden tan and startling mermaid eyes and pale, bright primrose hair. She was taller than most of our village males, high-breasted and fearless and friendly, with an Amazon's walk that showed off those long, long legs of hers, and her shapely and sinewy ankles and feet. You watched her stride past, and your own knees turned to water. And when you looked straight into the sea-blue stare—and if ever you spoke to her you had to, for she could and would have looked a tiger innocently in the eye—you drowned.

So that was what the Landons brought into Cleave Court with them, and them as ornery a pair as you could find in an ephemeral and slightly shady business. He was a townie to his finger-ends, playing at being a sort of sub-squire with commercial connections, a big fleshy bloke with thinning black hair and a moist eye. When I first saw him I wondered how his wife ever came to hire a girl like Kirsten; but I think it was her sheer bland vanity that made her blind to the possibilities. She was a blonde, too, I suppose not yet thirty, but a string-coloured blonde with no sap in her, everything about her slightly withered, though to give her her due she had good enough features, and was the type to look much the same at sixty as she did at thirty. But alongside Kirsten she vanished; it was as simple as that.

A novelty is a novelty, and at first the whole village took up Kirsten and made itself attentive to her, the women ahead of the men. They asked her to join this and that, they invited her to tea; and Kirsten responded, up to a point—the point where she got bored. There was no doubt about it, women in the mass were not for her. She preferred the company of men any day, and pretty soon the women noticed it. That did it. They drew off warily and really looked at her. Then they looked at their menfolk, and saw what by that time they expected to see.

A time-bomb, that was Kirsten. At first we never even noticed the clock ticking. But before Christmas we all knew, and we were all waiting for the explosion.

I reckon within three months she'd been out with every young fellow in the place, and a good few not so young, provided they were unattached, and sometimes even if they were very firmly attached. There'd been more than one fight over her by then. When they fought she shrugged and walked away, losing interest. If she'd joined in I calculate she could have settled which way most of the fights would go, without even ruffling her hair. But she didn't like upsets, she liked everything to be sunny. I suppose she was hardly ever known to pass up an opportunity or refuse a date. She smiled on everybody alike, looking them straight in the eye and drowning them in that private ocean of hers; and I doubt if it ever dawned on her how the women had drawn off and closed their faces against her. Seen from behind the shutters, her very walk was provocation, her body a blatant challenge. Kirsten was pure sex. How she could have the face to be devout into the bargain, and go regularly to church, was something that baffled them completely.

Kirsten went home for Christmas, and the female half of the village prayed she wouldn't come back, and the male half agonised, hoping that she would. And she did, in the New Year when the first heavy snow was receding. Our Mildred was one of the first to see her after her return. They met in Dr. Clegg's waiting-room, and I remember Mildred going on about her afterwards, how Kirsten told her she'd had a bit of trouble after the jet flight over, and Mrs. Landon had sent her to Clegg because she said no irregular haemorrhage should be neglected, but Mildred's theory was that that was a cover-up for something very different, and what was the betting the Landons would soon be shipping her off home again in a hurry, before her condition began to show? Which will indicate to you the state of female feeling at that time. If she had begun to display signs of pregnancy, there wasn't a married or engaged woman in the place who wouldn't have been giving her man hell. Including our Mildred. She isn't a bad-looking girl at all, after our dark, squat fashion, but it was a sad day when young Ted Blantyre from the garage up at Croft started measuring her lumpy legs against Kirsten's magnificent under-proppings, and let Mildred catch him at it.

Whether anything ever got round about that rumour I can't say. It never did to me, from any other source; but after Christmas there was something new in the tension that centred round Kirsten. All the men were like cocks preening and

strutting in a sort of premature Spring. The kids first, and after them plenty who
should have known better, started boasting openly of their sexual revelations
with her. It was the done thing to have had Kirsten. And, my God, one could
believe that to have had her would be an experience out of this world, like matching
with a Valkyrie. And through all the hates and rivalries engendered by her she
walked radiantly as ever, flaunting her high breasts and her pale hair and her
grand, brazen face, with the white-hot passion of men and women following her,
and scorching the very footprints she left behind her.

Then came the night of the big snow, in February. All our roads out were
blocked completely. We no longer have a railway, as I've said. But by this time,
like our ancestors—and we get closer to them every season—we know enough
to stock up before the winter closes in, and have developed ways of surviving.

Snow couldn't keep Kirsten indoors. She came from a country of winter and
darkness. There was a dance that night in the Institute, and Kirsten loved to
dance. She walked from Cleave. The snow had hardly begun then; there was a
sharp wind blowing, and minor drifts were building up, but she strode through
them like a goddess, unescorted and unafraid, with her dancing shoes in the
outsize handbag on her arm, and her marvellous legs cased in thigh-boots.

The first I knew of the affair was when the 'phone rang at one o'clock in the
morning. I crawled out and went down to the office, and it was Mrs. Landon on
the line, clipped and shrill, very uneasy.

"Oh, Sergeant Moon, I'm so sorry to get you up at this hour, but we're so
worried about Kirsten. She hasn't come in yet. The dance was to end at midnight,
wasn't it? And with this blizzard, anything could happen. My husband had to
abandon the car at Miller's Corner, and walk all the way from there, and he's
been back as far as the main road since, and along the lane, and not a sign of her.
I'm so anxious …"

Landon had been at a sale in Shrewsbury, it seemed, and only made it back
home around half past twelve, since when he'd struggled part of the way towards
the village in search of his missing nursemaid, and no luck. And by that time
blizzard was the word for what we had, a horizontal northeaster that was flaying
the open surfaces bare and burying the vulnerable places fathoms deep. One
gets to know where all the marooned cars will be, and where the sheep will
huddle in the hills. Between us and Cleave, I could have numbered the stretches
where a homing girl might founder.

"Stay up," I said, "and we'll work our way out to you. Someone here may
know if anyone started home with her."

I wouldn't have left a dog out without hunting for him that night. I knocked up
our two constables, and Joe Egan from next door, and young Ted, because our
Mildred gave me a sort of claim on him, and anyhow he'd been at the dance, and

would hardly be in bed yet. He came down to us clumping in rubber thigh-boots, ready for anything, and stared at us pallidly from under a cut eyebrow when he heard Kirsten's name.

"She went off early," he said, "hardly turned eleven. On her tod. She shoulda been home long since."

We went to look for her, two of us the shorter way by the fields, three the long way by the road and the lane, because even Kirsten must have had some respect for such weather. Visibility was nil by then. There was no air, just a shifting veil of snow, driving parallel with the ground. We shoved our way crosswise through it, sprouting icicles and breathing snow. And all the way I was thinking of Kirsten disseminated into air, enlarged to fill the night, afloat over us on the tension of the withering wind. But she was flesh and blood like the rest of us, and the cold could kill even the marvellous winter women of the north, even her.

We'd hardly started Buller and Crowe and Joe Egan off by the road, and were crossing the lane by the lych-gate, when the church bell started to toll.

You'd have thought it was a gun trained on us, the way Ted and me pulled up standing. Six bells our church has, but this was just one of them, the biggest, banging out slow, single strokes. Nobody has to tell our natives what a passing bell is, we still toll for our people when they go. Some other customs we've shed only since the last war. Give us ten more years, and this one will be gone after the rest; but not yet.

I turned and made for the church in a hurry. The doors are never locked, night or day, summer or winter, it's a tradition with us. I was pounding up the path to the porch, when the reverberations of the last stroke shook away into the silence, and left the nave still quivering. One rope was still swaying gently when I turned the torch on it. There was nobody there. I listened and there was no sound. I went all round the place. The vestry door was unlocked, too. The bell-ringer could have been anywhere by that time. Maybe one of the youngsters, too lit to go home after the dance—But no, not a night like this, I thought. They're witless, but not that witless.

Whoever he was, he was gone. And we had a girl to find. We went back to the job of finding her. Everything else could wait.

It took us three hours to find her. We made it to the Cleave drive, and Landon met us there, plastered white, and shaking like a leaf inside his big shaggy coat. We separated again in all directions, inside the grounds and out. Though if she'd ever got that far she would have made it to the door.

No, it was out in the lane, a quarter of a mile away, that we found her at last drawn back into the corner of a field gate. The wind had shifted a point to the north, and started demolishing the drifts it had built. Powdered snow came off the dunes like spume. A hem of dark cloth showed that had been hidden before.

We uncovered her, digging with our hands. She lay on her back with her face turned up to us, and her head at an impossible angle. There were fingermarks on her throat, but she hadn't died of strangulation, and her face, startled, indignant, frozen in outraged alarm, wasn't marred. Her clothes were tumbled and torn, but she had put up fight enough to preserve everything but her life. It wasn't the cold that had killed Kirsten. Her neck was broken. Her nails weren't going to tell us anything, either; she had on sheepskin mitts, elasticated at the wrists. Her big handbag lay against the gate. It hadn't been touched; we never entertained the idea that it would have been. Nobody had wanted to rob her. There was, after all, only one way Kirsten was likely to die.

We got the private door of the Cleave gardens off its hinges, and lifted her on to it to carry her back to the village. There was hardly any snow under her, the grass and the ground showed through; she must have been lying there since before midnight. We staked a tarpaulin over the place where she'd lain. By morning that would be buried, too, the way the snow was still coming down, but we knew now where to find what evidence there was.

It wasn't far off morning when we got her back to the police station. A proper mortuary we haven't got, but we'd made shift more than once when we were cut off in other winters, and had to dig dead men out of their buried cars. I knew the roads would be closed. I didn't know, until I tried the telephone, that the outside line would be down, but it was. We were on our own with this murder; and for that it was the first time.

Molly was up and waiting for us, and so was Mildred. Not a soul in the place could have slept through that bell tolling. Nobody said much, but Molly's eyes followed me about the place wherever I went, and Mildred's followed young Ted, and didn't miss the split eyebrow or the bruises that were coming up on his cheekbone and chin, or the look in his eyes that took no account of her watching him. He knew she was there in the room, pouring tea, and that was about all she meant to him. He'd just seen the last of Kirsten.

I left them gulping tea, and went down the village to get Dr. Clegg. He was our local G.P. from years back, and used to carrying the total load when we were isolated, and in any case the official police surgeon was ten miles away and out of reach. He came down grumbling like a grizzly bear—and looking a bit like one, too, with his brindled hair on end and a huge brown woollen dressing-gown draped round him—and wanted to know what I thought I was doing, getting him up so early, after two late calls the night before, and Mrs. Dent's baby due any minute. When he heard, he went back upstairs without a word, and was down in two minutes, dressed and ready. There was no wife to complicate his comings and goings; she'd been dead for thirty years, died soon after he married her. Jenny Crowther did for him, days, and a sister from Birmingham came over now and again to see that everything was in order. He'd never looked at any woman again, bar professionally.

He didn't ask what had happened to Kirsten. What could have happened to her but a passionate sexual assault that turned fatal? Women like her don't die of old age or accidents, or freeze submissively in any weather. When we got back to the station he took his bag into the mortuary room back of the office—it used to be a cell once—and shut the door after him.

So then there were just the four of us sitting round our kitchen table over another pot of tea, Molly and Mildred on one side, young Ted and me on the other. Buller was in the office typing a preliminary report, and Crowe had gone off to see the M.C. from last night's dance; and Joe Egan had slipped home to get ready for work, because Joe is a cowman, and cows won't wait.

I said: "Now suppose you tell us what happened at the dance last night, before we hear it from someone else. You might as well, we can see the scars, and if you don't talk, she will." And Mildred didn't say a word. When girls keep their mouths shut, look out. They'd gone to the dance together, that I knew. She'd been home soon after eleven, by herself. And when did Ted ever fight over our Mildred?

He looked up at her, and she looked back at him, and you'd have said there went any prospects of that marriage ever coming off, but the next minute you'd have sworn, with more conviction, they'd never get free of each other as long as they lived. Love or hate, comfort or kill, they'd never claw their way loose. And when I took one quick glance at Molly, she was staring straight at me, and, my God, her face looked just the same.

"He pinched her off me," young Ted said. He looked at Mildred and looked through her. "I'd asked her for that dance, what business did he have shoving his face in? Across the floor like a shot, the minute the band struck up, and had her out on the floor before I could get near."

"It was *me* you took there," said Mildred in a thin voice, "remember?"

"I'd asked her for this one dance. How many did I have with you? And he cut in on me ..."

"And she let him," Mildred said, and laughed.

"He?" I said.

"George Tranter. He pinched her from me ..."

His voice went up, higher and higher, keening without tears. He stared into my girl's eyes, and told us all about it, how they'd fought, on the dance floor until they were hustled out, and then in the snow. And when the fight was over, and they were both marked and dishevelled, and both feeling pretty stupid, back they'd gone into the Institute, and Kirsten wasn't there any more, Kirsten had shrugged her shoulders and walked out, bored with their adolescent tantrums.

"Did you follow her?" I asked.

He looked down into his linked hands on the table, and said: "Yes, as far as the stile up the fields. It was snowing hard, and blowing like hell. She wasn't anywhere. She'd gone by the road. I knew it was no good. I went back."

And Mildred had left, too, of course, supposing he even noticed. And that would be about—what?—eleven-thirty at the latest?

"So what did you do then? Go back to the dance?"

But maybe George Tranter had also set off after her as soon as he realised she had walked out on them; and maybe he went by the road. All inflamed with his wrongs and his battle, ready to confront her as Ted had been ready. And Kirsten so large and fair and scornful, Venus ankle-deep among her puny admirers!

Harry Clegg came in through the office, so quietly that we almost didn't notice him, and sat down wearily in the corner by the fire, and reached for the tea-pot.

"I went back again," Ted said in a low, even voice, watching our Mildred with every word. "By the road, this time. I went after her, and I overtook her. I told her I loved her, and always should, as long as I lived, like she bloody well knew without being told, ever since we'd first been together. I told her I didn't care how many others there'd been, but there weren't going to be any others ever again, only me. I told her I'd see her dead first ... and she said, then I'd have to, wouldn't I? *And I did!* She was laughing at me, and then she choked, and crumpled up in my hands with her head all on one side. And I kissed her, and she never moved or breathed. *I killed her!*" said young Ted, and his voice was thin and low and chilly, and all the time he was looking with narrowed eyes at our Mildred. "I dropped her there in the gateway, and left her lying. I killed her! Now charge me!"

I could have asked him how he managed the dead-bell from the wrong side of the lych-gate, but I never said anything, and nobody else did, either. He looked across at Harry Clegg, warming himself at the fire, and he said: "Her neck was broken, wasn't it? *Well, wasn't it?*" He was a hefty youngster, he knew his own strength all right.

"That's right," Harry said mildly, "her neck was broken. That's what she died of. If it matters, it was quick. And most likely accidental."

"Accidental! Like trying to take her ... right there in the snow ...?"

"Then I suppose," Harry said in the same tone, "the child she was carrying was yours?"

Everybody saw Ted go rigid, and everybody saw him recover. After all, nobody's ever *known*, before. "Yes, it was mine," he said. His tone said: "Whose else would it be?"

Harry said heavily and absolutely, in a tired voice: "*She was a virgin.*"

We didn't rightly hear, or we didn't rightly understand, not for a moment. No, it was impossible! That creature all devilment and provocation and allure, the magnet that had dragged at us all …

Ted was the first to admit anything, because Ted knew. He gave one hopeless look round the lot of us, and his bruised face crumpled. He put his head down in his arms on the kitchen table and burst into tears. Poor kid, he'd never had anything from her, she'd never known she owed him anything, and now she was out of reach for ever. Out of reach of all of us. She'd sheared clean through all our pretensions with her terrible honesty, to make her exit in triumph. Kirsten was a virgin!

"There's no doubt?" I asked.

"What do you take me for?" said Harry. "They'll all swear the opposite, let them! They're all liars, every one. You all had her labelled. Well, you'll have to get used to a new label. I tell you the girl was a virgin."

I knew him, and I knew it was the truth. "You'd better get home, lad," I said to Ted, "and sleep it off."

What can you make of women? Mildred cooked breakfast for him. I'd have sworn he wouldn't touch it, but he ate it and looked round for more. Mildred walked him home, and probably saw him to bed, too, and all the time with that closed looked of triumph and revenge on her face. And it was Mildred who called the garage and told them he wouldn't be in that day. And he bore it all, and never hit her. The makings of a marriage there, after all. Of a sort! Not so unusual a sort, God help us!

I don't know which of them gave the show away, but the grapevine had the news about Kirsten before the day was out, and something queer was going on among our snowbound womenfolk. Suddenly Kirsten emerged a heroine. Every woman in the place walked round with a countenance of secret, vengeful joy, eyeing her man, as the priest eyes the sacrifice. The girls glowed in silent exultation, the village Romeos slunk into hiding. Everybody knew they were fools, dupes and liars, and Kirsten after her death an ally and champion of her sex, outstanding in the war against men. Who had shaken and shamed them as she had?

You think you've seen the sex war in action? You don't know the half. You had lifelines on the world, we had none. You knew ways out of the closed circle, we went round and round on a treadmill from which there was no escape. And then, you never knew Kirsten.

Mind you, nobody admitted to knowing anything. We had at least a veil of silence and decency. Until the next day, which was Sunday.

Unless you know a church like ours, you won't understand. Parts of it are Saxon, parts Norman, the newest bits Gothic from the fourteenth century, and it clings to every tradition from Alfred on down. A leper squint? There's one in the south porch. A sword-stand? We've got that, too, and not one but two thirteen-sconce cressets, from the days when the church was lit by oil-flares in stone bases. And hanging high on the wall of the south aisle we keep twelve maiden garlands. You don't know what they are? Neither did I when I first came here. They're crude crowns of paper flowers on wire frames, with white paper glove-shapes pinned into them, and white ribbons with the names of the girls they commemorate. Girls who died virgin, spinsters of this parish. Our latest is dated July 5th, 1934, Emily Weston, aged 18. The oldest, gone dingy brown and brittle as ash with age, dates back to 1780, but the name's faded clean away, and we don't know who she was.

But this Sunday morning there were not twelve crowns, but thirteen, and against the dusty dimness of the other twelve the last one exploded like a Roman Candle. All the plastic daffodils and tulips from all the packets of washing powder in the village had gone into the making of that garland, not to mention a real pair of white nylon gloves. There was a white ribbon dangling from the apex where the bars of flowers met, and a name inked on it. Too high to be readable—they must have brought in a ladder to put the thing in place—but nobody needed to ask whose maiden crown that was.

The show of colour nearly stopped the choir in its tracks, and ripped the processional hymn ragged. The vicar turned whiter than his surplice. He was a man, too. Maybe he hadn't joined the hunt, but not because he hadn't heard the horns calling. Every woman in church—and there were many more than usual—glowed with terrible triumph and disdain; they were all in the know, every one of them. All the men drew in their heads like tortoises and shrank over their hymn books, remembering their idiot brags and struttings, and knowing the women were remembering them, too.

So now it was out in the open. Every marriage was going to be a silent battlefield, and every engagement total war.

We got through morning service somehow. After everybody'd gone I wanted to take the thing down, on the pretext that it might be evidence, but the vicar wouldn't have it. He stood there like Horatius keeping the bridge, staring through the church wall and away to where some inward vision showed him Kirsten still, and he said in a great voice:

"She was a virgin, and she is there by right." And I knew that nobody was going to find the courage to displace Kirsten's memorial.

There was nothing for it but to get on with the job like the day before, the hard way. We put in a long day of it, going doggedly from house to house checking the movements of every man in the place from just after eleven on that Friday night. In the village itself it wasn't so bad, but when it came to the farms and scattered farm cottages around, we had to dig our way through to meet the locals digging themselves out. Mercifully it didn't snow again. But we got back late in the evening with sore feet and aching legs, and a list as long as my arm of men who might have killed Kirsten. Not forgetting Landon, who had made his way home alone and on foot after midnight; or George Tranter, who had never gone back to the dance after the fight, and hadn't been heard letting himself in at home, so that no one could confirm the time he gave; or, for that matter, young Ted, though I was pretty sure his being right there beside me when the bell began to toll let him out. Still, it didn't *have* to be the murderer who rang for her, even if it was a ninety-per-cent certainty.

Ted was with Mildred in our front room, heaven help him, but I think he was even glad of her. Better somebody who knew the whole of it, he hadn't got any farther to fall, and with a wall at his back he could begin to fight back. Having Molly sit down opposite me at the kitchen table with a book she wasn't even pretending to read had the same effect on me. Nobody had any secrets around here any more; she knew every time the image of Kirsten strode across my mind, and every time I went down into the sea of her eyes. She watched me going through my list of males, and smiled terrifyingly.

"You'd do better asking the women all those questions," she said, and it was the first remark she'd volunteered all that day. "They might get you somewhere. You can cross off all those stupid kids who went about flexing their muscles and pretending they'd had the mastery of that girl. Which of 'em did she ever let come near enough to guess whether she was a virgin? Not even the last!"

And she was right. When it came to imagining the final collision between Kirsten and her murderer, how many of our lads matched up? Eighty per cent of them she could have pulverised with one hand. This one she had fought till she died, and he'd never got his way.

"How could he know," said Molly, slamming her book shut and leaning over the table at me with her eyes narrowed as if she hated my guts, as maybe she did, "how could he know she was a virgin? As soon as he realised he'd killed her he dropped her and ran. It wasn't then he found out, oh, dear, no! This one happened to know already!"

"He didn't have to know at all," I said. "Everybody in the place knows now, you women have seen to that, but nobody'd decorated the poor girl with a plastic halo then. He didn't have to know."

"Oh, no?" she said. *"He rang the bell for her, didn't he?"*

"What's that got to do with it, for God's sake?" I said. "He knew she was dead, that's for sure."

"He knew more than that. He had to! And he was the only one who did, then. What sort of copper are you?" she said, spitting like a cat. "Never thought to count the strokes, did you? Six tolls that bell gave. I know it, if you don't. Six was the peal for a girl who died virgin. You may have forgotten it, but he didn't. And he knew it was her due! And nobody else did! Nobody would have believed you then if you'd suggested it, would they? But he *knew*!"

I got up from the table and walked across the room to the door like a wound-up mechanical doll. As I passed her she was going on as if she didn't know how to stop, like the beginning of a big thaw: "Who's the one person who *could* know? Not a lover! That's the whole point, isn't it, that she never had a lover, that she wouldn't have let one of the lot of you touch her that way ... All that seeming brazenness of hers that got her her bad name ... all just what it seemed, if we could have believed it, just honesty and friendliness and trust—only she was too innocent, and too fearless. ..."

I shut the door on her and walked away slowly down the road. It was dark, and the east wind was still blowing, whisking a fine spray of snow off the roofs, but suddenly it seemed as if the edge was off the frost.

The one person who *could* have known! Had Molly thought of that by herself, or had Mildred reminded her?

Harry Clegg was just coming rushing out of his gate in a hurry when I got there, with his bag in his hand, clumping in his huge Wellingtons. He pulled up when he saw me, but only in the brisk way of somebody checking for an instant before continuing his flight.

"Looking for me? The Dent baby's on its way in a hurry at last, her mother just sent for me . . ."

"Can't keep the Dent baby waiting," I said. "When you get back I'll be sending for you, too, Harry. I'd like a fuller report. On Kirsten."

Then he settled, letting his big coat droop round him like a crow folding its wings. He heaved a sort of quiet sigh, and stood looking at me with a half-relieved, half-resigned smile. And in a moment he said: "What was it? Not that it could have been any other way in the end. I'd have told you, just as soon as the road's open and we can get another medical man in."

"It was the bell," I said. "Six tolls for a virgin."

"You got round to that finally. I wonder," he said, "if that's why I rang it. It could have been. I wonder!"

"Not me," I said. "It took the women to put a finger on that."

"Well, I'm not sorry," he said gently. "Let me take care of Joan and her baby, and then if the weather report's right I reckon the telephone line may be working and the road open tomorrow." And he stood there quiet for a minute, and then suddenly he said, quite conversationally, but in a voice I can't forget: "I'm a live man, too. They don't realise ..." And after another minute: "I never knew it could happen to me. She shouldn't have been let out alone, she must always have had her death on a short lead, walking on her heels. I was on my way home from a damn-fool call up at Coulters'—woman's a fool, hysterical if she cuts her finger—Kirsten ... I picked her out of the drifts, and steered her back in the right direction, and I never knew it could happen to me, not till she put her arms round me . . . in pure gratitude . . . not knowing there was anything to be afraid of ... That was her trouble, she never knew she was deadly. She didn't even know she was playing with fire. . . ."

I thought of all the years of abstinence, and of Kirsten clinging to him in the snow, hugging him, laughing, her hair whipped across his face, and her high breasts crushed against him, an innocent without the sense to put a guard on her devastating friendliness ... And who was the victim and who the destroyer I shall never know.

"Better get along to Joan," I said. And he said: "I'll call you afterwards," and went off headlong in the dark to his job.

He called me in the small hours. The baby was a boy, and mother and child were as fit as frogs, and he was at my disposal. I said: "It'll keep till morning," and he said: "I'll be here."

I went round in the morning. I took my time. He was dead, sitting in his surgery with an empty glass at his elbow.

The only announcement we made about it was that Dr. Clegg had died suddenly. There'd have to be an inquest, of course, and they'd have to find that he'd taken his own life, but nobody in our village would ever say a word to suggest that his suicide was connected with Kirsten's death. And after a few days' interval we could make the formal announcement that the murder case was closed to the police's satisfaction, and no prosecution was contemplated.

Everybody would know, of course, but we don't tell all we know. Not even to one another.

The thaw began that day, the doctors from the next village could get through to us, and the outside 'phone lines were working again. Molly looked at me as though she hadn't slept well, but wasn't blaming me for it, the women began, slowly and carefully, to speak civilly to their men again, and life felt its way cautiously into gear and went on where it had left off. The thaw began, a slow thaw. But a sure one. Come Easter I reckon Mildred and young Ted will be getting married.

It might be better, in a way, to take down that thirteenth maiden garland and burn it, but nobody ever will. Nor will anybody ever own to knowing anything about it, when the stray summer visitor asks. She lived here and died here, and we won't excise her from our memories though we may from our mouths. As long as any of us survive who lived through her catastrophic impact, she will remain a legitimate part of our history and our experience. But one we don't talk about either to strangers or among ourselves.

So now I suppose I'd better write "Finis" to this story, and then put a match to it.

THE TRINITY CAT

He was sitting on top of one of the rear gate-posts of the churchyard when I walked through on Christmas Eve, grooming in his lordly style, with one back leg wrapped round his neck, and his bitten ear at an angle of forty-five degrees, as usual. I reckon one of the toms he'd tangled with in his nomad days had ripped the starched bit out of that one, the other stood up sharply enough. There was snow on the ground, a thin veiling, just beginning to crackle in promise of frost before evening, but he had at least three warm refuges around the place whenever he felt like holing up, besides his two houses, which he used only for visiting and cadging. He'd been a known character around our village for three years then, ever since he walked in from nowhere and made himself agreeable to the vicar and the verger, and finding the billet comfortable and the pickings good, constituted himself resident cat to Holy Trinity church, and took over all the jobs around the place that humans were too slow to tackle, like rat-catching, and chasing off invading dogs.

Nobody knows how old he is, but I think he could only have been about two when he settled here, a scrawny, chewed-up black bandit as lean as wire. After three years of being fed by Joel Woodward at Trinity Cottage, which was the verger's house by tradition, and flanked the lychgate on one side, and pampered and petted by Miss Patience Thomson at Church Cottage on the other side, he was double his old size, and sleek as velvet, but still had one lop ear and a kink two inches from the end of his tail. He still looked like a brigand, but a highly prosperous brigand. Nobody ever gave him a name, he wasn't the sort to get called anything fluffy or familiar. Only Miss Patience ever dared coo at him, and he was very gracious about that, she being elderly and innocent and very free with little perks like raw liver, on which he doted. One way and another, he had it made. He lived mostly outdoors, never staying in either house overnight. In winter he had his own little ground-level hatch into the furnace-room of the church, sharing his lodgings matily with a hedgehog that had qualified as assistant vermin-destructor around the churchyard, and preferred sitting out the winter among the coke to hibernating like common hedgehogs. These individualists keep turning up in our valley, for some reason.

All I'd gone to the church for that afternoon was to fix up with the vicar about the Christmas peal, having been roped into the bell-ringing team. Resident police in remote areas like ours get dragged into all sorts of activities, and when the area's changing, and new problems cropping up, if they have any sense they don't need too much dragging, but go willingly. I've put my finger on many an astonished yobbo who thought he'd got clean away with his little breaking-and-entering, just by keeping my ears open during a darts match, or choir practice.

When I came back through the churchyard, around half-past two, Miss Patience was just coming out of her gate, with a shopping bag on her wrist, and heading towards the street, and we walked along together a bit of the way. She was getting on for seventy, and hardly bigger than a bird, but very independent. Never having married or left the valley, and having looked after a mother who lived to be nearly ninety, she'd never had time to catch up with new ideas in the style of dress suitable for elderly ladies. Everything had always been done mother's way, and fashion, music and morals had stuck at the period when mother was a carefully-brought-up girl learning domestic skills, and preparing for a chaste marriage. There's a lot to be said for it! But it had turned Miss Patience into a frail little lady in long-skirted black or grey or navy blue, who still felt undressed without hat and gloves, at an age when Mrs. Newcombe, for instance, up at the pub, favoured shocking pink trouser suits and red-gold hair-pieces. A pretty little old lady Miss Patience was, though, very straight and neat. It was a pleasure to watch her walk. Which is more than I could say for Mrs. Newcombe in her trouser suit, especially from the back!

"A happy Christmas, Sergeant Moon!" she chirped at me on sight. And I wished her the same, and slowed up to her pace.

"It's going to be slippery by twilight," I said. "You be careful how you go."

"Oh, I'm only going to be an hour or so," she said serenely. "I shall be home long before the frost sets in. I'm only doing the last bit of Christmas shopping. There's a cardigan I have to collect for Mrs. Downs." That was her cleaning-lady, who went in three mornings a week. "I ordered it long ago, but deliveries are so slow nowadays. They've promised it for today. And a gramophone record for my little errand-boy." Tommy Fowler that was, one of the church trebles, as pink and wholesome looking as they usually contrive to be, and just as artful. "And one mustn't forget our dumb friends, either, must one?" said Miss Patience cheerfully. "They're all important, too."

I took this to mean a couple of packets of some new product to lure wild birds to her garden. The Church Cottage thrushes were so fat they could hardly fly, and when it was frosty she put out fresh water three and four times a day.

We came to our brief street of shops, and off she went, with her big jet-and-gold brooch gleaming in her scarf. She had quite a few pieces of Victorian and Edwardian jewellery her mother'd left behind, and almost always wore one piece, being used to the belief that a lady dresses meticulously every day, not just on

Sundays. And I went for a brisk walk round to see what was going on, and then went home to Molly and high tea, and took my boots off thankfully.

That was Christmas Eve. Christmas Day little Miss Thomson didn't turn up for eight o'clock Communion, which was unheard-of. The vicar said he'd call in after matins and see that she was all right, and hadn't taken cold trotting about in the snow. But somebody else beat us both to it. Tommy Fowler! He was anxious about that pop record of his. But even he had no chance until after service, for in our village it's the custom for the choir to go and sing the vicar an aubade in the shape of "Christians, Awake!" before the main service, ignoring the fact that he's then been up four hours, and conducted two Communions. And Tommy Fowler had a solo in the anthem, too. It was a quarter-past twelve when he got away, and shot up the garden path to the door of Church Cottage.

He shot back even faster a minute later. I was heading for home when he came rocketing out of the gate and ran slam into me, with his eyes sticking out on stalks and his mouth wide open, making a sort of muted keening sound with shock. He clutched hold of me and pointed back towards Miss Thomson's front door, left half-open when he fled, and tried three times before he could croak out:

"Miss Patience. . . . She's there on the floor—she's bad!"

I went in on the run, thinking she'd had a heart attack all alone there, and was lying helpless. The front door led through a diminutive hall, and through another glazed door into the living-room, and that door was open, too, and there was Miss Patience face-down on the carpet, still in her coat and gloves, and with her shopping-bag lying beside her. An occasional table had been knocked over in her fall, spilling a vase and a book. Her hat was askew over one ear, and caved in like a trodden mushroom, and her neat grey bun of hair had come undone and trailed on her shoulder, and it was no longer grey but soiled, brownish black. She was dead and stiff. The room was so cold, you could tell those doors had been ajar all night.

The kid had followed me in, hanging on to my sleeve, his teeth chattering. "I didn't open the door—it was open! I didn't touch her, or anything. I only came to see if she was all right, and get my record."

It was there, lying unbroken, half out of the shopping-bag by her arm. She'd meant it for him, and I told him he should have it, but not yet, because it might be evidence, and we mustn't move anything. And I got him out of there quick, and gave him to the vicar to cope with, and went back to Miss Patience as soon as I'd telephoned for the outfit. Because we had a murder on our hands.

So that was the end of one gentle, harmless old woman, one of very many these days, battered to death because she walked in on an intruder who panicked. Walked in on him, I judged, not much more than an hour after I left her in the street. Everything about her looked the same as then, the shopping-bag, the coat, the hat, the gloves. The only difference, that she was dead. No, one more thing! No handbag, unless it was under the body, and later, when we were able to move her, I wasn't surprised to see that it wasn't there. Handbags are where old ladies carry their money. The sneak-thief who panicked and lashed out at her had still had greed and presence of mind enough to grab the bag as he fled. Nobody'd have to describe that bag to me, I knew it well, soft black leather with an old-fashioned gilt clasp and a short handle, a small thing, not like the hold-alls they carry nowadays.

She was lying facing the opposite door, also open, which led to the stairs. On the writing-desk by that door stood one of a pair of heavy brass candlesticks. Its fellow was on the floor beside Miss Thomson's body, and though the bun of hair and the felt hat had prevented any great spattering of blood, there was blood enough on the square base to label the weapon. Whoever had hit her had been just sneaking down the stairs, ready to leave. She'd come home barely five minutes too soon.

Upstairs, in her bedroom, her bits of jewellery hadn't taken much finding. She'd never thought of herself as having valuables, or of other people as coveting them. Her gold and turquoise and funereal jet and true-lover's-knots in gold and opals, and mother's engagement and wedding rings, and her little Edwardian pendant watch set with seed pearls, had simply lived in the small top drawer of her dressing-table. She belonged to an honest epoch, and it was gone, and now she was gone after it. She didn't even lock her door when she went shopping. There wouldn't have been so much as the warning of a key grating in the lock, just the door opening.

Ten years ago not a soul in this valley behaved differently from Miss Patience. Nobody locked doors, sometimes not even overnight. Some of us went on a fortnight's holiday and left the doors unlocked. Now we can't even put out the milk money until the milkman knocks at the door in person. If this generation likes to pride itself on its progress, let it! As for me, I thought suddenly that maybe the innocent was well out of it.

We did the usual things, photographed the body and the scene of the crime, the doctor examined her and authorised her removal, and confirmed what I'd supposed about the approximate time of her death. And the forensic boys lifted a lot of smudgy latents that weren't going to be of any use to anybody, because they weren't going to be on record, barring a million to one chance. The whole thing stank of the amateur. There wouldn't be any easy matching up of prints, even if they got beauties. One more thing we did for Miss Patience. We tolled the deadbell for her on Christmas night, six heavy, muffled strokes. She was a virgin. Nobody had to vouch for it, we all knew. And let me point out, it is a title of honour, to be respected accordingly.

We'd hardly got the poor soul out of the house when the Trinity cat strolled in, taking advantage of the minute or two while the door was open. He got as far as the place on the carpet where she'd lain, and his fur and whiskers stood on end, and even his lop ear jerked up straight. He put his nose down to the pile of the Wilton, about where her shopping bag and handbag must have lain, and started going round in interested circles, snuffing the floor and making little throaty noises that might have been distress, but sounded like pleasure. Excitement, anyhow. The chaps from the C.I.D. were still busy, and didn't want him under their feet, so I picked him up and took him with me when I went across to Trinity Cottage to talk to the verger. The cat never liked being picked up, after a minute he started clawing and cursing, and I put him down. He stalked away again at once, past the corner where people shot their dead flowers, out at the lych-gate, and straight back to sit on Miss Thomson's doorstep. Well, after all, he used to get fed there, he might well be uneasy at all these queer comings and goings. And they don't say "as curious as a cat" for nothing, either.

I didn't need telling that Joel Woodward had had no hand in what had happened, he'd been nearest neighbour and good friend to Miss Patience for years, but he might have seen or heard something out of the ordinary. He was a little, wiry fellow, gnarled like a tree-root, the kind that goes on spry and active into his nineties, and then decides that's enough, and leaves overnight. His wife was dead long ago, and his daughter had come back to keep house for him after her husband deserted her, until she died, too, in a bus accident. There was just old Joel now, and the grandson she'd left with him, young Joel Barnett, nineteen, and a bit of a tearaway by his grandad's standards, but so far pretty innocuous by mine. He was a sulky, graceless sort, but he did work, and he stuck with the old man when many another would have lit out elsewhere.

"A bad business," said old Joel, shaking his head. "I only wish I could help you lay hands on whoever did it. But I only saw her yesterday morning about ten, when she took in the milk. I was round at the church hall all afternoon, getting things ready for the youth social they had last night, it was dark before I got back. I never saw or heard anything out of place. You can't see her living-room light from here, so there was no call to wonder. But the lad was here all afternoon. They only work till one, Christmas Eve. Then they all went boozing together for an hour or so, I expect, so I don't know exactly what time he got in, but he was here and had the tea on when I came home. Drop round in an hour or so and he should be here, he's gone round to collect this girl he's mashing. There's a party somewhere tonight."

I dropped round accordingly, and young Joel was there, sure enough, shoulder-length hair, frilled shirt, outsize lapels and all, got up to kill, all for the benefit of the girl his grandad had mentioned. And it turned out to be Connie Dymond, from the comparatively respectable branch of the family, along the canal-side. There were three sets of Dymond cousins, boys, no great harm in 'em but worth watching, but only this one girl in Connie's family. A good-looker, or at least most of the lads seemed to think so, she had a dozen or so on her string before she took up with young Joel. Big girl, too, with a lot of mauve eye-shadow and a mother-of-pearl mouth, in huge platform shoes and the fashionable drab granny-coat. But she was acting very prim and proper with old Joel around.

"Half-past two when I got home," said young Joel. "Grandad was round at the hall, and I'd have gone round to help him, only I'd had a pint or two, and after I'd had me dinner I went to sleep, so it wasn't worth it by the time I woke up. Around four, that'd be. From then on I was here watching the telly, and I never saw nor heard a thing. But there was nobody else here, so I could be spinning you the yarn, if you want to look at it that way."

He had a way of going looking for trouble before anybody else suggested it, there was nothing new about that. Still, there it was. One young fellow on the spot, and minus any alibi. There'd be plenty of others in the same case.

In the evening he'd been at the church social. Miss Patience wouldn't be expected there, it was mainly for the young, and anyhow, she very seldom went out in the evenings.

"*I* was there with Joel," said Connie Dymond. "He called for me at seven, I was with him all the evening. We went home to our place after the social finished, and he didn't leave till nearly midnight."

Very firm about it she was, doing her best for him. She could hardly know that his movements in the evening didn't interest us, since Miss Patience had then been dead for some hours.

When I opened the door to leave the Trinity cat walked in, stalking past me with a purposeful stride. He had a look round us all, and then made for the girl, reached up his front paws to her knees, and was on her lap before she could fend him off, though she didn't look as if she welcomed his attentions. Very civil he was, purring and rubbing himself against her coat sleeve, and poking his whiskery face into hers. Unusual for him to be effusive, but when he did decide on it, it was always with someone who couldn't stand cats. You'll have noticed it's a way they have.

"Shove him off," said young Joel, seeing she didn't at all care for being singled out. "He only does it to annoy people."

And she did, but he only jumped on again, I noticed as I closed the door on them and left. It was a Dymond party they were going to, the senior lot, up at the filling station. Not much point in trying to check up on all her cousins and swains when they were gathered for a booze-up. Coming out of a hangover, tomorrow, they might be easy meat. Not that I had any special reason to look their way, they were an extrovert lot, more given to grievous bodily harm in street punch-ups than anything secretive. But it was wide open.

Well, we summed up. None of the lifted prints was on record, all we could do in that line was exclude all those that were Miss Thomson's. This kind of sordid little opportunist break-in had come into local experience only fairly recently, and though it was no novelty now, it had never before led to a death. No motive but the impulse of greed, so no traces leading up to the act, and none leading away. Everyone connected with the church, and most of the village besides, knew about the bits of jewellery she had, but never before had anyone considered them as desirable loot. Victoriana now carry inflated values, and are in demand, but this still didn't look calculated, just wanton. A kid's crime, a teen-ager's crime. Or the crime of a permanent teen-ager. They start at twelve years old now, but there are also the shiftless louts who never get beyond twelve years old, even in their forties.

We checked all the obvious people, her part-time gardener—but he was demonstrably elsewhere at the time—and his drifter of a son, whose alibi was non-existent but voluble, the window-cleaner, a sidelong soul who played up his ailments and did rather well out of her, all the delivery men. Several there who were clear, one or two who could have been around, but had no particular reason to be. Then we went after all the youngsters who, on their records, were possibles. There were three with breaking-and-entering convictions, but if they'd been there they'd been gloved. Several others with petty theft against them were also without alibis. By the end of a pretty exhaustive survey the field was wide, and none of the runners seemed to be ahead of the rest, and we were still looking. None of the stolen property had so far showed up.

Not, that is, until the Saturday. I was coming from Church Cottage through the graveyard again, and as I came near the corner where the dead flowers were shot, I noticed a glaring black patch making an irregular hole in the veil of frozen snow that still covered the ground. You couldn't miss it, it showed up like a black eye. And part of it was the soil and rotting leaves showing through, and part, the blackest part, was the Trinity cat, head down and back arched, digging industriously like a terrier after a rat. The bent end of his tail lashed steadily, while the remaining eight inches stood erect. If he knew I was standing watching him, he didn't care. Nothing was going to deflect him from what he was doing. And in a minute or two he heaved his prize clear, and clawed out to the light a little black leather handbag with a gilt clasp. No mistaking it, all stuck over as it was with dirt and rotting leaves. And he loved it, he was patting it and playing with it and rubbing his head against it, and purring like a steam-engine. He cursed, though, when I took it off him, and walked round and round me, pawing and swearing, telling me and the world he'd found it, and it was his.

It hadn't been there long. I'd been along that path often enough to know that the snow hadn't been disturbed the day before. Also, the mess of humus fell off it pretty quick and clean, and left it hardly stained at all. I held it in my handkerchief and snapped the catch, and the inside was clean and empty, the lining slightly frayed from long use. The Trinity cat stood upright on his hind legs and protested loudly, and he had a voice that could outshout a Siamese.

Somebody behind me said curiously: "Whatever've you got there?" And there was young Joel standing openmouthed, staring, with Connie Dymond hanging on to his arm and gaping at the cat's find in horrified recognition.

"Oh, no! My gawd, that's Miss Thomson's bag, isn't it? I've seen her carrying it hundreds of times."

"Did *he* dig it up?" said Joel, incredulous. "You reckon the chap who—you know, *him*!—he buried it there? It could be anybody, everybody uses this way through."

"My gawd!" said Connie, shrinking in fascinated horror against his side. "Look at that cat! You'd think he *knows*. . . . He gives me the shivers! What's got into him?"

What, indeed? After I'd got rid of them and taken the bag away with me I was still wondering. I walked away with his prize and he followed me as far as the road, howling and swearing, and once I put the bag down, open, to see what he'd do, and he pounced on it and started his fun and games again until I took it from him. For the life of me I couldn't see what there was about it to delight him, but he was in no doubt. I was beginning to feel right superstitious about this avenging detective cat, and to wonder what he was going to unearth next.

I know I ought to have delivered the bag to the forensic lab, but somehow I hung on to it overnight. There was something fermenting at the back of my mind that I couldn't yet grasp.

Next morning we had two more at morning service besides the regulars. Young Joel hardly ever went to church, and I doubt if anybody'd ever seen Connie Dymond there before, but there they both were, large as life and solemn as death, in a middle pew, the boy sulky and scowling as if he'd been press-ganged into it, as he certainly had, Connie very subdued and big-eyed, with almost no make-up and an unusually grave and thoughtful face. Sudden death brings people up against daunting possibilities, and creates penitents. Young Joel felt silly there, but he was daft about her, plainly enough, she could get him to do what she wanted, and she'd wanted to make this gesture. She went through all the movements of devotion, he just sat, stood and kneeled awkwardly as required, and went on scowling.

There was a bitter east wind when we came out. On the steps of the porch everybody dug out gloves and turned up collars against it, and so did young Joel, and as he hauled his gloves out of his coat pocket, out with them came a little bright thing that rolled down the steps in front of us all and came to rest in a crack between the flagstones of the path. A gleam of pale blue and gold. A dozen people must have recognised it. Mrs. Downs gave tongue in a shriek that informed even those who hadn't.

"That's Miss Thomson's! It's one of her turquoise ear-rings! *How did you get hold of that, Joel Barnett?*"

How, indeed? Everybody stood staring at the tiny thing, and then at young Joel, and he was gazing at the flagstones, struck white and dumb. And all in a moment Connie Dymond had pulled her arm free of his and recoiled from him until her back was against the wall, and was edging away from him like somebody trying to get out of range of flood or fire, and her face a sight to be seen, blind and stiff with horror.

"You!" she said in a whisper. "It was you! Oh, my God, *you* did it—*you* killed her! And me keeping company—how could I? How could *you!*"

She let out a screech and burst into sobs, and before anybody could stop her she turned and took to her heels, running for home like a mad thing.

I let her go. She'd keep. And I got young Joel and that single ear-ring away from the Sunday congregation and into Trinity Cottage before half the people there knew what was happening, and shut the world out, all but old Joel who came panting and shaking after us a few minutes later.

The boy was a long time getting his voice back, and when he did he had nothing to say but, hopelessly, over and over: "I didn't! I never touched her, I wouldn't. I don't know how that thing got into my pocket. I didn't do it. I never. . . ."

Human beings are not all that inventive. Given a similar set of circumstances they tend to come out with the same formula. And in any case, "deny everything and say nothing else" is a very good rule when cornered.

They thought I'd gone round the bend when I said: "Where's the cat? See if you can get him in."

Old Joel was past wondering. He went out and rattled a saucer on the steps, and pretty soon the Trinity cat strolled in. Not at all excited, not wanting anything, fed and lazy, just curious enough to come and see why he was wanted. I turned him loose on young Joel's overcoat, and he couldn't have cared less. The pocket that had held the ear-ring held very little interest for him. He didn't care about any of the clothes in the wardrobe, or on the pegs in the little hall. As far as he was concerned, this new find was a non-event.

I sent for a constable and a car, and took young Joel in with me to the station, and all the village, you may be sure, either saw us pass or heard about it very shortly after. But I didn't stop to take any statement from him, just left him there, and took the car up to Mary Melton's place, where she breeds Siamese, and borrowed a cat-basket from her, the sort she uses to carry her queens to the vet. She asked what on earth I wanted it for, and I said to take the Trinity cat for a ride. She laughed her head off.

"Well, *he's* no queen," she said, "and no king, either. Not even a jack! And you'll never get that wild thing into a basket."

"Oh, yes, I will," I said. "And if he isn't any of the other picture cards, he's probably going to turn out to be the joker."

A very neat basket it was, not too obviously meant for a cat. And it was no trick getting the Trinity cat into it, all I did was drop in Miss Thomson's handbag, and he was in after it in a moment. He growled when he found himself shut in, but it was too late to complain then.

At the house by the canal Connie Dymond's mother let me in, but was none too happy about letting me see Connie, until I explained that I needed a statement from her before I could fit together young Joel's movements all through those Christmas days. Naturally I understood that the girl was terribly upset, but she'd had a lucky escape, and the sooner everything was cleared up, the better for her. And it wouldn't take long.

It didn't take long. Connie came down the stairs readily enough when her mother called her. She was all stained and pale and tearful, but had perked up somewhat with a sort of shivering pride in her own prominence. I've seen them like that before, getting the juice out of being the centre of attention even while they wish they were elsewhere. You could even say she hurried down, and she left the door of her bedroom open behind her, by the light coming through at the head of the stairs.

"Oh, Sergeant Moon!" she quavered at me from three steps up. "Isn't it *awful*? I still can't believe it! *Can* there be some mistake? Is there any chance it *wasn't* …?"

I said soothingly, yes, there was always a chance. And I slipped the latch of the cat-basket with one hand, so that the flap fell open, and the Trinity cat was out of there and up those stairs like a black flash, startling her so much she nearly fell down the last step, and steadied herself against the wall with a small shriek. And I blurted apologies for accidentally loosing him, and went up the stairs three at a time ahead of her, before she could recover her balance.

He was up on his hind legs in her dolly little room, full of pop posters and frills and garish colours, pawing at the second drawer of her dressing-table, and singing a loud, joyous, impatient song. When I came plunging in, he even looked over his shoulder at me and stood down, as though he knew I'd open the drawer for him. And I did, and he was up among her fancy undies like a shot, and digging with his front paws.

He found what he wanted just as she came in at the door. He yanked it out from among her bras and slips, and tossed it into the air, and in seconds he was on the floor with it, rolling and wrestling it, juggling it on his four paws like a circus turn, and purring fit to kill, a cat in ecstasy. A comic little thing it was, a muslin mouse with a plaited green nylon string for a tail, yellow beads for eyes, and nylon threads for whiskers, that rustled and sent out wafts of strong scent as he batted it around and sang to it. A catmint mouse, old Miss Thomson's last-minute purchase from the pet shop for her dumb friend. If you could ever call the Trinity cat dumb! The only thing she bought that day small enough to be slipped into her handbag instead of the shopping bag.

Connie let out a screech, and was across that room so fast I only just beat her to the open drawer. They were all there, the little pendant watch, the locket, the brooches, the true-lover's-knot, the purse, even the other ear-ring. A mistake, she should have ditched both while she was about it, but she was too greedy. They were for pierced ears, anyhow, no good to Connie.

I held them out in the palm of my hand—such a large haul they made—and let her see what she'd robbed and killed for.

If she'd kept her head she might have made a fight of it even then, claimed he'd made her hide them for him, and she'd been afraid to tell on him directly, and could only think of staging that public act at church, to get him safely in custody before she came clean. But she went wild. She did the one deadly thing, turned and kicked out in a screaming fury at the Trinity cat. He was spinning like a humming-top, and all she touched was the kink in his tail. He whipped round and clawed a red streak down her leg through the nylon. And then she screamed again, and began to babble through hysterical sobs that she never meant to hurt the poor old sod, that it wasn't her fault! Ever since she'd been going with young Joel she'd been seeing that little old bag going in and out, draped with her bits of gold. What in hell did an old witch like her want with jewellery? She had no *right*! At her age!

"But I never meant to hurt her! She came in too soon," lamented Connie, still and for ever the aggrieved. "What was I supposed to do? I had to get away, didn't I? *She was between me and the door!*"

She was half her size, too, and nearly four times her age! Ah, well! What the courts would do with Connie, thank God, was none of my business. I just took her in and charged her, and got her statement. Once we had her dabs it was all over, because she'd left a bunch of them sweaty and clear on that brass candlestick. But if it hadn't been for the Trinity cat and his single-minded pursuit, scaring her into that ill-judged attempt to hand us young Joel as a scapegoat, she might, she just might, have got clean away with it. At least the boy could go home now, and count his blessings.

Not that she was very bright, of course. Who but a stupid harpy, soaked in cheap perfume and gimcrack dreams, would have hung on even to the catmint mouse, mistaking it for a herbal sachet to put among her smalls?

I saw the Trinity cat only this morning, sitting grooming in the church porch. He's getting very self-important, as if he knows he's a celebrity, though throughout he was only looking after the interests of Number One, like all cats. He's lost interest in his mouse already, now most of the scent's gone.

COME TO DUST

My wife's Aunt Filomena is the oldest of a big family, of which Fran's Mum is the youngest, and I reckon there must be twenty years between them. The old girl's all of seventy-five now, but indestructible, and in her time she's run through three marriages, one divorce and two widowhoods, the second one highly profitable. But for that, she might have been having a look round now for her fourth, but ending up with half a million, even in dollars, has tipped the scale in favour of settling back into solitary luxury and putting her feet up. She's holed up in California, and not likely to do much cavorting about the world any more, but she's lost none of her volcanic energy, or her genius for disrupting the affairs of her scattered family from a distance.

That side of Fran's family comes from Turin. Her Mum's name, before she married an Englishman over on business, was Emilia Cecchini, and the Italian influence remained dominant. All the Cecchinis are born managers and administrators. North Italians are like that, not small, dark and private, like south of Eboli, where Christianity stopped, but big, assertive and blonde, everything the Italians are not supposed to be. Moreover, by instinct they sing in harmony, just like small dark Welshmen, while the small dark southerners, who physically resemble Welshmen, are despairingly monodic to the last forlorn degree. How do you make sense of that?

To get back to Aunt Filomena, the doyenne of the lot. In her affluent retirement, with a married son not far away, money enough to buy all the attendance she wants, and no worries, she has developed a new hobby. Hobby? Obsession! She keeps a family tree complete with all the third and fourth generation, all but herself and Cousin Paolo left behind here in Britain and Europe, mostly in Italy. And she loves to buy presents for this one and that one, as the fit takes her. She's the wealthiest of the bunch, and granted she's generous, she loves to spread the joy. With the kids she does pretty well. Maybe she's in her second childhood, and understands what children like. With the rest of us she has a marvellous knack of discovering white elephants.

The trouble is, she has got hooked on auctioneers' catalogues, and has them sent to her in advance from all the main houses, goes through them with eyeballs bulging, picks out the most appalling specimens of expensive kitsch, and despatches her orders to agents wherever the sales are taking place, London, Zurich, New York, Amsterdam, Florence—you name it!—to bid for the most God-awful pieces, provided they're labelled "important," which means fashionable and hellishly expensive. Then she has them sent to such relatives as she feels would best both love and deserve them.

I am never sure whether this is pure, misguided benevolence, or plain mischief.

Anyhow, that's how we happened to get Aunt Filomena's nineteenth century copy of an (alleged!) earlier French *bonheur du jour* delivered to our unoffending bungalow in a quarter of an acre, in the second-best district of our prosperous and genteel market town, as a birthday present to Fran.

You have never, but never, seen such a monstrosity. Its only admirer throughout has been the long-haired nit who helped the driver to lift it inside. He thought it was wonderful. Afterwards we wished we'd asked for his name and address, he could have given it to his old Mum for a Christmas present. The driver was a pro who regularly delivered for the firm, he averted his eyes as he helped to carry it in. He was accustomed to the better trade. If he said six words during the whole transaction, that was about it. He accelerated away from our gate as if he feared we might call him back to take the thing away before he could escape.

So there it stood in our hall, out in the open to be viewed from every side, and Fran and I circled warily round it looking for a place from which it might look better, but there wasn't one. There wasn't a prospect that pleased. Like man, the thing was vile.

A *bonheur du jour* is, or should be, a lady's writing-desk, where she is supposed to sit down in the morning, full of housewifely energy and importance, to write her letters, her menus for the day, and any notes she may think necessary, perhaps her diary, too, if she has a bent that way. Mostly the French ones were light, elegant and decorative in a graceful, restrained way. This thing was bloated, heavy, with two tiers of drawers, on either side a kneehole, and one long, shallow drawer above the knee-space; and above the writing surface a raised back panel flanked by two more very small drawers.

It wasn't simply that it was covered all over with ornamentation that bore no relationship to its shape, but mainly that the shape itself was all wrong. Every proportion was false by just that fraction that turned it into horrid caricature. The ornamentation was a bonus. All its edges, pedestals and writing surface alike, were finished with frills, like okra pods—no, more like some obscene lizard; and all its surfaces except the back were inlaid with vari-coloured veneers and bits of coloured glass in intricate patterns. I won't say every small oblong had a different design—I daresay they ran out of ideas here and there, and slipped in a duplicate— but certainly there was no pattern or symmetry in their arrangement. As a finishing touch, all the frills were gilded at the edges. And there it sat and leered at us.

"And I shall be expected to write and *thank* her for it!" Fran said, bitterly but resignedly.

What can you do? Kith and kin are kith and kin, and you can't deliberately hurt their feelings. Everybody who's ever had a most unwelcome present delivered in good faith knows the procedure. The difficulty is to sound cheerfully grateful without going overboard into such fulsome appreciation that it defeats its own end. But Fran has a warm corner for Aunt Filomena, and a kind heart, and she manages to make it ring true.

Well, we may have looked our gift horse very dubiously in the mouth, but at least we did make an honest effort to find a suitable stable for it. The note that came with it gave a full description but a vague and incomplete provenance. The thing had, like so many nineteenth-century pieces, two concealed drawers, hardly worth calling secret, since a seven-year-old could have found his way in, once informed there was something there to be found, but private enough unless you knew they were there. They were built into the tops of the two pedestals, and all you had to do was to open the visible top drawer, slip your fingers inside the top of it, press up a tilted slip of wood there, and draw it forward, and out popped a section of the apparently solid inlay immediately under the writing surface, to reveal another shallow drawer. When you pushed it in again the wooden catch clicked home and fastened it closed, and the awful expanse of inlay showed complete again.

Fran made a determined effort to take it seriously and make use of it. "It's meant for writing on," she said, "and I'll use it for writing. If we have to give it house-room, let's make it earn its keep."

She moved all her notepaper, envelopes, pens, ink and what have you into the drawers, all very orderly and neat. She even insisted on using the secret drawers, all her pens and pencils, stapler and stamp-book in the left-hand one, her bottles of blue and red ink in the right. I forget how we even came to have red ink, I think it must have been when I was map-making for a client at the office. Anyhow, Fran stood it for fully three weeks before she gave up. That thing was the wrong height for writing on, no matter what chair or stool you used, the desk wouldn't accommodate her typewriter, and the frilly edge was hideously uncomfortable under the wrist for writing by hand.

So then we tried the most obscure corner of the living-room, but it wasn't obscure enough, the thing managed to obtrude ominously wherever we parked it. Then we stuck it out in the hall, where at least we weren't obliged to look at it all the time, but it still contrived to get in the way, and Fran said it grinned at her every time she passed it.

I don't know why it took us so long to realise that we weren't forced to go on enduring the thing. Aunt Filomena had long ago had her letter of thanks, and was some thousands of miles away in California, and never likely to cross the Atlantic again, so how was she ever to know whether we continued to cherish her gift, or threw it out thankfully and forgot about it? Where ignorance is bliss ... Of course she'd never know!

"Do you really think we could?" wondered Fran, brightening at the very thought. "I'd feel mean, somehow, if we sold it. All I want is to get rid of it, not to turn it to profit. If we gave it away I shouldn't feel quite so base."

It was getting round into December then, and our annual riot of fund-raising events for the mayor's great Christmas charity appeal was in full swing, so I said why not donate Aunt Filomena's *bonheur du jour* to the Lions' auction for the good cause. And we did.

Nobody bid for it.

Tommy Anslow, who ran the do, said he thought it was too upstage for his customers, and it was a shame, really, not to put so remarkable a piece into its own kind of sale, and we'd better take it back for the present. So we did.

Well, if we couldn't get any of our respectable neighbours to take it, we could throw it open to the less respectable. *Somebody* had to have that sort of taste, surely. So we did what we'd done once or twice before when we installed new furniture and wanted to get rid of the old, we put the thing out by the gate, with a notice saying: *If you fancy this, please take it and welcome.*

It had always worked before. Things vanished like magic. Not this time. After some days it snowed, so we took it in again as far as the porch. In a proper house it could have been hoisted out of sight into the attic long before then, but modern bungalows don't have attics. It was still in the porch, like an astronaut stuck in the air-lock, when Ben and Meg came to spend Christmas with us.

Ben is Fran's younger brother, and where girls are concerned more Italian than the Italians. He is also a dealer in antiques, prints and ceramics mostly, though he does a little with furniture, too, when he drops on something he likes. He wasn't going to like Aunt Filomena's writing-desk, that was for sure.

And now I suppose you're thinking in terms of Frances and Benjamin for these two half-breeds? Not a bit of it. She's Francesca, and he's Benedetto. I told you the Italian side was dominant. Ben is elegant, handsome and promiscuous, at least as far as eyes and tongue are concerned, but dead practical, too, and had the sense to marry Meg, his girl-Friday, who knows as much about prints as he does, and almost as much about ceramics. Meg is thin, plain, exquisitely dressed on next to nothing, with a sardonic turn of speech, and the cool nerves any woman with a wandering-eyed husband needs. She is imperturbable, with good reason. She knows not only that Ben will always come back, but also that he'll always come back with renewed pleasure.

The pair of them took one look at the exile in the air-lock. Meg continued to study it with detached interest. Ben closed his eyes and shuddered.

"What," he demanded, with his eyes still closed, "is that?"

"That," said Fran, almost smug in her despair, "is Aunt Filomena's *bonheur du jour*, and my last birthday present from her."

Ben opened one eye, cautiously, and closed it again. Meg said: "More of a *malheur du jour*, wouldn't you say?"

Ben said at once, as soon as he could get both eyes open: "Get rid of it! No one can be asked to live with that. I don't care if it did come from Aunt Filomena. She's never going to erupt on your doorstep, and what the eye doesn't see the heart doesn't grieve. Get rid of it!"

Over drinks, over dinner, over the first far too early carol singers elbowing and giggling on the doorstep, we explained that we'd already tried to get rid of it, without success. It kept coming back like a song. Or like garlic!

"You've got a bulk-garbage disposal arrangement of some sort," said Ben ruthlessly, "you must have. Every council has. What's that thing but bulk-garbage? Chuck it out, before it turns you peculiar. No use being sentimental where your sanity's at stake."

It took a bit of getting used to, but I could see Fran warming to the idea. And Meg said placidly: "She was cheated, anyhow, I'll bet. It isn't worth even its curiosity price. Much better let her dream she gave you something precious, if eccentric. She's never going to know any better, is she?"

We were coming up to the last pre-Christmas visit from the bin-boys then, and we looked at each other, and visibly thought, well, why not?

Our friendly neighbourhood dustman is a glorious patriarch by the name of Augustus, believe it or not. He isn't, of course, our only dustman, he's the gaffer of the regular squad, and the monarch of our local tip, which he keeps with the strict neatness and precision of a Puritan prelate. Which he almost is, for he's a local preacher of an elder school, too benevolent for hell-fire, rather of the "Lord-knock-a-brick-out-and-let-glory-in!" persuasion. Even in orange overalls he has a regal look about him. In visage he's weather-beaten and benign, with grizzled, wiry hair, and a five o'clock shadow that begins to manifest itself around noon. In build he's stocky and powerful, and composed entirely of right angles, as befits so foursquare a character. And like all the delivery and service men around the town, he's on terms of warm mutual respect with Fran. Fran elicits Christian names as an expert waiter draws corks, with no effort at all.

"And they're due tomorrow," said Fran, delighted. "The last collection before Christmas." They're not allowed to ask for Christmas boxes, but she always manages to slip them one, and usually has a glass of something warming and a mince-pie handy.

So Augustus came in and viewed the family incubus thoughtfully over his mince-pie, and gave judgement.

"I tell you what," he said, "I'll have it took up to the tip for you, and pop it under cover there, where folks who come to dump stuff can see it, and it'll be out of the weather, and we'll see what happens. You'd be surprised how folks who wouldn't give things another look on a market stall or put out by a gate, like you put this, will pounce on 'em and haul 'em away like treasure when they find 'em on the tip. Some of what gets fetched away that road we get back later, when they come to their right senses. But the thought of picking up something for nothing, and having *discovered* it, as you might say … They get carried away. No reason why something that's no good to you shouldn't be some good to someone else, is there? When I get something that might catch somebody's eye, I let it lie in full view a few days, and as often as not it gets fetched away."

All of which we already knew, though we'd never expected to have to take advantage of it. Our local tip is a decorous distance out of town, among open fields, covering a large plot of waste ground that's been pitted with old surface mining and earlier shallow shafts. They're gradually levelling it off, and the first quarter or so is already smoothed and tidied and under grass, and there Augustus and his myrmidons have a hut, and a large covered port for lorries and plant while on the job, and that's where he puts such cast-off objects as he thinks worthy of survival if some inquisitive visitor fancies them. I go there sometimes to take massive loads of hedge-brushings or other garden rubbish, and it's quite amazing what people do throw away. No wonder some of it gets reclaimed by more thrifty-minded people. Not that I could imagine anyone falling upon our contribution with glad cries. But they could always bulldoze it in, if all else failed.

"You don't know how grateful I'll be," said Fran fervently, "to see the back of it. Will it be all right if we drive it round there tomorrow?"

"Bless you, ma'am, no need for that," said Augustus. "I've got a van coming round this way this afternoon. My lads will pick it up on their way out there."

It seemed his lads were a somewhat motley lot at the time, due to a 'flu bug that was running round the district in full cry. So many of the regulars were down with it that he'd had to take on some casuals, a scratch lot including a few students not too proud to take a dirty holiday job. He admitted they weren't doing too badly. Certainly the pair who called to pick up the *bonheur du jour* in the afternoon seemed brisk and willing enough. One dark young fellow, and one fair, in borrowed orange overalls. They eyed the thing with interest, and didn't say no to a mince-pie each. Fran was so happy to be getting shot of the horror that she never stopped talking. She even demonstrated one of the "secret" drawers and how to open and shut it, the left-hand one, from which she'd long since removed her pens and stamps and stapler. They were fascinated. They popped their fingers in, pressed the catch, sprang the drawer open and clicked it shut several times, ran a finger along the almost invisible join, and remarked, truly, that whether you liked the thing or not, a lot of fairly expert work had gone into it. Which is true of a lot of artifacts which had better never have been started at all, but are put together to last almost for ever.

"Just the job, that," said the fair one, "for keeping your diamond studs in."

"Or your love letters," offered the dark one. He was showing the usual reaction to Fran, and I wouldn't swear he hadn't one eye on Meg, too, who may not be so obviously decorative, but draws plenty of male eyes, all the same. "You're sure you want to part with it?"

Fran said yes, emphatically she did, and never to see it again. And with that they seized it boisterously, hoisted it, and galloped out jauntily to stow it in their van, and off it went at last. We closed the door on it, and heaved a concerted sigh of content at seeing the last of it.

"Students!" said Meg reflectively, having weighed up our deliverers as she watched them depart. "Now I wonder what those two are studying? Womankind, to judge by the dark one's roving eye. Such a bright blue eye, too. I saw it wink at you, Fran."

"So did I!" admitted Fran. "Do you think I overdid the grace and charm? I was so darned pleased to see them, I suppose I practically fawned. Even when Augustus promised, I could hardly believe I was really going to be rid of that awful thing. It's a wonder I didn't kiss the pair of them, I'm so grateful."

"Be grateful to Augustus," I said. "I don't know that I'd mind you kissing him—just once at New Year, maybe, for auld lang syne. It would be worth it to see his face."

"Good-looking lad, though," said Meg thoughtfully, "that dark one. Well, now we can all breathe more easily. And Aunt Filomena just as happy as ever!"

It's quite extraordinary how much more spacious the house seemed without that lumpish nuisance. We went back to our Christmas preparations with lighter hearts, and Ben and Meg set off on their round of friendly calls in the neighbourhood, and left us to it. There were three more fund-raising events the day before Christmas Eve, and then the gala concert and supper on Christmas Eve itself, where all the takings would be handed in to Roddy Hughes, who is treasurer. I avoid committees like the plague, but Fran is on the Ladies' Committee, and inevitably gets roped in among the voluntary helpers, catering, selling tickets and programmes, serving the buffet supper and what have you. Even lady guests of our committee women are drafted unless they're good at dodging. Meg is excellent at dodging. She says it would cramp Ben's style if she occupied a place anywhere but in the discreet background on social occasions.

You know what these do's are like, they must be much the same everywhere, with all the local talent competing for a place on the programme. The male voice choir sings, the chamber orchestra plays, the best of the amateur and semi-professional singers bring out their ballads and duets, and the evening ends with a grand carol-sing led by the Town Hall organ, which happens to be quite a good one. As the bar is open well before the performance begins, and for a half-hour interval midway, we can sing like nobody's business by the finish, and a good time is had by all. It's a very dressy occasion, too, which adds to the pleasure for the eyes.

Fran went along early to sell programmes and help organise the buffet, and then joined us before the show began. Ben fought his way to the bar for drinks for Meg and himself—I was driving—and came back with his chin on his shoulder and a thoughtful look in his eye.

"Who's the blonde in the blue dress?" he asked Fran when she joined us. "Behind the bar. Local girl? I don't remember her last year."

There were two or three girls helping the professional barman behind the bar, all volunteers, all young and attractive. Evidently one of them had already taken Ben's critical eye. No beating about the bush with Ben, he goes straight for what he wants.

"Oh, that one!" said Meg. "I was wondering which of them it would be. Not bad, not bad at all!"

"I don't know her name," said Fran. "I think she came with Mrs. Grant." Mrs. Grant is the secretary of the Ladies' Committee, and quite capable of recruiting any young female relative who happens to be spending Christmas with her. "They arrived together. Probably a niece or something. I don't remember her from last year, either, and yet I do feel I've seen her somewhere before. She *is* fetching, isn't she?"

The girl was just abandoning her bottles and glasses and emerging to go into the hall and take her seat. The blue dress was floor-length and fluted from the hips, long-sleeved and high at the neck, very demure indeed. Her hair was almost primrose-fair, and cut short in a smooth, feathery style that set off good cheekbones and a wide forehead, and eyes, viewed at that distance, several shades darker than the blue of her gown. Not bad at all! There were plenty of fluffier, fancier, more elaborately dressed girls around, but Ben goes for quality and style.

There was no pursuing her then, it was time to take our places. But when the first half had gone off smoothly and we came out for the interval, there she was behind the bar again, and somehow, as soon as Ben and I had provided our womenfolk with their chosen poison, Ben was lost again.

By that time Roddy Hughes had the ticket and door takings all corralled, plus the three sums handed in from the previous night's fund-raising events, and was shut up with a couple of helpers in the office at the rear of the hall, feverishly totting up the lot and committing it to the office safe in its locked bag, since there'd be no banking it until after the two-day holiday. The takings from the bar and the sale of raffle tickets would have to wait to be totalled up separately afterwards. Everybody was already acquiring a smug glow of virtue at duty done. Ben's blonde girl emerged from the bar with a tray of drinks for the backroom boys and a black coffee for Roddy, who loses his ability to add up after even a mild dose of alcohol. And guess who loped gracefully ahead to open all the doors for her and escort her back again, blushing. There were rivals in the field by then, but they were up against something out of their class.

Meg smiled and said: "Not to worry, he thrives on competition. It's competition that keeps him safe, and confirms his judgement at the same time. You don't suppose he really wants anything to come of it, do you, beyond a perfume and a rose-leaf? It's a *clair-de-lune* thing, a *fête galante* thing. He dances to an imaginary mirror. So—I hope!—does she. Though she does look a bit young and innocent for it," she ended doubtfully.

I don't think she need have worried, the blue girl, shy and quiet though she might be, was clearly enjoying herself and well able to cope. Ben rejoined us for the second half not displeased with his own image, but disapproving strongly of the boisterous attentions of one or two of our local young bloods. They tend to get a little above themselves on such occasions. Didn't we all, once?

It was pretty plain that Ben had his private plans to corner the girl at supper, after we'd all sung ourselves hoarse and sufficiently admired the sound of our own voices. In the milling throng ferrying their plates hungrily along the buffet tables I did catch a glimpse of the primrose-coloured head once or twice, but by the time we'd stacked our plates and picked up our wine and found a reasonably protected corner from which to survey the scrum in comparative safety, I'd completely lost her. Worse, so had Ben. He's taller than most of us, but even with that advantage he'd begun to wear a frown of mingled frustration and concern. He slipped away back to the buffet, with a sharp eye cocked either way as he went, to check on those who came late, or went back for refills or more wine, but no girl. Cinderella had left before the end of the ball, wiser than in the fairy tale.

"And I don't see that clot who was pestering her in the interval, either," said Ben, vexed. "I hope she hasn't gone off with him. I wouldn't trust him as far as I could throw him."

"If she came with Mrs. Grant," said Fran reasonably, "she'll have left with Mrs. Grant, and I know *she* left as soon as she'd had a word with Roddy Hughes and seen the records and the money into the safe."

So that's how the evening ended. We all went home about midnight, and more or less shut the business of the world out for the next two days. You know how it is at Christmas. No newspapers, the news on telly and radio cut down to size, and nobody bothers to turn it on, anyhow. No offices to attend, no banks to deposit in or borrow from, no business letters to answer, no nothing to spoil the calm. Except that Ben, still preoccupied, took himself off on Christmas morning for a walk, and went to church instead. He came back considerably aggrieved, and confronted Fran with: "I thought you said that girl was staying with Mrs. Grant."

"I said she arrived with Mrs. Grant," said Fran, interested. "Why? Isn't she?"

"I had a word with Mrs. Grant after church," said Ben with dignity. "Wished her the usual, asked if she was tired after last night—you know the line." No one can shoot it better with middle-aged ladies. "Then I asked if her guest had enjoyed the gala. *What guest?* So then I had to describe her. She's nothing whatever to do with the Grants. Mrs. Grant thought she was with Mrs. Forster."

"So then," said Meg, sweetly smiling, "I suppose you passed the compliments of the season with Mrs. Forster. No dice?"

"Mrs. Forster," said Ben flatly, "thought she was with Fran. Nice, helpful girl, but never seen her in her life before."

"And yet I still feel that *I* have, somewhere, some time," said Fran, after the subject had otherwise been dropped, even by Ben, though he was still brooding.

The day after Boxing Day, usually slow and reluctant to start up again, actually went off like a bomb that time. Two bombs! For when Roddy Hughes went to the Town Hall in the morning to collect his big leather bag of money and take it to the bank, unlocking the door of the office, unlocking the door of the safe, and fingering forth his little key to unlock the bag itself, quite unnecessarily, for the pure pleasure of taking a look at all that delectable loot, he found he had no lock in which to insert it, no bag, no money, nothing on the shelf. Admitted it was an old safe a seven-year-old could probably have opened, if ever it had entered his head to try, but nobody had ever questioned its security before, and until now nobody had robbed it.

The sensation ran round the town like wildfire. The second bomb made no great noise anywhere but in our bungalow, but there it drowned out the other. It was a letter from Aunt Filomena in California. Cousin Paolo, she wrote, had had to fly over to Turin on family business, and he proposed to return via London, and come and spend a few days with us in the New Year before flying home. And she had asked him to bring back up-to-date photographs of us all, and of the house. In particular she looked forward to seeing how her *bonheur du jour* had fitted into our home.

In panic and recrimination we wasted at least ten minutes, everyone accusing everyone else of stupidly urging the jettisoning of the thing, on the grounds that Aunt Filomena would never know, when there were so many ways in which she might find out. Then Fran said: "Shut up, and *do* something! We know where it is, don't we? It can just as easily come back, can't it? There's only one thing to be done, take the station wagon and go and fetch it."

"It's been out in the weather for a week," I said feebly. "And how if somebody's adopted it and made off with it? That's what we wanted to happen."

"Ha!" said Fran scornfully. She knew it better than that. "It'll still be there, where Augustus put it, and he said under cover. Get going!"

So Ben and I leaped into the station wagon and drove off to the tip to retrieve the horrid thing.

Our tip must have the biggest inland resident colony of seagulls anywhere short of the central European breeding grounds. They live there all the year, doing a useful job of scavenging and tidying up the area, but you have to watch your heads when you drive in through the gate to the edge of the levelled and grassed part, because at the sound of a car they go up in their thousands like a snowstorm in reverse.

Augustus came out of his hut just as we pulled up. He had a grievance of his own, because the usual had happened, and half his squad who should have shown up for work that morning were stretching the holiday a little—possibly only for this one day, but he darkly suspected some of them wouldn't clock in again until after New Year. It was an old human failing, and Augustus accepted it in a spirit of Christian resignation. One of his temporaries, at any rate, had shown up for work, for the fair boy who had helped to remove the writing-desk emerged from the hut to help us reload it. No doubt he thought we were looney, but we didn't bother to explain to him. We did to Augustus, after he'd led us to the spot where the thing lurked, as evil as ever, and none the worse (or better!) for its stay among the garbage.

"Well, it's worth a little self-sacrifice to keep the lady happy," he said gravely. "And probably the gentleman won't be visiting this way for some years, after this." It was kind of him to point out so soothingly that our suffering need only be temporary. "It would be a shame to wound her feelings, when she meant it as a generous act." And he looked up rather warily into the sky full of seagulls and threatening frost or snow, and murmured: "—thou dost not bite so nigh, as benefits forgot!" You can always rely on Augustus to have a line of Shakespeare ready for most occasions.

We hoisted the horror into the station wagon, and drove back home as if we expected Cousin Paolo to be on the doorstep ahead of us. We parked the desk dubiously in the least offensive position in the living-room, and Fran drew a finger along the top and decided that we ought to polish it up a bit after its week in the cold and the dust. That was when she opened the top pedestal drawer on the right, to wipe away the rim of dust left where it didn't fit flush, and let out a yell of pure surprise that brought us all crowding round.

The drawer wasn't empty, as it had been, but full of crumpled blue fabric that looked like silk jersey. Meg leaned and plucked it out, and it uncoiled in her hands into the unmistakable shape of a full-length dress, high-necked and long-sleeved, dirty now and creased, and with a great, blackening reddish stain all over breast and shoulder.

Ben was the first to recognise it. He gave a yelp of horror, and grabbed it away from Meg. "My God, whatever … This is *hers*! Look at it! It's the dress that girl was wearing on Christmas Eve. For God's sake, what's happened to her?"

"You're crazy!" snapped Meg, rather fending off belief than expressing any real doubt. "It's just a dress someone threw away. Why should it be hers?"

"It *is*!" Ben insisted. "I'd know it again anywhere. That poor kid …"

"It is," Fran echoed him hollowly. "Look here!" And she plucked a pale, smooth hair from the shoulder of the dress, and even the hair was dark at one end from whatever had dried there.

Ben fell upon the other three drawers and dragged them out, to reveal a few more pathetic relics hurriedly shoved into hiding there, a long white evening slip, a pair of silver-grey nylon hold-ups, the kind of stockings that need no suspender belt, and a soiled and draggled lacy bra with one broken shoulder-strap.

"Hers!" said Ben hoarsely. "They must be …"

We stood and gaped at the wretched little collection, all spoiled and befouled as they were, and couldn't choose but think of the wearer, perhaps similarly violated and abandoned, there among the garbage.

"Let everything lie," said Ben after a long silence. "This is police business now. That …" He stabbed a finger at the ominous blackish red stain, dried into a crust at the edges. "*That*—is blood. Don't mess with these things any more than we already have, just leave them. Bill, you'd better …"

"I know," I said, and made for the telephone to dial 999.

They came, first Sergeant Green, whom we all knew, and later an inspector and others. We had to tell them the whole story of how the *bonheur du jour* had been banished and then hurriedly fished back again. What we'd found inside we didn't have to tell them, every item was there to be seen, and by that time we were all quite certain of the girl who had last been seen wearing them. But there was nothing more we could tell them about the girl herself, except that so far we hadn't found anyone who knew who she was, or where she'd come from.

"It does look," said Sergeant Green, "as if we've got something worse than a robbery on our hands now. Queer we should get two such cases dropped on us together, a quiet place like this. Though if there's any connection between the two, so far I don't see it."

They put every article of clothing carefully into a plastic bag, picked a few more short fair hairs from the neck of the dress, noted that the zipper at the back was wrenched out of place, as though the dress had been torn off her by force, and went off with everything to get forensic reports, and to interview Augustus and get him to show them exactly where the desk had been standing while it remained at the tip. The few taciturn remarks they exchanged in our hearing gave little away, except that they were taking the matter very seriously.

"No pants, you notice. No vest or anything—if they wear them under this sort of gear. It was a cold night."

"Could be still on the body."

"No coat, but it would be bulky, and if she was wearing fur it would be worth making off with, of course."

We hadn't seen whatever coat she'd been wearing, but the cloakroom that night had been bulging with furs.

"And no shoes. If there was a struggle she may have lost those. We'll look for them on the spot."

"Some devil dragged her in there," Ben said bitterly, "and then raped and killed her. Maybe she had to take that road past the tip to get home ... Maybe this chap offered to escort her, and then ..."

They didn't say anything to that. But that same day they began to search the tip, the whole great, unpleasant slope of it, where tipping was currently going on, where a body could most easily be covered from view. If her clothes were there, she couldn't be far away.

And still, though the whole town was boiling now with rumours, and everyone who had attended the gala was being questioned, still nobody could say who she was, or where she'd come from. Nor where she'd gone to, either. They had bulldozers carefully turning up the recent layers, and policemen wading among the debris, and dogs, and every resource you can think of, but they didn't find the blonde girl, nor her missing shoes. Augustus looked on with sorrowful dignity, shook his head, and murmured something about "golden lads and girls all must ..." But he didn't like seeing his beautiful orderly tip either used for such vile purposes as murder, or so torn to pieces by the law.

But if they didn't find a body, they did find the leather bag in which Roddy Hughes had locked the entire proceeds of all our charity events. Still locked—it was the one lock which had defeated the thief. But empty, of course. He'd used a knife to slit it open, and he was now between seven and eight hundred pounds richer than he'd been ten days previously, and in mixed, easily usable currency, too. But if there was plain sign that the thief had been here, did that also prove him the murderer? There's a lot of our town dump, it looked like being a very long job sifting all of it.

In the end it turned out not to be necessary.

It was two days later when Sergeant Green came to see us again, and asked if he could take another look at our *bonheur du jour*.

"You see," said he mildly, "we've now had the forensic reports on those clothes, and there are several interesting things to note. To begin with—that dark stain on the dress. I don't know if you noticed that there wasn't a mark on the slip she wore under it. That stain isn't blood, after all. It turns out it's red ink."

"Red *ink*?" echoed Fran, wide-eyed; and suddenly she gave a sort of strangled squeak, and plunged upon Aunt Filomena's gift, and plucked open the top pedestal drawer on the right side. "Of *course*! Since ball-pens I hardly ever use even blue ink, let alone red. When they fetched this away I clean forgot ..."

She sprang the catch and hauled open the shallow drawer hidden above. Two ink-bottles rolled ponderously about the space within. The blue ink had had its cap screwed on firmly enough to remain sealed while rattled along in the van, but the red had not, and its entire contents had dyed the base of the drawer, and seeped through the seams to drip steadily into the drawer below, providing a puddle into which the crumpled dress had been stuffed in a hurry. When it was heaved about, the bottles had fallen over, the motion of the van had kept them rolling, and worked off the loose cap.

"Then *no blood*!" breathed Fran, and looked up hopefully at Sergeant Green. "So it may not be as bad as we feared?"

"Well," said Sergeant Green deprecatingly, "there's also the matter of the fair hairs. There were three or four caught in the zipper, as it happens. That jammed it, that's why it had to be ripped apart by force to get the dress off. And as it turns out—they're not hairs at all—well, not human hairs. They're nylon. So I thought, if I may have another look at where everything was stowed ... And that little trick you just did, ma'am—would there be another like it this other side?"

Fran was staring at Meg and Meg was staring at Fran, and their mouths and eyes hung wide open, and there was some frantic reassessment going on inside their heads. And then they both began to speak at once.

"Fran—it was the *left* one you showed them . . ."

Fran stared through her, and said: "I *said* I kept thinking I'd seen her before . . ."

"A blue and roving eye," said Meg in a faint voice.

"Those two were the only ones I showed how to open them ..."

Then Ben and I caught the infection, and started connecting, too, and that didn't make things much clearer for anyone listening. Ben said: "The fair lad's there all right, he helped us load ..."

I said: "I'll bet the other is one of the defaulters. Augustus can tell us."

The whole discussion didn't seem to be getting anywhere, or providing much enlightenment for Sergeant Green, so Fran pounced on the left-hand pedestal, opened the upper drawer, slid in her fingers and sprang the catch.

There were just three things in the secret drawer she had demonstrated for Augustus's young men: a smooth, blonde, feather-cut nylon wig, and two buxom falsies to pad out the bra.

He'd worn his own underwear, of course, and the long-skirted, fluted dress, dexterously managed, was perfectly adequate to hide his shoes. He'd probably have taken the dress away with him if he hadn't wrecked the zipper getting it off.

He never clocked on for work with the bin-boys again, naturally. They tried to trace him by the clothes, but it was no go. Nobody in this town has set eyes on him since, and I doubt if anybody ever will.

Cousin Paolo never showed up, after all, he rang up from Heathrow to say that an urgent business deal had cropped up in New York, and he couldn't afford to let it slip through his fingers, so he was taking an immediate connection for home. Next year, perhaps, he said.

Augustus has smoothed out all the nasty holes and furrows the police made in his nice, tidy tip, and put out of sight, among other eyesores, Aunt Filomena's *bonheur du jour*. Henceforth cousins from California, if they ever do turn up, will have to take us as they find us—hospitable but defiant.

Ben has gone off blondes.

LET NOTHING YOU DISMAY!

The girl in the patched jeans and the voluminous black sweater got off the bus from Comerbourne at the stop opposite the Sitting Duck at ten minutes past seven in the evening, on the twenty-third of December. It was too early then for the landlord to be doing much business in the bar, too late for any delayed shoppers or honest folk coming home from work to be about the single street of the village, and only one other passenger descended from the ancient bus, and scurried away at once into the darkness, to vanish with the crisp click of a gate-latch and in through a house door just beyond the pub. There was no one to notice the arrival of the girl in Mottisham, and by the time the bus rattled away up the valley road towards its final halt at Abbot's Bale, a mile further towards the Welsh border, she, too, had vanished into the tree-shrouded darkness of the lane that climbed the slope behind the church.

The long cleft of Middlehope climbs the valley of a border stream, dwindling as it mounts, until the river shrinks into the spring that is its source, the final village of Abbot's Bale is left behind, and nothing remains but the bare moorland and occasional marsh of the watershed between England and Wales. The local bus, family-owned and driven, turns about at Abbot's Bale after its final evening run, the driver has a meal, a break, a gossip and a single pint at the Gun Dog before driving back down the valley to Comerbourne, which is home. Why go further? Over the two bleak miles of the crest there are no houses to be served. The road goes on, and winds its way down to civilisation again on the other side, but for practical purposes Abbot's Bale is the end of the road.

Even at the more congenial level of the village of Mottisham, population is still sparse, in spite of some new development on the lower slopes, and there was no one abroad to see or hear the girl in the patched jeans as she walked briskly up the winding lane, past one or two lighted cottage windows, towards one of the older houses on the fringe of the village. She was small and lightly built, almost silent on the unpaved road surface, almost invisible in her dark clothing. The night was moonless and overcast, relatively mild for December, though there might well be frost later, in the small hours.

She had left the few lights of the village behind, and the stone wall of a well-treed garden began on her right hand. Fifty yards along the wall was pierced by a modest, square-pillared gateway, its white gate wide open on a drive flanked by old shrubberies. The girl turned in there, and proceeded confidently up the drive until it curved to the left, and for the first time brought into view, clear-cut against the sky and rearing out of the cloudy shapelessness of old trees, the line of the roof and the square bulk of the upper part of the house. A solid, respectable, middle-class house, probably mid-Victorian, a silhouette cut out in black paper against a mount just perceptibly less black. And profoundly silent, to the point of menace.

The girl halted in the cover of the trees, and stood a moment perfectly still, contemplating the unrelieved darkness. Not a light in the entire bulk, outside or in. Even the heaviest of curtains could hardly have sealed in light totally, had there been any to conceal. Still, you never know! The girl marched on boldly, climbed the steps to the front door, and rang the bell. For a moment she stood listening, an ear inclined to the door, but not a sound of any kind responded from within. Appearances were confirmed, the house was empty.

She descended the steps again, and without hesitation set off by the path that rounded the corner of the house, and made for the back premises. Evidently she already knew the ground well enough to know where she could find what she wanted. The garden was old, closely treed, cover available close to the walls on every side but the front. Round at the rear there was a small, rather high window, the kind to be found in cloakroom or scullery or larder, and this one probably as old as the house, never replaced by a more modern and more secure one. Under the bushes that crowded near it the girl dumped the duffle bag from her shoulder, rummaged inside its outer pocket for a moment, and produced a long nail-file. Reaching the latch of the window was no problem. An old creeper that covered half of the rear wall had its formidable roots braced almost under the sill, and took her light weight without a quiver as she climbed nimbly to the casement and levered the file in beneath the latch. It rose obligingly easily, and she drew the window open, held by the gnarled stem of the creeper, and slid one slim leg over the sill. The rest of her small person folded itself neatly and followed, and a moment later she was standing on the tiled floor of a small room, apparently a cloakroom, listening to the silence as it settled again gradually after the small agitation of her own movements.

She was in, and she had the house to herself.

Moving with unruffled confidence, she let herself out into a dark passage, and felt her way along it with fingertips brushing the walls, past a kitchen door and towards the front of the house. By this time her eyes were becoming sufficiently accustomed to the darkness to distinguish faintly the broad sweep of the banister rail of the staircase in the wide Victorian hall, and feeling her way along the wall parallel to it she found the light switch, and was hesitating with her finger on it when the first slight, disturbing sound came to her ears, and she froze where she stood, listening intently.

A car's engine, quiet and distant as yet, but not so distant as to be on the main road, on the other side of the house from the narrow lane by which she had come. It was coming gradually nearer, cutting through from that road by the short piece that would bring it round to the lane, and to the gate. Her acute ear caught the check and change in the note as it turned into the drive, and the sudden cautious crescendo as it rounded the curve. No doubt about it, someone was at this moment driving up to the front door—No, correction!—*past* the front door, and on round to the right, deep into the cover of the trees. Wheeling, backing and turning now. Ready for a quick departure?

The girl took her finger hastily from the lightswitch instead of pressing it, swooped round the ornate newel-post, and went scrambling up the stairs, hands spread to feel her way, and into the first bedroom on that side of the house. The large window showed as a shape of comparative pallor, the curtains undrawn, and prolonged acquaintance with the night had given her a fair measure of vision by this time. Peering down into the open between the house and its encircling trees, she could distinguish movement and form even when the car lights were switched off. Not a car, though, a van, middle-sized, elderly, backed unobtrusively into cover before it halted. And a minute later, after profound, listening silence, the cab doors opened quietly, and two figures slid out and crossed like shifting shadows to the window immediately below the one where she crouched in hiding.

One of them spoke, but it was only a wordless murmur. But when the second figure stepped back briefly to look up at the face of the house she saw that he carried something under his arm, and the something had the unmistakable shape of a gun. Shotguns they were carrying, these days, and this was the precise outline of a man with a shotgun, used to it, and probably all too ready to use it at the drop of a hat. A flicker of light reflected briefly from under the wall. They had a torch, and were using it to locate the fastenings of the window. A minute later she heard the sharp, tinkling fall of glass. They were in the house with her.

She took a moment to consider both the room she was in, and the alarming possibilities. They had brought a van, that meant larger plunder, pieces of furniture, antiques, silver. But not a very large van, not the kind to accommodate half the contents of the house. They were after chosen pieces. Probably they knew already what they wanted, collectors' pieces, whatever they had customers for, or could most profitably find customers for. Professionals specialised, handling only what they knew best. And here she was in a bedroom filled with good furniture, and she had better not stay there, if she could find a less likely place to provide desirable loot. And meantime …

She crossed the room to the dressing-table, detected by the ghostly gleam of mirrors. Where they found the light to reflect as they did she had no time to consider. She found what she was searching for in the second drawer, a roll of soft Indian leather as thick as her wrist, tied with brocaded ribbons. Without staying to untie it and confirm what was within, she could feel the shapes of bracelet and brooch and necklace through the silky folds. With luck they wouldn't even look for this, if clocks and china were what they fancied, but she meant at all costs to retain it if she could. She stuffed it down the neck of her sweater, made for the door, and opened it cautiously to listen for what was happening below.

They had not ventured to put on a light, but seemed to know, even by the beam of a torch, carefully shaded, exactly where to find what they wanted. There were voices now, subdued but audible, one gravelly, laconic and professionally calm, one sharp and edgy, and distinctly disquieting in its suggestion of hair-trigger nervousness.

"Take this an' all, eh?" He was close under the stairs, handling glass by the sound of it, but still with the gun under his arm. The gravelly voice swore at him, but still low and placidly.

"No, leave it! Come on with this clock 'ere, and look sharp."

The edgy one came, as ordered, but still mutinous. "What you turning it up for? That's good stuff."

"Good stuff, but no buyer. Stick to what I know. Safer."

And there went the clock aforesaid, out through the open window, to be stowed away in the van. They were working fast and methodically. The two of them, now, were carrying a piece of furniture between them, very carefully. Some sort of cabinet. They were in and out of other rooms, there was no moment when she had any chance to steal down the stairs in their absence, and get back to the rear of the house, and the open cloakroom window. She would have to sit it out, somewhere as safe as possible, and hope for them to go. How if they decided to come and continue their hunt upstairs?

The girl retreated warily along the dark landing, feeling her way against the wall. Down below her the shaded torch beam focused on the foot of the stairs.

"What's up there?" demanded the nervous voice, uneasy about time passing.

"His coins. Worth a packet sold in one go."

"Dead risky!" hazarded the doubter, but he was already on the stairs.

"Got it all set up, safe as houses. They're going west."

The girl felt behind her, softly opened the rearmost bedroom door, let herself in with feverish haste, and closed it behind her. Flattened against the wall behind the door, she heard them enter the bedroom she had quitted. There were a few minutes of silence, and then the sound of wood splintering, and a murmur of satisfaction. They had got what they had come for. Collectors sometimes allow their pride and joy to be viewed and recorded, whether in professional journals or regional television news programmes, and expert thieves digest and remember every detail. But now surely they would leave, and she could make her own departure once they were clear of the house.

They were out on the landing again with their loot, they must be nearly as eager to leave as she was to hear them go.

"What else they got up here, then?" wondered the edgy voice, turning towards where she hid, instead of away. "Might as well take a look."

"We got what we know we can deal with," said his mentor sharply. "Doesn't pay to take risks out of your depth. Come on, let's get out of here."

A hand grasped the outer knob of the door. The girl gripped its fellow on her side with both hands and all her strength, and struggled to prevent it from turning. It seemed that his touch had been no more than tentative, and for a moment she managed to hold it fast. But that was her undoing, for at once he said, with rising interest: "Locked! Let's have a go, then!" and she heard him lay his shotgun aside, leaning it against the jamb of the door to have both hands free. The next moment the knob turned, jerking her hands away, his shoulder thudded heavily against the wood, and the door flew open so violently that he shot half across the room, and let out a yell, suddenly thrown off-balance. The door, flung back hard against the girl's body, rebounded again with a dull sound that should have covered the gasp the blow fetched out of her, but did not quite cover it. The professional of these two had acute hearing. In his business he needed it.

"Hi up! What's here?" He was inside with them in an instant, the shotgun braced under his right arm, the torch in his left, sweeping the room. He kicked the door shut, and spread both feet firmly to bring the barrel of the gun to bear on the intruder. There was one instant when the girl gave herself up for lost, and as instantly recovered when the alarm point passed and nothing happened. All over in about half a second. Thank God it was the professional, not the lout, who held the gun, and his nerves were considerably stouter than his colleague's, and his wits quicker. The beam of the torch swept the girl from head to foot, and the most dangerous moment was past. Not that she could reckon on that as the end of danger, but at least it hadn't wiped her out on sight.

"Well, well!" said the expert, slowly lowering the barrel of the gun, but holding her pinned in the ray of the torch. "Look what we've found!"

His mate was certainly looking, dumbstruck and plainly in a state of panic which would have been her death if he had been holding the gun. "My Gawd!" he babbled, still breathless and splayed against the wall. "How come she's here? You said they was gone for hours. What we goin' to do with 'er now? She 'as to go, or we're goners. What you waitin' for? We *got* to ..."

"Shut up!" said the elder shortly. And to the girl, standing mute and still and very wary in the beam of the torch: "Who the hell are you?"

She had a vague view of them both now, at least their bulk and shape, even glimpses of features in the diffused light. The older man was stocky and square and shaggy, in what seemed to be overalls and a donkey jacket, middle-aged and composed, even respectable-looking, like an honest transport driver working late, a good appearance for a professional burglar. The other one was young, large, unshaven and lumpish, with a general bearing between a cringe and a swagger. Hard to account for why so competent a pro should tolerate so perilous and probably unreliable an aide. Perhaps they were father and son, and there wasn't much choice, or perhaps the lout had his own peculiar skills, like breaking open doors, or battering people to death if they got in the way. Anyhow, there they were, and she was stuck with them.

"Well, I'm not the missus here," she said, venturing close to sounding tart, "that's for sure. Nor the parlourmaid, neither."

"No, you for sure ain't," allowed the interrogator. "So what are you doing here?"

"Same as you, if I'd had the chance," she said resignedly. "If you hadn't come butting in I'd have been off a long time ago. You're one of a kind yourself, it seems, you should know another when you see one. What else you think I'd be doing here?"

"You reckon?" He was not impressed, but he was willing to think about it. "You got a name?"

"Not one you'd want to know, no more than I want to know yours. What's the use of names, anyway, wouldn't mean nothing to you. I told you what you asked me."

"What you wasting time for?" demanded the younger man feverishly, and laid a hand on the stock of the gun, but his companion held on to it and elbowed him off. "Get rid of her and let's get out of here. What else can we do with her now? She's nothing but trouble, whoever she is."

"Shut up!" repeated his elder, and kept his eyes unwaveringly upon the girl. "Two of a kind, are we?" he repeated thoughtfully. "How'd you get in here, then? Go on, show me!"

"Through a back window, round by the kitchen. Go on, have a look for yourself. I left it open, ready to get out again quick. Bent me nail-file, levering up the latch. Go on, see for yourself if you don't believe me. I left my duffle bag under the bushes, outside there. Go on, send him to have a look! I'm not telling you lies. Why should I? I got nothing against you. I know nothing, I seen nothing, and sure as hell I'm saying nothing."

The elder man hesitated for a long minute, and then abruptly jerked head and gun in the direction of the stairs. "Come on down, and go softly on the way, I'll be right behind. I dunno yet. Go on round the back, Stan, and see. How big is this window, then? I never spotted none we could use."

"I got through it, didn't I? Show you, if you like." She was feeling her way down stair by stair ahead of him, only too conscious of the shotgun close behind, and devoutly grateful that it was not in the younger man's hands. "*He*'s too big to get through, though. Pays to be a little person, on these capers."

"You done many?" He was sceptical but open-minded.

"None round here before. Never strike twice in the same place. Like lightning!" she said, testing the water a little deeper.

"Come from round here?"

"Not me! I came in from Brum, tonight. Came up here by the bus, and I aim to go back by the bus. He comes back down the valley about half past nine."

The young man Stan, however suspicious and uneasy, had done as his chief instructed, and made off ahead across the hall, out through the window they had forced, and round to the rear of the house. She felt somewhat reassured in his absence, however brief it might be. This one at least was a professional, and elderly, and professionals who have survived to reach middle age have normally done so by avoiding unnecessary complications like murder.

"How long were you in here ahead of us?" he asked suddenly. They had reached the foot of the stairs, and could hear Stan's steps faintly crisping the gravel outside.

"About a couple of minutes. Frightened me to death when I heard you driving in. I thought the folks were coming home too soon."

"Get what you come for?"

"Bits and pieces," she said, after a momentary hesitation. Whatever she said would be a gamble.

"Down the neck of your jumper?" And when she was silent: "What's your preference, then?"

"You got what *you* come for," she said, reluctant and aggrieved. "You wouldn't grudge me a ring or two, would you? I don't trespass on your patch, you might as well leave me mine. What you got to lose? We're both bound to keep our mouths shut, we're in the same boat. I never been inside, and don't intend to go, but you could shop me just as easy as I could you."

Stan was coming back, sliding in through the open window to dump her duffle bag in front of his leader. "It was there, sure enough, slung under the bushes. The window, an' all. That's how she got in. So what? You can't trust women."

"Why not?" she said indignantly. "We *are* in the same boat. I can't grass on you or anybody without putting my own head on the chopping-block. I broke in, as well as you."

"It takes some thinking about," said the elder, "except we don't have time. Sooner we're out of here, the better."

"Then that's it," she agreed firmly. "So let's get going. And you can give me a lift out to the main road, where the bus stops. Wherever you're heading, you've got to go that far to get started."

"I say make sure," insisted Stan. "If her mouth was shut for good we'd know where we were."

"Yes, up the creek without a paddle," said his leader with decision. "What, with a body to get rid of? I'm driving nowhere with that in the van. Leave it here? It wouldn't be silence you'd be making sure of. If you're ambitious to be a lifer, I'm not. Come on, let's get the van away while we're safe. Pick up your bag, kid, and hop in the cab. Might as well drop you off. Sooner you was in Brum than hanging around these parts."

In the cab of the van she was glad to see that Stan did not mind taking the wheel. That was a relief. He couldn't very well commit murder while he was driving, and she had the elder man in between.

The first few house lights of the village came into view. At the crossroads she would get down and walk away, still in one piece, still with the soft roll of leather and its contents snugly tucked away inside her sweater.

"Where will you be slipping a catch next?" the man beside her asked, as civilly and normally as if they had just picked up a young hitch-hiker out of the kindness of their hearts, and felt it only courteous to take an interest in her prospects.

"A hundred miles away, for preference," said the girl. "I'm going to enjoy my Christmas first. Never work at Christmas. This'll do, drop me off here."

It was under the light, just opposite the Sitting Duck. She dropped her bag out first, and jumped down after it, lifted a hand in ambiguous acknowledgement, and stood a moment to watch which way the van turned into the main valley road. Uphill, towards the border and the watershed. That made sense, small chance of being intercepted on that road on most winter nights.

The van, hitherto just a shape in the dark, took on form as it drew away along the road. The rear numberplate was muddy, but perfectly legible.

The girl watched it for only a few seconds. Then she crossed the road and went into the Sitting Duck.

The bus which would presently set off on its last trip of the evening, down the valley and back to Comerbourne, was parked at this hour just aside from the minute open space which was the centre of the village of Abbot's Bale, leaving the green free for an assembled crowd surprisingly large for so apparently modest a community. At this hour of the evening most of the shepherds and hands from all the surrounding farms would in any case have been congregated here in the Gun Dog, but on this evening they had brought wives and families with them, for the church choir was carol-singing for charity on the green, and there was warmth, welcome and the harvest of a dozen farm kitchens to be found in the church hall, on sale at nominal prices for the same good cause that was stretching the lungs of all the local choirboys, and filling the night air with a silver mist of frosty breath. The driver of the bus was sitting in a corner settle in the bar over a pie, along with Sergeant Moon, who was the law in Middlehope, rather than merely representing it, and without whom no function could be a complete success. The driver, a conscientious man, was making his single pint last as long as possible. Or if, for once, he had exceeded it, no one was counting. Sergeant Moon was on his second when the landlord called him to the telephone.

He came back in a few moments to haul the driver out with him into the night, and shortly thereafter the driver was seen to climb into his bus and move it several yards lower down the valley road, clear of the full-throated assembly presently delivering "The Farewell of the Shepherds" to the listening night, and there to stow it face-forward up the considerable slope of the hedge-bank, and abandon it, tail looming over the empty road. At the same time Sergeant Moon was seen to emerge from the yard of the Gun Dog with a red and white traffic cone in either hand, and place them judiciously in the fairway, a few yards below the point where the bus's rear loomed out of the hedge. A third such cone, brought out to join the first pair, completed a sufficient barrier on this narrow road.

The next thing that happened was that a word in the ear of the Reverend Stephen and his choirmaster unaccountably shifted the singers to a position in the middle of the road, instead of neatly grouped on the triangle of green, and effectively blocked the way to all traffic. Their horn lantern, reared on a long pole, stood out like a battle standard in the midst.

They were in the middle of "Good King Wenceslas," with the leading bass cast as the king, and the star treble as the page, when the sound of a motor climbing the slope was heard, and Sergeant Moon, hands benevolently clasped behind his back, and legs braced apart, took his stand in the middle of the road, and turned about at the last moment to confront the battered van with a large hand and a benign smile, as it baulked, hooted, and stopped. His pace as he approached it and leaned to the window was leisured, and his smile amiable.

"A happy Christmas to you, too, sir, I'm sure! Sorry to hold you up, but you see how it is. This is for the Salvation Army. They'll be finished pretty soon now, I'm sure you won't mind waiting."

"Well, we need to get on, officer," said the elderly man in the passenger seat. "Got a long way to go yet. You sure they won't be long? You couldn't clear a way through for us?"

The tension within the cab, which had smelled strongly of panic as soon as the window was rolled down, seemed to ease very slightly at the seasonal greeting.

The barrier seemed to have nothing to do with anything more menacing than some village choir collecting for charity. Sergeant Moon radiated placid reassurance.

"They can't keep the kids out too late. They'll soon wind it up now. The bus has to leave on time, some of 'em will be travelling down the valley a piece. Soon be on your way now."

The Sergeant had already located the shotgun, laid along the seat behind the driver and his passenger, and covered from sight with a rug, but the shape of the stock showed through. It would not be simple to produce and level it quickly from that position. All the same, the driver was getting distinctly more jumpy with every second, drumming his fingers on the wheel and twitching his shoulders ominously. The older one was tough enough to sit it out, but he was getting worried about his mate's liability to blow up at any moment. The Sergeant was glad to observe the three or four solid villagers emerge from the yard of the inn and amble innocently into position a few yards down the road. If anyone abandoned ship and ran, it would be in that direction, since there must be some fifty or more people deployed in the road ahead.

> "God rest you merry, gentlemen,
> Let nothing you dismay ..."

sang the choir imperturbably, embattled round their lantern banner.

The bus driver had climbed into his cab, and was watching with vague, detached interest. The man at the wheel of the van stared ahead, and had begun to sweat and blink, and curse wordlessly, his lips contorting. The older man kicked at him sidewise, and precipitated what he was trying to avoid.

It all happened in a second. The young man loosed the wheel, uttered a howling oath, shoved his mate sideways, and grabbed for the shotgun. At the same instant Sergeant Moon waved a hand, and the service bus, brakes released, rolled ponderously but rapidly down the slope of grass, and careered backwards directly towards the front of the van.

A shriller yell followed the first, cutting through the carol with a note of utter hysteria. The shotgun, hurled aside as suddenly as it had been seized, and still somewhat tangled in the rug, went off with a tremendous bang, fortunately spattering nothing more vulnerable than the roof of the van, as Stan fought his gears and tried to back off in a hurry, and failing, stalled his engine, flung open his door, and hurtled out and down the road, to be engulfed in the arms of a six-foot shepherd from one of the hill farms, ably supported by the cellarman from the Gun Dog.

"God rest you merry" was never finished. The choir broke ranks with a view halloo, and piled into the affray with enthusiasm, in case the van should yet serve to extricate its remaining occupant, by some feat of trick driving. But the professional knew when he was beaten, and had sense enough not to aggravate matters when they were past mending. The bus had braked to a halt at least a foot short of his right front wing, but still he sat motionless in his place, staring bitterly before him into the unexpected revelry, and cursing with monotonous, resigned fluency under his breath.

Sergeant Moon reached in unresisted, and appropriated the shotgun. Large, interested locals leaned on either door, grinning. The Sergeant moved round to the back of the van, and opened the rear doors.

"Well, well!" he said, gratified. "Aladdin's cave! Won't the Harrisons be pleased when Father Christmas comes!"

The girl in black silk evening trousers and bat-winged, sequinned top sat, cross-legged, in front of the fire she had kindled in the living room before her uncle and aunt had returned from their dinner party, and recounted the events of the evening for them with relish as she roasted chestnuts. It was no bad start to a Christmas vacation to be able to take her elders' breath away, first with shock and dismay, then with relief and admiration.

"So you see, it's all right, you'll get everything back safely. I did rescue your jewellery, I was determined they shouldn't have that, but all the rest will be back soon. Sergeant Moon has been on the phone already. I knew he'd manage everything, somehow, and I did warn him they had a gun. But isn't it lucky for you that I decided to come down a day early, after all? I did ring you, but you were out already. And anyhow, I knew how I could get in. Now who was it said I'd never make it as an actress?"

"But, for God's sake, girl," protested her uncle, not yet recovered from multiple shock, "you might have got yourself killed."

"Well, that's what I was trying to avoid! I was there, and they found me, I didn't have much choice. When you're cornered, no use coming apart at the seams. You have to use what you've got—same as Sergeant Moon had to do. And I *had* broken in, and I suppose I *did* look every inch the part. Anyhow, they believed it. Finally!" she added, somewhat more sombrely. "I admit there *were* moments ..."

"But you're taking it all so coolly," her aunt wondered faintly. "Weren't you even afraid?"

"Terrified!" said the girl complacently, and fielded a chestnut which had shot out upon the rug. "But I tell you what—as soon as my folks get back from Canada I'm going to put it to them they should let me switch to drama school. I always said that was my natural home."

THE FRUSTRATION DREAM

Have you ever had the frustration dream? I wouldn't mind betting that you have, I fancy few people escape it all their lives. But you might not recognise it, let alone call it by that name. I have a tendency to categorise dream patterns, a hangover, perhaps, from my abortive studies in philosophy, which never came to anything. There is, for instance, the flying dream, in which you tire of such tedious means of progression as walking, and take off from the ground, or sail comfortably from a cliff-edge without so much as thinking about it beforehand, or realising that it is not the usual prerogative of humanity. Natural optimists regularly fly in their sleep. Pessimists fall into pits instead.

The frustration dream comes in several variations. The most frequent, perhaps, is of setting out to go somewhere, and finding that roads shrivel into narrow lanes before you, and narrow lanes into paths blocked by bushes and briars, rocks, stones, fetid puddles and even nastier obstacles. A slightly different form of the same type is of looking forward eagerly to some particular treat, and rising to dress for the occasion with special care. Whereupon everything you attempt to put on, even supposing you can find it at all, is either crumpled in the laundry-bin, or tears at a touch, or suddenly develops foul stains. Women must go through legions of laddered tights if they suffer from the frustration dream.

Another kind is the dream of being just settled in a hotel somewhere, going out for a walk, and finding that you either can't find your way back to the hotel and can't even remember its name to ask someone, or if you do rediscover the place, you can't recall the number of your room, and can't find any spot in miles of corridors that even looks like the right door, or any person around to ask.

Another familiar version is of falling in front of a moving vehicle—mine was usually a steamroller—and being quite unable to move hand or foot to get up and evade it. For hours you watch the approach which seems to cross only about one yard of road surface.

Yet another is of being with a companion, on some business absolutely vital—in any surroundings, the locale doesn't matter, though usually indoors, and in a fairly complex building. Your companion goes away for some innocent purpose demanding only a few moments. And never comes back. And because this is important and must be completed, you go looking for him. The building about you does as the roads do, folds up in dark passages and gloomy corners, empty rooms vary the monotony, your search becomes ever more frantic.

248

Well, you get the idea. And the really absolute law that applies to all these dreams is that they never have any ending, never a solution. When you set out to go somewhere, you never arrive. If it's the variation where you're dressing for a ball, you never even set out. You never find your lost hotel or your vanished room. You never get run over by the steamroller, though you never get to your feet and run, either. And whatever you're searching for, you never find it. The frustration dream never has any conclusion. You just wake up out of it, still lost, still half-dressed, still yelling for help, still desperately hunting for what is lost. Lost for good. Balked and exasperated and aggrieved, you start off on the wrong foot for the day, even though you thought you were glad and relieved to find it was a dream. You're still cheated of a solution.

You never get used to it. But you can, I think, develop a kind of internal defence that can wake you out of it before it gets too maddening to endure. Or so I thought, until the time when it happened to me while I was wide awake, and I couldn't break out of it, and it did have an ending.

It's several years back now, before I was married. Indeed, if I hadn't been thinking of marriage, and working up the courage to broach the subject with Laura, it might never have happened to me. I was working with a firm of architects outside town then, before I joined up with Martin in Birmingham, and we set up the partnership. I had a small flat in the conversion of some old minor spa buildings, and once a month half a dozen of us who had been juniors together for the New Town Development Corporation used to meet in Breybourne for a meal or a pint or two. I didn't run a car then, more because the buses were frequent and convenient than because I couldn't afford it. I was being canny with my savings with a view to matrimony and house purchase, and somewhere ahead, a family.

So on this particular autumn evening we'd been dining at our favourite place, a crumbling old pub on the edges of old Breybourne, which had the best food in the town. A little later in the transformation of Breybourne, we suspected, the Golden Spur was pretty certain to go the way of many other fine buildings left over from the old town and in the way of profitable development. It wasn't listed, though it probably should have been, and it wasn't really so outstanding as to arouse protests, so we made the most of its cuisine while it lasted.

We ate early, because two or three of the bunch had long drives, and it looked as if it might turn foggy with the dark. We broke up about nine, since mist was hazing all the street lights already, and it looked as if the forecast would be accurate; and I walked towards the bus stop intending to take an earlier bus, but in no hurry, since I didn't have to drive. There was something curiously Dickensian in strolling the streets of the old town under those haloed lights, even if they weren't gaslamps, and that surviving quarter was a maze of narrow lanes, sudden corners, and narrow Victorian shopfronts, some still lit even below, some gleaming above through drawn curtains, for here small dealers and craftsmen lived above their shops. The few people I met could have belonged in Dickens, too, going hurriedly home, almost furtively because of the windless silence and the gathering fog, shadows in a shadowy world.

I had plenty of time, or thought I had, and had never really explored this quarter, so I was tempted to turn aside and take a more leisurely look at it now, the narrow frontages that ran back and back into remote and complex rears, built over and built on over centuries, huddles of invisible, complicated chimneys up there on top, sudden extensions skyward of the cramped house-fronts that sported below such unexpected and secretive show-windows, one here and there still lit at this hour. The highly professional enclaves of very old towns, where the jewellers and gem-cutters and locksmiths and pawnbrokers and money-lenders operated, kept no closing hours against customers of substance. Much of their business was done in the twilight, not by reason of any dishonesty, but because it was personal, private and vulnerable. Something of that era—how far back? Back, certainly, to before the expulsion of the Jews—lingered here in this autumnal and half-obliterated evening.

One of the alleys actually still had its medieval cobbles, and deep-rutted stone laid for where the cart-wheels would have run. And there was a small rounded bay window in one of the narrow frontages, a Victorian modernisation that had probably replaced stone mullions. It was still lighted, a solitary gleam in the dark, and it caught my eye by the glitter of cut stones within. Of all shop windows to leave lighted after closing, a jeweller's, I thought, and stopped to examine what was on show. No great value at risk, probably, except that most of it was antique, some Victorian jet and onyx, and some semi-precious stones of the more modest kind, in older settings, and period pieces have become fashionable again lately, far beyond their value in commercial terms. But there was one quite lovely amethyst pendant, five stones of excellent colour and finely cut, in delicate silver filigree. Without a chain, but most women have an assortment of chains to suit all occasions.

I like amethysts, and by that time I had discovered that Laura liked them, too, and frequently wore shades of iris and lavender that cried out for this kind of embellishment. A pity it was well past any closing time, and would it be there if I dropped in here next time?

I don't know why I tried the door, since I knew it would be locked.

Only it wasn't. It gave at once, and the attached bell rang loudly and clearly, startling me into stepping back instead of forward. But what was the good of retreating, now? People here lived over the shop. Better go in and at least warn the jeweller that he'd left his wares open—some of them, at least—to any opportunist who happened to come along and try his luck. And in any case, waiting within for attention would prove I was no such raider. And who knows, if the boss was actually working late in his back room he might not be averse to making a late sale. He might even knock a bit off the price in gratitude for the warning.

And Laura's birthday was only three weeks away. I went in, and closed the door behind me to produce another alerting peal.

The shop was lighted only by the incongruous fluorescent strip in the window, and its corners retreated into obscurity, even though it was small and as much workshop as sales depot. A curtained door sealed it off from the back premises, there were closed cupboards built in behind the single counter, the glass showcase which had been emptied, evidently the more valuable pieces put into a safe for the night, I thought. Clean, worn and bare, totally without glitter, the kind of shop where a man could reasonably look for a fair bargain.

A woman came in through the rear door, drawing the curtain aside with a rustle of rings and folds, and releasing a faint odour of dust. The sort of woman who went well with that sort of shop, fairly tall, erect, in forgettable black, possibly forty years old, and not at all bad looking in a severe way, her face oval, and looking pale in the dimness. She did not switch on another light. Nor did she seem surprised at seeing a customer at this hour. The bell had called, and she came in response to it. And sparing of words, too, for she left it to me to open contact, merely standing before me with her head inclined and a faint smile, inviting approach.

"Good evening," I said. "I was surprised to find the shop open at this hour. Did you know the door was still unlocked?"

"I worked late," she said. Her voice was very quiet, low-pitched and without resonances. "But I had forgotten. Thank you for reminding me."

Well, since I was there, and she was there, I might as well ask.

"I just happened to be passing, but there is an item in your window I should like to buy, if the price is right. And if you'd be kind enough to make a concession for me, even at this hour, I may not be this way again for some time."

She came forward then, and turned towards the window. "I have cashed up. But of course … Open is open for business!" She had a smile as distant as her voice. Her short, straight hair was dark, maybe black, her eyes large and dark. She looked her years, but she was still handsome. "Which piece is it you liked?"

I told her, and she lifted it out, and stood for a moment cupping it in one palm. Then she looked up directly at me, and really smiled, a momentary warmth shining through her tiredness. She had worked late, and it showed.

"It is for a gift?" she said, very softly.

"If I can afford it," I said cautiously.

She priced it at £60, her eyes steady on me, and I knew by the workmanship in the filigree setting it was worth more, possibly a great deal more. I had that much cash on me, and no card, as it happened, and in any case this was a curious, once-only transaction between us two, to be sealed and shaken hands on here and now. It was almost as if she and the shop itself would have vanished utterly if ever I came that way again. Outside, the fog was thick. Even here within, outlines seemed to have softened and melted in mist.

I gave her the money, and she checked it into tomorrow's takings in the empty till.

"I'll find a lined box for it," she said. "Wait just a moment. I'll be back." She went away through the curtained door, and I heard her footsteps diminuendo along a paved passage, but only for a few paces. And I waited. The earlier bus would have gone by that time, but I had plenty of time before my usual one, even allowing for delays due to the fog. So I ranged about the little shop and looked at the other bits in the window, and the empty velvet pad that lined the showcase, and the array of cupboard doors in the panelling, and the swirls of shifting fog outside in the alley. And listened to the silence. And waited.

But she didn't come back. It took me a long time to begin to feel uneasy, because it had all been so ordinary, after all, a fortuitous find and an unexpected sale. Nothing to write home about. But I'm not a very patient person, and there was little entertainment there to keep me interested, and I began to be irritated first, then uneasy, and then so annoyed that I might have walked out and shrugged off the whole thing, but for the fact that my £60 was shut into the till, and she had gone away with Laura's amethyst pendant in her hand. Reasonably enough if she had a selection of boxes from which to choose, and wanted the most suitable one; but I wanted that pendant. So I couldn't leave. And time ran on, and I began to think of my bus.

In the end I opened the door through which she had vanished, and called through it, rather tentatively: "Are you there? I have to go!" I didn't know a name for her. "Please hurry! The box doesn't matter, I'll find one."

I was looking into a stony passage, unlit, with the shadows of doorways deepening the dark on one side, and beyond, what seemed to be the foot of a staircase. Absolute silence beyond there. I called again, and the shaken air lay like a faintly stirred blanket heavy over me. Groping, I opened the nearer door, and found a light switch on the wall inside. A shabby, ordinary living-room, furniture old but once good, everything neat and clean but somehow impersonal. The second door was a jeweller's workroom, with a large, solid bench, tools, a little furnace, an air of having been quitted for the day some hours ago, with everything austerely put away until tomorrow.

Under the stairs a dusty cupboard with a vacuum cleaner, brooms, all the paraphernalia of a modest household; no way of lighting it, I identified the nature of what it held by falling over and into the various traps. Close to it, working backwards through a convoluted and bewildering depth of house, two empty closets and a small, bleak kitchen. This place was very old, and I was falling backwards through history in plumbing its depths.

And there was no one there, and in every corner the dank feeling that there had never been anyone, or not for centuries. And no amount of exasperated calling raised any answer but a hollow echo that went batting back and forth from every wall ahead of me, apparently into infinity.

I don't even know why I went on, except that the impetus of setting out on such a search makes it difficult to slow down, and almost impossible to stop. And I wanted my property. But perhaps even more, by that time, I wanted to set eyes once again on that quiet woman, and see for myself that she did exist, and that she was just as material and practical as she had been in the shop. Whatever the reason, I went on up the stairs. The first room there was a double bedroom, quite well furnished, but with wardrobe doors hanging open. After that the usual disintegration of the frustration dream set in, through rooms shrinking in size, ever more deserted and dusty, and at last narrow and empty. The house was very, very old. Floors swayed up and down, and creaked. There were tiny windows which had been sealed shut for centuries.

I came back to the stairhead, and peered again into the bedroom, where I had done no more than look in, and see that it was empty. This time I went in, switching on the light, and advanced to the bed. And beyond it, on the flowered carpet between bed and window, there she was, the vanished lady in black. She lay contorted, limbs tossed wide, as if she had been seized by the throat and flung down forcibly. Her head was turned a little aside, on her right cheek. Her face was suffused and discoloured, her throat bruised. Every detail leaped into my eyes stunningly in the sharp light, and I knew she was dead. While I waited below, she had been dying above. From here not a sound would carry below. So short a time it takes to end a life.

I say I knew she was dead, and I did, but it took an age to believe what I knew. And while I was staring helplessly at what I had been searching for, and wishing I had awakened before I ever found it, the door closed behind me, and I heard the key turn in the lock.

And while I was wrenching at the handle and refusing to believe it wouldn't turn and let me out, the light went out. I was left alone with a murdered woman, unable to get to a telephone, unable to break out of this room and this dream and run for it back to reality. The frustration dream had broken all the rules by arriving at last, by finding what was lost, and with all my appalled senses and soul I wished it had not.

It must have been a couple of hours before they came; and *they* were the police. All that time I'd been trying to pick that lock, with every possible thing I had about me that resembled a tool, but without success. There had to be a telephone somewhere downstairs, if only I could get to it. But it seemed someone else had used another telephone to warn the local constabulary that lights had been going on and off in the Ames house in a somewhat suspect way, and the caller thought there might have been a break-in.

So they told me, when they had forced the lock of that bedroom door, and firmly, but with the sort of gentleness (or caution?) you use towards a case of precarious mental stability, escorted me downstairs to await transfer to the local police station. Held on suspicion of murder. What else could I expect? Alone in that huge, rambling labyrinth with the dead woman—a natural suspect if ever there was. The fact that we were locked in, and the key was certainly not in there with us or I would have used it, did not prove that I had not killed her, merely that someone else, offered the opportunity, had turned the key to make sure I stayed to be arrested. Though I wasn't actually arrested, merely held for questioning.

I told them the whole story, not being sure what to tell and what to leave out if I hedged. The entire progression of my evening, complete with times, when I had left the Golden Spur, the names of all my friends who would confirm it, and so to the shop and the pendant. Yes, the pendant—where was it? I hadn't seen it since, and I remembered to tell them that my £60 in the till would speak for me. I checked and signed a long statement before they locked me in a cell, still uncharged. They let me call my boss. At that time of night he couldn't have been very grateful, but he came up trumps and promised police bail next morning if they'd allow it.

Then they locked me in. I didn't have any dreams that night, but then I didn't have much sleep either.

The boss was as good as his word, and bailed me out next morning. To tell the truth, I was surprised they let me out so complacently, seeing the state of the case, but they weren't giving anything away, just turning me loose with the request-cum-warning that I should remain at their disposal while enquiries continued.

Two days later Detective-Sergeant Sharp came to see me at my flat, after office hours. I'd got used to his poker face by then, and didn't want to jump to any too hopeful conclusions.

"It's all right," he said, "you're off the hook. We've got our man. Picked him up at Heathrow, with all the good stuff and all the cash from the safe in his luggage. Her husband! He was still in the house when you barged in, of course, he's the one who locked you in, he's the one who telephoned us to go and get you an hour and more later, when he was well on his way south. The business was hers, you see, came of generations of jewellers in that house. Seems things had been going awry between them. Anyhow, she seems to have had reason not to put much trust in him, for she'd changed the combination of the safe. You should see that safe. Built into the panelling feet deep, super job. It took him ages to break into it after he'd killed her, or he'd have been away before ever you blew in and spoiled things."

I mulled that over, and objected suddenly: "Wait a minute! How *could* he have been off the scene before I came? She was alive then, she was in the shop with me. She answered the bell."

He didn't answer at once, he was looking at me as though I'd said something at once pertinent and lunatic. "Well," he said then, "as a matter of fact, we didn't really think much of you as a suspect after that first night. If then! But certainly not after that. There was the fact that someone had been there to lock you in with her, and who was it likely to be but the husband who just didn't seem to be around any more from then on? Then next day, when we went over the house, sure enough we found your notes in the till, the safe cleaned out, the best of the male clothes from the wardrobe gone. And this—" He took from his pocket and laid before me the amethyst pendant, opening out the tissue paper in which he had wrapped it. "This we found about seven yards along the downstairs corridor from the shop."

It didn't make sense. None of it made sense.

"I can't hand it over," said Sharp, "not yet, anyhow, but I rather think by rights this is yours. You paid the price tag."

I said that I didn't think she would want it, now. I'd have to buy her something else.

"Perhaps you're right," he said. "But of course, it was after the post-mortem that we knew you were out of the picture. By all the signs, she was dead by nine o'clock at the latest, probably before. About the time you and your mates were coming out of the Golden Spur, Ames was strangling his wife in the bedroom over the shop."

He didn't wait to reason, or listen to reason, he got up and made for the door. There he looked back to where I sat struck dumb. "I shouldn't even try," he said kindly. "Just be thankful."

So there you are, and make what you can of it. I don't know! The bell rang, and she came to serve a customer, just as she must have done for years. Do you suppose that they have, for a limited time, like an echo that sounds quite realistically but then dies away, the faculty of lingering on in a corporeal echo? Just for a brief while only, before they make sense of death, and leave? She only got a few yards along the passage before she dropped the pendant. And it was a long stone passage, and I only heard the first seven or eight footsteps, before they died away. Well …

Women are strange. I didn't tell Laura the whole story, I left out all about the time of death, but she read the reports at the police-court hearing, so she knew. And when I said I hadn't wanted to accept the pendant because of its associations, she said, why not?

"You did her no wrong," she said. "You helped to get justice for her, if that was what she wanted. And there was a moment of contact, remember what you told me. When she looked at you, and asked: Is it a gift?, and went off to find a pretty box to put it in. She saw a young man buying a present for his girl, and just for a moment it gave her pleasure. In a way," said Laura, "you were the last person to see her alive."

THE MAN WHO HELD UP THE ROOF

Mind you, I've said nothing! I don't actually know what, if anything, Pete found out about Tolchard; I don't *know* whether there was anything to find out in the first place. All I know is there were these rumours. And even if Pete did get on to something about his foreman, you're not entitled to deduce from that that what happened to Pete was a direct result. Are you? *Or are you?* And even if Pete did threaten to put a spoke in Tolchard's profitable wheel, and brought the result on himself, it doesn't follow that what happened afterwards had anything to do with it. Not that I know what really did happen, thank God!

You have to find out by trial and error in this world the times when not to know. If there's any fear of finding out, positively finding out by touch or sight, shut at least one eye, quick, preferably both, and clench your hands and touch nothing. Knock about enough, and you get quite good at not knowing. So good, that now I never shall know, and sometimes, I swear to God, I can't keep from wondering.

We were building this great big office block at some intersection I'm not daft enough to name, in some city you won't know, anyway. Shiltons was a big company, and kept its skilled men, and I'd been in one of their crews a year, so I knew what was said about Tolchard. But then, they always do say these things. There's always a Tolchard, bigger than a bull and louder than thunder; the guy the world rests on, Atlas in person, the one who can lift anything and make anything work, the one who sets the standards other folks fall by. And there's always plenty to hate him. I hated him. You couldn't do other. He was too big, too loud and too effective. So they always have tales about this kind of men, how they knock off at least fifteen per cent of the stores on any job they work on, how they've been feathering their nests all the thirty years they've worked for whoever it is they work for. Everybody knows about the dumps they salt away in corners, and the lorries that drift in at night and ship the freight away. Only don't ever sit and watch. You might find out if it's true, and it's better just to pass it along softly, like the rest, and never to know. I'm telling you, lay off!

Pete couldn't lay off. And look what happened to Pete.

Those two came wandering in together on to the job, Pete and Abram. We used a lot of labour, and it moved around a lot. These two moved in while the ground floor was going up, all that concrete and glass and chrome and God knows what. Pete was from somewhere west, a great, blond lad nearly as big as Tolchard, only a lot better-looking; and Abram was a world wanderer and a

257

gypsy, he'd have been a gypsy wherever he'd got himself born. It was in Ireland, as it happens. He was a quiet one, though, not a talker, proud and silent and fastidious as hell, and he loved Pete the way brothers are supposed to, and seldom do. They'd been halfway round the world together, and that brings people pretty close, especially such dissimilar people. And what could you do but love Pete, anyhow? He was so clean and straight he made you see that man had really fallen, and from what a height! If he'd seen it himself you'd have been delivered, but he was as innocent as the children. And like the children, he made you afraid.

Maybe that was what it was. Maybe he made Tolchard afraid.

It was Tolchard who set them on. At first he didn't take any special note of them, but after a while he got to watching Pete with a sort of thoughtful smile on the quiet, and then he took him into his own outfit. They were just raising the pillars that were to hold up the ceiling of the main entrance hall. Faced stone, two storeys tall; a flash job, built up of hollow stone rings and then filled with concrete. Twelve of these things, there were to be, and the capitals for the tops were lying outside under tarpaulins already. It looked like a well-preserved corner from Karnak, or somewhere. Well, it was a temple, too, in its own way. A bank was having one half the ground floor when the block was finished, and a shipping company the other half.

So Pete worked with Tolchard, while Abram was left slogging with us on the site work outside. Anything Tolchard could lift, Pete could lift, and anything Tolchard attempted, Pete could do after him, and sometimes better. And he accepted what looked like the old bull's friendship and liking, because he was honest himself. But we'd never known Tolchard like anybody, least of all a young chap who was his match. And we wondered. And Abram wondered the most. Or perhaps he didn't wonder, he only didn't want to let on to Pete what he knew by instinct.

Anyhow, all I know is, one night Tolchard kept Pete back a good hour after we finished, because I was with Abram down in the canteen, waiting for him. When he came he looked thoughtful and distant, and wouldn't talk. He was so short to question that even Abram let him alone.

And the next day, when they were hoisting one of the stone rings of those pillars, fifteen feet up, the tackle slipped and let the thing fall. It fell on Pete. By the time they got it off him he was unconscious. He died in hospital the same day, without coming round. Abram sat by him to the last moment, waiting for a word, but he never opened his eyes, and he never spoke.

At the inquest there was a perfectly good explanation for the failure. As works accidents go, it came out looking more excusable than most. But Tolchard was bossing that crew. And I know that, mostly, plant did what Tolchard told it to do.

The firm buried Pete. He didn't have any family, only Abram.

Most of us had thought Abram would take up his anchor and pull out, now that he was on his own, but he didn't. He stuck around, working on the job just the same as ever, and saying nothing to anybody about Pete, and precious little about anything. Only once did he open up to me, and that was when I was walking home one night in the dark, past the site, and ran slam into him by the fence there, staring over it at those great, topless pillars, looming over the place where Pete had been crushed to death.

I said something to him then, I don't know what, something awkward. I hadn't ventured before.

He turned his head and looked at me along his shoulder, and he said: "Tolchard murdered Pete."

It wasn't as if we hadn't wondered; but when somebody says it you don't believe. I said: "Oh, come off it, why should he want to? He picked Pete for his own crew. He *liked* him!"

"Like hell he liked him! What's crooked can't abide what's straight."

"But even if that's true, why should he want to kill him? There wasn't any reason. He had nothing to gain."

"I think he had. You know why? Because Tolchard was trying to get Pete to help him shift a load out. That last night, he thought he'd got him nicely to the right frame of mind, and could open up to him. His mistake! Pete wouldn't touch it, and wouldn't let it alone, either. And that's why Pete had to go."

"It makes no sense," I said. "Tolchard's been operating for thirty years, he didn't need Pete. Why should he choose him, of all people? The last man in the world for a crooked job!"

"I'm telling you, because what's crooked can't abide what's straight. He didn't need him, but he wanted him! He wanted him dirtied and broken in, and no better than *he* was. Seeing Pete around the way he was, that was something Tolchard couldn't bear. It made his life not worth living. If he couldn't have him dirtied, he had to have him dead. Because Pete had told him straight he wouldn't stand for Shiltons being robbed, now he knew the score. Tolchard could straighten the account with them himself, or Pete would do it for him. Why? Because he couldn't help it. Because what's straight can't abide what's crooked, either!"

He said all this so quietly you'd have thought we were just jawing about the job, or something. And there was that weird, roofless hall of pillars staring at us over the fence. They were going to run the concrete next day, and fill those shells. A couple of days, and the capitals would be hoisted into place, and we should be raising the scaffolding a stage for the next storey.

"Do you know all this from Pete?" I asked. "Or are you guessing?"

"I know it from Pete," he said, and smiled. "He didn't tell me, but I know it. And I've just told Tolchard what I know. I take on where Pete left off."

"You didn't learn much, did you?" I said, only half believing him. "If we have to dig you out of a collapsed trench tomorrow, you'll need no telling why, will you?"

"I'll need no telling," he said, and smiled that hollow smile again.

But that wasn't what happened the next day. Not this time. What happened the next day was that Tolchard never showed up on the job. When they contacted his lodgings they found he hadn't been back there overnight. Nobody knew anything about where he was or why he hadn't shown up, but the job couldn't wait around for him. Shiltons' manager put a new boss on the crew, and they went ahead with filling the columns according to plan.

When we had our break I went up with Abram to watch them running the concrete. They'd reached the last pair of pillars by that time, and were bringing up the crane to hoist the capitals into place. Things went smoothly without Tolchard.

And after that day everybody stopped wondering why he'd disappeared; because they found out, as soon as they began to go carefully into the accounts and stores, that he'd left back-tracks everywhere, to the tune of a small fortune. But they never did find his tracks forward. The police came into it, and the hunt was on for months, and never has been officially closed. They wondered what had persuaded him to run just at that moment, but Abram kept his mouth shut, and I said nothing, except to him, and that was only to say: "Well, nothing fell on anybody that time."

He smiled, a tight, dark smile, and said: "No?" I didn't know what that was supposed to mean. I still don't. What I really couldn't make out was why Abram should seem satisfied with that sort of half-justice; because look at it how you would, Tolchard had got away with it.

Things went on just as steadily without him; he wouldn't have liked that. He liked to be the one who props up everything, and to believe that things would come to pieces if he turned his back. They didn't come to pieces. We finished the job finally. The bank moved in, the shipping company moved in, and we moved out.

Abram quit Shiltons after that job was completed. He didn't say where he was going, he didn't say he'd write. Even if he had said it, I wouldn't have believed him. He wasn't the writing kind.

But we did go for one last drink together, the morning he was leaving. And on the way to his bus we passed the new building, and stopped to look in at the main hall.

The place was alive by then; there was a porter on the doors, and a lot of busy, important-looking folks running in and out of the lifts. The twelve pillars looked fine, too massive, if anything—they were three feet in diameter, heavy even for that height—but very impressive. Abram stood looking at them in silence for some time, and presently it seemed to me that he was looking specially at one of them, the second on the right from the doorway.

"So that's the one you carved your initials on," I said.

"That's the one!" said Abram; and in a minute he turned back to the door, and led the way out. "Had to take a last look at my handiwork." And he laughed, short and quiet, and the laugh left him with a queer sort of smile afterwards. Not exactly a smile, perhaps. Call it what you like, I never saw it but the once. And to tell the truth, it bothers me even more than remembering what he said, just as we turned our backs on that intersection for the last time.

"When you come to think of it," he said, "he should be satisfied. He always did think he was the bloke who held up the roof."

SOURCES

"Dead Mountain Lion," *Everywoman*, 2 parts, November-December 1954.

"A Lift into Colmar," *Good Housekeeping,* 4 parts, April-July 1956.

"At the House of the Gentle Wind," *Everywoman*, 2 parts, October-November 1956.

"Breathless Beauty," *Good Housekeeping*, 2 parts, April-May, 1957.

"A Present for Ivo," *Everywoman*, 2 parts, December1958-January 1959.

"Guide to Doom," *This Week,* November 10 1963.

"The Golden Girl," *This Week,* August 16 1964.

"Hostile Witness," *This Week,* December 27 1964.

"With Regrets," *The Week*, May 30 1965.

"Maiden Garland," *Winter's Crimes 1,*1969.

"The Trinity Cat," *Winter's Crimes 8,* 1976.

"Come to Dust," *Winter's Crimes 16,* 1984.

"Let Nothing You Dismay," *Winter's Crimes 21,*1989.

"Frustration Dream," *2nd Culprit*, 1993.

"The Man Who Held Up the Roof," previous publication (if any) unknown.

THE TRINITY CAT

The Trinity Cat and Other Mysteries by Ellis Peters (Edith Pargeter), edited by Martin Edwards and Sue Feder, is set in Times New Roman and printed on 60 pound Natural acid-free paper. The cover illustration is by Gail Cross, and the Lost Classics design is by Deborah Miller. *The Trinity Cat* was published in August 2006 by Crippen & Landru Publishers, Norfolk, Virginia.

CRIPPEN & LANDRU, PUBLISHERS

P. O. Box 9315, Norfolk, VA 23505

E-mail: info@crippenlandru.com; toll-free 877 622-6656

Web: www.crippenlandru.com

Crippen & Landru publishes first edition short-story collections by important detective and mystery writers. The following books are currently (August 2006) in print in our regular series; see our website for full details:

The McCone Files by Marcia Muller. 1995. Trade softcover, $19.00.

Diagnosis: Impossible, The Problems of Dr. Sam Hawthorne by Edward D. Hoch. 1996. Trade softcover, $19.00.

Who Killed Father Christmas? by Patricia Moyes. 1996. Signed, unnumbered cloth overrun copies, $30.00. Trade softcover, $16.00.

My Mother, The Detective by James Yaffe. 1997. Trade softcover, $15.00.

In Kensington Gardens Once by H.R.F. Keating.1997. Trade softcover, $12.00.

Shoveling Smoke by Margaret Maron. 1997. Trade softcover, $19.00.

The Ripper of Storyville by Edward D. Hoch. 1997. Trade softcover. $19.00.

Renowned Be Thy Grave by P.M. Carlson. 1998. Trade softcover, $16.00.

Carpenter and Quincannon by Bill Pronzini. 1998. Trade softcover, $16.00.

Famous Blue Raincoat by Ed Gorman. 1999. Signed, unnumbered cloth overrun copies, $30.00. Trade softcover, $17.00.

The Tragedy of Errors by Ellery Queen. 1999. Trade softcover, $19.00.

Challenge the Widow Maker by Clark Howard. 2000. Trade softcover, $16.00.

Fortune's World by Michael Collins. 2000. Trade softcover, $16.00.

Long Live the Dead by Hugh B. Cave. 2000. Trade softcover, $16.00.

Tales Out of School by Carolyn Wheat. 2000. Trade softcover, $16.00.

Stakeout on Page Street and Other DKA Files by Joe Gores. 2000. Trade softcover, $16.00.

The Celestial Buffet by Susan Dunlap. 2001. Trade softcover, $16.00.

The Old Spies Club by Edward D. Hoch. 2001. Signed, unnumbered cloth overrun copies, $32.00. Trade softcover, $17.00.

Adam and Eve on a Raft by Ron Goulart. 2001. Signed, unnumbered cloth overrun copies, $32.00. Trade softcover, $17.00.

The Sedgemoor Strangler by Peter Lovesey. 2001. Trade softcover, $17.00.

The Reluctant Detective by Michael Z. Lewin. 2001. Signed, numbered clothbound, $42.00. Trade softcover, $17.00.

Nine Sons by Wendy Hornsby. 2002. Trade softcover, $16.00.

The Curious Conspiracy and Other Crimes by Michael Gilbert. 2002. Signed, numbered clothbound, $42.00. Trade softcover, $17.00.

The 13 Culprits by Georges Simenon. 2002. Trade softcover, $16.00.

The Dark Snow by Brendan DuBois. 2002. Signed, unnumbered cloth overrun copies, $32.00. Trade softcover, $17.00.

Come Into My Parlor by Hugh B. Cave. 2002. Trade softcover, $17.00.

The Iron Angel and Other Tales of the Gypsy Sleuth by Edward D. Hoch. 2003. Signed, numbered clothbound, $42.00. Trade softcover, $17.00.

Cuddy – Plus One by Jeremiah Healy. 2003. Trade softcover, $18.00.

Problems Solved by Bill Pronzini and Barry N. Malzberg. 2003. Signed, numbered clothbound, $42.00. Trade softcover, $16.00.

A Killing Climate by Eric Wright. 2003. Signed, numbered clothbound, $42.00. Trade softcover, $17.00.

Lucky Dip by Liza Cody. 2003. Signed, numbered clothbound, $42.00. Trade softcover, $17.00.

Kill the Umpire: The Calls of Ed Gorgon by Jon L. Breen. 2003. Trade softcover, $17.00.

Suitable for Hanging by Margaret Maron. 2004. Trade softcover, $17.00.

Murders and Other Confusions by Kathy Lynn Emerson. 2004. Signed, numbered clothbound, $42.00. Trade softcover, $19.00.

Byline: Mickey Spillane by Mickey Spillane. 2004. Trade softcover, $20.00.

The Confessions of Owen Keane by Terence Faherty. 2005. Signed, numbered clothbound, $42.00. Trade softcover, $17.00.

The Adventure of the Murdered Moths and Other Radio Mysteries by Ellery Queen. 2005. Numbered clothbound, $45.00. Trade softcover, $20.00.

Murder, Ancient and Modern by Edward Marston. 2005. Signed, numbered clothbound, $43.00. Trade softcover, $18.00.

More Things Impossible by Edward D. Hoch. 2005. Signed, numbered clothbound, $43.00. Trade softcover, $18.00.

FORTHCOMING TITLES IN THE REGULAR SERIES

Murder! 'Orrible Murder! by Amy Myers

The Mankiller of Poojeegai and Other Mysteries by Walter Satterthwait

A Pocketful of Noses: Stories of One Ganelon or Another by James Powell

Thirteen to the Gallows by John Dickson Carr and Val Gielgud

The Archer Files: The Complete Short Stories of Lew Archer, Private Investigator, Including Newly-Discovered Case-Notes by Ross Macdonald, edited by Tom Nolan

Quintet: The Cases of Chase and Delacroix, by Richard A. Lupoff
A Little Intelligence by Robert Silverberg and Randall Garrett (writing as "Robert Randall")
Hoch's Ladies by Edward D. Hoch
Attitude and Other Stories of Suspense by Loren D. Estleman
Suspense – His and Hers by Barbara and Max Allan Collins
[Untitled collection] by S.J. Rozan

CRIPPEN & LANDRU LOST CLASSICS

Crippen & Landru is proud to publish a series of *new* short-story collections by great authors who specialized in traditional mysteries:

The Newtonian Egg and Other Cases of Rolf le Roux by Peter Godfrey, introduction by Ronald Godfrey. 2002. Trade softcover, $15.00
Murder, Mystery and Malone by Craig Rice, edited by Jeffrey A. Marks. 2002. Trade softcover, $19.00.
The Sleuth of Baghdad: The Inspector Chafik Stories, by Charles B. Child. 2002. Cloth, $27.00. Trade softcover, $17.00.
Hildegarde Withers: Uncollected Riddles by Stuart Palmer, introduction by Mrs. Stuart Palmer. 2002. Trade softcover, $19.00.
The Spotted Cat and Other Mysteries by Christianna Brand, edited by Tony Medawar. 2002. Cloth, $29.00. Trade softcover, $19.00.
Marksman and Other Stories by William Campbell Gault, edited by Bill Pronzini; afterword by Shelley Gault. 2003. Trade softcover, $19.00.
Karmesin: The World's Greatest Criminal — Or Most Outrageous Liar by Gerald Kersh, edited by Paul Duncan. 2003. Cloth, $27.00. Trade softcover, $17.00.
The Complete Curious Mr. Tarrant by C. Daly King, introduction by Edward D. Hoch. 2003. Cloth, $29.00. Trade softcover, $19.00.
The Pleasant Assassin and Other Cases of Dr. Basil Willing by Helen McCloy, introduction by B.A. Pike. 2003. Cloth, $27.00. Trade softcover, $18.00.
Murder – All Kinds by William L. DeAndrea, introduction by Jane Haddam. 2003. Cloth, $29.00. Trade softcover, $19.00.
The Avenging Chance and Other Mysteries from Roger Sheringham's Casebook by Anthony Berkeley, edited by Tony Medawar and Arthur Robinson. 2004. Cloth, $29.00. Trade softcover, $19.00.
Banner Deadlines: The Impossible Files of Senator Brooks U. Banner by

Joseph Commings, edited by Robert Adey; memoir by Edward D. Hoch. 2004. Cloth, $29.00. Trade softcover, $19.00.

The Danger Zone and Other Stories by Erle Stanley Gardner, edited by Bill Pronzini. 2004. Cloth, $29.00. Trade softcover, $19.00.

Dr. Poggioli: Criminologist by T.S. Stribling, edited by Arthur Vidro. 2004. Cloth, $29.00. Trade softcover, $19.00.

The Couple Next Door: Collected Short Mysteries by Margaret Millar, edited by Tom Nolan. 2004. Cloth, $29.00. Trade softcover, $19.00.

Sleuth's Alchemy: Cases of Mrs. Bradley and Others by Gladys Mitchell, edited by Nicholas Fuller. 2005. Cloth, $29.00. Trade softcover, $19.00.

Who Was Guilty? Two Dime Novels by Philip S. Warne/Howard W. Macy, edited by Marlena E. Bremseth. 2005. Cloth, $29.00. Trade softcover, $19.00.

Slot-Machine Kelly. The Collected Private Eye Cases of the "One-Armed Bandit" by Dennis Lynds writing as Michael Collins, introduction by Robert J. Randisi. 2005. Cloth, $29.00. Trade softcover, $19.00.

The Detections of Francis Quarles by Julian Symons, edited by John Cooper; afterword by Kathleen Symons. 2006. Cloth, $29.00. Trade softcover, $19.00.

The Evidence of the Sword by Rafael Sabatini, edited by Jesse F. Knight. 2006. Cloth, $29.00. Trade softcover, $19.00.

The Casebook of Sidney Zoom by Erle Stanley Gardner, edited by Bill Pronzini. 2006. Cloth, $29.00. Trade softcover, $19.00.

The Trinity Cat and Other Mysteries by Ellis Peters (Edith Pargeter), edited by Martin Edwards and Sue Feder. 2006. Cloth, $29.00. Trade softcover, $19.00.

FORTHCOMING LOST CLASSICS

The Grandfather Rastin Mysteries Lloyd Biggle, Jr., introduction by Kenneth Biggle

Masquerade: Nine Crime Stories by Max Brand, edited by William F. Nolan, Jr.

The Battles of Jericho by Hugh Pentecost, introduction by S.T. Karnick

Dead Yesterday and Other Mysteries by Mignon G. Eberhart, edited by Rick Cypert and Kirby McCauley

The Minerva Club, The Department of Patterns and Other Stories by Victor Canning, edited by John Higgins

The Casebook of Jonas P. Jonas and Others by Elizabeth Ferrars, edited by John Cooper

The Casebook of Gregory Hood by Anthony Boucher and Denis Green, edited by Joe R. Christopher

Ten Thousand Blunt Instruments by Philip Wylie, edited by Bill Pronzini

The Adventures of Señor Lobo by Erle Stanley Gardner, edited by Bill Pronzini
Lilies for the Crooked Cross and Other Stories by G.T. Fleming-Roberts, edited by Monte Herridge

SUBSCRIPTIONS

Crippen & Landru offers discounts to individuals and institutions who place Standing Order Subscriptions for its forthcoming publications, either all the Regular Series or all the Lost Classics or (preferably) both. Collectors can thereby guarantee receiving limited editions, and readers won't miss any favorite stories. Standing Order Subscribers receive a specially commissioned story in a deluxe edition as a gift at the end of the year. Please write or e-mail for more details.